VIKING CONQUEROR

THE HARDRADA SAGA, VOLUME 5

JC DUNCAN

Boldwood

First published in Great Britain in 2026 by Boldwood Books Ltd.

Cover Design by Colin Thomas

Cover Images: Colin Thomas

Map Image: Flintlock Covers

A CIP catalogue record for this book is available from the British Library.

Paperback ISBN 978-1-83617-786-9

Large Print ISBN 978-1-83617-785-2

Hardback ISBN 978-1-83617-784-5

Trade Paperback ISBN 978-1-80656-355-5

Ebook ISBN 978-1-83617-787-6

Kindle ISBN 978-1-83617-788-3

Audio CD ISBN 978-1-83617-779-1

MP3 CD ISBN 978-1-83617-780-7

Digital audio download ISBN 978-1-83617-781-4

This book is printed on certified sustainable paper. Boldwood Books is dedicated to putting sustainability at the heart of our business. For more information please visit https://www.boldwoodbooks.com/about-us/sustainability/

Boldwood Books Ltd, 23 Bowerdean Street, London, SW6 3TN

www.boldwoodbooks.com

GREECE AT THE TIME OF HARALD HARDRADA
0 50 100 150 MILES
Belgrade
River Danube
DELYAN'S UPRISING
BYZANTINE EMPIRE
BLACK SEA
Thracia theme
Bulgaria theme
Macedonia theme
Constantinople
Skopje
Ostrovo
Via Egnatia
Mosynopolis
Voden
Dyrrhachium
Thessaloniki
Thessaly theme
Hellas theme
AEGEAN SEA

CAST OF CHARACTERS

The Kingdoms of Norway, Sweden and Denmark

Afra the Constant: Elder of the bandit brothers in Harald's service, known for his persistence.

Anund Jacob: King of Sweden from 1022-1050.

Einar 'Thambarskelfir' Eindridesson: Powerful Norwegian noble, advisor to King Magnus.

Eric 'Sveitungr' Alvarsson: The narrator, Harald's closest companion and follower.

Eystein Orre: Norwegian nobleman and staunch supporter of Harald.

Finn Árnasson: Brother of Kálfr but had not joined his brother in rebellion against King Olaf.

Harald 'Hardrada' Sigurdsson: King of Norway 1046-1066, half-brother of King Olaf, and claimant to Danish and English thrones.

Ingvarr Hakonsson: Son of Hakon.

Jarl Hakon: Petty jarl, on his way to join King Magnus barefoot in his campaign to the Southern Isles.

Jarl Halfdan: Lord of Tinghaugen.

Jarl Torvald: Petty jarl, friend of Hakon.

Jarl Rognvald Brusason: Exiled lord of Orkney, follower of Olaf and Harald.

Kálfr Árnasson: Enemy of King Olaf, victor of the battle of Stiklestad.

Magnus: Illegitimate son of King Olaf, later King Magnus I 'the Good' of Norway 1035-1047.
Magnus Haraldsson: Son of Harald Hardrada, King of Norway as Magnus II 1066-1067.
Magnus Olafsson: Grandson of Hardrada, King of Norway as Magnus III 'Barefoot' 1093-1103.
Olaf (Saint Olaf) Haraldsson: King of Norway 1015-1028, half-brother of Hardrada.
Olaf Haraldsson: Son of Harald Hardrada, King of Norway as Olaf III from 1067-1093.
Rurik: Varangian guardsman, follower of Harald since Stiklestad.
Stykarr: Harald's second marshal.
Sweyn: Jarl and then King of Denmark.
Tjodolv Arnórsson: Skald of Harald's court when he was king of Norway, his favourite poet and storyteller.
Thorir the Cuckoo: Younger of the bandit brothers. Known for his thievery and disguises.
Thorberg Árnasson: Third brother of the Árnasson clan, supporters of Harald.
Paul and Erlend Thorfinnsson: The inseparable brothers and Jarls of Orkney.
Tore of Steig: Norwegian noble, supporter of King Magnus, and then early defector to Harald.
Ulfr Ospaksson: Varangian with Harald Hardrada, one of his senior warriors and later his marshal.

Kingdom of England
Harold Godwinson: King of England.
Tostig Godwinson: Exiled brother of Harald, once earl of Northumbria.

The Kyivan Rus
Elisiv: Daughter of Yaroslav, first wife of Harald Hardrada and Queen of Norway.
Olga: Daughter of minor Rus nobility, wife of Eric Alvarsson.
Yaroslav the Wise: Grand Prince of the Kyivan Rus.

The Byzantine Empire
Georgios Maniakes: Byzantine nobleman and general.

Michael IV the Paphlagonian: Emperor of The Romans.
Michael V: Successor of Michael IV as emperor.
Petar Delyan: Bulgarian rebel and self-proclaimed emperor.
Theodora Porphyrogenita: Sister of, and perpetual rebel and plotter against, Empress Zoe.
Zoe Porphyrogenita: Empress consort, wife of Emperor Romanos Argyros and then Michael IV.

PREFACE

At the conclusion of *Wolves of the Empire* in the early summer of 1042 AD, Harald Sigurdsson had just participated in the short and vicious palace coup and counter-coup in Constantinople that resulted in the Empress Zoe claiming near total control of the empire alongside her sister Theodora. That relationship would go on to have its own fascinating adventures, calamities and intrigue, as the sisters ruled the empire unchallenged for another decade together. But that is not Harald's story.

Harald had hoped that by helping Zoe finally gain control of the city, he would be rewarded and free to leave. Perhaps he knew Zoe too well to ever truly believe it, and he planned his escape should she refuse to let such a powerful and useful subordinate go. Harald was ordered by Zoe – with the implicit choice of obeying or death – to be rid of the threat of the deposed former boy-emperor Michael V, telling him to 'end his line and ensure he never sees the light of day again.' Harald found a way to comply with the wording of the order without completely breaking his oaths by murdering the emperor. He mutilated and blinded Michael V, ending his line and ensuring he never saw the light of day again, but leaving the poor young man alive.

He knew how Zoe would react and, having raided the imperial treasury to claim the rewards he saw as his by right, he and 200 of his most loyal Varangians fled the city by ship, trying to escape Zoe's furious wrath. In the straits of the Golden Horn, on the verge of reaching freedom, that wrath caught up with them when Zoe's men raised the harbour chain, catching the latter of their two ships.

Harald, Eric and all who were lucky enough to be on the lead ship were forced to watch, helplessly, as the second ship containing their friends was caught and burned, with its entire crew massacred.

Harald was now free to sail for Kyiv, with only half the men and treasure he had expected to have at his command, and his plans for regaining his throne through force, bribery and politics facing ruin.

But Harald Sigurdsson was not a man to accept defeat, not a man to be put off by setbacks or tragedy. Harald had an unquenchable thirst for power and glory, and an unslakable desire to regain the throne he saw as his by right, that of Norway where his beloved half-brother Olaf had once been king.

So Harald is sailing north, and while the smoke of his friends' floating pyre still hangs in the air behind him, and his men sit shocked in their benches, the great Prince of Norway is focused only on returning to the path of his destiny, one that will lead to the crown of Norway, and a small green field beside a river known as the Derwent.

The world will change at the battle of Stamford Bridge, but to reach that field of destiny, Harald has to overcome his latest disaster using the only methods he knows how: an iron will, a predatory cunning, and the blood and despair of his followers and enemies alike.

This is the final chapter in the life and adventures of Harald Sigurdsson: The Hardrada, the King of Norway – The Last Viking.

PART I

THE CROWN

1

TINGHAUGEN, NORWAY; SPRING 1098 AD

'Everyone be seated!' Jarl Halfdan called out to the packed crowd in the open field at the edge of Tinghaugen where, the next day, the great festival and meeting of the Frostating was to be begun. The Frostating was the great Thing meeting of northern Norway, and the King would present his plans for the year, hear council and attend to the politics of the region and kingdom.

That final day was the day of gathering, where the last of those who planned to attend the Thing were arriving, where political horse-trading and temporary alliances formed, old ones broken or reaffirmed, and positions decided for the great meetings of the next day.

But politics was not why so many men, far more than on any of the previous days, had gathered on the meeting field. No, the town was abuzz with one thing and one thing only: that Eric Alvarsson, known as 'The Follower' – the lifelong companion of King Harald Hardrada – was going to tell the story of his final battles and his glorious death.

For four nights Eric had been telling the story of Harald's great adventures, from the battle of Stiklestad seventy years before, through his time in the Kyivan Rus and his tumultuous service as a mercenary in the Eastern Roman empire. On the first night a few dozen men had listened in rapt attention as Eric told the tale in the great hall. By the second night word had spread, and half a hundred men or more listened. This continued each day, more and more men coming, until the day the King himself arrived to listen to the tale. There were so many men that they had to sit outside on benches in the afternoon sun, and later packed the hall to standing room only.

And now, on the final day, Eric sat on the meeting field under the ancient tree that marked the speaker's place, looking utterly at peace, leaning in and grinning at a joke he had just told the young man – a boy, even – sitting near to him.

Ingvarr, son of Jarl Hakon, the boy who had first asked Eric about Harald and spurred him to begin his epic tale.

Eric looked up as Jarl Halfdan roared for everyone to sit and be quiet. Getting everyone to still was difficult; getting them to be quiet was not. They were all there to listen, not to be heard. The time for their voices was the next day; this afternoon was the time for them to open their ears, for perhaps it would be the last time anyone would hear the story of the great king from one who was actually there to witness his deeds.

Jarl Halfdan finally judged that the crowd was still enough for his liking. As if on some hidden signal, King Magnus, grandson of Harald and their sworn ruler, appeared around the last building with his closest followers and supporters and strolled towards the speaker's bench near Eric. Everyone rose to greet him.

'What a fine day the Lord has blessed us with,' King Magnus said with a smile, waving casually at the assembled ranks to sit.

Even Eric stood, despite his long years and ancient knees, and Magnus held out an arm in greeting. 'I am glad to see you are ready to start, Eric. I apologise for keeping you all waiting – I have a great many men who wished to meet with me before tomorrow.' The young king gave a knowing nod to the tail of lords and wealthy men who filed in behind him.

'I was not waiting even for a moment, Lord King, I was merely enjoying sitting in the sun and having good conversation.'

'Excellent. Well, we have much to do, and I am keen to hear the conclusion to your story. Come to the speaker's bench and complete your tale.' The King gestured to the crowd. 'I will be deposed if I do not allow it.' He joked, although there was not much humour in his voice.

Men laughed, not sensing the tension Eric made no impression that he had detected it either and smiled, walking over to the King and taking his place in front of the simple wooden bench where any man, king or commoner, who wished to speak at the Thing would take their place and wait.

But he did not sit – he nodded his thanks to the King who sat down to one side and smiled shyly at the audience.

'I am so, so humbled that so many of you have come to hear the story of King Harald,' Eric began, 'for it is one that all men of Norway should know.' He grinned. 'I know it has taken longer than I said, and even longer than you expected, but such is the way of very old men, so I beg your forgiveness.'

He nodded deferentially to the King. 'But I know that if I do not complete the tale today, being deposed will be the least of my concerns.'

Men laughed at that, too, because Magnus had not been good at hiding his impatience to get the tale completed so that he could get on with the usual pre-event politicking and celebrations.

Eric leant on his thick walking stick and turned his head to the nearest bench. 'Now, Ingvarr, remind an old man – where was I in my tale?'

Ingvarr looked taken aback as hundreds of sets of eyes, all the great men of the kingdom, turned to him, waiting for him to speak.

'You were telling us about your escape from Constantinople,' he finally managed to say breathlessly.

Eric's smile faded a little and he nodded slowly. 'Of course. No wonder I put it from my mind.' His hands clenched on the top of his walking stick and he looked out over the crowd. Not at them but above them, where his old eyes focused on some unseen horizon as his ever-sharp mind dredged up the events to relate them. 'That was the worst day of my life, until Harald's last. Well, we need to arrive at that point, so let me begin.'

2

THE KYIVAN RUS; SPRING 1042 AD

No one had spoken as we sailed out of the straits and into the Black Sea. I was white and shaken with grief, and most of the men on their benches were in shock, listless and subdued. A hundred of our friends and comrades, men who had been our brothers in a dozen battles across the entire empire, had been burned before our eyes in a handful of moments.

It was not just the loss of men we loved, for we Varangians were used to death and loss – it was that we were the greatest warriors in the circle of the earth. We knew that individually we were mortal – far too many of us had died to believe otherwise – but we believed from extensive experience that as a group we were nigh on invincible, that it would take all the power of kingdoms to take us down.

Empress Zoe had killed a hundred of us, in moments, with a mere word of command to raise the harbour chain, and the breath of her navy's Greek fire. It was a shock we simply could not process. We were not just mortal, we were *fragile* compared to the power of the Greek empress.

I knew half the dead men by name, but it was the loss of Afra that gored me the deepest. He had been my closest friend, for Harald, as I have told you many times, was not truly my friend. I had watched Afra burn, even as he smiled at me across the water between our ships in his final moments, making his peace before the empire took his life.

That smile haunts me... How brave does a man have to be to find peace in that moment, with the flames and death coming for him, in a boat full of wounded, screaming, burning men? What strength of character is required? I have been close to death many times, and not once was I smiling.

But he'd had enough. Maybe he only found that courage for my benefit, to give me the strength I needed to go on and do my duty to Harald. Maybe he knew watching him wave and scream and beg for help would have broken me, because help was impossible.

I don't know and can never know. In my dreams sometimes I still see him – not his death or his pain but standing there in the soft sunlight under the golden domes of Miklagard, serene and strong. It was his great gift to me – that I awake not in horror or fear, but in the knowledge that he made his peace before death came for him. I tell you, as the veteran of two dozen battles, so few of those who die are so lucky to have found the same.

Harald had the decency to keep silent, other than to give orders, although I could see he was not in shock, not in mourning. Harald had no use for those emotions, so he did not entertain them. He was angry. He was almost in a rage, although he controlled that too. Not, I suspect, because his men had died – he was quite used to that – but because he had needed them and the wealth their ship had carried, and all his plans were in danger, adrift on the Black Sea as we crossed it headed for Kyiv. A huge chunk of his hard-earned fortune had gone down in those flames. Greek divers would be recovering it from the charred timbers in that shallow water and returning it to Zoe within a day. That, I am sure, is what hurt him the most.

I did not speak to him either, for I blamed him entirely, and perhaps unfairly, for the disaster we had just left behind. What would I have done differently? Nothing, I am sure, but still, I blamed him because Zoe was not there to hate, and it had been Harald who had got too close to Zoe and thus led us to that end.

Harald had run across the knife's edge in his dealings with the imperial family in those desperate, blood-soaked days, and as an honest old man, aware of his own failings, I can tell you it was nothing but a miracle of skill and politics that he got even half of us out alive.

But I was not a wise old man, I was an angry bereaved one, so I blamed him and I grieved and sulked at the opposite end of our ship.

Bah, let us move on from that sadness, for the sun is being good to us and we are all sitting in the presence of our friends. I know you all want to hear of

Harald's final campaign, which at the time we sailed away from the empire of the Romans was still twenty-five years off, so I must move at a pace that would make the sun blush as it sears its way across the sky.

It was an uneventful journey to Kyiv, and by the time we arrived at the white city on the hill I had recovered enough to allow Harald to give me orders without glaring at him like a petulant child. We docked at the commercial harbour beneath the bluff on which the palace of Grand Prince Yaroslav stood, and Harald sent a message informing him of our arrival and asking permission to land and find somewhere to store our possessions.

We did not allow the prince's tax inspectors on board while we waited for word. They stood on the dock, angry and impotent, helpless against a hundred sullen, angry armed men. We could not allow them to find the sheer quantity of riches in our ballast, lest word spread and someone gathered enough armed men to think they could come and take it.

We needn't have worried – we were welcomed soon enough, and in the proper way, and given escort of the royal guard whom Harald had once commanded to transport all our belongings to the very barracks where we had lived all those years ago when we had served the Prince of the Rus.

Look, I will not tell you of Kyiv again, for I have told you before and it was all very much the same as the previous time. We were bored, we were cold in winter, and the men got into more trouble than Harald would have liked. The only part that matters is what happened between Harald and Yaroslav, for that decided his future plans.

We were summoned to the palace for the formal reception the day after our arrival, along with a number of other dignitaries, and I saw that Yaroslav looked older. He was delighted to see Harald, and broke protocol by coming down from his throne and embracing my prince.

'Come! I am so glad you have returned, Harald, and with such wealth and honour! Ha! Come to my chambers and speak with me.'

The prince's chamberlain scurried over, looked desperately worried and upset. 'My lord, what of the rest of the dignitaries waiting to be received?' he said, waving at the small line at the back of the hall.

Yaroslav waved the man away in irritation. 'They can return tomorrow. None are so important as the future king of Norway.'

It was calculated to offend, of course, but also to allow men who would undoubtedly gossip to hear those words spoken, and to see Harald's special favour. Everything Yaroslav did was calculated, as I learned more and more every time I was in his presence.

'See to the men, Eric,' Harald said, looking over his shoulder. I bowed and turned to leave the hall as Harald and Yaroslav went off with the prince's attendants.

I was deep in thought as I left the reception hall, wondering what Yaroslav would tell Harald and wishing I was there. Making my way down the hallway outside I nearly ran into a well-dressed woman who I did not notice until too late.

'My apologies,' I said in Greek, for I did not speak the Rus language and everyone at court spoke Greek. Everyone who mattered, anyway. I stepped to the side to continue, barely looking at her as my mind was still elsewhere.

But suddenly she swiftly stepped back and to the side to block me again, and I looked up in surprise, realising that I was being accosted deliberately.

That surprise, of course, was nothing compared to the surprise, horror, shame and... happiness that I felt when I saw who she was.

'Olga?' I croaked. The face that looked back at me was beautiful and taut with anger. My wife, or the woman who had once been my wife. I was not even sure. I had not seen her for so long, not heard from her for years. Not thought about her for... too long.

'I... I thought you had left.'

'And I heard that you had died. Several times, in fact. But now you are here, and I have to hear about it from a maid?' she said in an acid tongue, hands clasped in front of her body. I was wracked with shame. I had been so deep in my grief on the return to the city that I had not even considered that she might be there, or, if I am honest, she had not crossed my mind at all. I had virtually wiped her from my thoughts years before, when I heard that my wife had left Kyiv and was no longer receiving the things that I sent to her.

'I... I am so sorry. I came to see you a few years ago, but they told me you had left the city and, well, that you did not want to hear from me again.'

'Of course I didn't!' she snapped. 'You left, telling me you would send for me, and all I got for years was silver and letters giving excuses. Then I heard rumours that you were all dead, then nothing for years. The money you had sent ran out.' Her hands wrestled with each other in pent-up fury. 'Do you know what happens to a penniless widow of a foreign mercenary in this city if she has no one to look after her?'

I gasped like a landed fish, because I had not considered that at all. 'I thought I had sent enough.'

I winced as I said it, because it was the most pathetic, cowardly thing I ever said in my life, and her eyes flashed with anger. I had abandoned my wife and all through my time in Sicily sent her nothing and had barely considered what that meant.

'You had not,' she said, icily.

I gulped and hung my head like a sick dog. 'I apologise, Olga. I have abandoned you and shamed myself.'

There was silence as she stood there, glaring at me. I waited like a man for execution as she took a deep, measured intake of breath. 'So what are you going to do about it?'

I dared to glance up again. 'Uh... I don't...'

She sneered. 'You don't know?'

I shook my head. 'I have a great deal of silver now, I could...'

'Silver? Is there nothing you think cannot be solved with silver!' she said furiously. 'Did you imagine that when I married you all I wanted was the occasional bag of silver and to be left to fend for myself, and now you offer to do that *again*, as an *apology*?'

Oh, to have been in the thickest fighting in the worst battle in that moment. I would have rather been in Afra's ship as the Greek fire consumed it than be in the burning glare of Olga's righteous rage.

'What else... What can I do? I accept my wrongdoing, Olga, but I cannot expect your forgiveness, so all I can offer is to help you recover. What do you hope for from me?'

'Hope for?' she said, raising her chin. 'Honour, or is that too much to hope for? I expect you to honour your commitment.' Her hands were now still, her fury cold and restrained. She stared at me intently, the way Harald might when he was angry. I took a moment to understand, slow as always.

'You... you still want me to be your husband?' I asked, shocked.

'I am told you are a man of honour.' She shook her head. 'Although it is so long since I saw you take an honourable action that I don't know if I believe it.'

'I am,' I croaked, cringing. 'Or, at least, I try to be.'

'Good,' she snapped. 'Then you will take me to be your wife again, because no one else will due to your actions. You made a commitment to me, and I expect you to carry it out.'

'You want to remain married to me, after all I have done?'

'In fact, we will have to have our marriage re-established, legally. I had it recorded as ended when I heard that you had died.'

'Oh,' I said dumbly. Then my brows furrowed. 'So... how did you survive?'

'I did what I had to,' she said with clenched teeth, and my heart sank. 'I was a young widow, childless and not high-born. I found an old nobleman who wanted a second wife to warm his bed. And I went with him to his lands.'

My mind dulled as she spoke. I found myself, ridiculously, feeling betrayed and jealous.

'He died. His family rejected me and declared I was never truly his wife. I returned to the city, a twice-widowed woman beyond her thirtieth year, with no hope and no options, to work once more as a maid in the palace, waiting until they would have put me in the laundry to spend the rest of my years.' It all came out of her in a rush, anger and humiliation, the rage of it all, and my guilt washed away all of my jealousy. 'Then I heard you were in the palace again, and...' She gestured at me irritably.

'I'm so sorry, Olga.' I meant it with every bone in my being, and I think she saw it. She softened a little, just a crack in a great stone wall of resentment.

'Do not be sorry – simply promise you will not do it again,' she replied.

'So, you truly want to stay with me?'

'I have no choice, and if you are a man of honour as you claim, neither do you.'

I sagged. 'If you live with me because you have no choice, what future is that?'

'Better than the others you left me with. And maybe, with time, you will prove you are the man I remember you being.'

I nodded slowly. 'I can be that man.'

It was all too much for me, too sudden. I had no notion of what I expected to happen, no idea how to deal with it, but it felt in that moment like a lifeline to a drowning man. I was completely lost after our time in the empire, dreading Harald's next action, and with nothing in my life that was mine, just service. Suddenly, the idea that I might have a wife again was invigorating. Perhaps it was a fragment upon which I could build a life that was *mine*.

Apart from anything else, despite her anger and my shame, Olga was still the woman I had fallen for in my childish passion.

'So, I will have to find us accommodation, somewhere suitable. It might take me a day or so.'

'Good. I will gather my possessions. Get us somewhere with two bedrooms.'

My head sank again but I nodded. 'I understand. I know that you would not want to share a room with me.'

'No,' she replied, and for the first time she looked nervous. 'The second is for my son.'

'You son?' I said, stunned.

'Yes. My second husband managed to have a son with me before the useless man died. His family rejected me and the boy both.' Her eyes narrowed and her neck tensed. 'He will not be rejected again. He is now *your* son. He is too young to remember his first father, and we will never speak of him again. Do you understand?'

I stared wide-eyed at her, the breath knocked out of me. It was all too much, too outrageous, but I had just enough sense to know I deserved it. 'I understand.'

'Swear it,' she snapped. 'Make one of your oaths and know that I will hold you to it.'

I blinked rapidly, wondering for a moment if I should refuse and reject this lioness of a woman who had me so thoroughly cornered. I had never known how strong she was, and perhaps she only became that way because I forced her to.

She was staring at me intently, her stress and anger written into every faint line in her face. Proud, desperate. The decision was suddenly easy. I reached for my sword, but it was not there, of course.

I reached out for her hand instead. She almost recoiled but then let me take her soft fingers in my rough, scarred hand.

'I swear to treat your son as my own, and that I will never abandon either of you again.'

She cracked a little and nodded, squeezing my hand in hers, her visage of anger and resentment melting a little into relief. 'Good,' she said. And then she wrenched her hand from mine and turned before I could see her tears. 'Send word to the servants' quarters when you have somewhere for us to live,' she said, and she disappeared around the corner before I could even reply.

What a woman she was. Well, as I have said, this is not my story, but I am proud to tell you I kept my word to Olga, from that day, until the day she died just a few short years ago. My sons are not here today – they are not warriors because I did not raise them to be, and Olga would not allow it – but I am proud of them, and I kept my word to them also. God as my witness, it is the one thing I can truly be proud of in this world.

* * *

It was not long before Harald returned to the barracks that had been provided to us. It was in chaos as the previous occupants – mercenaries under Yaroslav's employ – had been rudely turfed out. Our men got settled in, taking our wealth up to the palace to be stored in the treasury with everything else Yaroslav had kept for us over the years.

Harald looked dark and furious, and my heart was glad of it, because that meant we were not immediately marching to war.

He looked at me, assessing me, perhaps wondering if I was still too angry to talk to him.

'What did the Grand Prince say?' I asked, by way of peace offering.

'That he cannot support my bid for the throne of Norway, not at the moment.'

I made a show of being disappointed. 'Ah.'

'And with the men and gold we lost, I cannot do it directly without him, or, worse, against him.'

'So… what do we do?'

'He made an offer.'

I tensed; that could not be good.

'He would give me the men, support and treasure I need if I would help him in a campaign against the empire.'

I opened my mouth in shock. 'He plans to campaign against the empire?'

'Yes, immediately. He intends to seize on the weakness and chaos left by the death of two emperors and the recent wars. He thinks now is the perfect time to strike.'

My heart sank. 'And he wants us to go with the army and help him.'

'Yes. He knows we could help him take the city, for our knowledge of it is invaluable, and for that help he would offer me the crown of Norway, aid me in getting rid of his ally Magnus.'

I was horrified. 'So we have to return to the empire, to wage war?'

Harald looked at me. 'What would you think of that?'

I shook my head, all the terrible outcomes flashing before me. 'Harald, we might end up fighting against the Varangians, our own friends and comrades. Apart from our own feelings and honour, the men might refuse and abandon you.'

He nodded slowly. 'That is exactly why I refused.'

'You… refused?' I was even more stunned, and it was a day where I thought nothing else could surprise me.

'Yes.' He nodded gravely. 'It was not a good meeting.'

'He offered you the crown of Norway for your help defeating Zoe, and you *refused.*'

He nodded again irritably. 'I will not lead our men to war against our old brothers. Never. I am disappointed that you think I would.'

'So what did he say? Must we leave?'

'I made a compromise to allow us to stay.'

'That can't have been cheap.'

'It wasn't. I will hand over one-third of the treasure we brought back from the empire and give him advice on how best to defeat Zoe. Us and our men are to join his forces and stay here to help guard the city while his army is on campaign, but he promises they will never have to fight against the empire.'

'And in return?'

Harald looked at me grimly. 'He doesn't have us killed and take everything, and, in the future – when the time is right – he will help me take the throne of Norway.'

'In the future?' I said, almost excited by it. It was terrible news for Harald, for it meant doing nothing. But it was excellent news for me, because it meant we were not going back to war, and I would be able, for the time being, to keep my new oath to Olga.

'Yes,' he said with a furious sigh. 'And I have no idea when that will be.'

'So what will we do?'

'We will train and keep the men active, and I will search for allies who could help me.' He nodded at the wall behind us. 'You'd better get the men ready to be settled in for a while. We could be here for a year or more.' He stood and then stopped. 'Oh, and I also agree to marry one of his daughters, the youngest.'

I wracked my brain. 'Elisiv?'

He nodded.

'But she is a child?'

'Not any more, she is a young woman now. I will marry her next year, after the proper procedures.'

'So we are staying here for some time as his guests while he secures his alliance with you and waits for the right time to use you.'

He grimaced at my wording but did not protest. 'Indeed.'

I gulped and nodded, and as he stood he gave me an odd look. 'You almost look happy, Eric. Why? This is everything you have worked for too being delayed, is it not?'

'Yes, but... Uh. I also had a difficult conversation in the palace, and I also made a promise that I was not entirely happy to make, one that commits me for a few years too, at the least.'

Harald looked completely confused. 'You did what? How?'

'It's quite difficult to explain,' I said, gesturing him back to his seat as he glared at me.

'Explain anyway,' he snapped.

I did my best to smile disarmingly. 'Well, I found Olga – or rather, she found me.'

Harald's brows rose. 'Olga? That serving girl you married last time we were here?'

I smiled helplessly. 'Yes.'

'And... what did you promise? God, Eric, we have been here barely an afternoon!'

I shrugged helplessly. 'Well... it seems I am also getting married again.'

3

Harald and I went to Kyiv to get an ally and an army to conquer Norway, but instead we both ended up married and guarding another city.

Olga and I went to the bishop and had our marriage re-established. Harald spent a year courting Elisiv, going through all the formal steps required at a speed that infuriated him but pleased the girl, who was strong-willed and hard to satisfy much like her father. They married in a grand week of ceremonies in 1043, a full year after we arrived, which Yaroslav also used as a celebration of the start of his campaign against the empire.

He sent his son, Vladimir, to make war against Zoe because he himself would not risk going. The Rus captured some Roman cities around the north side of the Black Sea, but when their fleet tried the same on the northern Anatolian shore they were surprised by an imperial navy near Constantinople and annihilated. The survivors reported their ships being overwhelmed with the devil's own fire, and that their army ashore was crushed by a Varangian-led army. It turned out that a year had been more than enough for the fearsome Zoe to establish control of the empire and its strength had rebounded, its army and navy peerless once more, far more than a match for Yaroslav's mercenaries and militia.

I tell you, I thank God for Harald's wisdom in not sending us on that ill-fated campaign because we would have had to face either Greek fire or our old brothers, and the thought of either sickened me.

Instead of war, I spent my time training with the men, and in my personal battle to earn Olga's forgiveness so that our life would not be spent together in hostility and mutual dislike. It was the most difficult campaign I ever fought, filled with more hardships and setbacks than Sicily, the fortress of her heart more difficult to reduce and capture than Syracuse itself. Eventually, little by little, I won my way back into her love.

Hah! You see, my only skill is not as a great warrior – I am a great husband and lover also. Perhaps, in my more honest moments, I accept that skill is far more important.

Anyway, by the year 1044 we had a daughter, a blessing that finally cemented us together as truly husband and wife again, and I found immense joy in starting to raise our children instead of being at war, our tiny, round-faced daughter and our son. *My* son, you see.

While I stayed in the city Harald was kept busy by Yaroslav, first in advising and training his army, and then on errands and diplomacy around the kingdom. I think Yaroslav knew that if he left Harald to fester in the capital he would be nothing but trouble, so Harald took his irritation and disappointment on tour, doing Yaroslav's bidding while his patience thinned and thinned.

While my marriage flourished, Harald was incapable of making his anything other than an arrangement of alliance, and vacillated between ignoring his new wife – she was too young for him to really bond with – and writing her letters and poetry telling her how much he wished she would return his love more freely and passionately.

Yes, while I was a great warrior and lover, Harald was hopeless when confronted with a wife who was not a great and powerful woman in her own right. He had no idea how to deal with a closeted princess who had never seen the world beyond the city walls.

By the year 1045, Harald's patience had worn out, and Yaroslav had abandoned his campaign in the southern Black Sea as unwinnable. Zoe and Theodora, with Zoe's new husband Constantine – apparently the very man Harald had negotiated with in the hippodrome to end the uprising three years before – had managed to turn the empire's fortunes around in remarkable fashion, securing the allegiance of all the themes, rejuvenating the finances, and strengthening the army, navy and borders.

Should we have been surprised? Probably not. Zoe was an extraordinarily capable woman, and she did what she had always promised to do: brought stability and strength to the empire in a way that had been missing since the death of her first husband.

The defeat dulled Yaroslav's ambitions, and thus the usefulness of keeping an increasingly petulant and irritable Harald around the palace.

In early 1045, Yaroslav called us to the palace for a meeting to decide the future of Norway, and we both knew what it was likely to mean.

'He is going to help me take the throne, finally,' Harald said as we strode up the hill in our finest regalia, with an escort of forty bored men of our warband.

'Or kill us,' I said nonchalantly.

Harald glanced at the men around us. 'And have to deal with these men afterwards? I doubt it. Easier to send me away than try to kill me.'

I nodded carelessly because I agreed. I felt no danger that day. I felt only happiness at how my life had changed, and the knowledge that our time in the city must be coming to an end. It was finally time to go home, one way or another.

* * *

Yaroslav received us in his chambers, the ones that had become so familiar to us in our previous stay in the Rus.

'Sit,' he said crisply, with a surprisingly warm smile, after the formalities. We sat on the chairs facing him and he stretched with a sigh. 'I do not know when I became old, I only know that it has happened now and cannot be denied any longer.'

Harald smiled thinly. 'You are not so old, but I would consult with Eric – he is my expert on the subject of feeling so. He never ceases to complain about it.'

Yaroslav barked out a laugh and winced as he stretched his damaged leg out, scratching at his knee. 'He is a pup still compared to me.'

'I know that, but from his complaints, he would never accept it.'

I just smiled and rolled my eyes a little. It was not my place to argue or even speak in that meeting of princes.

'I think it is time that you went home,' said Yaroslav suddenly, losing his smile in a moment and looking at Harald carefully.

Harald straightened. 'I agree, my prince. But the question is, in what way?'

'You don't have the treasure or the men to take the country by force,' Yaroslav said.

'I know it,' Harald agreed grimly.

'And after my war with the empire, neither do I,' the prince added with a glower. These were two men who did not take failure or inability to do what they wished well at all.

'So how can I return? Magnus would never allow me to live in Norway in peace – he would know I was always going to be a threat.'

'I know that too, so I have made an arrangement.'

Harald looked up, surprised. 'An arrangement?' His surprise turned to anger. 'I know nothing of an arrangement being negotiated.'

Yaroslav held up a hand to forestall Harald's anger. 'Nor would you have, for it was conducted in utmost secrecy.'

'With whom?'

'King Anund Jacob,' Yaroslav said softly, 'My brother-in-law, who is now also your family by marriage.'

Harald stared at him and then looked down, his eyes flickering as he considered it. King Anund had sheltered us after Stiklestad and was a friend and ally of Olaf but had not been willing to risk open conflict with Norway's rulers, and their overlords Denmark, so had forced us to flee east.

'King Jacob is finally willing to confront Norway?' Harald asked.

'Yes. After the death of Cnut's sons, he worries that Magnus is becoming too powerful.'

Now, I shouldn't need to remind most of you of our nation's history, but this being over fifty years ago, let me at least say that Magnus had taken Norway from Cnut's sons with Yaroslav's and Jacob's help. When Harthacnut also died, Magnus claimed the crown of Denmark in 1042, making him ruler of both countries.

Harald leaned back, considering it. 'So you no longer have enough control over Magnus.'

Yaroslav smiled sadly. 'He is not the quiet boy you remember. He has grown quite independent, and no longer heeds my command, especially since my recent defeat.'

It was an astonishing admission from a man such as Yaroslav, one that would never have been made in company he did not trust.

'So Jacob is worried, and wants to reduce the power of Norway, and you want to be rid of me.'

'Neither is entirely untrue,' Yaroslav said with a tilt of his head. 'But you are now my family, and Magnus is not.'

It was that simple to Yaroslav. He was building a continent-spanning empire of family ties. One other daughter was married to the new king of Hungary, while the younger two were being actively courted to other European princes.

'But Norway under me would not be weaker than under Magnus. Why would King Jacob welcome that?' Harald asked.

'Is Sweden part of your ambitions?'

Harald shook his head. 'Denmark and England.'

Yaroslav spread his palms. 'Precisely. And whose help would you benefit from in taking those realms?'

'King Jacob's. So he trusts I will not have conflict with him.'

'He will want your oath on that too, of course.'

Harald nodded slowly. 'That would be acceptable.'

'And I have agreed to treat you as an enemy if you break it,' Yaroslav said quietly.

Harald looked up but said nothing.

Yaroslav smiled humourlessly. 'I am a little reduced, but, I think, still not a man you wish to be enemies with, even if you would turn on the people who sheltered you when you needed it and helped put you back on the throne. Would you be so dishonourable? I think not.'

'I would not,' growled Harald in assent.

'Good, then it is clear. Jacob will help you bring Magnus to heel, you will have your Kingdom, if you have the ability to claim it, and I will secure peace and allies on my western side while I continue my work in the south and east.'

Harald nodded. 'I accept.'

Yaroslav chortled. 'Your acceptance was not really the question – we are only discussing the arrangements.'

Harald swallowed his anger at Yaroslav asserting his dominance once again. 'So, what is your intent?'

'You take your men, your gold and your ships and sail north. I will have men escort and guide you, ensure you receive all the help you need. You should be in Sweden by autumn. After that, it's up to you. But that is the way you prefer it, I think.'

'It is.'

Yaroslav held out his hand, offering it to Harald to take to seal their pact. 'Then I wish you the best, Prince Harald. I think you are ready to be king.'

'I have never not been ready.' Harald said, and his eyes were full of fire again.

* * *

We sailed from Kyiv a week or so later in our ship, with another one following on behind. Why another? Our single ship was too heavily laden to pass the narrow and shallow rivers of the Rus, and we had acquired additional... *baggage*. Harald and I were not the only men to be leaving Kyiv with a wife or family. We had been there for three years, and the men had grown bored. You know how it is.

Let us not talk of the journey, for even now I see the sun moving through the sky and your patience thinning. Suffice to say it was boring, and we only lost one woman to foolishness and drowning on the trip, and one man to a fall on rocks while climbing the riverbank who received a caved-in skull. A good passage, by any standards.

We arrived in Sweden by autumn as Yaroslav had promised we would, and King Jacob gave us the welcome we were promised. Our people settled in while Jacob and Harald plotted their campaign against Magnus for the next year.

Sweyn, a Danish jarl who was Cnut's nephew and claimed the throne of Denmark, was already with Jacob. He had led a failed rebellion in 1043, and had fled to Sweden to find a new ally. Harald had little regard for him and intended to discard him the first chance he got, but was willing to use him to help secure the Norwegian throne.

So the two men planned their campaign, and I had a second son, which, let me tell you, brought me nothing but joy.

I shall not relate the campaign of 1046. It was extremely uneventful, and this is not the story you came to hear. We sailed to the Danish islands and raided them mercilessly, trying to force Magnus to come and face us where we would be able to defeat him in battle and take the country. We went to Roskilde and burned it, slaying the men who remained to fight and taking women as captives to goad the Danes further. But despite devastating the lands, Magnus did not come out to face us, and we left before winter with nothing of substance achieved.

In the summer of 1046, Magnus stunned us all by sending a peace delegation to Sweden to offer terms, despite the fact that we had not defeated him in battle. True, we had raided and burned some important towns and gained a few minor victories over local forces in Denmark, but we had not touched Norway to avoid upsetting Harald's future subjects, and the war was far from conclusive.

But yet, he sent envoys anyway. He is known as Magnus the Good, and with some fondness. He earned that name by keeping the peace in the kingdom, and by forgiving his enemies and the murderers of Olaf after he gained the throne in 1035, rather than committing a campaign of revenge as Harald would have. I suppose this was an extension of that reputation. Regardless, Harald found it incomprehensible and quite cowardly. It completely soured his opinion of Magnus, who, by all accounts, had grown to be a good leader and fearsome warrior with a reputation for clearing the decks of enemy ships at the head of his huskarls.

Harald should have respected him for that, even liked him, but hearing Magnus had forgiven the killers of his brother Olaf in order to secure peace was unforgivable. Harald would never have done such a thing.

'It must be a trick,' he said as we gathered to hastily discuss our strategy before meeting the delegation.

'Perhaps he simply knows he cannot win,' I suggested. 'He is choosing diplomacy rather than risk defeat in the field.'

'Nonsense. He is the King, and he has fought and won three major battles in the last three years. He knows how to fight, and he can raise a large army. He would not surrender without fighting even once,' said Ulfr dismissively.

'I cannot be sure. Perhaps he is brave in battle, but a coward in matters of rule. In any case, we will hear what he has to say and beware of trickery or deception.'

* * *

Well, we went to King Jacob's hall and Harald met with King Magnus's men. I was not there for their meeting, but Harald came out of it barely concealing his excitement.

'He offers me discussion of co-rule in Norway in exchange for peace,' he said, almost giddy. 'He is a coward, as I suspected. He is weak from the war with Sweyn and is desperate.'

'And for Sweyn?' I asked.

Harald shook his head. 'Nothing.'

'But you made a pact with Sweyn to oppose Magnus together, and now he forces you to break it. See? He may be a coward, but he is no fool. It is a trick to dishonour you.'

Harald looked at me. 'I have agreed to nothing, so I have broken nothing.'

I narrowed my eyes. 'You have agreed to meet Magnus to discuss it?'

'Yes.'

'That will be seen as betrayal. How can you hope to gain the trust of the Norwegian lords if your first act here is to break an alliance?'

'I never said I would not talk to my nephew. It is only betrayal if I discard my pact with Sweyn to make another with Magnus,' he replied with a grin.

I narrowed my eyes, seeing from Harald's glee that he had a plan. 'I do not understand.'

'If Sweyn breaks our pact first, I will not be held to it any more.'

'How will you get him to do that?'

'By leading him to believe I have already betrayed him.'

I glared at him. It was a typically devious ploy for Harald, and one I knew would lead to trouble. But I could not argue.

Harald nodded over his shoulder to the main area of the hall, where men were already gathering, and where Sweyn sat with a circle of his friends, watching us like a hawk.

'He is watching us?' Harald asked, not turning to look.

I nodded, not taking my eyes off Sweyn, and I saw Sweyn frown from across the room.

'And he sees you looking at him with that angry expression?'

I nodded.

Harald laughed softly. 'Good, then the first step is already done. He now believes it is likely I have betrayed him.'

I looked back at him, eyebrows rising. 'The whole point of this little conversation was to use me to bait Sweyn?'

'Yes,' he nodded emphatically.

I scowled. 'I dislike this.'

'I knew I could rely on you to, and he will see it and interpret the way his mind is telling him.'

Harald motioned to Ulfr with one hand and the big Icelander came over and leant in to listen closely as Harald leant in too, only exaggerating the air of conspiracy.

'I want you to gently spread a rumour that I have agreed with Magnus to turn on Sweyn and kill him in return for the crown of Norway.'

Ulfr's eyes widened. 'Is that true?'

Harald subtly shook his head. 'No, but I want everyone to think it might be. Choose the men carefully, keep it vague, tell a few different versions of the story. By the end of tonight, I want confusing and contradicting rumours on the tongue of every man in town.' Harald nodded to himself in satisfaction. 'Sweyn won't know what to believe, but his conclusion will be inevitable – that I am about to betray him.'

'Harald,' I hissed. 'We are in a hall with him all evening, you will be dining with him. What if he makes a move against you?'

'In King Jacob's hall? He will not. Jacob would string him up for violating his peace. No. He will do nothing except grow more and more angry and suspicious.'

'Then he will come for you afterwards!'

Harald leaned across the table until he was a mere handspan from my face. 'Eric, my old friend,' he said softly, with that wolfish smile upon his face. 'I am relying on it.'

* * *

'What did Magnus's envoys offer us then?' Sweyn said to Harald as they sat at the King's table later that night.

Sweyn had been practically beside himself with nerves and angst as he sat next to Harald, who, conversely, was boisterous and loud, entertaining those around him with the very tales of the empire that I have related to you in the last few days.

Finally, the Danish pretender had summoned the courage to try and pry into Harald's intent. No doubt his men had told him of the rumours spreading through the hall. Ulfr had done his job well, and many men were staring at Harald wide-eyed and whispering among the crowd.

Harald waved the question away dismissively. 'Oh, nothing of interest. They are practically begging for peace, offering us silver and grain.' He slapped

Sweyn brusquely on the shoulder. 'They are weak. One more campaign and they will be forced to fight us or surrender. Don't worry.'

'Don't worry?' asked Sweyn, tension written deep in the lines on his face and in the downwards curl of the corner of his mouth. 'I should have been present for the negotiations.'

Harald shrugged. 'If there had been serious negotiations, I would have called for you. But I dismissed them as pointless talking.'

'If you dismissed them, why are they still here?' Sweyn asked, pointing at the Norwegian delegation sitting at a table on the other side of the King.

'For appearances. If we sent them away, we would seem unreasonable.'

'Then why do they look so pleased?'

'Hmm?' Harald pretended his attention had slipped and then smiled. 'Oh, I told them we would consider it and that peace was what we sought. No need to waste an opportunity to weaken their position further.' He nodded and looked away rudely, signalling the conversation was over.

Sweyn looked anything but reassured, as I know Harald intended.

'I do not like being removed from these negotiations, Harald,' he hissed, barely controlling his anger. 'Men are saying you have sold my claim to Denmark for your own interests in Norway.'

Harald paused and turned to regard Sweyn carefully, and all amusement was gone from his flinty glare. 'Which men are saying that? Bring these liars before me so that I may hear their accusations and respond. None were in that room besides me, so none should dare speak of it except to honour my words.'

He had spoken calmly, but even Sweyn was taken aback by the anger in his face.

He waved weakly at the hall. 'It is rumours and gossip. No man would stand before you and claim it.'

Harald looked confused. 'Then why pay it heed? Drunken men say many things that are not true, and that they do not mean.'

Sweyn looked a little embarrassed, but he did not back down. 'My claim to Denmark is the most precious thing I own. I merely defend it, even if it is from rumours, rumours that impinge my reputation. What is the most valuable thing to you, that you would not defend it if men threatened it so?'

Harald considered it for a moment, then nodded. 'Land Waster, my standard, is the most valuable thing I own.'

Sweyn was surprised. 'Your flag? You are the richest man in all the north, and your most valuable possession is your battle-standard? Why?'

'Because men know of it, and know that wherever it goes, and whoever it is raised against, I will be victorious. A claim to a throne is just words unless you sit upon it. But under that flag I have never been defeated, and that reputation is more valuable than all the gold in Rome,' Harald said carefully.

Sweyn's cheeks coloured as the obvious insult bit home. He had failed in three attempts to defeat Magnus in battle, despite his reported skill and courage. Harald comparing Sweyn's thrice-failed claim to his own famed success in battle was a humiliation that was not lost on Sweyn, or the dozen or so men now listening to the tense exchange.

Sweyn tried to brashly dismiss the insult. 'Bah, I will believe in its value when you have raised it against Magnus three times and been victorious. Until then, it is just a flag and an empty promise of battle I have yet to see.'

Harald was silent for a moment, as was everyone around us. 'I will not be lectured by you, cousin, on what to do with my nephew, or how and when to seek battle.' He stood. 'Perhaps I will do as those envoys ask and seek partnership with a man who has stood victorious three times on the field at the end of battle, not fled from it thrice in shame. Now we shall go and drink in our own company, rather than share this hall.'

There were gasps around the table at the insults, and Harald strode from the room in a furious rage, gesturing to us with a single turn of his hand to go with him.

All of us surged from the benches, leaving the stunned hall. As we got outside, I scurried to catch up with him, hoping to calm his anger.

I got alongside and saw that he was grinning from ear to ear, and I sighed.

'That should do it,' he said casually.

'I suspect so,' I muttered. 'What now?'

'Now I believe he will send men to kill me.'

'Then we must arm ourselves and prepare a defence,' I said grimly.

'No,' said Harald with a mischievous grin. 'We will not be seen to prepare first for a fight; it will look bad.'

'Then what do we do?'

'We gather the men and drink into the late hours of the night, drink and be merry, and make sure we are seen and heard doing so.'

I was completely lost, thinking Harald had lost his mind over the long three years without action. 'So what do we do when they come to kill you?' I asked, exasperated.

'Ah, that's the truly clever part,' said Harald, putting an arm around my shoulder with a pleased tone. 'We let them.'

* * *

'This is a stupid plan,' I grumbled for about the tenth time as Ulfr and I sat in our boat, holding our mugs of ale which I had barely touched.

'I know, but it is pointless arguing,' said Ulfr calmly.

It was late, and Harald and most of the men were around a huge fire on the foreshore at Uppsala, drinking, laughing, singing and generally making a great ruckus that could be seen from everywhere along the crowded anchorage and the shore beside it.

That, of course, was the point. Harald was demonstrating that we were not men preparing for a fight. We were, in fact, getting quite visibly drunk.

None of the watchers – and there were many watchers, for no one could sleep through that noise – would know the barrels our men were cheerfully drinking from were mostly water. Nor that many of the men were wearing light Roman maille under their cloaks, and weapons were laid out under blankets around the edges of the space, just in case Sweyn attacked us openly.

But Harald was sure he would not. That would be a foolish move, even for the angry Danish lord.

Finally, the party around the fire died as its flames receded, and half the men simply lay down where they were in drunken stupors. Harald made a great show of staggering to his ship with only a handful of men, making a great deal of noise, making sure everyone saw exactly where he went in the torchlight of his guardians.

Then, when they were aboard, Harald lay down in a makeshift bed near the stern under a sail stretched out to cover him against rain, and the torch was extinguished. A single man, visibly nodding off with exhaustion and drink, sat in the bow to keep watch.

'And now we wait,' said Ulfr nervously.

We were hidden in deep shadow, and I was sure we could not be seen. Nor could the dozen men lying uncomfortably in the bilge of our ship.

'Yes, now we can do nothing but wait.'

* * *

We waited for so long that I started to think nothing would happen. The single sentry in the bow of Harald's boat was loudly snoring, and the sail-covered area where he and his companions had gone to sleep was silent. Nothing moved within or along the shoreline.

'There,' whispered Ulfr, as our ship gently rocked with the movement of the waves. The sound of men grunting and wet slaps on the hull came from behind us. But I ignored it, for creeping along the shore in the shadows, almost invisible in the weak moonlight, was a small boat, headed for Harald's ship.

'Ah, they are here,' said a voice from behind me. I turned to see Harald's hulking form in the darkness, hearing the water streaming off him and dripping on the deck. Behind him, the rest of the half dozen men he had lain down with in the stern of his ship were huddled after their slow, cold swim from the other vessel. They had slipped one by one overboard on the side facing away from the shore, and crept their way through the water, barely keeping their heads above the surface so as not to be seen, until they reached us.

I shook my head at the ridiculousness of it, and we watched the small boat creep up to Harald's ship. There were perhaps four men in it, and they watched the snoring sentry carefully and I held my breath.

That man, I knew, was both sober and awake, and was essential to luring the killers into believing there was nothing out of the ordinary. Just a drunken, snoring sentry sleeping in the blood hour just before dawn. A fantastically brave man, for if the killers decided to slit his throat just to be sure, there was nothing he could do about it.

But they clearly decided he was not a threat and slipped carefully over the side in the moonlight and padded towards the stern, disappearing into the deep darkness under the sail. There was a series of thuds, and a hissed curse of anger.

'Now!' Harald said, and we all stood up and shouted into the night with alarm and anger, making sure we were as loud as possible. One of the men opened a cover where he had been carefully keeping a small fire tended, and we lit torches, picking them up and waving them chaotically.

Visible panic spread aboard Harald's ship and the four figures bolted out of the tent, suddenly lit up in the dim outer-reaches of our torchlight. They scrambled back into the boat even as the snoring sentry stood for his most crucial task, rising like an awoken god and launching his spear at them from mere paces away, skewering one of them through the side.

The three others abandoned their fellow to lie thrashing in the bottom of the ship, even as the lone sentry howled at them in anger and outrage but carefully avoided preventing their escape.

We finally got our ship moving, throwing off the rope that held the anchor stone in place, and clumsily poling our ship towards Harald's.

It was all quite a show, all done for the benefit of the hundreds who would be scrambling from their tents and bedrolls and coming to see the source of the alarm.

We got alongside Harald's ship, and scrambled aboard, making as much noise and confusion as possible. We did not want anyone to discern that the ship had been empty. Harald stood in the bow, shouting furious orders and summoning his men on the shore to arms.

Well. It was all quite fun, I admit.

By morning light all our men were armed and aboard our ships, and Jacob sent his own ship out to us to see what had happened. The worried-looking King was escorted aboard, and Harald solemnly showed him to the sleeping area in the aft end, where, in the middle of the steering platform, Harald's distinctive, gold-trimmed Varangian's cloak lay wrapped around a huddled form, an axe embedded in the cloak and what lay beneath.

The King drew in a breath of nervous anger as Harald carefully prised the axe free, and removed the cloak to show a sack of grain and a line of barrels beneath, arranged into the rough form of a man.

The similar fake men that had been under cloaks on either side had been cleared away.

'I left it untouched, so that you would see. Only my huskarl's caution in telling me to sleep elsewhere and leaving this pretence of my body saved my life from the assassins as my men slept around me.'

Jacob nodded gravely, taking it in. 'And what of the assailants?'

Harald shook his head sadly. 'My men killed one, the others escaped.' He pointed at the slumped form lying at one side of the ship.

'Only killed one?' Jacob said dubiously.

Harald looked embarrassed. 'We had... drunk quite a lot. More than we should have.'

'Hmm, so I heard.'

'Well, who is this man?'

'We do not know,' Harald said, shaking his head regretfully. 'None of us recognises him.'

We had needed at least one body, you see, to prove that we had not pretended the entire attack ourselves.

The King looked at the body thoughtfully. 'I know who you are thinking is responsible.'

Harald did his best to look neutral. 'I have no proof, my lord, and thus will not speak it.'

Jacob looked at Harald carefully. 'Good. It would be better if no rash accusations were made.'

'I understand.'

Jacob looked at the body again. 'I will see if he can be identified.'

That would be difficult, since the man had unluckily taken a really nasty facial injury shortly after his death.

Ha! I see you laughing. Well, that was Harald – every plan was more complicated than it needed to be, but his reasons were sound. It was not in our interest for the would-be assassin to be identified. We hoped Sweyn had been clever enough to use men he could not be linked to, but we had cut half through his head with an axe just in case. The mere belief that Sweyn had acted, the obvious conclusion everyone would draw, was enough for us.

'I suggest you leave Uppsala while I attend to this... incident,' said the King firmly. 'You can return later, when everything is calm and I have found the culprits.'

Harald inclined his head in deference. 'I think that would be wise, Lord King.'

King Jacob looked furious, and gave Harald a bitter look. He knew he was being manipulated, I think that was clear. He knew that Harald had wanted to leave without Sweyn and would not intend to return. He knew that his plan to weaken Magnus and control the balance of power in the north was hanging by a thread, and that now, inevitably, he would have to contend with Harald.

And he was not pleased with any of that, I am sure. But he had no choice. Sweyn had been foolish enough to be provoked, and his failed assassination had left an axe buried in Harald's cloak, the perfect proof of an alliance broken. Within the day, every man in Uppsala would hear that Sweyn had treacherously tried to kill Harald in his sleep. None would complain when Harald himself then declared the alliance over.

That was Harald, friends. He always found a way.

4

We sailed quickly, because of course we had prepared for it the night before and there was genuine concern that, with his ruse having failed, Sweyn might use his significant forces in the city to simply engulf us in a straightforward attack. Given that the alliance was now considered broken, King Jacob might not have even tried to stop him.

But nothing happened. Was Sweyn too slow? Too concerned about the aftermath? We will never know, for I never saw the man again.

We sailed our two ships south around Scania, laden with all our property, and then up towards Norway. We knew we were sailing into danger, and an uncertain future, so we left all our families behind. Elisiv, Olga, all those women who had come with our men from Kyiv. They would be safe with King Jacob until we returned, and it also served as a symbolic promise that we would not betray him. Harald was implicitly surrendering them as hostages to assure Jacob that he meant no quarrel, although I do not believe they ever actually agreed such a thing formally.

Either way, with just ourselves, our wealth and our weapons, we sailed to claim Harald's crown.

Now, Magnus had invited Harald to meet him at Konungahella, the old royal hall and meeting place of kings, in northern Scania, and I presume that is where he and his men were gathered, ready to move south to the islands to protect his southern holdings if required. So I was quite surprised when Harald ordered the steersman to sail past the inlet that led to the meeting place.

'We are not going to meet Magnus?' I asked.

'We are, but not immediately. It gives him too many advantages. There is no need for us to do exactly as he wants.'

'So where are we going?'

Harald looked at me with a soft smile. 'Home. To my father's old lands in Upplond.'

I looked away in concern at the shore. 'Magnus might see this as an invasion. Why risk it?'

'He will not see me travelling home with one hundred men as an invasion, nor will it be.'

'But it will worry him.'

'I intend it to. Look, Eric, imagine how desperate he must have been to send an invitation for talks to share his kingdom with me. He knows I have a vast fortune, and I know he must have been completely drained of wealth by five years of war in Denmark, and the destruction of his tax revenue there. I am not going to him as a supplicant, to be summoned to his chosen ground to receive his offer. When I meet him, it will be as near to being equals as possible, and we will make sure everyone knows it.'

He smiled and waved at the horizon, where Norway lay beyond sight. 'I am not arriving to beg for part of his kingdom – I am being invited here to buy it. Like a man at a horse market, I will go and inspect my purchase before I make it. I want to see what support I have, for gold alone cannot make me king if the people of my father's own lands do not accept it. No, once I have made it clear that I have the support needed to claim the title of king, only then will I meet with Magnus to arrange the terms, and trade peaceful transfer of power for the gold he needs.'

I nodded, for it made sense even to me, and I was always slow in matters of politics. 'It will certainly give you a stronger position,' I replied. I looked at him carefully. 'But it is not your intent to share your kingdom with Magnus.'

'Of course not,' said Harald with a guffaw.

'Then once this great agreement is made, how will you claim sole rule? A kingship cannot be so easily won from a man who is young and strong, with great support, all of which Magnus has. And he will have part of your wealth also. Merely killing him might lose you the support of the lords and the people, and it might require a war that destroys the entire kingdom to achieve that.'

Harald's smile faded and he nodded. 'I know it. And I cannot confide with you any clever plan to achieve the final victory, because I do not have one. I only know that within a few years of sitting in Sweden, raiding Denmark every year, my wealth and reputation would have been squandered, and Magnus simply had to avoid confronting me to gain victory and make me irrelevant, exactly as he did to Sweyn. While Magnus is my enemy, it is better to sit in Norway, earning taxes and weakening his own support, than sit in Sweden spending gold and making enemies of my own people.'

He smiled at me with calming confidence. 'I do not know what the opportunity will be, my dear Eric – I only know that it will come, and I will seize upon it.'

I slapped him on the back and set my own eyes on the horizon, glad that he had chosen a path that, for now, was not the path of war and loss. I had seen enough of both.

'I believe in you when you say it, Harald.'

'I know you do. Now, let us see if the people do too.'

* * *

We sailed north into the great fjord from where rivers lead in towards Upplond. We landed near Akre Gard, the old meeting place of the people of the southern lands. Now that little farming village is grown into the royal town of Anslo, but as you should know, it was just a collection of farms and a meeting place at the time.

Now, we could have paid the local karl to keep our ships safe at his dock, which he was well used to, for many who travelled to Upplond chose to leave their ships in the bay rather than make the difficult journey upriver. Our heavily laden ships, however, were too fat to make the journey, and full of too much valuable cargo to leave under another's supervision. So Harald split our force in two and left Rurik with fifty men to make camp there and guard the ships, and to bring much of our treasure ashore in secret and hide it.

It was a significant risk, but carrying such a huge load to Upplond would have been an enormous effort, and no less dangerous.

Anyway, taking risks were how Harald made himself king.

We carried what we could and headed north, five days' walking until we reached Ringerike, the land where Harald's father had once ruled as king, and where Harald had not set foot since he was merely twelve years old.

That was his first great challenge. Almost no one there had ever met him, although all, of course, knew who he was – he was one of the most famous men of Norway, even in his absence. At first, he found it hard to find anyone of note who would take him in as a guest. His father's old lands and holdings had long ago been given to other men, and nothing was left that was legally his own property to claim.

I think Harald had been hoping to be immediately welcomed home by his father's old people as a returning ruler and hero, but his father had died thirty years before, and most of the men who were in their prime and owning large lands there were barely old enough to remember their old petty king. Certainly, very few were old enough to have sworn allegiance to him at the time.

Morose, and quite angry, Harald pushed on northwards through his father's old lands, being treated with more concern than acclaim.

Things finally changed as we travelled up the western shore of Mjǫrs lake and reached the land where one of Harald's father's leading supporters had lived: Tord Guttormsson.

Harald had met the old man when he was a child, and although the man himself was surely dead, Harald held hope that his family would still welcome him.

We were met there by a young man who came excitedly out to see us.

'Harald Sigurdsson?' the young man said when I introduced us.

He had come down to the edge of his lands with a dozen armed men, which must have been all he could gather at a moment's notice, but that was not alarming – it was a perfectly normal reaction to fifty armed men arriving and asking for reception.

'Yes,' Harald said, stepping forwards. 'And who are you? I want to see the lord of this land. Who is it? Perhaps it is still Tord Guttormsson, or his sons.'

The young man did not look insulted as he bowed. 'I am Tore Tordsson, and I am the owner of these lands, although I would not call myself a lord without my King's blessing.'

Now, I see you all tense, and I hear your little gasps of protest. And yes, forgive me for speaking his name in your presence, King Magnus, I mean no insult. This was indeed the same Tore Tordsson of Steig who stood against your kingship, and whom you rightfully executed for his rebellion a mere three years ago. But I tell of him with care and import, because although he died in shame and dishonour, he was also the very first man of Norway to call Harald king and was essential to Harald's rise to power. So allow me to speak of him, a little, and not to venerate his memory but to be truthful as to the man he once was, and what he did for Harald's rise.

In any case, Harald looked at the boy Tore with renewed interest. 'You are Tord's son? But you are so young.'

'I am fifteen years old, Prince Harald.'

That struck home with Harald, I could see. That was the age he had been at Stiklestad. Suddenly the young man did not seem so young, and in his confidence and bright demeanour, Harald could see a little of himself, I think.

'Well, then you are a man before the law, and I am merely a guest in your lands,' Harald said graciously with a small bow. 'I would request guest privileges, and some space for my people to set up camp.'

'Oh, Prince Harald, that you shall have and more,' said Tore with a happy smile. 'Your men shall camp in my farm, and you shall sleep in my home and hall, be most welcome here and honour me by it.'

This was the first warm welcome we had received, and Harald was childishly pleased. 'Why are you so happy to receive me, Tore? For surely you know your King and I are at odds.'

Tore straightened a little. 'My father never stopped speaking of his love for your father and bade me follow his son if ever the opportunity came. You are not at odds with my King, Prince Harald, for I believe you have come here to be so.'

Harald looked at the enthusiastic young man and the dozen who followed him, carefully assessing them. Then he stepped forwards, slowly, closing to whispering distance, and found himself not so much taller than the proud young man. 'If I offered the chance to swear to me, what could you offer me more than yourself and your dozen men?'

Tore was not dissuaded by the soft insult. 'I can raise a hundred men from these lands for the leidang, and I believe I can sway many of the landowners in this land to your cause, with your help. There is much discontent with Magnus here – he does not give us the respect and position we used to be afforded, preferring the Danes and the men of Viken in the south. The bondes of

Upplond could be yours, Prince Harald, and I would be honoured to be the first to swear to you.'

Harald carefully considered it and nodded. 'There is no jarl here, correct?'

'No, Magnus does not allow it. He fears any man becoming too powerful in these valleys.'

Harald nodded. It made sense. Upplond was, and still is, a powerful and wealthy area.

'If I called a Thing for these lands, would the karls attend?'

Tore nodded. 'I believe so. They would want to hear what you have to say, and I would support you in calling it.'

Harald looked around, thinking for a moment. 'No, it would be better if you did not. I will see a more truthful representation of the feeling towards me if it is me alone that calls it.'

Tore looked taken aback for the first time. 'If you think so.'

Harald met the younger man's gaze again. 'Do not be insulted. It will give you the chance to be the first to pledge to me, in public, with none knowing before and thinking you are merely my servant.'

Tore's brows furrowed. Clearly his age and lack of title ate at him and his pride was pricked, but he nodded. 'As you suggest.'

Harald gestured up towards Tore's sprawling farm. 'Now tell me, whose support do I need to gain?'

* * *

Well, the Thing of Upplond, the Eidsivating, was not due for many months. But Harald sent out word to all the landowners of the valley that a Thing would be called at Ridabu to discuss the future of Upplond, and that all who wished to have a part in it should come. Ridabu was a symbolic choice – it had been the meeting place of the Eidsivating before King Olaf's time, before Olaf moved it to Eidsvoll, on the southern tip of the lake, as a political favour to the powerful men of that area further south.

By calling a Thing at Ridabu, he was subtly calling to, and sympathising with, those who might naturally see him as their enemy because of his association to Olaf, and also signalling respect to their traditions.

Despite that, the gathering was modest. Far from everyone who owned land in the area came – unsurprising since the notice given was short – but nearly a hundred of the wealthy landowners of the region came to listen to the son of the long dead petty king of Ringerike speak.

The gathering field there is very much like this one we sit in today. Nothing more than an ancient farmer's field, bounded by wood and stone, but without the benches Jarl Halfdan has been kind enough to set out for us here. Harald took the position at the head of the gathering, and he had no need to stand on a block of stone or a stump, for he was the tallest man there.

'I will not introduce myself. If you are here, it means you already know who I am. But given what I am going to ask for, I will tell you a little of what I have done. I served in the army of Yaroslav of Kyiv. I captured for him two great and two lesser fortresses at the head of my men. I became the commander of his royal guard, all before my nineteenth year. I went to Miklagard, the capital of the Romans, to join the Varangians, and in the service of the empire I won four great battles and seven lesser ones, and captured over a dozen fortified towns or cities and over fifty lesser forts. I became the commander of the Varangians. All this, before my twenty-fifth year. I became, through these actions, the most successful and wealthiest man of the North, and I have married a princess of the Rus, the daughter of Yaroslav, the most powerful man in the world.'

Harald said it all calmly, without overt pride or boast, as if he were listing items for a market sale. That always helped impress men, I have found. Those who feel the need to impress with their noise or bluster, rarely do.

He gestured to the men gathered at the side of the field in their maille and cloaks, but with their weapons stacked and piled to one side to make it clear they meant no threat.

'One hundred of my Varangians, the greatest warriors in the world, chose to follow me home for one purpose: to assume my rightful place on the throne of my brother, Olaf.'

'King Magnus is the son of Olaf, his claim is rightful,' said an angry voice from the crowd. There was a great muttering and, let us say, the exchange of strong opinions.

Harald waited for them to calm and nodded. 'The kings of the North are chosen for two virtues, and two virtues alone: a claim by right, and the ability to defend and enrich their people. Magnus has one, but he has failed utterly to provide the other. What glories has he gained? What wealth has he brought?' He looked at them with his hands outstretched. 'How many times has he raised taxes in Norway to go and defend the Danes?'

'He was victorious in every case!' a man protested.

Harald pointed at the man. 'Victory on the battlefield is only one aspect of success in battle. That is something I learned deeply in the empire. Tell me, karl of Norway, what benefit did you draw from those victories in Denmark? What glory or wealth did Norway gain?'

There was silence to that.

'Nothing,' said an angry voice. 'Three of my sons and half of my silver went south to Denmark three years ago, and only two of my sons – and none of my silver – returned.' The angry man spat on the ground.

'Exactly.' Harald's expression darkened and he shook his fist. 'A good king would not spend Norwegian lives and Norwegian silver protecting Danes who cannot protect themselves.'

There was a strong swell of agreement to that, almost completely drowning out any dissent, and I could see Harald was winning the crowd.

'I say the Danes should pay for their own protection in lives and silver, and the men of Norway should look only to the interests of Norway. My nephew Magnus has lost his way.'

'So what would you do, kill him?'

Harald looked appalled. 'No! I would say, let him be king of the Danes that he loves so much, and let there be another king in Norway, one who cares about the Norwegians in his heart, who lives here and protects these lands, who fights only for the glory of Norway. If Norway and Denmark are to be joined again in the future, let it be with them as our supplicants, subject to our rule.'

'You would be Cnut,' said a voice, laughing derisively.

'Yes!' shouted Harald. 'And why not? When since has Norway had such wealth and glory as when Cnut ruled all the lands around us? When has Norway bled so heavily as when Cnut spent our lives in England and Denmark and the northern islands?'

Harald shook his clenched fist, eyes aflame. 'Blood must be spilled for wealth and glory to be gained.'

The man shook his head. 'Glory? I care not for glory; it does not feed my family.'

'But wealth does,' Harald countered. 'Those who would only be sheep farmers are welcome to remain so and will not share in our success.'

The man furiously looked away, because few sympathised with him.

'So what do you suggest, Harald son of Sigurd?'

Harald nodded, looking out over everyone before answering. 'I would ask you to call me king, as once you called my father king. And, like him, I will be faithful to you, honour you, and lead you to prosperity.'

There was muted shock in the gathering, for the words of rebellion had been spoken and could never be unspoken.

'There are no petty kings in Norway any more, Harald. They are all dead or gone, and you cannot stand against Magnus with just us beside you. It is madness.'

Much of the audience, despite their obvious support for what Harald had said, agreed, nodding and adding their voices. It was one thing to complain about the King; it was another to go against him sword in hand.

'And you are right, but I will not be standing against him, I will be making terms with him,' he said, summoning Ulfr for his pre-planned display. Ulfr came over with another man, carrying a small barrel between them, both men grunting with the effort.

'This will not be solved by the shedding of Norwegian blood against Norwegian blood; this will be solved by the shedding of Roman gold.'

Ulfr placed the barrel on the ground and stood aside, and Harald, with a flair of flicking his cloak aside, raised his foot and kicked the barrel over.

There was a gasp as it crunched to the ground, and a wave of silver and gold spilled from it – coins and jewellery, bars and rings cascaded and scattered in a shocking, shining river of wealth at his feet.

Some of the coins bounced and rolled into the crowd across the hard ground, to be quickly grabbed up by the stunned audience, but Harald did not even look at them. Worrying about such trinkets was beneath him. Surely no man in that audience had ever seen such wealth before, and it was one of the wealthiest regions of Norway.

Harald stood with one foot on the barrel as the men chattered with each other in animated, roiling groups, staring wide-eyed at Harald's casual display of extreme wealth, pointing and gesturing at the riches and then at each other, until struggles broke out with the ferocity of their disagreements.

For a while I thought it might not even work, that their fear might overcome their greed, but then a voice called out for calm, surprisingly strongly.

'Respect yourselves, men of Upplond! And respect this gathering with your calmness.' A young man stepped to the front and waved to the crowd, who slowly paid attention and fell to something resembling quiet.

Tore walked serenely over to the barrel, also ignoring the riches at his feet, and faced Harald.

'My father served your father and did well from it. He was always safe and wealthy and never disrespected or abused. I, Tore of Steig, say that I would do for you what my father did for your father, and I would kneel to you and would call you my king.'

There was silence around the gathering. All it took was for one landowner of status to call a man king and he was king under the old customs. King only of the land that karl held, but a king, nonetheless. Of course, that custom has been erased with the rise of the unified crown of Norway – and a good thing that is too – but at the time, those words held real meaning.

It had taken twenty years, but Harald was now a king. It was that simple.

He looked at Tore, jaw tensing and eyes blazing, and he held up his hand to forestall the chattering of the crowd. 'I accept this offer, and I will take the oath of Tore of Steig, and make my own, as our fathers once did.' Then, slowly and deliberately, he took off his own cloak, his wonderful, richly woven Varangian cloak, and he laid it across his arms and offered it to Tore.

'I came here as a Varangian, and I leave here as a king. Take this Varangian cloak, Tore, so that wherever you may go, men will know that you wear the cloak of Harald king, and that you were his first subject.'

Tore smiled and took the cloak with a nod of gratitude, for it was a wonderful gift.

'Not only this poor cloak,' Harald said. 'You will take from my hands silver such that you can carry, so that all will know the riches that I will bring to those that follow me, and I declare that you shall never pay unto me or Norway taxes in silver again, as long as we both shall live.'

That was a shocking gift, for without taxes, a king has nothing but what he earns for himself. But such a thing did not bother Harald, for he had always been one to earn wealth with his sword. That would come back to hurt him later in his reign, but… that is another story.

Tore bowed and stood aside, putting the cloak across his shoulder, because it was too long for him to wear.

Then Harald looked out across the crowd, who were all eyeing the cloak, the casually scattered riches, and thinking of a life without taxes.

Do any of you doubt the outcome? Ha! Of course you do not. Most of the men present swore to him, right there and then. Some held out, of course. I am a little ashamed to say Harald used the implied threat of steel against them, where the promise of gold had failed. Those men all woke up in the following days to find Harald's warband of Varangians standing outside their doors in silent ranks, fully armed and armoured, watching quietly, refusing to speak or answer questions or demands to leave. They did no violence, but they made their point.

More men came to Harald to swear to him after that.

Harald handed out silver and gifts and recruited men. He called for men with their own good maille and weapons to join him, and he paid them well, and our little band grew from fifty men to a hundred men in less than a week. Not quite enough to be an army. Harald was careful not to raise an army, but certainly to form a hird fit for a king.

We moved south through the Upplond, Harald speaking at every gathering he could find or summon and using steel and silver to persuade the reluctant and the greedy alike. He found resistance, great resistance. The further south we went, the more popular Magnus was. And he *was* popular – don't let anyone tell you differently. King Magnus was known as Magnus the Good because although he took much in taxes, he was fair to the people and forgave his enemies. Very little Norwegian blood was spilled on his hands, and people liked him for it.

But people love silver more than kindness, and Harald had it in vast quantities, and spent it as we moved south. Not grossly, not foolishly, not giving away his fortune. He was clever as you know, and wise, and he showed men far more wealth than he gave them. He merely wanted them to get a taste of what was to come, not eat his entire hoard. It was enough, he knew, for them to see the treasure and be captured by its sheen. So again and again, in a dozen different towns, the same barrel of gold was kicked over in front of wide eyes and open mouths, and the stories of his generosity and wealth spread like seeds on the wind, drifting all through the kingdom, just waiting for the right ears to receive them.

5

AKRE GARD, NORWAY; AUTUMN 1046 AD

And so those seeds reached Magnus, as of course they were intended to do, and he sailed north to confront this man who also called himself king, although Harald was careful not to repudiate Magnus's title of Norway, and merely called himself King of Upplond.

We heard that Magnus was coming, and Harald immediately marched south with the men we had gathered – not enough to fight Magnus, but enough to show him Harald had true support and could not easily be taken or killed.

We met Magnus at Akre Gard, where Ulfr and his men we had left behind were encamped, raising our forces further so that we had over 200 men.

Magnus arrived with twice that, his ships filling the foreshore, anchoring in the traditional royal anchorage, and camping in the royal enclosure that was reserved there for such occasions, for it was an ancient meeting-place and Harald had chosen it carefully.

I went to meet Magnus's representatives, and a truce was agreed that no man, king or karl, should break under pain of being declared outlaw. Magnus brought all his men ashore and both sides disarmed and stacked their weapons in their camps. A joint feast was agreed, which Magnus, as King, would host.

It took two days to prepare, both in gathering animals and in preparing the feasting area. There was no hall there fit enough to hold us, so a great tent of woven sails was made, and benches and tables found or roughly made to hold over a hundred of the most important men. The other hundreds would sit around fires in the field and eat together as a sign of friendship. It was all carefully arranged, although I spare you the details.

Finally, the feast was called, and entire animals were roasted over open pits and every barrel of ale within thirty miles was collected and opened for the men to drink and celebrate the fact that none of them would die the next day.

Magnus sat at the head of the feast on a raised platform of wood, Harald on his right, with all of the right side of the tent filled with our men, and all of the left side with Magnus's men, all facing each other. Nobles crossed the tent to speak to friends and enemies, to make boasts and repair feuds. It was an opportunity for diplomacy, and threats or hostility were banned by the order of the two kings. Many came to see Harald, many who had never seen him before and wished merely to meet him out of curiosity, or those seeking patronage.

One of the nobles there took particular care to come and impress himself to Harald.

'I am Finn Árnasson, of Orlandet in Trondelag.'

'I know who you are, Finn Árnasson,' Harald replied with a smile. 'You were my brother's man.' His smile faded. 'Although you did not fight with us at Stiklestad, so close to your home.'

Árnasson nodded sadly. 'I did not know of the battle until it was over. I had pledged to meet your brother in Nidaros and intended to do so. As you well know, the people of that area were not expected to oppose him, and especially not in such numbers.'

'But your brother knew well enough, and he was present for the battle,' Harald replied. He was speaking of Kálfr Árnasson, Finn's brother, and the man who had led the rebels and killed Olaf along with Thorir the Hound.

'My brother knew because he organised the rebels, and he did not deign to tell me of his treachery, because he knew I opposed it,' Finn said, keeping calm amid the accusations.

'So, your brother – where is he? He still resides in your lands? He was Magnus's greatest supporter and sponsor. I last saw him in Kyiv, taking Magnus away to win him the crown.' Harald looked around. 'But I do not see him on the King's benches. Where is he?'

'My brother overreached and fell out of the King's favour,' Finn said with a sad nod.

'So your brother betrayed every king he ever served.'

Finn looked uncomfortable but did not deny it.

'And yet, you do not condemn him?'

'I oppose him, Prince Harald, but he is my brother, and I cannot condemn him. I pray for his repentance and forgiveness.'

King Harald nodded slowly, ignoring Finn's pointed avoidance of acknowledging him king. Finn was still sworn to Magnus, and in a difficult position. 'So, you are here to seek my forgiveness for him. That is a lot to ask for my brother's murderer. Too much, in fact,' Harald said sternly.

Finn shook his head. 'I do not ask for his forgiveness for he has not repented, and one must follow the other. I merely ask that you consider, as a good Christian and a leader, that you make a path to him earning forgiveness, however hard that path is to cut.'

Harald looked at Finn carefully. 'I suspect you do not expect this path to be cut by me alone, so what help do you offer?'

Finn settled in over the table. Now they were down to the real business.

'You need a powerful ally in the north, to counter the influence of Einar Thambarskelfir Eindridesson, who is King Magnus's foster father and foremost supporter. His is also the most powerful family in Trondelag, but my family are the second.'

'And what reason have you to choose me over Magnus?'

'Einar, in his jealousy and desire to remain in his position, has treated us poorly, and abused his relationship with the King to repress us.'

Harald grunted. 'So you wish to build a relationship with me to equally abuse.'

Finn smiled. 'You understand exactly.'

'And, if your alliance to me is fruitful, you hope eventually to persuade your brother to repent of his grievous sins and receive my forgiveness.'

'I do.'

Harald considered Finn carefully, weighing up the cost. He was not a man to forgive easily, and we hated Kálfr above all other men. The blood debt between us was vast and deep.

But... Harald desperately needed allies, especially in the north where they had hated his brother so much the very farmers had thrown themselves onto the swords of Olaf's warriors just to get at him and kill him. I remembered their hatred vividly. We needed friends in that place, lest Harald suffer the same fate.

Harald finally spoke. 'I accept your offer, Finn, although I warn you that your brother's path to forgiveness will be paved not with gold or words, but with actions. Repentance is nothing if merely uttered by the tongue. As Christ himself showed – you must bear your cross despite the heat and the thorns.' Harald leaned in, his face deathly serious. 'Do you know, Finn, that I have visited the very place where our saviour was crucified?'

Finn's eyebrows rose. He had clearly not known.

'Yes, it is true. I have been to the Church of the Holy Sepulchre. I have prayed at Christ's tomb and knelt at the spot where he was killed. I swear to you, by those holy places, that your brother will bear his cross and suffer my judgement before he is forgiven, and it will not be easy.'

Finn swallowed and bowed his head. 'I accept your judgement, King Harald.'

'I'm not your king – not yet.'

Finn met his eye again. 'Yes, you are.' He stood and left, moving on down the tables.

* * *

It was a good feast, honestly, given that it took place in a field and the weather was not as good as we could have hoped. Halfway through, Magnus stood and brought in twenty men carrying bundles of weapons and equipment, and for a moment we were alarmed. But he went to our side of the tent, at the head of his men, and came to me, as I was sitting next to Harald, and I stood and found myself face-to-face with him, who I had known as a boy, and found now to be a kindly-faced and confident man.

He said nothing to me, but he turned to his men behind and took a fine sword, a really well-made weapon with a good leather scabbard decorated in brass and silver, and he pressed it into my hands. 'A gift for you, so that you may better protect your king.'

It was a clever thing to say for he did not clarify which king he meant, and it was a clever gift because it showed both generosity and respect, which are the two things all men crave.

'Thank you, King Magnus,' I said with a genuine bow of gratitude, and he moved on to the next man, taking a fine shield, rimmed in iron with a snarling wolf on the front, and pressed it into his hands. 'A gift for you, so that you may better protect your king,' Magnus repeated.

And so he went down the entire side of our tent, giving each man either a fine sword, shield, helmet or rich cloak, until everyone had met him, and received a gift from his own hand.

I watched Harald, and you might think he would be angry at Magnus's clever display, but he was not. Harald, above all things, loved a good opponent. He had little respect for Magnus forgiving his enemies, especially the enemies who had killed King Olaf, but he knew Magnus was no fool. That feast proved it. Really, the entire event was just them sizing each other up, examining each other's determination and intellect.

Finally, Magnus came up to Harald, and his hands were empty. All were watching with great care and quiet, because the fate of Norway hung in the silence.

'Kinsman, which gift will you take from me?' Magnus took out from his cloak a reed. Just a common reed as would be found beside a river, and he broke it into two equal halves, showing the room.

Harald looked at Magnus carefully, a little confusedly perhaps, even if he tried not to show it.

Finally, he pointed at one of the broken halves. 'I will take this one in your right hand, as you have given all my men great gifts with that hand tonight, and they seem otherwise equal.'

Magnus handed over the broken reed. Turning and facing the room. 'With this half reed, I give you half of the realm of Norway, with all the taxes and properties due to it. I declare that you will be king everywhere in Norway with the same rights as I. As the first king between us, I will have precedence in all things where honour is given, I will take the central seat in all gatherings of nobility, and where we go together the benefit of royal estates, moorings and docks shall be mine. In return, you shall support and strengthen my power and that of Norway, for I have raised you to a position no man thought we could both occupy.'

He gestured to his side of the tent, where many of them looked openly shocked. 'Rise, and greet Harald Sigurdsson, King of Norway.'

The men in the tent, on both sides, obediently rose and acclaimed Harald as Magnus held his hand, and I could see that Harald was moved, deeply. He was shocked, I think, to finally have the title he had craved for so long, despite him and Magnus having discussed this deal in advance.

For all his life since Stiklestad he had wanted one thing alone: the crown of

Norway, and now it sat upon his head, even if its circle included his young nephew.

We cleared away the tables, joined the benches together so that the men of each side could drink and celebrate together as the men of Norway they were.

We got riotously, shamelessly drunk and, for one night, I think Harald was truly happy.

* * *

Three days later we held another feast, this time hosted by Harald. He was careful not to exceed the feast of Magnus and replicated it in every way as to not upset the new-formed alliance. The same tent was used, with the same tables and benches, and a very similar feast was served with ale and mead.

Harald was left sitting there in contemplation, and my eyes wandered to Magnus's side of the tent, where I saw the old man Einar watching us carefully, clearly having been watching the entire time.

He may have been old, but Einar Eindridesson was a big man, powerfully built, close to rivalling Harald for his size. But he was fat as well as strong, and his earned name 'Belly-shaker' was both an insult to his size and the fact that his fearsome mass and strength made men's stomachs churn when they had to face him in battle. Despite being twice Harald's age, I suspected not all his strength had left him, and certainly his ruthlessness and ambition had not.

As the meal ended, Harald stood and waved Ulfr into the tent on the side of Magnus's party, and a dozen men followed him with wrapped parcels. Harald went to the first man on his fellow King's side, and, taking a Roman-cast gold bar from Ulfr, offered it to the noble. 'With this wealth, may your service to the King of Norway be repaid.'

Harald used the same clever language as Magnus – an amusing riposte, for he did not say which king he meant.

And it was a fine gift, worth more than a good farm, and the noble's face was flush with gratitude.

And of course, as Magnus had done, Harald moved down the line, handing out bags of silver, rings of jewelled gold, a gold-scabbarded Roman sword, and other treasures from his personal wealth. And to each man he praised them for their loyalty and service to the crown. That was his own clever message, you see. That loyal service would be repaid by him, for he knew it had rarely been repaid by Magnus.

Finally, when every one of Magnus's men in the tent had their gift, he sent Ulfr out into the field beyond with several chests full of silver coins, to distribute to those who had not a seat in the tent, to whooping roars of appreciation and men calling out his name in thanks.

Magnus smiled at the display, for it was so humorously and diplomatically done as to match his own gifts but not greatly overshadow them.

Then Harald set out two chairs in the central space, quite far apart, and gestured to Magnus. 'Come, kinsman, and take a seat with me.'

Magnus came down happily and sat opposite Harald, and Ulfr laid blankets out covering the entire space between them. Then, one by one, dozens of our men came in carrying boxes, chests, barrels and sacks, and emptied them onto the blankets.

It was all Harald's remaining wealth. Every bit of it, and the total together, which even I had never seen in one pile, was shocking. Even Magnus, who was so good at remaining calm, was wide-eyed and astonished. The rumours of Harald's wealth did no justice to its scale. It took our men a long time to arrange it all, and the tent filled to the brim as word of what was happening spread through the field.

Finally, the outrageous pile of silver, gold and valuables was all set out, and Harald just sat there smiling softly.

'King Magnus, three days ago you conferred a great gift on me, one half of the realm of Norway, which you had won from our enemies with great honour and courage. Today, I repay your generosity and split with you my wealth which I won in the same peril and honour, each to take and do with their share as they choose.'

He leaned forwards and gestured to the pile. 'It would please me if you would make the first choice of item, and then we shall have the rest weighed and divided fairly according to its value.'

Magnus could not avoid showing his excitement and pleasure, and he stood and examined the pile carefully. Finally he selected a heavy golden cup the size of a man's head. 'I choose this cup, from which I shall drink to toast our rule.'

Harald smiled. 'A well-chosen gift. I took that cup from the tent of the rebel Emperor Petar Delyan, after I slew him in battle. It is one of the more valuable items I own.' Then his smile faded a little. 'Tell me, nephew – what can you offer me as gift that can rival its value?'

Magnus looked a little taken aback by the challenge, and he thought about it as he put the magnificent cup down by his chair. Then he shook his head sadly. 'We have been at war defending the realm for so long that all my gold and silver taken in plunder and taxes is spent. There is nothing of value left to me to rival this, other than this ring I have on my own hand.' And he took a fine gold ring off his own finger and proffered it to Harald.

Harald did not look impressed, and hundreds of men watched in concern, for the tone had shifted as Harald had picked his moment to try and appear superior and reduce Magnus.

'That does not approach the value of what I gave you with that cup, which I took from an emperor.'

'Oh, Harald, but to *you* it does. Calm your pride and use your eyes. Do you not recognise it? For I had this ring from the hand of a king beloved by us both, who had it from another king before him. When it sits upon your hand, it will be the ring that has passed between four kings of Norway, all of them kin.'

Harald paused, his face draining a little, and he looked at the ring again, all his hostility and bravado stilled. 'By God, you are right. This is my brother Olaf's ring, who received it from my father in tax and as a gesture of his loyalty,' he said, half in wonder. He looked abashed. 'I was wrong, King Magnus. I have nothing left of my father or my brother, so to me this is a gift more valuable than any other.'

He closed his hands around the ring gently, reverently, looking down at it with more emotion than I think I ever saw him display before or since. I can tell you, to demonstrate to you how much that ring meant to Harald, and how it utterly silenced his usually unrestrainable aggressive spirit, that he wore it from that day until the day that he died, and it was his most treasured possession.

Then Magnus broke the laboured silence by standing and gesturing to one of his followers. 'Work with King Harald's men to split this wealth fairly and without conflict and then take my property to my ship and set no guard upon it, for we have nothing but friends and loyal men here.'

I tell you truthfully, it was hard not to admire Magnus, for he was a good man and a wise king. He came away from that meeting looking like a great king who had faced down the famous Harald Sigurdsson and lost no honour in the process, and none called him coward for giving away half of his kingdom, for they all knew it avoided a war that would have been terrible in its bloodshed and destruction beyond anything Norway had experienced before.

He was called Magnus the Good, and I swear to you, he earned that name.

6

Well, you all know that relations between Magnus and Harald broke down very quickly after they were separated for a while to go about their business. I shall not relate to you the squabbles and petty arguments, the criminal actions and accusations by men of one side or the other trying to earn their ruler's favour. Harald was careful to tax very slightly too much for his share. Not enough to be proven, but enough to aggravate matters. Magnus was careful to enforce the image that he was the superior king, and Harald merely his subordinate.

Both men needled at each other relentlessly, and all the great men of the land competed for the affections of one or the other, desperate to prove their loyalty. Skalds made songs and poems uplifting one and subtly insulting the other, and more than one lost their lives for it.

It was during this time that Tjodolv Arnórsson came to be in Harald's court at Anslo and was his favourite skald and his true friend. I did not know him well nor like the man, for he was overtly a sycophant, but in fair judgement I must also say his loyalty was true and strong, as later events would prove. He was also, without a doubt, one of the most talented of skalds, and many of you will be familiar with his songs and poems, many of which are still performed in these days.

Harald sought vengeance on those who had wronged him in attacking his brother Olaf. He most wanted vengeance on Kálfr Árnasson but could not because of his alliance with Finn and the rest of the Árnasson family. Kálfr had fled to Orkney anyway, not believing that Harald would spare him, which infuriated Harald further.

Kálfr Árnasson's flight to the Orkney islands was particularly aggravating for Harald because he fled to stay with his kin there, who jointly ruled the islands with Rognvald Brusason, whom Harald loved and had hoped to win over to his side along with the battle-hard men of those islands.

But Rognvald, bless him, was true to Olaf's memory and refused to welcome Kálfr, and it spurred a conflict between the lords of Orkney that Rognvald eventually lost. He was killed by Kálfr's men in an ambush after having won several small victories against them. Harald was affected badly by that but would often remark that Rognvald was the truest of his followers, who died fighting Olaf's enemies even fifteen years after King Olaf's death, and was thus the most honourable of men. His hatred of Kálfr only grew, burning deep within him.

All this conflict and killing caused great anger across the kingdom and worked very poorly for Harald. He was causing strife where none had existed, and Magnus's popularity grew and grew as Harald carried out his campaign of excessive taxation and settling of scores. I think it was Harald's theory that any conflict was good, because it increased the chance that something would happen that would allow him to gain the throne, and that peaceful existence was the death of his dreams.

Honestly, I think that was true, and it might even have worked – but fate had other plans, and matters were resolved much more quickly than I think any of us expected.

* * *

In 1047, less than a year after they agreed to share the throne, Sweyn invaded Denmark again using the distraction of the two kings of Norway who were focused on each other. He forced the people of several of the larger islands into obedience, and Magnus and Harald united to raise the leidang, the army of the nation, and sail south to defeat him before Magnus's control was lost permanently.

Now why, you might ask, would Harald sail south to save Magnus's kingdom of Denmark from Sweyn?

Well, because he wanted the kingdom for himself, and if Magnus died, Harald would have the strongest claim to its throne. If he let Sweyn take over, he would have to conquer Denmark by force. It was in his interest to sail with Magnus and help him secure his realm. You see? Sometimes politics is so easy even I understand it. Now you – yes, you, I see you at the back laughing at me. I may have failed so many times to understand Harald's plans, but you are sitting in a field listening to an old man tell impossible stories, and you are not even drunk yet by way of excuse. So who, I ask, is really the fool?

Well, our fleet that year was not so large but sailed to Denmark uncontested and we marched about in Fyn and Skjaeland enforcing Magnus's control. Wherever we went, Sweyn fled long in advance, and we progressed slowly, as each town and area had to be put back under Magnus's control. Harald would have scoured the whole land, as indeed he later did, but Magnus wanted to rule those people, not conquer them, so only in a few cases did he use violence against those who were known to support Sweyn openly, as to set an example.

There is only one event during that campaign worth speaking of, and you all know what it was. The history of our country, and all of the countries around the western sea, was decided there.

Harald was with Ulfr and me planning the next day's march in some nameless town in the middle of Skjaeland, south of Roskilde, when a messenger from Magnus arrived.

'The king feels unwell. He will rest here tonight, and we will march when he feels ready tomorrow. Await his signal.' And with that said he left abruptly, because the messengers between the Kings were routinely rude and brusque with each other, and the two Kings very rarely spoke in person.

Harald snorted in annoyance. The campaign was nothing like one that he would have commanded, but he was without a doubt the subordinate since we were in Magnus's realm, not Harald's.

'Another day's delay,' he exclaimed angrily, throwing his half-empty waterskin to the ground in disgust. 'Sweyn need not even flee from us. He must merely hope our men die of old age before his.'

'Shall I convene the leaders?' Ulfr asked.

I should explain, things were done very differently in Harald's army in Norway to the way he had commanded the Varangians. As King, he had men of his own personal hird, who were commanded in the field by Rurik, and then most of the men who followed him were commanded directly by their local lord, who was loyal to Harald. It was a far less organised and disciplined system than Harald was used to, and I know he hated it for its inflexibility and ponderous system of orders.

He could not command the men directly; he had to debate somewhat with their leaders, and whatever was agreed was conferred to their men. It is a system any of you who has gone on campaign will be familiar with, but I want you to understand that for Harald, after ten years fighting in the highly structured armies of the east, it was infuriating. He appointed a marshal to organise the leaders, and he chose Ulfr. And a good choice it was too, for Ulfr was brave, skilled and loyal. Perhaps if Styrbjorn had survived to return with us he would have been a better choice, but alas...

'No, we will not convene a meeting to talk about it. Merely pass the message that we are staying here for an extra day. Make sure supplies and firewood are organised.' Harald looked at Ulfr's reproachful stare and sighed, waving at him irritably. 'Yes, I know, you will do that without my command.'

'It is not the place of a king to worry about firewood,' Ulfr said. 'Not when you have those to do it for you.'

'It is my place to worry about everything, Marshal. But fine, go and do your duty, and tell me if there is anything I need to address.'

'Yes, Lord King,' Ulfr said with a small smile, because none of us were used to calling him king even if he had taken to it so easily. For some of us, he would always be the bright young Varangian commander.

Harald turned to me and his face was odd, like his annoyance had passed and he was deep in thought.

'I will organise the evening meal,' I said, for I really had no role in Harald's army other than to advise him, and help manage the lesser commanders and supplies.

'You are not my steward.'

'No, but it will give me something to do while you grumble and complain about Magnus, which you can do as well without me here.'

Harald did not smile, which annoyed me, but he waved me away without a word and went to his tent with Rurik. I found his mood odd, but Harald was always under a great deal of conflicting pressures.

* * *

The next day we sat and waited, and Harald paced irritably, often deciding to send for word on the King's condition, but always changing his mind, as Magnus's people would only tell us when they decided to, and respond poorly to demands for information.

Finally, as the afternoon arrived and his patience wore thin, he sent Ulfr, who returned looking disturbed.

'What did they say?' Harald asked.

'Nothing.'

'They refused to tell you the King's commands?'

Ulfr looked at Harald carefully. 'They refused to speak to me at all. In fact, I think there was no one there who *could* speak to me.'

'What do you mean, no one there? How can there be no one there? Has Magnus left?'

Ulfr shook his head. 'No, but the King's quarters were in a very strange state. I think all his lords are in his tent, and there were servants and karls running about everywhere, looking panicked and harried.'

'The King's illness must be serious,' I said, and Harald looked from Ulfr to me.

'I don't like it. Send word out to all our men – get ready to break camp.'

'Break camp?' I looked at him in confusion. 'Why would illness make us break camp?'

Harald looked away. 'I just want to be ready for anything.'

Rurik went to talk with Harald, and then he ran off to stir the hird from their tents.

* * *

It was not long before Magnus's camp stirred into a great commotion, and no one came to speak to us. Harald was increasingly angry, and finally he lost his temper.

'Rurik, put the hird in formation. We are going to their camp to demand an answer. Something is very wrong.'

'All of the men… Should we be ready for a fight?'

'Fully armed. Be ready for anything but make no hostile intent. Let's go!'

Well, let me tell you, to march into Magnus's camp fully armed with 200 men was about as hostile an intent as could be displayed in the atmosphere that existed between those two Kings. They camped separately for good reason.

I expected us to be stopped at the edge of their camp, but not only did no force assemble to block us, no one even asked us who we were. The camp was in chaos, men going everywhere. Some were packing their tents, and I was afraid. There were no good outcomes to what was happening.

We marched through their camp in formation, and although men avoided us warily, none confronted us, and some did not seem to care about us at all.

'This is all deeply wrong,' Ulfr said.

Harald just grunted and increased the pace.

We quickly came to the King's quarters and found Einar Thambarskelfir talking in hurried tones with a group of four or five of Norway's leading men. They looked at us nervously as we arrived, and several sent men off at a run, presumably to summon their own forces.

'I come with no intent of violence, Einar,' Harald said, holding up both hands to make it clear.

'Then why now of all times, and why with so many men?'

'What do you mean, why now?' Harald asked, and Einar and one of the other lords looked at each other nervously.

'You have not heard? Then why are you here?'

'What have I not heard, Einar? Speak now, I am one of your Kings and I demand an answer.'

Einar looked at Harald darkly, and his hate was written deeply. 'You are not *one* of our Kings, Harald Sigurdsson.'

Harald was stunned, outraged. 'Do you finally declare your treason against me, old man?'

Einar shook his head. 'God sees fit that you are our *only* King now.'

Harald huffed but his rage faltered and he leaned forwards, raising a finger. 'Speak clearly. Magnus is dead?'

Einar turned and looked at the other lords and nodded. 'His illness took him.'

My mouth hung open and Rurik cursed like a whore. Harald had the decency not to smile in triumph. He instantly leapt into his commander's role.

'Then we are in peril and must act quickly. We must calm this nonsense in your camp, get the army together, and quickly enforce my leadership on Denmark before Sweyn acts to try and steal the crown. Gather all the leaders.

We must go to Roskilde and then to Viborg and hold a Thing in each town to secure our rule.'

Einar looked at the ground nervously, and then at his fellows for encouragement. None of them could look Harald in the eye, and Harald started looking nervous for the first time. My hand drifted to the hilt of my sword. There was the stink of rebellion in the air and suddenly I was glad of the 200 men behind us.

'Einar!' Harald snapped, and finally the man found his courage and faced Harald.

'We have already met and decided. We will not support you in your claims on Denmark. Magnus gave his commands, and we obeyed them. We will take his body home to be buried properly with his father and leave the Danes to their own fate. We are tired of foolish wars in this cursed land. If you wish for their throne, take it yourself. I would rather follow good King Magnus home in death, than follow you or any other king alive in a foolish campaign here.'

Harald was furious, his face turning red and his whole body tensing and preparing for violence.

'You refuse to acknowledge that I am King,' Harald said, the words practically forced out of him in a growl.

Einar looked sullen and shook his head. 'I acknowledge you as King, Harald Sigurdsson: King of Norway, and I will recognise you as such when we are there. But this is not Norway, and my duty, my final promise to my foster-son and liege, was to escort his body home. His army wishes the same, and we will return him safely to his father, for we loved him. You could learn a little about that, the love of your people, oh great King Harald.'

And with that Einar nodded at the other lords to go, for clearly the situation was escalating towards violence.

'This is an outrage. We came here to determine who would be king of Denmark, Sweyn or Magnus! You committed yourself to this campaign and you think you can merely leave before it is decided?'

'Oh, Harald, how sorely you misjudged Magnus with your treatment of him and your views of his courage. He knew exactly who you were, and he did nothing but think of protecting Norway from you. You thought yourself clever in undermining him, but he was always ahead of you, leading you like a sow to market, doing whatever was needed to save our people from your destructive character.' Einar shook his head in fury and spat on the ground. 'You accuse me of breaking my word, kinslayer? I swore to support Magnus in this campaign until the dispute with Sweyn was decided. Open your eyes, fool-king – the kingship of Denmark *is* decided. Magnus sent word of his support for Sweyn's claim and that he dropped his own claim in his final hours. If you rely on inheriting Magnus's claim you have nothing, for he rescinded it. You could oppose Sweyn anyway, but I expect the people of Denmark will choose him over you, although I would be nothing but pleased if you stay here to contest it and never darken our shores with your rule again.'

And then Einar stalked off, leaving Harald speechless with rage in his wake, and the men around him standing there too scared to move or breathe for the depth of insult Einar had pronounced on him.

Finally, I dared to approach Harald. 'We must return to our camp; there is nothing we can do here.'

Harald nodded curtly, jaw clenched, humiliation writ in pained lines across his face. He turned on his heel and strode back down the path, our men scattering out of his way and then reforming in his wake.

'What does this mean?' Ulfr said nervously, looking at me.

And I returned his stare with deep, heavy sadness, my dreams of a peaceful life with my family dying in my mind.

'The only thing it could mean for a man like Harald: war.'

* * *

'Harald we *must* return to Norway,' I said, beseeching my furious King.

'If we return to Norway, Sweyn will secure rule in Denmark before we can ever return! No, we must march with all haste to Viborg, demonstrate our power and will, and have me declared king before Sweyn can do so!'

'And then Sweyn will have himself declared king in Roskilde, or anywhere else – Aarhus! Who knows!'

'So? We will march to defeat him.'

'With one third of our army? The rest are leaving as we speak!'

Harald turned on me furiously. 'With one thousand men, with one hundred, hell below, with ten alone I will resist this injustice and this treachery. That *boy* Magnus gave away my rights, to a traitor? It cannot be allowed to stand! Maybe it will take us months, maybe years, but we will secure this kingdom, and to do so we must start *now*!'

'And what of Norway!' I shouted back at him, shocking the assembled commanders who were loyal to Harald. 'What will that snake Einar and his allies do if we do not return immediately? Will they claim another heir to Magnus, and we will return weakened by war to a nation divided with two kings once more? No, Harald, you must not stay here and fight for Denmark, you *must* secure your home and your throne first or surely lose it all. You have no support here in Denmark, have had no time to build it. Norway is the only place you can hope to rule this year. Please, I beseech you, shed your wounded pride and go home while you have a throne to go home to!'

I stared at him, all my willpower and desperation forcing me to meet his furious, roiling, wounded hate. And it was not hatred for Einar in that moment, it was not hatred for Magnus or for Sweyn. It was for me. I was the one finally taking the kingdom of Denmark from him, I was the one stealing his dream, by daring to say what he and all the others around us knew to be true.

I was killing his ambition. I, the man he counted loyal above all others. And it broke both our hearts together.

'If I leave Denmark to Sweyn and return to Norway where only one in three lords counts me as a friend, I will not be able to return and take the throne here this year,' he said, his voice almost a whisper of grief. 'My chance will be gone, perhaps forever.'

I put my hand on his shoulder. 'I know it. But fuck Denmark. Go home to your brother's throne. Finally, you will sit alone upon it, as he would have wished for you. Remember his words, Harald, so many years ago.'

Harald's eyes moistened and the fight sank out of them. 'I remember them, Eric. That you were to protect me, and I was to listen to you, because you were wise beyond your years.'

I nodded, feeling his grief and sharing it. 'Let's go home, Harald.'

Harald looked around the gathering, and saw their averted gazes, and their hope that he would agree. There were a great many worried men in that circle, worried that they would not be able to return home if another king took power, for he would cleanse the land of any who supported Harald.

Harald breathed hard and stiffened. 'So be it.' And his anger swelled and returned. 'But this is not the end. I will not surrender my rights here. I will return next year to claim my throne and damn any man of Norway who does not support me.'

'Harald,' I pleaded quietly.

He held out a hand to silence me. 'No, Eric. Not this time. I have done as my brother bade me and listened to you, but I am King and I will make the final decision. We will go and secure my throne, as you ask, but I will not resign myself to the loss of Denmark through this treachery and cowardice... Never!' he hissed, and my heart sank.

Was that the moment I lost him? I don't know. It felt like it at the time, and it has felt like it ever since.

7

TINGHAUGEN, NORWAY; SPRING 1098 AD

'You are a fool, Eric, if you believe King Magnus simply died. All men know that Harald poisoned him,' called out a loud voice, dripping with scorn. The current King looked up in surprise at the man calling out so rudely and interrupting Eric's tale, but then raised a curious eyebrow to the storyteller.

Eric looked unperturbed and stared at the man who had interrupted. 'How long have you been listening to my tale, brave young man?'

'For two days,' the man called back.

'Two days? Huh. And how old are you? Much less than thirty years, I think. So your father was perhaps a child when these events took place – maybe your father was still in your grandfather's sack – and yet you think to tell me I am a fool for my telling of events that I witnessed, that I should not believe a man I lived with for most of my life and knew better than any other man?' Eric laughed warmly. 'Yes, a brave young man you are indeed to say something so stupid in front of so many.'

Laughter rang across the field and the man's smirk shattered, his face reddening with anger.

The fool pressed his case instead of backing down.

'I do not need to have been there to understand you were blinded by your closeness. Magnus was young and healthy, and then, at the moment Harald wanted him to die and was present to cause it, he died.'

Eric nodded. 'All of those things are true, but none of them prove Harald did anything.'

'Then how do you know he did not?' The man sputtered, drawing himself up.

Eric just smiled and let the moment draw out a little as the nervous young warrior stood there, angry and embarrassed.

'Harald never broke an oath he made in all the time I followed him in the Rus and in the empire. He was exceedingly clever, as you have heard, in finding ways around his word without directly breaking it, but he treated the idea of breaking them outright as sacrilege. So I know he did not kill Magnus.'

'Why? Was he oathsworn not to kill him?'

Eric shook his head. 'No, he took no such oath. But I also suspected he had killed Magnus and questioned him. He swore to me that he had not.' Eric shrugged. 'So I know that he did not.'

The man snorted. 'He lied to you.'

Many of the men in the audience bristled at that. King Magnus straightened in his chair. It was one thing to accuse Harald of committing a crime – Harald was somewhat famous for his views that the laws did not really apply to him, and for committing outright murder. However, murder was a quietly acknowledged tool of kings, as was lawbreaking. But to accuse him of lying? That was a direct assault on the dead king's honour.

The fool was in dangerous water, and he did not seem to know it, so angry was he at his humiliation.

Eric's smile had disappeared, and he stared at the young man. 'You think I do not know that it is possible Harald lied to me? That he killed Magnus with poison and concealed it from me because he was afraid that the secret might escape and the nation renounce him?'

'That is exactly what I think he did. If he had told you, you might have told others, and the nation would have rejected the killer of King Magnus the Good.'

'Then I say to you that you have never known loyalty and honour, and are, in fact, an honourless man,' Eric said, standing, his face stony.

The young man gaped in outrage and then looked around and saw that there were few sympathetic faces in the crowd that was watching the exchange. He gulped, but he was still young and proud. Too proud.

'What reason do you have to question my honour? I should cut you down for it!'

Eric laughed, throwing his arms to the side to expose his chest. 'You are welcome to try, fool! I say you have no honour because if you did, you would understand why I have said that I know Harald did not kill King Magnus. I was Harald's sworn man, his loyal companion. He gave me his word that he did not kill the king, and he is not here to explain himself. What kind of man would I be if I did anything other than defend his honour? I say that Harald's words are true because he is not here to say so himself, and thus it is my simple duty. What kind of base, disloyal dog would I be if, in front of all these great men of Norway – Harald's kingdom – I said that his words were a lie, without any evidence other than the convenience of events and the opinion of a loud-mouthed pup?'

Eric leered at the furious young warrior and slowly raised his hand, pointing it like a spear at the accuser. 'That kind of man, *that* is what I would be. I know that you know no loyalty or honour because if you did, you could never be surprised that I defend my king's name and reputation. I have no evidence that Harald ever broke his word, but I declare with all the evidence a man could ever need that your word is worthless, your honour is meaningless, and your name shall never be written down or spoken by the skalds. Come, dog, and prove me a liar with words or actions, or begone from this place of honour and truth.'

The warrior's face went bright red at the sheer force and weight of Eric's words. He looked around, seeing nothing but contempt on the faces of the audience.

He made to step forwards towards Eric, fists balled in anger, but several men got up immediately and blocked his path, staring him down as Eric leered triumphantly past them.

'Back away or be put in the dirt,' one of the men said in a calm but loud voice.

The angry young man clearly considered it, but the second man put his shoulder next to the first, hemming him in.

'Will you fight us instead of an old man, coward?'

The warrior contemplated it, gone too far to save himself. But he had no chance against the two men facing him, and others were standing by. He would never reach Eric. He gave one last furious snort and turned on his heel, leaving the field to jeers and whistles of contempt.

When he had disappeared from view, King Magnus spoke. 'Whose man was that?'

A lord stood from the nearest benches, looking anguished. 'One of my followers, Lord King, he is...'

'Do not speak his name!' Magnus snapped, and the lord nodded and lowered his eyes to the ground in front of the King.

'That man shamed himself and this gathering, insulted my family, and will never be seen here again.'

The lord nodded vehemently and sat as Magnus gestured at him with his fingers.

Magnus shook his head. 'That was unworthy. I apologise, Eric.'

Eric bowed his head. 'It was not your doing, my lord.'

The King nodded and waved irritably for Eric to continue. Eric inclined his head and returned to face the audience. 'Now, where was I?'

'Calling a warrior a coward in public like that... He might have killed you. How did you know he would not?' Jarl Hakon asked loudly.

'Friendship,' Eric said with a smile. 'And because if he had killed me, you wouldn't have heard the rest of the story.'

There were laughs across the field, breaking the tension.

'And if they had not stood for you?' Jarl Hakon asked.

Eric laughed coarsely. 'Then I would have killed him myself!'

'How? You are not as young as you once were, and I am sure he is a good warrior.' Hakon said with a wry smile.

Eric's smile snapped out. 'No! He is a fool, and a fool can never be a good warrior. He might be skilled with a sword, he might be strong and brave, but every fool with a sword I ever met is dead, and I am alive. Nothing about that was going to change in this field today.' He shook his head. 'I had won that fight before it even started, and he was too foolish to know it. Bah.' Eric snorted, waving the air of the departed man away like a foul smell. 'He was not worthy to face me.'

Hakon held his hands up in mock submission. 'I believe you, Eric, and I would not dare contradict.'

Eric smiled and clapped his hands together. 'Good – you are learning! Now, shall I continue?'

* * *

We returned home from Denmark separately from Magnus's followers, for Harald was too angry to go with them. That was a mistake, and it looked bad for him to the people, who were distraught about Magnus's death. Far more so than we expected. There was an outpouring of grief across Norway about his untimely demise, for almost all said that his rule had been just and prosperous and admired the young king for both his efforts to keep peace, and his decisive victories when war was forced upon him.

Harald did not react well to what he saw as the disloyalty, and although no pretender stood against him and in that winter's Things all the regions of Norway stood and confirmed that he was their King, he was not well-liked.

He immediately started planning his campaign to Denmark, where Sweyn had indeed claimed the throne by way of his relation to Cnut, and was proclaimed King without resistance.

But planning such a campaign was hard, and meant taxation of the people, and taking their men away again for war. It was the fifth of the last seven years that the leidang had been called to war, a highly unusual frequency, as you will all know, for it has not been called now more than five times in the last thirty years in this era of stability and peace.

Everywhere that we went to raise taxes and men we faced resistance; everywhere the welcome grew more and more cold. He was compared very poorly to Magnus, and it hurt him deeply. He was a brilliant military commander, intelligent beyond almost any other man, but in understanding of men's love and loyalty and the politics of keeping a nation happy, he was sorely lacking in understanding and experience. I am not afraid to tell you this, because an old man like me cannot be afraid of the truth, and although he is rightfully loved and remembered well now, at the time, it was a dark cloud in Norway wherever he travelled, and even loyal men made excuses not to greet him.

The Danes, hearing of his troubles and assuming foolishly that they would never see him again, mocked him from across the water. Harald heard a story of how the Danes celebrated his tenuous hold on Norway by cutting cheeses into the shape of anchors and throwing them into the sea to float to Norway, saying that Harald would never have the courage to bring his ships to Denmark and moor them there again, so anchors of cheese were all he needed as he would never cast a real anchor on Danish shores again.

A strange insult, but the Danes are very strange people. Regardless, Harald took that disrespect very poorly, and, if they could have known what it would lead to, I am sure the Danes would have eaten their cheese instead of making jokes with it.

As you can expect, after all the humiliation and insults, nothing could dissuade him, not even me, and in 1048 we went to Denmark on campaign, and we harried it. We did not just raid and loot, to my regret – we devastated and burned it like it was those rebel lands in Greece I told you of last night. We killed anyone we found, took everything of value, and salted the very earth behind us. We tore wounds through those islands so deep and so bloody that some areas have not recovered to this very day. All driven by Harald's anger, as much as being a strategy to lure Sweyn out to fight.

Einar and his allies did not send a single man to aid us, flaunting their disrespect of Harald and their unwillingness to support his campaign in any way. But Harald had the choice of going north in a very dangerous move to subdue his wayward northern provinces, one that could lead to another civil war like the one that had killed Olaf, or to go to Denmark. So, of course, he chose to confront Sweyn.

But still, Sweyn, new to his kingship, did not come out to face us; he had learned from Magnus how effective and frustrating that strategy could be, and we did not leave any settlement alive that could support us for the winter, so we had no choice but to return home.

Harald carried great riches back to Norway, and was generous with them as was his way, and he earned the loyalty of a lot of men who had been dubious. He also ensured that future campaigns would attract a great deal more enthusiastic participants. Nothing can draw men to war like the lure of silver and a commander who knows nothing but victory.

Harald learned from the mistakes of his first year, because he was not a fool, and spent a great deal of thought on these matters. He made attempts to improve his position further in Norway. He married Thora, daughter of Thorberg Árnasson, one of the great men who had followed Magnus, and sister of both our great enemy Kálfr Árnasson and our ally Finn Árnasson. It was a very clever match, for the people mistrusted his foreign queen Elisiv, and the Árnasson family was large and powerful and the marriage secured their closeness to him.

He did not discard his Elisiv; he simply lived with two wives and kept them on two royal estates so that they never came into conflict. His marriage with Thora may have been entirely political to start with, but he was very affectionate to her, and she quickly bore him two sons, whom he called Magnus and Olaf. That was wise politics, let me tell you, and went a great way to smooth over the ill-will that many people held for him, by honouring their memories in that way. Elisiv only bore him two daughters, Queen Ingegerd who still sits aside the throne of Sweden today, and poor Maria, whom Harald loved the most of all his children, and whose heart was so bound to his that she would die when she heard of his death. It pains me to think of it, for what a future she should have had.

You may wonder why I dismiss two years of Harald's early rule with so few words, but it was because I was spending most of my time building my estate, near Tore's in Upplond, and raising my young sons and daughter. Harald did not campaign in 1049, and I was glad of the peace, for I was truly tired of the business of war and starting to wonder what my place by Harald's side even meant to either of us, except that perhaps we were both clinging to the ghost of the past. A ghost with the face of King Olaf.

Having improved his position somewhat at home, Harald made his plans to campaign again in Denmark in 1050, and made sure it was known. He wanted the Danes to be afraid, he wanted them to demand Sweyn come out and face us. No more stories of anchors cut from cheese were heard from Denmark that year. Instead, they prepared their ships for the water and cut wood for spears and arrows. Among all the people, the knowledge that a great confrontation would take place became more and more certain.

Finn brought his brother Kálfr back to Norway, having persuaded him to end his self-imposed exile. I was not there, but the two of them met with Harald at Finn's estate, and Harald made an accommodation. Kálfr would support him in his campaigns and pay an extra tax as compensation for the murder – although they would not call it that, for declaring he had murdered a king would result in being outlawed – and they parted ways.

When I saw Harald next, he refused to talk about it, I suspect because it angered him so much that he had been forced to make peace with his most hated enemy.

To our surprise, a messenger from Sweyn came in the winter, and he did not come offering peace or compromise.

'Sweyn Estridsson, King of Denmark, invites the traitor Harald, son of Sigurd, to do battle to resolve their claims, at the Gaut river at the boundary between Norway and Denmark, five months hence, on the first full week after the solstice. To the victor: the crown of Denmark, never to be disputed again.'

Harald did not show his surprise. 'That is a noble offer from Sweyn and the Danes. You may tell him that I will meet him in battle, and long to finish our dispute in the honourable way.'

He gathered us together once the envoys were gone: Rurik, Ulfr and I, for we were the only men of importance with him during the quiet winter months, when most men stayed at their own estates. In fact, I was only there by chance, as I visited Harald from time to time as was my duty.

'This suits me well,' Harald said with a smile. 'Perhaps too well. Why would Sweyn offer battle when he has no need to?'

'His people have suffered greatly from our previous campaign, and we have carried away a huge amount of their wealth,' I said uncertainly.

'What we have carried away is only a fraction of the wealth of the Danish people,' Harald said, 'and that only from Fyn and Skjaeland. Surely, the people there cry out to him to protect them, but the great lands of Jutland and Scania? They hold the power and have not yet felt the edge of our blades. Why would they risk this, for a King with such a poor record in battle?'

'They must think it is to their advantage, but I don't see how,' I agreed. 'They have wisely avoided battle with you for years. What has changed?'

'Nothing that I know of,' Harald said.

'Perhaps it is a distraction, and they will invade Norway while we are in the south.'

'That is possible, but if true, why would they invite us to battle on the border with Scania, and not further south where we would be too far away to help our homeland?'

'Because to invite us for battle deep in their lands would be overly suspicious?' Ulfr mused.

'I agree,' said Rurik. 'If they want us to go to battle there, it is to our disadvantage, and thus we should not.'

Harald nodded. 'They will know I cannot refuse the chance of battle. What will men say of me when I have sought it so desperately, and refused it when the chance arrives? So, we must determine what advantage they seek.'

'An alliance,' I said, rubbing my chin.

'An... You think he wants to make an alliance?'

I shook my head brusquely. 'No, I think he must have made an alliance. He will not face you with the power of Denmark alone. He must have an ally.'

Harald hummed and leant back, thinking it over. 'King Jacob – could he turn on me?'

'If he thinks you have become too powerful, surely he could. It is his way, and Sweyn has long had his support.'

'But I am his kin – I am married to Jacob's niece.'

'Such ties have been sacrificed before, for lesser goals. He knows how dangerous you are, Harald. He might well have chosen Sweyn over you. I think this is the most likely reason. The chosen site of battle is close to Sweden, and it would be easy for them to take an army there beyond our notice in the spring,' I replied.

'Then what shall we do?' Ulfr said.

Harald smiled. 'If it is true, we should be glad if all our rivals gather in one place together, for it saves us finding them one at a time.'

'You told Yaroslav you would not fight King Jacob,' I cautioned.

Harald shrugged. 'I am not. I am going to fight Sweyn, and if King Jacob is foolish enough to join on the other side, I can only respond.'

'They will have a large army.'

'They will, so we will raise a large leidang. Half of the fighting men of Norway,' Harald said firmly. 'That is what we will need.'

'Half!' My eyes widened. That was perhaps over 10,000 men, 200 ships. Five times what we had raided Jutland with. The largest army of Norway gathered since Olaf's time. Such large armies were not often gathered in Norway, and still are not, for very good reason. It is extremely difficult to entice so many lords to bring so many of their followers, incredibly expensive to feed and supply them, and a nightmare to organise 200 ships into anchorages, camps and movements. Armies are small in the north for good reason. This is not the empire of the Romans.

'How will you gather so many, let alone campaign with them?' I asked, deeply concerned.

'I will promise them silver, glory, and more quietly, make it known that any lord who refuses to send his fair portion will be taxed extra to support the effort and excluded from all rewards of battle in the future.'

I gulped. He was stretching his blooming power and popularity to the limit, perhaps beyond the limit. 'There are so many barriers to this, Harald. We must convince them all, we must secure the supplies and manage the fleet and...'

Harald smiled and put his hands on my shoulders. 'Calm, Eric. We marched in the empire with five times this number. We learned their ways – let us teach a little of it to the men of Norway, so that they are all the greater for it.'

I just nodded dumbly, I could see there was no dissuading him. Harald moved to Ulfr. 'Marshal Ulfr, you are capable of supplying this army if I provide the silver and the authority, are you not?'

Ulfr smiled nervously. 'Of course, King Harald.'

'Good.' Harald nodded. 'Then we shall prepare. We must attend the Things and make our plans clear to the people and gain their support, as soon as the spring thaw comes.'

'Which Things?' I asked, and Harald turned to me, his smile broadening.

'All of them.'

* * *

Ah, when Harald gets an idea, he does not let go. He was as good as his word, and as soon as the snows started to recede and the Thing meetings were held all over Norway to welcome in the new year, Harald and I raced about Norway in two ships with just a hundred men, arguing his case to the people in every corner of the land.

Harald was so animated, so confident, and so liberal with his promises of wealth, that we did not struggle to gain the agreement of the lords of Norway to support his campaign. Aye, I remember Harald standing in this very spot, under this very tree, at the Frostating of 1050, forty-eight long years ago when few of you were even sucking air, and many of those alive still at their mother's tit. I tell you, he could rouse a crowd like no other, and even in the land of his enemies – for the people of this region were Einar's family and supporters and thus Harald's undeclared opponents – they were so impressed by his courage in arriving here to speak with only a hundred men, that some of them even agreed to follow him. Although Einar, of course, did not.

The Árnasson clan was there and promised a thousand men to Harald's cause. A thousand! It must have been every man they could raise, and boys beside, but they owed Harald a great debt because Kálfr Árnasson was standing there, in the open, mere miles from where he had killed Olaf, and Harald smiled and acknowledged him like a friend in front of Einar and all his followers, who naturally pledged only the minimum to avoid accusations of cowardice.

* * *

By the time the campaign season arrived, we had more than 200 ships gathered in the seaside towns south of Anslo, the new royal town Harald had started building at the site of his great conference with Magnus four years before. In the great fjord there, in some places you could practically walk from one shore to the other across the decks of ships, so many were gathered. It was quite remarkable, and Ulfr had bought every spare bushel of grain and market-ready animal in all of southern Norway. The pockets of farmers everywhere in those lands were heavy with silver, and they loved Harald for it.

But keeping so many men together can only be achieved for a short time. The real warriors would happily campaign for a season, but most of the leidang were farmers and fishermen of course, and they arrived expecting a single battle and then to go home to their families and harvests, neither of which could do without them for long.

So as soon as the appointed time was close, we sailed south in a great mass, stretched out over ten miles of sea, hugging the coast past Viken, where we stopped for the night twice, before arriving at the mouth of the river Gaut, two days before the battle was due to be joined.

I stood in the bow with Harald, as he angrily scanned the scene that lay before us.

Nothing. There was no one there. Even the town at the mouth of the river was abandoned.

'The cowards did not come,' Ulfr growled.

'We are two days early; they may yet arrive,' Finn said without conviction.

'No. This is their land. If they were bringing their army here, they would be here for many days in advance preparing,' Harald said angrily. 'We have been tricked, but not in the way I expected. If they are not here now, it is unlikely they will come at all.'

'So what is their purpose in drawing us here?' I asked.

Harald chewed his lip nervously. 'It could be as you said those months ago, that this is a ruse to leave Norway undefended.' He gestured towards the shore to our east and north. 'Maybe they are marching into Norway overland, even as we stand here.'

'That would take weeks – surely not. And we could cut them off from sea, and if we put men ashore, by land too.'

'I know, it does not make sense. But if not, then what?'

'You are overthinking it, my king,' Ulfr said with a dismissive tone. 'They are simply cowards or failed to raise a sufficient force to face you. You always credit your enemy to be as cunning as you, and it is rarely the case. It is far more common for men to make empty boasts they cannot live up to, than conduct clever ruses.'

'You might be right,' Harald said with a snort of derision.

'So what do we do?'

'Well, we go ashore. I will not let it be said that on the appointed day, I was not here. Maybe the fool Sweyn is merely late. I will give him fair chance to arrive on time and face me.'

'And if he does not? The army cannot sit here for more than a few days – we will run out of food, and I bet a fistful of silver that abandoned town is completely bare of it,' I said.

Harald sighed irritably. 'I know. If battle is not offered in two days' time, we will have to send the army home.'

'It will make you look bad, to have promised glory and sent them home empty-handed,' said Ulfr.

'I know.' Harald paused and then laughed. 'Perhaps that was all this is. Another way to delay and confound me.' He shook his head. 'I was thinking like an honourable man. Does Sweyn care if we call him coward? No, of course not. He simply wanted us *here*, not destroying his lands. He thinks this buys him a year, that we will have to go home and that next year fewer men will follow me if I promise battle again. The bastard. You see Ulfr, he is clever. He adopts a strategy so dishonourable I did not even consider it.'

Ulfr spat in disgust. 'This is not the way kings should behave.'

'So we go home and return next year,' I said, almost relieved.

'Absolutely not,' Harald said. 'We will send home those who must return and take our best men and the men of southern Norway to raid. We will punish the Danes for this dishonour!'

'Harald, we didn't plan for a long campaign *or* bring supplies.'

He thumped me on the shoulder. 'Remember our campaign against the rebels in Greece? Or against the pirates in the Anatolian hills?'

I nodded.

'Well, we never had more than a day's food there, did we? No, we took what we needed from the land, and we moved on.'

I pointed at the town before us. 'They have warned the people here and surely left nothing for us.'

Harald turned his wolfish grin on me, the predator's grin, the one I loved and hated. 'They have warned the people *here*. But I bet you your fistful of silver they have not done the same in Jutland.'

I nodded, relenting. I could see what was happening and that nothing could stop it.

Harald turned to us in glee, slapping his hands together. 'We are going Viking in Jutland, and not ponderously marching about to seek battle, but to sail and raid, fast and deadly, in the old way. Come! Let's make camp and find sixty good ships of men to come and scour Jutland with us.'

8

The Danes did not arrive to give battle, and Harald released the levy troops to go home, keeping only the southern lords and their warriors, the most loyal and the closest to home, to supplement his own.

Kálfr stayed with us with a hundred men, even though Finn returned home with most of their clan. Kálfr needed to prove himself and his dedication and Finn needed to ensure their lands were not left for long without any protection lest Einar Thambarskelfir cause trouble. The old northern lord had kept the peace since the death of his foster son Magnus – so far – but it was no secret to anyone that he hated Harald, and probably wished to overthrow him, although he was savvy enough not to make it publicly known.

He also, I am sure, suspected Harald had killed Magnus somehow, with poison or trickery, and that was a heavy blood-debt, however misguided.

With sixty ships, three thousand men, and barely enough food for two days, we sailed west towards Jutland. We fell upon that rich, untouched land with a fury and a speed that the Danes were utterly unprepared for. We arrived in the dawn at Aarhus and gutted it, shattering its hastily formed militia, taking everything we could and being back at our ships before the midday sun was up.

We sailed south along the coast, Harald sending ships off in groups to raid every village and town we passed, smothering that coastline in attacks that no army on land could possibly respond to, and everywhere we went we were victorious. We let survivors go with the same message everywhere.

'Tell your King we came because he did not.'

Eventually, word spread that the entire coast was in peril, and pickings became slimmer and slimmer. So on south we went, sailing ahead of the news, far down the peninsula, far beyond any raids of recent years, towards the great city of Hedeby, the root of Danish wealth in southern Jutland.

Hedeby is barely known today, but that is because of what we did in that year. At the time we darkened the horizon outside their shores with our sails, it was the richest town in Jutland, perhaps in all of Denmark – the trading centre for all of the southern part of the western sea and as far east as the Rus. Traders there came from Alba and England, from Francia and Saxony – even from the Roman Empire itself, although I have never sailed that route and do not understand how ships can sail west from Sicily and yet still come to our shores. Apparently, there is a passage somewhere down there, where the great ocean of the Romans joins the great ocean of the west, and it must exist, for Roman goods do arrive here when traders are brave enough to make the journey.

Rich towns are well-defended, and at Hedeby we faced our first true test, for they had been warned we were about, and their defenders outnumbered ours.

It was a stern test, but Harald relished it.

Hedeby could not be raided from the land. It had good, stout walls and a ditch. An army much larger than ours would be required to besiege it while its defenders were armed and ready. So we came from the sea, for no wall could protect the acre of docks and harbourfront that faced the lake that led to the sea, and no local force could summon sixty ships to face ours on the water.

So we rowed all the way up the river and into the lake the town sat upon, and came at them from the water, with axes and maille and the war cries of Norway, and God bless those brave souls who stood to face us because they proved themselves far better men than Sweyn that day.

We touched the dock first, as Harald insisted, and he was among the first men to leap onto the planks of the harbour. The men of his hird competed to go with him, so of course, I had to be among them too.

We landed on the hard, even boards with a roar as arrows and spears streaked over our heads going both ways. I was a pace slower than Harald – two paces, if I am honest with myself, because I was already an older man and had not fought a proper fight for nearly ten years.

We were met almost at the water's edge by the men of Hedeby, with their shields proudly in line, their shining helmets on their heads, and their spears and swords reaching out to meet us.

Did I make a great hero of myself in that battle as I did in the stories I told you over the last few days?

Ha! How little you all know of battle if you believe so. It amuses me to think of it, that I was once the greatest swordsman of the Varangians, perhaps in all the empire, because you should have seen me hit that dock, forty years of age, and the first thing I did was trip over a spear embedded point-first in the boards, and fall flat on my face in front of both armies.

Well, we cannot all be heroes all the time.

I was lucky, for the enemy were not advancing, and few enough men were pressing from behind that I was not trampled into mush, as men who fall in battle so often are. I struggled to my feet, far more embarrassed than hurt, and found Harald was already laying into the enemy line with his great axe, Rurik and a dozen other warriors of his hird at his sides, and none in the shocked Danish ranks could stand against his power and fury.

You see, while I slowed and grew fat with age, working my farm and raising my children, Harald trained with his guards, and he was a towering mountain of muscle, and even in his mid-thirties, still only a hair past his prime.

It was quite glorious to watch, I assure you, as the King of Norway, unfettered and filled with battle-lust, broke through the Danish line with so few men, and scattered the enemy, howling like the pagan gods of old.

And then I was catching up to him, the army of Norway at my heels and my sides, and we smashed into the rest of the Danes, and for thirty heartbeats there was a real contest, with wounds and strikes on both sides, but I felt their line bowing, and I kept having to step forwards to maintain the pressure so I knew we were winning.

I have told you, many times, that in nine battles out of ten the first line to start giving ground first will lose the battle. All men know this, and as soon as they start having to edge back, they think less of killing you, and more of how they are going to escape when their army collapses.

That hasty line quickly gave way. We ran to catch up with Harald, puffing and sucking to get air into my already burning lungs. The enemy fled as we organised our men, who were still arriving by the hundred, into formations to attack the town itself. More Danes flooded out of the town's streets, coming down from the walls and the outer defences to face the sudden, unexpected landing in the harbour.

We made our line, five or six men deep, and we fought them again at the edge of the town and that fight was harder than most, because these men were defending their homes and there was nowhere left to run. They were brave, those men of Denmark, and skilled for what they were, but they were mostly levies, and we were the veterans of the east, victors of twenty battles against the greatest armies of the empire's many enemies, and a few hundred Danish townsmen could never have stood against us. Never.

We hammered into their lines, and for the first time in that battle I found myself in the front of the wall near Harald and laid my sword upon an enemy for the first time in years. I found it wildly terrifying and invigorating. The struggle was hard, and men around me were taken down by Danish steel, even as we wreaked great slaughter into their ranks. But I kept my shield on my shoulder, my sword busy around its edges, and my head down, all as I had once taught new recruits. And I was lucky, for no enemy blade found me. Sometimes battle is that simple, friends. Just do the right things and get lucky, no heroics. I was too old to be a hero, and too young to accept death for the sake of trying.

Finally, the Danes broke, and we surged over their bodies and chased after the ones who fled into the town.

Well, I don't think I killed anyone in that battle, although there was blood on my sword and my spear was gone, stuck in some unlucky Dane's leg so deep I left it there as I passed him. But when I went to recover it, I found he had died from another man's blow to the neck. Could I claim that as my kill, for I am the one who put him on the ground? Well, it does not matter what you think, for I do not count it. It was still true that I had not killed a man in combat since I left the service of the empire.

Once the enemy were utterly routed, I finally caught up to Harald, blown and sweating, as Harald gave his orders. 'Loot this town. Take its wealth, its trade-goods and take women as captives. Then burn it to the ground. I want the smoke of its destruction seen from all across their kingdom. We will make the Danes regret the day they called us out for battle, only to leave their wives to pay the price.'

I went up to him with a smile. 'A great victory, Harald.' I was shocked when he rounded on me with a furious expression.

'Where were you, Eric?'

I stopped dead in my path and frowned. 'In the fight.'

'But not at my side?'

'I was... trying to get back to you.' I tried to brush it away with humour and laughed shallowly. 'You are a very hard man to keep up with in battle.'

'That is not good enough,' Harald snarled, full of genuine anger that bit me deeply. 'I heard you fell as we landed and were too slow to get back to my side. It is a disgrace for the man who stands beside me, the great Eric Alvarsson of the Varangians, to make a fool of himself and me in front of our army. What will men think? That everything they have heard of us is a lie?'

'I...' I was shocked, angry, and ashamed. 'I apologise.'

He looked me up and down in disgust. 'Years away from campaign have weakened you, made you soft. If you are to stand at my side in battle *that* is where I expect you to be, do you understand? You need to get back your fighting form. Train, be worthy of being known as a man who goes into battle at my shoulder, not following me about falling on your face in front of the army.' He shook his head, unable to look at me any further, and simply went back to shouting his orders, leaving me gaping at his back as men looked away from me with embarrassment.

Oh, it was a hard moment for me, I needn't tell you. And it was true. Eight years without a proper fight had weakened my body for war the way my injuries and grief in the east had weakened my mind. But I had never felt the scale of it until then.

The men carried out his orders gladly, however much they discomforted me. True, I was angry with the Danes for their dishonour, but as I watched chains of terrified, mauled women and children being taken down to the docks and unceremoniously dumped into our ships, I could not help but think there was no path that led from that to Harald ruling Denmark. How could the people ever forgive such an act and suffer him to be their king? Only as slaves, not as followers and subjects.

Perhaps Harald knew it too. Perhaps he had given up the idea of ruling Denmark and only saw it as a source of power and revenue. I don't know. I just know that I saw nothing good in the faces of those weeping women and felt nothing but distaste when I saw how some of them had been used before they were piled into the ships. Come now, I was an old soldier and it was nothing I had not seen before. But these were not some foreign enemies of the empire. These were Danes who should have been like cousins to us, even if they were cousins with whom we had fought and quarrelled since before the memory of men.

Bah, the regrets of an old man. Complaining about the way men behave in war is as futile as shouting at the tide not to come in. They have done the same to us and worse. We are not good cousins or neighbours, we people of the north.

We loaded up our ships with our loot and our captives, and we made camp outside the city as it burned deep into the night, the light of its fires turning the dusk into an orange hell of smoke and dancing shadows. I tried to sleep through the stink of smoke, and the screams of those who were still clinging to life or begging for death. It was an evil omen, if ever there was one.

We sailed the next morning, for we were worried about being caught in the lake by a Danish force. Even a small fleet could close the river that led to it, and we would be like fish in a willow trap.

So although the men were weary, and many wounded, we sailed out into the sea and a day north until we found a good, sheltered bay, and there we made camp to rest for a couple of days.

On the first day in camp Harald summoned Kálfr Árnasson, who had conducted himself well with his men in the battle, for if he lacked honour and loyalty, he certainly did not lack for courage in battle.

'Take your men north of here a few miles, over the ridge, and watch the northern road so that we are not surprised by an army coming for us.'

Kálfr looked at Harald sternly. 'You assign me this task because it is a dangerous and lowly task and you hope to humiliate me, but I will do it anyway to show my loyalty. And if I were truly your enemy, I could betray you and not report an enemy coming.'

'I give you this task because I do not wish to share a camp with you. And I know I can trust you with this task, because your brother's life depends on it as much as mine. Would you sacrifice your brother to kill me?'

Kálfr shook his head. 'I would not do anything to kill you, King Harald. My acceptance of your rule is absolute.'

Harald regarded the man coldly for a while. 'Only because I won.'

'The most important factor in deciding who is king,' Kálfr said with a small bow of his head, and then he left before Harald could insult him further.

* * *

We stayed there for another day, resting and celebrating our victory. We were not in a hurry to sail. There was no other large settlement nearby that could send relief, and we had taken a significant number of wounded in the fighting. Men needed time to rest and enjoy the fruits of their victory.

On the second day I was near Harald's tent, still sulking like a child over my humiliation, when four of our men escorted a mounted messenger into Harald's presence.

'Lord King, this man claims to bring a message for you. He came riding in from the north,' the guards said to Harald with a bow.

Harald nodded and waved at the messenger. 'What message, and from whom?'

'King Harald, I bear a message from King Sweyn.'

Harald grunted in amusement. 'Then you are wasting your time. King Sweyn promises battle and honour and delivers nothing. Why would I care what he says?'

'King Sweyn is three days north of here with his army. He regrets being late for the appointed day at the Gaut, but he offers you the same battle now, if you await his arrival, to save any more towns the unforgivable fate you wreaked on Hedeby.'

The smoke on the horizon to the south still marked where the smouldering ruins of Hedeby lay, and we could all see it from where we sat.

Harald looked at the man and laughed. 'Now he wishes battle, when most of my army has gone home and the rest is tired from victory and plunder? Hah! What a fool. Tell King Sweyn I will deign to defeat him next year, if he has the courage to face me. A king should be a keeper of promises, not a speaker of excuses. No, begone.'

'I will repeat your words to my King.'

The messenger gave a curt, disrespectful nod, and turned to remount his horse. Harald watched him go with amusement and then carried on speaking to the men gathered around him.

But I was disquieted. Something about the messenger and his message had disturbed me, and it took me a while contemplating it to work out what. Suddenly it dawned on me, and I stood, staring at the path where the messenger had disappeared, off to return to his King.

Three days' march away. Three days.

I walked over to Harald in a hurry, all thought of my shame banished.

'Harald,' I said sharply, interrupting the conversation without hesitation.

All of them looked at me in annoyance, and Harald's look darkened, but he gestured to me irritably. 'What?'

'There is something wrong. That messenger has deceived us.'

Harald snorted. 'He has changed nothing. I care nothing for what he has said, so how has he deceived me? Sweyn is three days away, probably halfway from Aarhus following the trail of news of our raids, so we will sail tomorrow.'

'He is not three days away,' I said, suddenly certain of my thoughts.

Harald's gaze softened and he looked at me carefully. 'Explain yourself.' He was still angry, but Harald was too smart, and too experienced, to refuse to listen to me just because he was angry with me.

'The messenger, he knew we had burned Hedeby. If Sweyn is three days away to the north, how could a man on a horse have come from him knowing we were here and that we had burned the city two days ago?'

Harald straightened and looked at me, and then around the circle, thinking. 'Curse the sky, you are right.'

Ulfr looked at me and then at Harald. 'The smoke would have been visible for dozens of miles.'

'Not from three days' march away,' I said. 'How long would it take word to get to Sweyn, and then for a man on a horse ride to meet us?'

'Three days, at least. Maybe four,' said Finn.

'And we burned Hedeby the day before last,' I said. 'If he was three days north, he could not know about Hedeby yet and have time to send us a messenger.'

Harald stood. 'He offered a battle he knew I would refuse, so his message to me was pointless. Unless...' He looked around the camp, where the entire army was visible, and then back to the north, where the messenger had disappeared.

'Unless he is almost upon us and merely wanted to know our strength and condition without alarming us,' I said, fear prickling at my chest and sucking at my breath. Sweyn's whole army would outnumber us several times, and we were in no condition to fight a battle if he arrived immediately. Nor could we flee through the lake to the sea with our ships laid up and full of plunder if the way was blocked. It would be a massacre.

Harald turned red and looked at me. 'My apologies, Eric. You have saved me once again.' He turned to Ulfr. 'Get the army to our ships, abandon anything we don't need. We sail immediately. Go!'

The other lords did not waste a moment in debate and ran off, scattering like cats at the bark of a hunting dog.

Harald alone did not abandon the place we were standing, for he had no duty other than to give orders. He looked at me in shame. 'I am sorry, Eric. I shamed you and you did not deserve it.' He offered me his hand to clasp.

I smiled softly and walked over to him and clasped it. 'I did deserve it, Harald. I am a fool for thinking I could still keep up with you in battle. You do not need me lumbering around in battle, disrespecting our reputation.' I tapped my head. 'But although my body has gone soft, my mind is still there, I think.'

Harald laughed softly. 'And I shall remember it. Perhaps it is time, now that I am no longer a mercenary commander but a king, that you also should adapt. I should make you my chamberlain, like the emperors and the princes of the Rus have. No longer my right hand in battle and standard bearer, but my foremost advisor. A position more suited to both of us.'

'Ulfr is your advisor.'

'Ulfr is my marshal, my sheepdog of lords, and the best in the land at that. He is ruthless and unyielding, but he does not have your sharpness, Eric, nor your nose for trouble.'

'Finn then?' I said awkwardly.

'Finn is his own man with his own lands – loyal for sure, but still not bound to me like you.' He gave me an odd look. 'Why are you refusing my offer and trying to suggest others? Have I wounded you so badly?'

I shrugged. 'I dislike the responsibility. I have always failed at every formal title and position you ever gave me. I like merely being Eric the Follower.'

Harald drew me in with a laugh to embrace me. 'The greatest of followers. Fine, have it your way. I will not name you to a title but never let my sharp temper drive you from my side again, even if you do not stand by my side in battle any longer.'

I nodded, relief pouring through me, for being out of Harald's favour was a terrible thing for me.

'Come, the men are preparing our ship. Walk with me down to it and let all men see that we are united.'

'Should we not run?' I said, looking nervously around at the emptying camp and the dozen rushed looking hirdmen who were packing Harald's things into makeshift bundles and running down to the shore with them.

Harald smiled and thumped me on the shoulder, gesturing down to the ship with a defiant grunt. 'A king does not run from his enemies,' he said, and we set off to the ships at a stroll.

I looked at him suddenly. 'We must send word to Kálfr. His men are directly in the path of the enemy, and if we leave them, they might...' I stopped, because I knew in that moment that Harald must already have come to the same conclusion. Of course he had. He considered everything.

Harald's eyes did not deviate from the ships ahead of us. 'I sent word to Kálfr. Do you not remember? That is what I will say if men ask. I will not remember who, precisely, because the chaos was great. But I am sure I remember sending someone, and you remember seeing me do it.'

I pursed my lips. My hatred for Kálfr was almost as true and raw as Harald's. But he had a hundred men with him, good men of Norway and allies of ours. But I knew that argument would not sway Harald. He had sacrificed a hundred men before for far less gain than the death of a blood enemy.

'Finn might not believe you.'

'Finn will have no choice. We will say it, and no man can counter it.'

'We need his willing alliance, even if he cannot claim it in public. You might lose him.'

Harald shook his head. 'I do not believe so. I am married to his sister, and he needs my family and my patronage more than he needs a traitor brother.'

'Harald, I think you misjudge the situation. This might lose you your only ally in the north.'

Harald looked at me with stone-cold eyes. 'Then so be it. As long as no man can claim before a lawgiver that I murdered Kálfr, I do not care. And anyway, he might have the sense to flee and follow us. His fate is in God's hands now. Let the Lord punish him or not, as he sees fit. I pray he has no mercy, for I also will have none on my enemies. I would trade any ally for men to know that, Eric: that I have no mercy on my enemies and never will. I am not Magnus the Good, forgiver of enemies; I am Harald Sigurdsson, the thunderbolt of the north. That is what the Danes call me. Let all men understand why.'

I shivered, because his resolve and his confidence were so imposing and unbreakable. This was a man whose will was a natural force of its own. But that is why he was great, even when he was making mistakes. And I cannot claim I was not hoping Kálfr would fall to Danish steel. Did I think it was worth the lives of a hundred of his men?

Yes – yes, I did. They were all knowingly following a kingslayer. They made their choice, and Harald made his. God decided the rest.

We reached the ships in silence and one of the lords from Viken ran over and waved at the two empty ships that Kálfr had left on the shoreline. 'Kálfr's ships – what shall we do? Do we wait for them?' The man asked, and Harald waved at the northern treeline.

'I have sent word to him. He will be here soon and follow us. But we need to put to sea in case the enemy appears.'

The lord nodded and turned to run to his ship.

Harald looked at me. 'Do you wish to protest my decision?'

I met his confident stare with my heart at peace. 'No, King Harald. I do not.'

* * *

The fleet set off in a disorganised huddle out to sea, some ships slower than others to get moving, but we were all afloat before anything stirred in the tree-lines near our abandoned camp where most of our tents stood empty and forlorn, pots of food still bubbling over untended fires. It hurts, to leave good equipment behind, but the value of everything we had plundered from Hedeby outstripped the value of some camp equipment by a hundred times, so it was no great loss other than in pride and a few cold nights under the stars ahead of us.

It looked like we might have left early but, sure enough, in the very next inlet, a forest of masts became visible. A Danish fleet at anchor not even ten miles north of us. There must have been 200 masts there, three times our number. A huge army – Denmark's entire force, and possibly an army of Sweden too.

Harald swore. 'I should have had scouts out far enough. Did we learn nothing in the empire? What a fool I am.'

I tried to mollify him, although it was true we had become complacent. 'We could not have expected them to come so quickly.'

'The rules of the empire's army are followed at all times precisely so they cannot be surprised, nor failed by bad judgement.' He shook his head, furious with himself. 'We need to apply more of what we learned in the empire. With their methods, and our men?' He shook his head at me wistfully. 'We could rebuild Cnut's empire before we even grey our beards.'

My stomach churned. I had hoped, vainly, that he had dropped his close-held plans for conquering all the lands that bordered the western seas.

'My beard is already greying, Harald.'

'Yes,' he said, ignoring the dissuasion. 'But you are terribly old indeed.'

'Sail!' someone shouted, pointing at the enemy fleet.

Sure enough, one of the masts nearest the sea was sprouting a sail.

'I was hoping they would be slower to react,' said Harald quietly. 'They should have been marching to attack us.'

Then another sail sprouted, and half a dozen more. Within a short time as we watched, helpless and glum while we passed the closest point to the enemy fleet and continued sailing past, the entire enemy force put to sea.

'They must have had men watching us pack up and leave and turned the army around immediately,' I said, with what I admit was no helpfulness at all.

Harald was silent, watching the vast enemy fleet put to sea and turn into our wake, five or so miles behind, following us like a flock of seagulls following a fishing boat. Cutting off Kálfr's still beached ships and giving chase.

* * *

'They will catch us before dark.' Ulfr said quietly. And even I could see the sails were getting bigger. It was happening fast enough to almost watch them grow over the white-flecked waves, for our ships were all over-laden and slow.

'We cannot fight them,' I said quietly to Harald. 'We should make terms.'

'Make terms?' he said, looking at me almost in confusion. 'What terms?'

'Offer the return of their goods and women, offer payment – it doesn't matter. Send a ship back to offer them terms, or when they catch us, it is over. However much better our men are, this is not a battle we can win. Not even you.'

Harald clenched his jaw and nodded. 'You are right.'

I let out a terse sigh of relief. 'Thank you.'

'But your method is wrong. Negotiation is not the answer and will lead to our total capitulation. No, we will simply give them what we offer, and it will save us.'

'What?' I said, nervous again. 'What do you mean?'

Harald looked down the ship, which was the largest in our fleet and held a full belly of goods and women from Hedeby, the poor wretches huddled together among their looted town's former riches.

'We will make the offer in a manner they cannot refuse.'

9

Ulfr's face was grim as he checked the ropes tying the crying woman to the barrel of salt fish, but he grunted in satisfaction and shoved both together over the back of the ship. There was a cry and a splash that choked it off, and then the woman surfaced, wailing and sputtering, as the barrel carried her away in our wake.

Another woman was brought up, this one tied to a bundle of furs.

'Wet furs will sink with her,' I said to Ulfr morosely, looking at the woman, who was young and terrified, eyes pleading with me.

'I know,' said Ulfr, who kicked the woman off the deck into the water without even looking at her.

I winced and looked away at the trail of misery in the wake of our fleet. Every ship was doing the same, for all knew that the heaviest ship would be taken first, and the moment they had seen Harald start to cast the plunder overboard, they had all raced to copy him.

Tying the women to the jettisoned cargo was not an act of mercy by Harald.

'They might not stop to pick up good swimmers or the bodies of those who could not,' Harald had said. 'Tie them to the cargo. Let the Danes row past screaming women by the hundred if they may. I do not believe they will.'

'You would run them under the keels of your ship before you gave up the chase on such an important enemy,' I said, unsure.

Harald looked at me with those eyes of flint and anger and shrugged. 'True, but Sweyn is not me. They will stop.'

'They will give up their kingdom for 500 women?'

'They are weak.'

Well. He was right.

The Danish fleet fell into total disarray as they came upon the first of the half-living jetsam we left in our wake. Sails veered out of line or were dropped, and ships behind swerved to avoid the mess in front. The last pair of children was pushed carelessly into the sea, tied to a crate of some sort. That was a mercy by our crew; the crate would float well.

Our ship was empty of prisoners, as were most of the ships in our fleet. Now lightened significantly we were noticeably faster, but despite the chaos behind us, and how many enemy ships were tearing their sails down and stopping to take onboard survivors, many ships kept coming, for we did not have enough prisoners to give them. At least a hundred ships followed.

'If they catch us, maybe we can defeat one hundred, but the others will come close behind, and they will only be more vengeful,' I said bleakly.

Harald's gift had not worked.

Harald watched for a while, and he could see that the enemy was still catching us, and even though evening was approaching and no fleet could chase through the night, they might still catch us before dusk.

There was still loot in our ship. The most valuable of the haul we had taken from Hedeby. Silver, silks, iron, weapons and other such things that men were the least willing to lose. Unfortunately, all such things of value weigh a great deal.

Harald walked over to the diminished pile and the men watched him glumly. He picked up a silver chalice, a fine work worth as much as half a good trading ship.

'Do you think we will not see such riches again?' he said, smiling at the men and looking around. 'I tell you, I have gained such a bounty a dozen times in my life, and greater ones half a dozen besides.' He casually flicked it over their heads and into the water without even looking, as if it was nothing. 'It is only the silver of one town, and we will gather this much and more next year, and the year after, and every year until there are no enemies left to fight. But there is no price I would not pay to see you home to your families again. Let us leave these cowardly Danes, and by our payment to the sea, they will know our determination and be awed by it.'

And then he stooped down and picked up a small chest that clinked with coin, and I closed my eyes in pain as he walked to the side and cast it out.

I knew how much that hurt Harald, although he showed not a care at all. The kingship runs on silver, and he was taking from the very men he had promised to enrich, taxing them the spoils of their victory and throwing it into the sea in front of their very eyes.

You would think they might have rebelled at that moment and killed him for it, yes?

Bah, a foolish thought. As Harald understood, most men wanted to live more than they wanted to die in ships weighed down with silver.

They all got up from their benches and helped, casting the riches of a generation out of our ship, and all around us in the fleet, we saw others do the same. I could not help but think of Afra, who had died in a ship weighed low with Harald's riches, all those years before in the Golden Horn of Constantinople, consumed in fire as their lives were ended because of the sheer quantity of wealth they carried. Maybe Harald had learned from that, or maybe he felt quietly guilty and never again wanted to see ships full of his men die for his silver.

I know, I am not such a fool. You have heard how Harald was. It was far more pragmatic than soothing his conscience. He knew he could survive the loss of silver, but he needed those men for the next campaign. Norway cannot simply raise another army like the empire could. Men were more precious than metal.

If it had been the other way around? What he would have done does not bear thinking about, but men would have been left bobbing in our wake as we sailed our treasures home. That is the king he was.

The precious cargo went into the sea as did the spare food and anything else, leaving a trail for ten miles of the richest, fattest crabs in all the circle of the world. Men kept their gold on their bodies; nothing would part a man from his golden jewellery, especially earned in battle. They would rather die wearing it than cast it into the sea.

But everything else other than our weapons and our oars was gone, and finally, the enemy sails stopped getting bigger. As the darkness started to come, those sails were taken down and the enemy turned back into the wind and started rowing back to the rest of their fleet.

We had escaped. Is there honour in it? No. But in letting us escape, the enemy had ensured they would have to fight us again, and against a king who had been humiliated despite his victory and would be twice as terrible on his return.

'They deceived me, twice,' Harald muttered angrily, still watching the enemy fleet swallowed by the gloom.

I said nothing; he was not really talking to me.

'I will never allow it again,' he said, and then I saw that he was, in fact, now looking at me. 'Never let me do that again, Eric. That is your task from now on. My arrogance nearly cost us everything, and I have paid a price in silver and honour that I am not willing to pay again. Your duty is to guard me against it, do you understand?'

I nodded firmly. 'I understand, my King.'

He stepped down into the hull of the boat, and went to go and talk to the men, suddenly his voice clear and sounding in high spirits, because that is what the men needed and that is the general Harald was.

Ulfr gave me a side-eyed expression from the steering oar where he was taking his turn, but he said nothing as I raised my eyebrow at him.

'Don't be so shy, Ulfr. What is it you want to say?'

Ulfr shook his head. 'I know you better than Harald does. You can't keep that promise you just made.'

I was annoyed. 'What do you mean by that? I've kept every promise I ever made to him!'

'I know. Trust me, of all men *I* know. But I'm also a man who once reached my end with my duty to Harald, and I see the same thing in you.' He looked me dead in the eye. 'You know it too, Eric. You just haven't found the courage to tell him yet.'

That hit me like a spear, because it was true. I had felt it since Magnus had died and Harald had not been satiated by claiming the throne he had always said was his ambition. Not one tiny bit. In that moment, and on that boat, I had felt the same thing: that Harald knew no end to his ambition, and service to him was a bottomless pit I could never fill, nor escape from if I allowed myself to fall in. It was not how I wanted to spend my life; it was not the promise I had made to Olga.

Ulfr shrugged knowingly and went back to looking forwards, trying to keep our course correct in the dying light. 'When you leave him, make sure you do it deliberately, Eric, at a good time. Don't let it burn you through like it did to me and come at the worst time. You owe him that much at least.'

I furrowed my brows and glared at him, for pride if for nothing else. But he wasn't gloating. My old friend was just saying the facts as he knew them.

'How did you recover from losing your will to serve him?' I asked quietly.

Ulfr thought about it for a while and finally he spoke. 'When I failed him and broke my oaths, you all stepped forwards and put yourselves under the lash for me.' His eyes creased a little as he remembered that time, eight years ago, when the men of the 7th bandon had shared his punishment, and saved his life.

'I came back to his service not for him, but for all of you. And that is when I realised it had been all that mattered to me all along. I had never truly cared for Harald's ambition; I was not risking my life for his crown. No, I was there for you – my brothers.' He gestured to the men in the ship before us. 'These are my brothers, and my duty is to protect them, even from Harald. That is why I serve.'

I thought back to that town square in Greece, the heat and the dust and the smell of shame and fear. I had been the first to place my body over Ulfr's, because he was my brother and he had been worthy of it. Not because of Harald. It had been to *spite* Harald. It had always been true. I served Harald not just to protect him, but to protect him and his men from his worst excesses. I cared nothing for his ambitions, and I had not for a long time.

'So the problem you have, Eric, is that service is no longer the thing you care about the most, is it?' It was not an accusation; it was asked with kindness. 'I used to watch you, how you would work so hard to keep as many of us alive as you could. And we loved you for it. Now... now I see that all you wish for is to get home. Saving him, saving us... it's just a way of ensuring you can, and Harald doesn't see it because he is not a man like us. He thinks you are saving him from himself, because of your love and loyalty to him. But you are not, are you?'

I glared at Ulfr resentfully but shook my head. 'No,' I said, and the word burned me like acid.

He nodded. 'Then your time is done.'

'And you?' I asked. 'When will your time end?'

Ulfr smiled happily. 'Never.'

'Never?'

He nodded. 'You all saved my life that day, my brothers. I will not leave Harald's service while even one of you remains to serve alongside, to do my best to watch over and protect them. So I will serve King Harald until the last man leaves, or I die. It is a worthy life redeemed.'

'They do not need you to do this. All men who serve Harald do so because they choose it.'

Ulfr's smile only deepened. 'I do not do it because you or they ask me to, Eric. Just as I did not ask you to lay your body on mine to take those lashes that still mark your back. In fact, I told you that you were a fool.'

I smiled. 'You did, and I was.'

'And now I am the fool,' Ulfr replied. 'And you are free to go back to your family. My honour is satisfied, and your agreement is not required. Let me take the next lashes of Harald's ambition, for I can see you are done with it.'

I shivered at the thought of it. 'He will never let me go.'

'He will. It might take him a winter of sulking to understand, but he will. He is a king and a conqueror, but at the core, he is your friend, and he is as loyal to you as you are to him. He will let you go, if you have the courage and sense to do it properly.'

I looked around the ship, seeing if anyone was watching us, or listening, but we were alone by the steering oar, and the waves and wind were enough that I could barely hear Ulfr myself.

I put my hand on his arm on the steering oar. 'Thank you, my friend.'

'For what?'

I searched for the right words, for it was difficult. 'For taking your turn at the lash,' I finally said. He grunted quietly and I let go of his arm and walked away, because my mind was whirling, and on that crowded ship I needed to find a space to myself to think.

* * *

We sailed back to Norway in low spirits, but without much trouble. Six ships were separated in the night, which is inevitable in such situations. We later found out they were caught by King Sweyn's fleet. Sweyn confiscated everything they had but then freed them after extracting promises that they would not return to Denmark in arms again, an act that angered Harald more than if they had been executed, for it showed Sweyn as merciful where Harald had been ruthless. Of Kálfr's two ships, however, we did not immediately hear word. Either he had been killed, or he had realised Harald's intent and fled. Perhaps even he had pledged himself to Sweyn. We did not know.

The news of Harald's defeat – for everyone saw it as a defeat, even though we had won every battle and destroyed a Danish city – stirred up the trouble-makers, sensing a weakness in Harald's position with his reputation and coffers injured by the costly campaign.

Harald went on a tireless campaign of diplomacy and threat for all the late summer and autumn, travelling around the entire country, from the southern tip upwards, putting himself in the face of every man of importance and enforcing their loyalty through a mixture of flattery, promises, pressure and implicit threats.

It was exhausting, although it was mostly successful. One particularly reluctant lord in the Upplond was persuaded to promise his support through the simple measure of Harald staying in his hall with a hundred men and refusing to stop enjoying his hospitality until he received it. The lord had two choices: pledge himself to Harald's next campaign, or be impoverished.

He repeated this trick several times, and it was brutally successful. He also executed several men for treason or insult and gave harsh interpretations of the law where he saw fit, often favouring himself in ways that others disagreed with. All of it was to force the people to bend to his will. He gained no love in that expedition, I tell you. Men knelt to his face and whispered in fearful discontent at his back.

The last place we travelled was Trondelag, where we knew our reception would be the coldest. We arrived in Orlandet at the entrance to this very fjord, where the Árnasson clan ruled, and Harald expected a fine reception. No one came down to greet us at the dock, beyond a half-stray dog that yapped at us for the invasion, and scuttled away with a howl when it got a boot to the nose.

'This does not bode well,' Harald said, looking down the road towards Finn's hall. There was nothing else to say, and we both knew why.

We set the men to camp near the dock and went to the hall with a dozen men and found it standing almost deserted. Finn had not simply refused to meet us – he was not even at home, despite having been sent message to prepare for our arrival weeks before. Nothing could be clearer to indicate his anger, and it was a humiliation of Harald within eyeshot of his worst enemy across the bay.

Eventually we cornered a worried-looking servant girl.

'Where is your master?' Harald demanded, and the poor thing quailed, almost unable to speak with fear.

'Lord Árnasson?'

'Yes!'

'Which... which one?' the girl asked. It was a fair question; there were six living Árnasson brothers, assuming Kálfr was still counted as alive.

'Any of them will do!' Harald snapped. The girl pointed a hasty finger up the road that led inland. 'Lord Thorberg and Lord Arni are at their hall, I believe.'

'And Finn? Where is Finn Árnasson?'

The girl just shook her head, and Harald scowled in fury and dismissed her with a wave. 'Then to the lesser brothers we go,' he growled.

We were halfway to the brothers' hall, Harald becoming angrier at the disrespect with every step, when we saw twenty men running down the road towards us, with two at their head. They were armed but not armoured for war. They stopped in the road and a very flustered-looking Thorberg came to meet us with a hurried bow, Arni at his side.

'My apologies, King Harald. I did not know of your arrival in advance.' He looked desperately nervous.

'What? I sent word to your brother weeks ago. Where is he? Does he refuse to meet his King?'

Thorberg looked distraught, glancing at his brother, who was grim-faced.

'Well?' Harald demanded.

'King Harald, our brother... Our brother did not tell us anything, other than that he was leaving. I apologise.'

'Leaving for where?' Harald asked, and the two of them could clearly not bear to tell us, but Arni eventually raised his chin and answered.

'Denmark,' he said with a nervous wobble in his voice.

'To Denmark! Why, to search for your brother?'

'No,' Arni said with a confused look. 'Our brother is dead. The Danes sent us his ring.'

Harald absorbed that news without missing a beat. 'So why has Finn gone there?'

Arni clenched, as if preparing for a blow. 'To pledge service to King Sweyn.'

Arni's instincts were good, for Harald went grey with rage, and nearly did strike the brother down such was his anger.

'Finn has betrayed me, and all of Norway! *Why!*'

'Lord King, I do not say I agree with him, but...'

'What? *Speak!*'

Arni gathered the courage. 'He says you broke your word and killed our brother.'

Harald snorted and huffed like a horse in battle, pacing back and forth in front of the two brothers, turning to look at them every couple of paces. 'I deny it, do you hear me? I deny it! Why is your brother too cowardly to face me and hear my denial?'

'He said your denial did not matter to him, and that if he remained, he would accuse you and you would kill him.'

'I would not have killed him!' Harald said, pointing at Arni in fury.

Arni just shrugged helplessly. 'It is what he said.'

Harald snorted again and looked away, teeth clenched. 'And what do you say, Thorberg, Arni? You lead the Árnasson clan now that your brother is dead.'

'Now that... Kálfr is dead?'

'No, now that Finn is dead,' Harald snapped. 'He has betrayed me, and thus he is dead. I declare it, and that all his property is now yours. So tell me, Arni, Thorberg. Do you accept my words and give me your loyalty?'

Thorberg nodded nervously. 'I do, Lord King. I do not agree with Finn, and our family will stand behind you, as those of us that remain here always have.'

'Kálfr died fighting the enemy?'

'He did, Lord King,' Arni said with a downcast expression.

'Then his sins are forgiven, and his quarrel with me is settled. You may speak his name with honour again.'

Arni looked up. 'Thank you, Lord King.'

'But no man will speak of the traitor Finn again. I declare him outlaw. Let any man of Norway kill him if they have the chance, on pain of becoming outlaw themselves if they fail to try, especially if he returns here. Do you hear my judgement?'

The two brothers nodded.

'Good, then I will spare you the humiliation of reading it at the Thing. Let it be whispered quietly, not shouted at the speaker's tree.'

The brothers looked relieved, grateful even, to be spared that. But truly Harald said it to spare himself the humiliation of having to stand and declare that his closest ally had betrayed him. Men would know anyway, and it would hurt him, but at least he would not have to say it in public.

The brothers were in no way prepared to host us, and Harald was too angry to stay, so we sailed for Nidaros and stayed at the royal estate there, even Harald not daring to provoke Einar by imposing himself on the powerful lord's hospitality. He was hoping to make an accommodation rather than start a war, and he knew Einar could not be cowed by threats and pressure.

We took the time to visit Olaf's grave, and check that his tomb was sealed and intact, before Harald had a service of prayer held there. I think that was for himself, not for show.

Harald then began to hold public hearings and meetings at the King's hall. He would hear complaints, judge criminal cases, and resolve other matters of the law, as is the normal way.

* * *

On the second day, having heard the King was present, Einar arrived with a fleet of nine ships and five hundred men, a brazen display of power. Harald and I watched from the eaves window of the royal hall, and he was sullen. 'Look how proudly he goes. Einar is undaunted by me. I can see that he still expects to be king.'

'He is just trying to retain power here; surely he does not intend to try and claim the throne?'

Harald muttered to himself, watching the small army land at the Nidaros docks. 'With such a display? He can only intend that.'

I was deeply unsure that was true, and I think Harald was very badly affected by Finn's betrayal and was becoming suspicious and untrusting of everyone. He cursed under his breath and walked away, going to his quarters.

10

NIDAROS, NORWAY; AUTUMN 1050 AD.

Einar did not deign to come and meet the King, as he should have. He just set himself up at his own estate on the edge of the city and held assemblies there as if he were a king, although he bade no man call him that. This was an outright refutal of Harald's authority, for although many of the town's citizens had come to pay homage to Harald the day he had arrived, many were then drawn to Einar's hall, embarrassing Harald, who sank lower and lower into his darkness and suspicion.

'He is just trying to provoke you,' I counselled Harald. 'Do not be bitten by it.'

'He is fanning the embers of rebellion, as his family and Kálfr did against my brother,' Harald furiously retorted.

He was like that for several days, holding increasingly poorly attended meetings in a dark and foul mood. Most of the business had been concluded, yet he refused to leave Nidaros, because to slink away with his tail between his legs without Einar paying homage was too humiliating. To go to Einar would be to recognise his supremacy, and to do nothing seemed his only option. Harald hated doing nothing with a great passion. He was a man of action, but we had one hundred men to Einar's five hundred, so any course of violence was completely out of the question.

It was perhaps on the fourth day when Ulfr came to Harald looking concerned. 'I have heard that Einar is pronouncing a matter of the law,' he said.

Harald looked up from his table, eyes glazing over with anger. 'What?'

'A thief was caught, one of Einar's men. He was being brought here to you for judgment, but Einar heard of it and had him seized and taken to his own hall. He heard the case in front of a gathering and pronounced sentence.'

'He seized the captive and held judgment without me, while I am in the city?'

Ulfr nodded.

'That is treason! I am the law while I am here. He should have been brought to me as I have heard other matters of dispute and the law while I am here!'

'He should have, my King.'

I glared at Ulfr, for it would have been better if he had not told the King, but Ulfr was not the sort of man to deceive his lord like that.

Harald rose from his seat in a cloud of fury, drawing alarm from the two dozen or more people who were in the hall to hear anything he might have to say, or make petitions.

'This is enough. Let us go down to Einar and have the law properly enforced.'

And so we gathered twenty or so men and marched through the city to Einar's hall, where there were perhaps a hundred people gathered, eating and talking on benches. It was a far larger crowd than had gathered to listen to Harald, and I saw the humiliation of that etched into his face.

Harald led us into the hall and everyone looked up. Einar had been laughing and talking with a couple of men who were standing in front of his chair, and he raised an eyebrow at Harald's entrance.

'Lord Harald. How pleasant to see you.'

'Your words are a lie, Einar, for if you found seeing me with your own eyes pleasant, you would have come to my hall to lay them upon me. I hear you are judging matters of the law, but how can you when the King himself is present, and you can speak nothing but lies?'

The hall fell silent, and Einar's smile faded a little.

'You are in my hall, Harald. That is not the correct way to speak. If you have a quarrel, let us resolve it peaceably.'

'You held your lawgiving assembly in public, against the traditions of our people, so I am happy to resolve it in public too.'

Einar looked Harald up and down, then stood to the side and gestured to the high seat he had been occupying. 'Come, then – sit in the speaker's chair, and speak to me of your concerns.'

Harald did not like the tone, which was calculated to goad him, but he did go and sit, and we occupied the benches on one side and Einar and his people the other, with the various other people trying to stay as far away as possible from the rival factions.

'You passed judgment on a thief, one who was being brought to me for judgment. This is not how the law should be given, and you know it. I want the man and his victims to be brought before me to be properly judged.'

Einar shook his head. 'Impossible, I am afraid.'

'How so?'

'I have passed judgment, and he has been banished for one year. Already gone from here.'

Harald scowled. 'Why, why did you seize him and prevent me doing my duty in judgment? By what arrogance or authority?'

Einar looked undeterred. 'Because I knew that you would not pass fair judgment upon him, for he is a kinsman of mine. You would have taken his life to spite me, over the theft of a little silver when he was drunk. I have heard of your judgments over the last days, Harald, and they are not just according to our laws. You have been harsh where mercy was needed, greedy where charity was required. A king's right is to pass judgment, but his duty is to follow the law fairly… and you have not.'

Harald's jaw flexed and twisted. 'You dare to judge not only the thief, but also your King?'

'Every man judges their king, Harald. That is what you do not understand. The people talk of their King; little else occupies their mind. They judged my dear son Magnus as good – that was their judgement on him, because he was fair and generous in his giving of the law.' Einar cocked an eyebrow at Harald. 'Do you know what they call you, Harald?'

'I do not care.' Harald hissed.

'Yes, you do.' Einar said confidently. 'In any case, they are calling you the Hardrada.'

I tensed. *Hard-ruler*. It was not a good name, or so I thought at the time.

'Is it any surprise to you that people come to me for assembly and judgment, where they can expect fair assessment and sentence from their lord who lives here, rather than King Harald Hardrada, who comes here for four days and uses the law as a whip to frighten his people, and a cudgel with which to extract their wealth?'

Harald leant forwards in his chair. 'It is the right of the people to grumble; it is *not* your right to usurp my power. In doing so you have crossed the line from an annoyance to openly opposing my authority, tantamount to an act of rebellion.'

Harald stood. 'You have pushed your limits too far, Einar, in attempting to show the people here that you, not I, are the authority on the law. You are powerful indeed, Einar, if you think you can rule the land rather than me, despite me having the title of king. But you are mistaken.'

Einar looked contemptuous. 'You are the ruler of the country, Harald, but I will not endure breaches of the law or mistreatment of my people by anyone, not even you.'

Harald's eyes blazed, but Einar was resolute and clearly would not be cowed by words, and his men outnumbered us in the hall, so there was nothing we could do.

'You have passed into usurpation of my rule, Einar. And I assure you, not only will I pass judgment, but you will think it harsh. You sit here so confidently because you have so many of your men about you, but I have all of Norway about me, and I shall return with them to judge you and all the people who flocked to you. You think you are saving them, but you are leading them to their doom.'

That got to Einar. 'You threaten war against me, Harald?'

'I threaten nothing. I tell you that my lawful authority will be enforced. You have two choices: submit to it by bringing me that thief, or await my return where I will enforce submission upon you.'

Einar stood, outraged. 'All this, for a thief?'

'All this for my honour and my rule! This is but a fraction of my determination to rule, Einar. You think being called Hardrada is an insult. You have no understanding, no conception of the things that I have done, suffered, lived through to wear the mantle of Norway's king. And you think I would surrender even a small part of it because you and your followers whisper a little behind my back, and call me Hardrada?' Harald laughed, booming and hostile, without a trace of humour.

'Oh, Einar. You have given me two great gifts tonight: a name that I love, and an excuse to end your troublemaking for good.'

Einar finally looked worried, and I could see that he had misjudged Harald's likely reaction. 'War is a foolish thing to declare when my men outnumber yours so badly.'

'I did not declare war, nor will you be able to pretend I did. I said that I would enforce your obedience to my rule, as is my right and my duty. All you need do is present yourself to me and pledge yourself, and no violence of any kind is required. If there is war, it will be on you, and all will know it. My followers and allies will not accept you as my replacement, so even if not for love of me, they will come north and erase your family's stain from the very soil,' Harald hissed, staring down at Einar. 'Be quick, for I leave in the morning, and I will return with judgment the like that you have never seen.' Harald gazed out over the hall. 'You have all heard it. If violence is done to me before I leave, it will be Einar who is the criminal, having declared himself a traitor.'

Then he strode from the room, with all of us leaving behind him. I glanced back and saw Einar looking deeply worried, and deep in thought. I almost felt sorry for him. He had never had the chance to understand who Harald truly was and had made a grave error in publicly usurping him.

* * *

We returned to the royal hall and Harald called Rurik over. 'Have half of the men prepare the ships and guard them. Be ready to leave at a moment's notice if there is trouble, even if it is during night. There is a good moon, and we can escape under its light if needed.'

'Do you think Einar will move against you?'

'I think he will do one of two things: that, or come to me to make peace. He cannot afford for me to leave with this matter unresolved – it would be the ruin of him, and he knows it.'

'I will prepare the men for a fight, but...' Rurik grimaced.

'I know,' Harald said. 'It is a fight we cannot win, that is why we must be ready to flee.'

Rurik nodded and left the hall at a run.

I looked at Harald nervously. 'Should we not just leave now?'

Harald shook his head. 'What people say happened here is important. If we flee now without Einar making a threat, it is cowardice, and that is not acceptable. No, he must move against us before we flee.'

I nodded. 'And if he comes here to make peace, what will you offer him?'

'Fair justice,' Harald said. 'As he asked for. I will ensure that peace is made between us. Norway cannot afford this conflict, not now.'

'Fair justice?' I asked with an eyebrow raised in suspicion.

'Yes, and I do not intend to discuss the details now. Get armed and ready and stay inside. We do nothing to provoke or seem hostile. Take a few men and keep a watch from the eaves and let us know if anyone approaches.'

I nodded reluctantly and took a few men into the loft to keep watch, wiggling holes in the thatch to see through, and peering from the small windows in the eaves.

* * *

It was evening before Einar came, and he had fifty or so men at his back. Not enough for it to be an attack but instead a deliberate matching of our forces so as to appear equal.

'They are here, fifty armed men, walking openly along the road under torches!'

'Come down, then,' Harald called to me.

I scrambled down the ladder and went to Harald, who was with Ulfr and a half dozen of his warriors, all fully armed, standing in the hall. Harald put his hand on my shoulder and leaned in. 'Go outside and meet him. Tell him I am willing to hear his offer for compensation and peace if he is willing to come in here and make it.'

I nodded nervously. 'He has a lot more men than you.'

'He will not come into my hall with fifty men looking for peace. The rest of ours are waiting outside and will face his and keep them out. Be ready for violence at a moment's notice.'

'As you say, Harald.'

Harald looked at me sternly in the torchlight, which was the only light in that hall that late in the evening. 'Eric, are you still true to me?'

'Yes, of course.'

'Then do not show any fear or disagreement. Whatever happens, you follow my lead. Do you understand?'

I nodded firmly. 'I do, my King.'

'Good.' Harald stood up again and pointed towards the door. 'Then go and meet him and invite him in so we can settle this.'

I went through the doors, closing them behind me, and found about forty of the warriors of the hird outside, waiting in two ranks either side of the doors. I nodded to them with what I hoped was a confident air. I knew many of them, there were blood-marked in their ranks, men who had followed Harald since Stiklestad, although only perhaps three, as so many had died, and others gone home to hang up their shields due to age or injury.

Over half of those men were Varangians though, men with half a dozen campaigns of experience, and I knew I could trust them in any fight with fifty of Einar's men. I would have put those forty up against any other hundred warriors in all the world. Well, except perhaps the Normans.

'Make no moves, no threats, no insults. This is a meeting for peace, not war,' I said, and men nodded and grunted their assent. Some even looked disappointed. Hah! Those men were wolves of war, always ready to be unleashed. 'But if violence is brought here, have no mercy. You are defending the King and all of Norway. We will cut our way to the ships, and we will stop for nothing!'

'Yes, Komes!' shouted Sigurd boisterously, who had been my second in command when I led the 7th bandon in the empire. And men laughed. I smiled at Sigurd, who beamed at me. That man was always up for a fight.

There was noise from beyond the open outer gate, and then Einar's party appeared, hesitating slightly when they saw our waiting, moonlit ranks, but then Einar found his courage and strode into the space with his only surviving son Eindridi at his side and their men behind.

'I am here to see the King,' Einar said loudly and confidently, as if he had not been summoned by threat of war.

I stood forwards and he looked at me. 'The King is willing to discuss an end to your disagreements and ensure peace. He awaits you inside. Your men, and ours, can remain here.'

Einar looked at me with remarkable confidence and nodded, but his son came past our men to stand by his side. 'Father, it could be a trap!'

Einar brushed him away with a casual wave. 'No, Harald is not a fool. With you out here and my men at your side, and 400 more at my estate across town, nothing will happen to me,' he said. 'The King offers me peace, and I am man enough to accept it. Wait here for me at the door, and keep your hands from your weapons, lest there be a tragic misunderstanding.'

Then he walked up to me. 'The King truly offers peace?' he asked, and I could see for the first time that the great man was more than a little nervous.

'He does,' I said with a firm expression. 'But you will meet him properly, in the royal meeting hall, as is correct for a lord petitioning his King. Take my advice, Lord Einar – be respectful, even in disagreement.'

Einar nodded slowly, regarding me. 'That is wise advice, Eric. I have heard much about you, and perhaps I should know you better. I look forward to it.'

'As do I. Come.' I gestured to the door and led him up the few steps.

I opened it for him and stepped through, and found most of the torches were out – only two on the far side cast flickering shadows as Einar stepped through the door behind me.

'It is dark in the King's meeting hall,' Einar said, with a calm bravado, even as I felt, rather than saw, movement behind me on both walls.

I turned to look at him, surprise on my face, even as three armoured forms came out of the gloom, helmets on and weapons in hand, and got between Einar and the door. I saw in shock that it was Harald himself, with two of his huskarls before him.

Einar wasted no time with words or anger; he ripped his sword from its sheath and ignored the blows the leading two men put into his chest and stomach, letting his armour take the worst of it.

Howling in outrage the old man launched himself at Harald with surprising speed and strength, taking Harald quite by surprise, and landed not one but two heavy blows on Harald before the King could defend himself.

But Harald's magnificent maille held, even under the sheer strength of Einar's blows, and he punched the hilt of his sword into Einar's helmetless face, ending the great howling in a sputter and a muffled curse. Then the two men who had jumped on Einar, who I could now see were Rurik and another Varangian, stabbed their seaxes into Einar's legs, below the armour, bringing the big man down to his knees in a heap with a roar of pain and outrage.

'*Father!*' came a terrified shout from outside, and Einar's son Eindridi came charging through the door, angling towards Harald's back.

I don't remember when I drew my sword, but it was already in my hand, and without hesitation I stepped in and cut Eindridi down with a blow that went from above my right shoulder and down, through Eindridi's face, neck, and into his mailled shoulder, all the force of my swing meeting all the speed of his rush, and the boy fell dead to the floor without making a sound beyond the thump of meat.

Einar howled in anguish at the sight of his son's corpse flopping to the floor, even as Harald cut the sword from the old man's hand in a spray of wood and fingers.

'Get outside and force them back!' said Harald to me, even as he raised his sword for the death blow. Numbly, I stepped over the body of the young man I had just killed and went out through the door, even as I heard the thump and gasp of the blow land behind me.

Our men outside had locked shields and covered the doorway, a powerful, disciplined mass, weapons in every hand. Beyond them, Einar's men huddled in anger and confusion.

'Begone! Your traitor lords are dead! Begone or die yourselves! That is the order of Harald King,' I shouted at them, blood-soaked sword in hand.

There were cries of anger and outrage from the armed band, but they had no leader and did not dare to attack our imposing wall of warriors.

'Advance! Push them clear of the gate!' I shouted, and our men stamped forwards in perfect formation, herding the disorganised band backwards, giving them no choice but to form their own wall or flee out of the gate.

They fled, and we stopped on the road outside.

Harald soon appeared. I looked at him in shock, shocked not that he had done such violence, but that he had not even warned me.

'Get everything we need, and we move to the ships. Go!' Harald ordered, and Ulfr took half the men back into the buildings to grab our equipment and wealth.

I just stared at Harald, who was flecked with blood. 'Was that really the only way?'

'It was,' he said gruffly. 'I will not tolerate usurpation of my rule, I will not tolerate rebellion or dissent. If we mean to dominate the nations around this sea, we must be united, as Yaroslav united his people. I will not make peace with those who see advantage in conflict with me.' He shook his head, and his teeth were bared. 'They will understand what you understand, Eric, and what Einar understood too late. I am not King Magnus the Good. I am King Harald, the Hardrada.'

* * *

Einar's people did not gather the wits or the courage quickly enough to come and stop us leaving, and we sailed north from Nidaros to the Árnasson estates, where they raised for us 500 armed men in case Einar's family came for revenge.

Envoys went back and forth between Harald and Einar's wife, and eventually peace was agreed, with exceeding reluctance on Einar's wife's part. But she had no choice. Harald paid compensation for the death of her son, and Einar's wife had to take it or enter a civil war her people didn't want and she could neither afford nor win.

She gathered a few followers and left. I don't know where to, probably Denmark.

With that, the resistance to Harald was shattered, his grasp over Norway was complete and total.

He took me and all of the blood-marked who were still with us on a ship to Stiklestad, and we walked up to the old battlefield and the rock where Olaf had died. It was quite difficult. We stood there, seven men who had been part of an army of thousands at that spot twenty years before. The only ones still together and fighting for Olaf's legacy. There was no sign of the battle in the field around us beyond a single rusty spearhead I spotted in the earth near my feet. It was as if nothing had happened in that terrible place, and that the country had not changed there forever.

'I thank you all for your loyalty,' Harald said, after we had prayed. 'It will be remembered through history. We promised to fight for Olaf here, and that duty, for us, did not end with his death on this spot. But now his throne is safe, his killers are dead, and his legacy is secure. King Olaf is a saint, and the Norway he intended to build is flourishing.' He looked around us with glistening eyes. 'You all ensured that, you and all our brothers who died at our sides over all these years.'

He went over and put his palm on the stone. 'Let us shed our blood here one last time, and then I shall release you all from my service, for I never want you to shed blood for Norway again.'

Some of the men looked surprised at that, but most were grateful. There wasn't a man there who wasn't at or past their fortieth year, except Harald.

He cut his outer forearm with his eating knife, and each of us stepped forward to embrace him, and let him mark our faces, as he had done with the blood of the traitor Thorir Hund on the day in Kyiv when Harald had killed him.

'That you have followed me this far is beyond value, but each of you shall go home a wealthy man.'

'We are wealthy already, Komes,' said Asel with a smile.

'More wealth has never hurt a man.'

'True enough,' said Sigurd.

'Leave me alone with Eric a moment. We will follow you down to the ship.'

They all went off together, quiet but happy, and I was left standing there with Harald in the fine afternoon sun.

'Twenty-one years,' Harald said softly, looking at the stone. 'It took me twenty-one years but I have returned to this place as King, and no man stands against me any more. Now, imagine what we can do with all Norway at our backs?'

I looked at him uncomfortably, for his eyes were shining and the wolf's smile was on his face. And I was tired. So tired.

'We can conquer whole nations, starting with the Danes. We will make our own empire of the north.' He looked at me sternly. 'Do you believe in it?'

'No,' I said.

'You shall. You will see it. We will build it together in Olaf's image.'

'Harald, I'm sorry but I can't. I have served you well, have I not?'

Harald looked confused. 'Yes, you have. My brother was wise beyond his knowing to put you at my side. That is why I need you to believe in this with me, to know it is our destiny. We have succeeded for a reason, and that reason is not yet achieved.'

'Do you still want my advice, Harald?'

'Yes! I will need it.'

I stared at him sadly. 'Then stay here. Rule the kingdom that you have won and seek no other, for it will never satisfy you. I cannot follow you on any further conquests.'

His face fell into shock. 'You cannot? Why!'

'I am too old, Harald. Too tired. I also have bled my last on foreign soil. I killed a boy who was barely a man for you last night Harald, without question. Do you know that is the first time I have killed a man since the battle in the valley of the Varangians, eight years ago?'

'I suppose I did not know that. Not even in Denmark?'

I shook my head. 'It made me sick. He was just a young man, another life wasted. I used to revel in the thrill of battle, of defeating my enemies. Now I sicken at the thought. I am not the warrior I was, and I am done with campaigning.'

'I do not need you for your sword, Eric – just for your support and advice.'

'My advice is to stay here and rule, and I can support you only in that. Simply stay here and be a good king, I beseech you.'

'You would betray me now, here, after all we have done!' Harald shouted, his anger finally boiling over.

My anger rose equally. '*Betray* you? You would say that here, of all places, on the very spot from which I followed you for half my life? Do not dishonour yourself with those words. I have served you like no other man alive!'

'And that makes your refusal to continue all the worse! You made a promise to my brother, in this very place, in this sacred spot!'

'And I have *kept* it!' I roared, pulsing with anger at how poorly Harald had taken my decision. 'I told your brother I would protect you and advise you, and we both know he meant for that single battle, and we both know it lasted for twenty years because we loved him. But here we are. I have brought you back, I have helped you earn your throne. I have killed for you, bled for you, travelled to the corners of the earth at your side. Damn you, Harald, let me go!'

'Go? And do what? What would a man like you do without war?'

'Live! And raise my children! I made a promise to my wife never to abandon her again and I intend to keep it. God knows the last three years I have already stretched that to its limits, campaigning in Denmark and following you around most of the year. I intend to stay at home, Harald, after all these years of suffering to earn the right to it.' I shook my head, exasperated. 'You should do the same. You have won this nation, so *rule* it. Be King, be a good King, and leave this madness of greed and conquest behind before it consumes you.'

'It is not madness to seek greatness, Eric. Did you learn nothing from our travels? Did you not see what can be accomplished by great powers, power beyond what can be drawn from Norway alone? Think what we could do with a united empire of the north! Think of what we could build, of the wealth and glory that could be ours!' His eyes were wild and his face red, remonstrating with me, gesturing to the lands around. It was heartbreaking. His eyes were wide open, but his ears and mind were closed.

'You learned all the wrong lessons from our travels, Harald,' I said, looking at him, crestfallen. 'I can be part of it no longer. If Norway is invaded, I will come and stand at your side to defend it. But I will not sail to a war of conquest again. I am going to go and raise my children, find my daughter a good husband, and make sure my sons have a father to guide them in life, as I once guided you.'

'Sons? You only have *one* son, Eric,' Harald hissed in his spite and shame.

I was rocked, unsteady on my heels, that Harald, with all his greatness and ambition, could say such a thing to me to wound me, so petty and low... I was torn from heart to head. I felt in that moment that I had given my life to a man who cared nothing for me. I told you, I am not sure he was ever my friend.

The silence stretched as I stared at him, heartbroken and furious. But he did not relent in his anger, his huffing and his narrowed eyes. In that heartless glare I saw only a hint of regret, but he was too proud and mighty to back down, too consumed in his greed for power and glory. I saw in his eyes that he would never understand, that he could never let go. And I felt broken and strangely released by it.

'You dishonour yourself, Harald. And you are no longer worthy of my service,' I whispered.

'I do not need the service of a man who cannot live up to his promise or his name. They call you Eric the Follower? You do not deserve it.'

I stepped forwards, right into his face, finger extended. 'Damn you, Harald, I *earned* that name.'

I felt that he might strike me down at that moment, but I did not back down, and he was too angry and proud to speak.

Finally, I turned and left, walking away down the slope, not even sure where I would go, for I would not return to his ship. I had left nothing there except my war equipment, and I didn't want that any more. My sword, my shield, my maille. It meant nothing to me. I had a purse of silver on my belt and a single aim in my mind: to get away from Harald before my service to him cost me my life, and return to my family, and my sons. My *sons*.

I did not look back, and Harald did not come after me. I walked all the way here to Tinghaugen and paid for a place on a ship to the south. I was still angry, but there was really nothing in my heart but relief and joy.

For finally, after twenty years of war, I was going home.

PART II

THE GLORY

11

TINGHAUGEN, NORWAY; SPRING 1098 AD

An awkward silence fell over the audience.

'You left him?'

Eric looked sadly at the young voice who had spoken the words and saw that it was Ingvarr. The young man looked upset, almost heartbroken.

'Yes,' Eric said with a sad nod.

'But... this whole tale is about how you followed him, your loyalty!'

Eric nodded. 'Yes. But it is also about Harald's imperfections, and ultimately, my own. I left him because my own family became more important than his ambitions, and I tell you, I do not regret it. It was the best decision of my life.'

Ingvarr looked dubious and a little hurt but fell into silence. The mood around the field did not improve.

Magnus finally spoke, and he looked a little irritated.

'I believed you were telling the tale of my grandfather's greatness, but now you speak of him as a tyrant. I am not sure why I allowed this to start, and I am even more unsure why I should let it continue.'

Eric looked at the King without fear. 'I can give you three reasons, Lord King, if you wish to hear them.'

The challenge was clear, and the King could not fail to meet it. He inclined his head reluctantly.

'Thank you, Lord King. Firstly, it is our tradition that a man of Norway, holding land, can speak his mind at the speaker's spot.'

'That is during a Thing. This is not a Thing but merely a gathering of friends,' the King said with a raised finger. 'And even at a Thing, men have the sense not to speak too freely about their kings' failings.'

'Ah, but men being afraid to speak their mind is mostly your grandfather's doing, and not, I humbly submit, his wisest legacy.'

Magnus's mouth curled a little. 'You said you had three reasons,' he grumbled. 'I hope the latter two are based on stronger foundations.'

Eric nodded more hurriedly. 'The second is that I only tell of his tyranny, which is well-known and spoken of still to this day, so that you may better understand what he achieved and how. I would be doing no service to King Harald by lying about that time, because many here remember it, and would know it to be a lie. If they know I am lying about one thing, the rest of the story becomes suspect, and thus worthless. I value honesty highly, as did Harald.'

Magnus stared at Eric for a long moment and then shook his head, leaning back. 'I accept that reasoning from your point of view, but it is not a good enough reason for me to allow you to continue to tell a tale that is only darkening the mood ahead of the Thing.'

Eric pursed his lips. 'I understand. Well, the third reason is that you all know I rejoined Harald, and thus my conclusion is not that he was a tyrant, nor a man worthy of scorn. I am here to tell you of his life, his greatness and his glory, and that is how the story ends. But only through understanding how Harald was at his worst can I possibly explain to these men the full height of his achievements. He was not a great king because he was a tyrant; he was a great king because he overcame his tyranny to achieve great things for his country, and the love of its people. Is that not something worthy of the tale?'

Magnus stared at Eric carefully, eyes flicking between Eric's as he considered it. The appeal was cleverly formed, because Magnus himself had used extreme methods to solidify his control over Norway, and by saying he would describe how a king could overcome that reputation to achieve greatness and the love of his people, Eric was offering him a gift and a branch of peace.

Magnus was too savvy to be instantly drawn, however, nor to fold to such an obvious appeal to his own desires. He stood slowly. 'I will consider it. Regardless, it is time we stopped to eat – the noon hour is upon us. I will return here on the next hour and if it seems correct, perhaps we will allow you to finish your tale.'

Eric bowed his head deeply. 'Thank you, Lord Magnus. I will await and respect your decision.'

The King had already decided and they both knew it, but Eric did not do anything to undermine it.

Magnus gestured to Jarl Halfdan as he walked away, and the lord of Tinghaugen followed him closely. They walked around the hall to the door that led to the Jarl's chambers, and the King went in without seeking invitation. The chambers were his for the duration of the Thing, by Halfdan's formal gift.

The interior was dark, but not so dark that they could not see, and the King walked past the table that was set on one side and stopped, putting his hands on a shelf and leaning into it.

'I have to let him continue,' Magnus finally growled.

'I believe you do,' Halfdan said with a nervous voice. 'It is too late to stop. It will look like weakness more now than before.'

'Oh, still the lecture in your tone, Halfdan,' Magnus snapped, turning to give Halfdan a sour look. 'I know you advised me to end this earlier, and perhaps I should have. But Eric is careful to introduce his opposition slowly. How clearly he was speaking out against the methods of my rule, methods I learned from how my grandfather ruled. He admonished me in front of all of them without even mentioning my name!' Magnus shook his head. 'And he pretends to be foolish and naive in the way of politics!'

'He is no fool.'

'Of course he isn't, otherwise my grandfather would not have kept him close for so many years. He is quite the master and has learned from some of the greatest men of his time. It is all a ploy.'

Halfdan frowned. 'Are we sure that is even the truth? He might be exaggerating his experiences.'

Magnus shook his head. 'No, it is the truth. My mother and father spoke of it in detail.'

'But your father Olaf did not keep Eric by his side?'

'No. And he did not explain why, but Eric was quietly and quickly pushed out of his court. I suspect my father did not trust him, or that Eric was too manipulative. Either way, he was not an advisor.'

Halfdan sighed. 'So if you cannot stop him telling his tale, we must focus on what he might say at the Thing.'

'Yes, that is the danger – that he takes to the speaker's bench and opposes my plans for invading England. You heard him, he just took pains to remind me and everyone listening that all men should be allowed to speak their mind at the Thing. He knew that was not a reason to allow him to continue today and feigned confusion, but no, it was quite deliberate. He is outright warning me he might speak against me if my plans are too ambitious or extensive!' Magnus slapped a jug of water from the table, ignoring it as it shattered against the wall, spraying the contents to dribble down the stones.

'He seeks to dictate my policy, manipulate me into cancelling my invasion!'

'We cannot be certain, but...' Halfdan looked at the King nervously. 'It does seem likely.'

'And I cannot stop him, I cannot judge him and I cannot kill him, because all of those would make me look weaker and his points stronger.' Magnus cursed under his breath. 'Damn him. I should have come here earlier.'

Jarl Halfdan looked at Magnus carefully for a while in silence as the King brooded. 'Perhaps you need to speak to him in private, my King. Perhaps you can convince him to support you. In fact, perhaps that is what he seeks – some recognition of concession in return for his support.'

Magnus raised his eyes to Halfdan in interest. 'Do you think such an old man cares about wealth or title? What could I offer him?'

Halfdan smiled. 'All he speaks of is reputation and legacy. You can offer him that, in a way. Offer to make him part of the court, to help him spread his tale. I don't know exactly, maybe he just wants to be heard by the King.'

Magnus looked a little dubious but nodded. 'It is worth trying, although it is not without risk. He might see it as obvious bribery, and reject it, even try to humiliate me for it.'

'Then make it not obvious.'

'How? He is too clever to do that in a single conversation. No, it will be obvious. More pertinently, he can secretively claim whatever he wants about that conversation. No, it is dangerous to publicly reward him with an audience when he has insulted me, unless it leads to his support. It will be an unspeakable humiliation if he speaks against me after that.'

Halfdan pursed his lips and spoke again hesitantly. 'There is perhaps a way we can prevent that after your conversation, if you feel he was not convinced. It is not perhaps one that you would like. I started preparing for this eventuality yesterday, in case it was needed.'

'You did what? You are already preparing my actions?' Magnus said with an angry expression.

'I apologise, but yes, because if you had decided now it would have been too late. I am merely giving you an option. I suggest you appear to be aligned with him. Have a conversation with him in private to appeal to him, and if he still defies you, we can use my preparation to limit the damage.'

Magnus furrowed his brows but stood up and relented, peering at Halfdan curiously.

'Then tell me, what is it?'

* * *

Eric was sitting in the sun, chatting with Jarl Hakon and Ingvarr while they shared some bread and mutton. Ingvarr finished quickly and wandered off, looking perturbed.

'Don't worry about him,' Hakon said as they watched him leave. 'He is young, and everything in politics is new to him. He sees the world in a very simple light.'

Eric smiled. 'Do not fear, for I am not concerned. Despite my age, I remember very well thinking the same way about things. What I said, or more how I said it, was deliberately crafted to challenge the way men think about Harald and his kingship.'

Hakon looked at him. 'Why is that? Why do you risk that?'

Eric smiled. 'Well, I can't tell you right now – that would ruin the story.'

'If King Magnus lets you complete it.'

'He will,' said Eric with a confident smile. 'If he does not, men will spend the entire Thing annoyed that they did not hear the end of the tale, and thinking about it, assuming the worst, and that is the last thing that Magnus wants.'

Hakon looked at him with concern. 'You are playing some sort of dangerous game, Eric.'

'I am merely telling him a story to pass the time,' Eric said nonchalantly.

Hakon gestured with a bit of bread at Eric, smiling. 'No one believes that any more.'

'Really, no one?'

Hakon used the meat-grease covered bread to gesture around the field, where several hundred men were sitting on benches or on the ground, or standing around talking, many still finishing their own meals. 'It is all any of them are talking about.'

'What is?'

'What you are really up to. What is the purpose of your story.'

Eric gave Hakon an innocent smile as the jarl finished the last of his bread. 'Well, if I had some sort of plan, that would be very good to hear.' He winked. 'Shame that I am just an old man telling old tales.'

Hakon licked his fingers and shook his head. 'You are a strange man, Eric.' He waggled a finger at Eric in mock warning. 'Don't disappoint my son; he has come to love your tale and think of you fondly. Whatever your purpose here is, don't crush his beliefs.'

'I don't intend to, but what beliefs are those?'

Hakon's look become more serious. 'That King Harald was a great and glorious king, and that we should all follow in his footsteps.'

Eric smiled softly and broadly, shaking his head. 'Don't worry, Jarl Hakon. I spent my entire life following in his footsteps, and that belief is the only one I have ever held to be unbreakably true. He will understand that, by the end. I hope you all will.'

Hakon gave Eric one last raised eyebrow and nodded in satisfaction. 'Good. Well...'

Then they both looked up as a gaggle of richly dressed men reappeared, with King Magnus at their head. The men in the field looked surprised at the King's sudden and early arrival; he usually waited for the whole gathering to be ready before he appeared. But the King looked in a bright and happy mood as he took his place beside the speaker's bench and looked out over the field.

'Well?' he said, slapping one hand down on his thigh. 'Shall we continue?'

There was a flurry as the audience scrambled to get back to their places.

Eric looked a little taken aback by the King's enthusiasm, regarding him with a raised eyebrow. Magnus turned his gaze to Eric and waved him forwards. 'Come, Eric. I trust my advisors as much as Harald trusted you, and they have convinced me the value of us hearing the rest of my grandfather's reign. So – the sun is moving, the day is turning. Let us begin.'

Eric got to his feet looking slightly perplexed. 'As you command, my King. Yes, of course.' He wiped his lips and hurriedly took a drink from his mug. Water, not ale.

Then he looked over the freshly assembled audience. 'Uh...'

'You were about to explain what drew you back to my grandfather's side,' Magnus interjected helpfully. 'How you regained your love and trust for him, or perhaps realised the error of your leaving?'

Eric bowed his head slightly. 'Thank you, Lord King. Yes. That is it, indeed.'

The King gestured to the space. 'Well, Eric Sveitungr – the field is yours.'

Eric bowed his head and turned to the audience, who were silent once more.

'I know the fact that I left Harald's service surprises you, and the fact that I returned to it might surprise you even more. But that is what was so magical about him, and why he was such a great man.'

'I have relayed to you that Harald ordered me to my death, several times, and how angry I was. You probably think that I am angry with him for that still, but I am not. You might think that I left because I could not forgive him, but I did. Or that I no longer loved him, but I loved him always. I left him not just because of his actions, but also my own weakness, because I could no longer bear the furnace heat of his ambitions, and what he was willing to do to achieve them. But that never changed the true nature of my bond to him.'

'Listen carefully, for this is what I have been trying to have you understand about Hardrada. He was not a great man because he was willing to order men to die for his ambitions. He was a great man because they *wanted to*.' His eyes swept towards King Magnus and their gazes locked. 'Every king and ruler of worth knows this is true greatness.'

Then he turned slowly back to the audience, earnest and intense. 'I want you to understand what I mean when I say great men like Harald are different to us, that merely being in their presence changes you, infuses you with the power of their souls and bonds you to them. I tell you this, because I must admit something terrible to you before I end my tale.'

All the mirth and joy left Eric's expression like blood flowing from a wound, leaving nothing but hardness and anger behind.

'The truth is, I wasn't just willing to die for Harald's ambitions, in my soul I *wanted* to give my life for his greatness.'

'So now I must tell of the great regret of my life. The story of how when the chance came... I failed to.'

12

RINGEVIRKE, UPPLOND; SPRING 1066 AD

For fifteen years Harald and I did not exchange another word. Fifteen years.

I saw him, of course, for every year I went to the Thing of the Upplonds at Anslo, and he was always there. I heard him speak, and sometimes I spoke at the meeting about one subject or another, so he heard me. But never a word to each other. Never. Not even one. For nearly as long as we had been together, we were strangers, and it was painful although I pretended otherwise.

He was too proud and hurt, and I was too proud and hurt, and we ignored each other like children.

And it was fear too, for what he had said haunted me: that my eldest son was not mine. I do not believe he ever repeated it, but he could have at any moment, and the King pronouncing that my son was not my heir would have been devastating to my family. That possibility hung over me like a cloud for all my years apart from him, always in the background, brought forwards every time I saw him at meetings.

And what did he do after I left his side? Well, you all know. Harald spent another twelve years campaigning in Denmark. He raided and harried them almost every year, draining Denmark of its warriors and its wealth, making the fighting men of Norway rich at his and Sweyn's expense. He achieved a great many victories, often against superior foes, and was never defeated in battle – but Denmark would not submit. Tough people, our southern cousins, and don't let anyone try and tell you different.

King Jacob died, and Yaroslav too. The great alliance of the north and the Rus fell apart so all that was left was the war of Harald and Sweyn, with no one to support either of them.

But it was not until 1062 that he managed to force Sweyn to finally fight him in the decisive battle he had always sought. The fleets met at Nisa, and although the battle was hard, Harald was victorious. But Sweyn escaped, and once more, to Harald's outrage, Denmark refused to submit.

Harald was finally forced to accept that they never would, and he made peace with Sweyn, each abandoning their claim to the other's kingdom.

For a few years, Harald returned home and ruled. But his endless and militarily successful campaigns in Denmark had created a nation of warriors who loved battle-won silver and did not know the taste of defeat. The greatest generation of warriors the north had seen for a hundred years or more. And they, like Harald, never lost their taste for conquest and war.

And I should say that Harald, for all my criticism of his greed for conquest, was a good king even if he was a hard one. He implemented many of the lessons of the empire into the governance of Norway and organised the nation in a way that made it wealthier and stronger. For the first time the entire realm acted as one – gone were the petty kings and internal wars of regions. Those reforms last to this day and are kept alive by his sons and grandsons. Norway is a better place for him having ruled it, and even if the path there cost us so much in blood and silver, it was worth the sacrifice.

And what did I do? I built my hall, I tended to my farms and my people, and I raised my children. I knew the love of my wife uninterrupted and returned tenfold, and for fifteen years I never took up a weapon in anger again, except a few times to deal with bandits and criminals, but that was rare enough. I would tell you of those wonderful years, but this is not my story.

So you all wonder, how did I end up on the field of Stamford Bridge with Harald? And here, my friends, at last we reach the final part of my tale. It began on a fine spring morning in my home, with a lone visitor at our hall, who wore the gold of a king, and the face of a long-lost friend.

'There is a party on the road to the hall, Eric,' said one of my men.

You see, I was not some great lord, but I was wealthy enough to have several servants and a dozen or so workers on the land around my hall. I taught the use of sword and shield to all those who were fit to bear them. We never had much trouble with bandits and thieves, I tell you.

So we quickly armed – not with helmets and maille, for no attacking party comes by road in broad daylight and allows themselves to be seen – but with swords and seaxes so that if some violence did occur, we could defend ourselves.

And we went down the road to the markers at the edge of my property. I saw that the party of men had stopped there, that it was large and rich, and that a single man was striding up the path towards us, not waiting to be invited in, with one of my people nervously hurrying along in his wake.

Ahh, I knew who it was immediately, even with my old eyes. No other man was so tall, nor could stride so confidently through another's land uninvited. Not that he needed an invitation, of course, for he was my King.

I gestured at my men to stop and went down to meet him alone, for if there was some conflict I wanted our words to be private. He stopped and waited for me, also alone, and as I approached him, I was angry, confused, worried... Above all I was happy. I was deliriously happy that he had come to see me, for I had started to believe I would die before we spoke again.

He stood there in all his finery, for even in travel he dressed as a king should, with a soft smile on his face. His hair was greying, his face was weathered and creased, his beard was streaked with white, but it was the same Harald. The fire still burned behind those bright blue eyes.

'How are your sons, Eric?' he said casually, as if nothing had ever changed.

How are your *sons*. Ahh, the *bastard*. He disarmed me with a single sentence. I wonder if he practised it on his journey, crafted it carefully, or whether they were simply the genuine words that came to his mind. With Harald's intelligence, you never knew.

It was an apology, or at least the closest he could ever come to apologising. It was a peace token, the most powerful one, because he was stripping himself of the very thing he had used to attack me. It was a heartfelt greeting, because nothing matters more to an old man than his sons.

Ahh, it stripped the years and layers of anger from me like a season in the sun strips old paint. It all fell away, unwanted and unneeded, and I was just an old man who was happy to see an old friend.

'They are well, thank you, my King,' I said, managing a smile and not a stutter. 'My eldest has a wife and a new son of his own now.'

'You have a grandchild!' Harald exclaimed, and I could see his surprise and joy were genuine.

I grinned, because it overjoyed me too. I had never expected to live to see grandchildren. 'Yes. My son was married last year, and he does not waste his time.'

Harald looked at me with a happy smile and then shook his head. 'How did we allow so much time to pass?'

'Because we are stubborn old fools.'

'We are,' he said with a nearly violent nod, and then finally stepped forward to embrace me, attacking me with it the way a bear might take down an ailing elk.

'Although I am still not so old as you,' he whispered in my captive ear. And then he laughed as I cursed him and struggled, beating helplessly on his ribs to force him to release me.

He eventually put me down, and it was nothing to do with my struggling. 'Can I come and be your guest?'

That is when I knew he needed something. It was his tone, I think, a hint of nervousness. But I did not care.

'Of course! You have always been welcome, even if you have been absent.'

'I have been busy,' he replied defensively.

'A king is always busy.'

'You could have come to see *me*!' Harald said as we headed off up the path like the old friends we never really were.

'A father is busy too,' I said. And we walked to my hall chatting like children who have been apart for a summer.

* * *

I made him and his people welcome in my hall, and I sent my workers to bring in two goats to slaughter and roast. I even opened a new barrel of good ale. I am generous, you see. A whole barrel!

'Olga!' Harald said, spreading his arms as my wife arrived in the hall. 'I am so happy to see you.'

'And I am happy to receive you, my King,' she replied with dignity, because she did not have a high opinion of Harald.

He took her hand and kissed it in the formal Rus way, which impressed me, and clearly impressed Olga too, for none of us had used it for two decades. He raised his head back up. 'Please, I am not King, not here in your home. You knew me when I was merely a mercenary captain and a boy.'

'You are a king everywhere you go in this country, but if it is your command, I will happily call you boy,' Olga said with a withering smile. Gods, she was so elegant. Age only improved her presence, let me tell you.

Harald chuckled at the play of words and nodded. 'I would be happy for that.'

'Then come, boy, and sit at my table.'

I think my mouth hung open a little, but Harald took the subtle punishment with perfect grace and meekly allowed himself to be led to his seat.

Ha! I speak so little of Olga because this is not her story, but my wife called Harald Hardrada *boy*, and he merely smiled at her submissively and did as she bade him! Can you believe it! What a woman she was, and how lucky I am for having lived with her.

It brings joy to my heart thinking of her, and tears to my eyes. Anyway, this is not my story.

So we sat and we talked of family and nothing, avoiding any politics or difficulty, and it was a wonderful meal. It was as if nothing had ever happened, and that we were dining at the barracks of the Varangians in Constantinople, or in Kyiv.

Finally, a comfortable silence descended as we sat, warm and satiated, and I turned to Harald to ask the thing that I had wanted to ask since he arrived.

'Why are you really here, Harald?'

He gave me a sideways glance and then a little grin from the corner of his mouth. 'Ah, to business then.'

I nodded. 'I have been beyond happy to dine and talk with you again, but I know you did not come here for meat and conversation.'

'Maybe I did? I thought coming here for your hospitality and conversation after all this time was worthy on its own, and I tell you, it was.' He smiled.

'But yet...' I said knowingly.

He nodded. 'Indeed. Wonderful though it is, as you have determined I do have another reason to visit.'

My wife gave me a look and stood. 'I should leave you boys to your peace negotiation.'

Harald moved surprisingly quickly to stop her, taking her arm lightly in his hand. 'I would prefer if you stayed, for it will save Eric having to relay my words to you and seek your opinion. Let's have you share it here, in front of me.'

Olga seemed a little taken aback, but she eased herself back down into her seat and Harald smiled and nodded, letting go of her arm. She was being done a great honour, being invited to stay and hear the King's counsel, and she knew it.

'Did you hear that King Edward is dead?' he asked.

Edward was the aging king of England at that time, you see.

I nodded. 'Even in this high valley, such news travels.'

'Well, then you already know the reason for my visit, or can guess at its main form.'

I sighed, staring into my empty ale. 'You intend to claim the throne of England.' I looked up at him sternly. 'Is this a sickness in you? You have only had three summers of peace and you seek war again?'

Harald held up his hands defensively. 'Hear me out, for this is not the same.'

I grumbled and rolled my eyes. 'Go ahead. Although I struggle to see why this would matter to me.'

'Magnus had a legitimate claim to the throne of England, as you know. I inherited it from him as his successor and kinsman.'

'That is dubious. I am sure there are better claimants.'

Harald wagged his finger. 'That is exactly the point. There are not. There are many claimants, but none of them good. The man died childless and brotherless.'

'So who sits the throne?'

'A man named Harold Godwinson, who had no claim at all other than he seized power when he had the opportunity.'

I smiled sarcastically. 'A man named Harold who seized power by his own accord? You must already love him. Are you sure you do not wish to be allies?'

Harald laughed. 'Yes, he sounds like someone I would respect. But regardless, my claim is better than his, and two others also make claim and have the possibility to enforce it.'

'Who?' I said tiredly, playing along with his game.

'Sweyn, who also claims it also through Magnus, and Duke William of Normandy, who was supposedly promised the throne by Edward, and is a distant relation.'

'So why does that have you so excited?'

'Well, William has made clear his intent to invade England and claim the throne. Sweyn makes similar noises, but he is too weak at the moment to do anything about it.'

'So William will invade and claim it?'

'He is too weak on his own. He cannot contend with all the power of England, not with just the forces of Normandy. He is looking for allies.'

'So you have made an alliance with him?'

'No.'

I stared at him, and his excitement was annoying. 'Then what?'

'Well, Harold is sitting in southern England with his army, waiting for William to finally gather enough forces to invade. This leaves the northern part of the country, where so many of our kin still live in the old Danelaw, vulnerable.'

'If you invade, Harold will come to face you.'

'He can't, not with the threat Duke William poses to his rich southern lands. But, more importantly, I have an ally in the north who can secure it for us and negotiate with Harold: his brother.'

'His brother?'

Harald nodded. 'A man named Tostig. He used to be the earl of the northern region, but he was deposed by Harold and Edward. He seeks the return of his lands, and he came to me looking for an ally. He knows the land, he knows the people and he has connections and allies there.'

I mulled it over. 'So what is your aim?'

'Well, it is simple – I will invade the north with Tostig while Harold and William face each other in the south. Once I have captured the north, with local allies and the support of the King of Scotland, my position will be too strong to oppose. Either Harold will be forced to make terms with me, and allow us to regain control of the Danelaw, or William will invade and defeat Harold, and I will make terms with him instead. Neither will be strong enough to remove us from the north once we are established, and recruit from our own kin there.'

I nodded. It was a sound strategy, although I still could not understand the reason. 'And what is the point?' I asked, looking at him. 'What does this gain?'

'What does it gain? Eric... Land, wealth, glory for our nation and the reintegration of our kin in the north of England! With all of that, Norway will be more powerful and more able to confront our enemies. We will rule the western sea entirely, from Vik to Orkney and the southern isles. We will control the trade, we will be able to move our influence south. Hopefully, we will be able to take advantage of any weakness in later years and take all of England and the other islands of Alba.' His eyes were sparkling with excitement.

'It is not an insane concept, Harald. But I still do not understand why you would do this. You are unlikely to live to see the results.'

'Legacy, Eric,' he said gruffly. 'My son Magnus is nearly ready to rule, and Olaf is nearly a man too.'

I nodded slowly. 'They need two kingdoms.'

'Exactly. If I leave them Norway alone, they will tear each other apart fighting over it. But if I leave Norway to Magnus, and England to Olaf, they can be allies, as Cnut's sons were allies, forming an alliance of the north that will overpower any enemy.'

'Like Yaroslav's sons,' I said.

'Exactly.'

Yaroslav was long dead by then, but his family still ruled or was married to the rulers in half a dozen great countries and formed an alliance that ensured the safety of all its parts. Yaroslav had built a legacy beyond conquest, a system of rulers that would safeguard his nation for centuries. Harald was thinking in long-term planning now, not his reflexive and fixated attempts to control the ruins of Denmark.

'So you are doing this for your sons?' I asked, still dubious.

'I am, and for all the sons of Norway. The warriors of this land are restless, Eric. They grew used to feeding off the fat of Denmark, and now they seek new conquests. Four years of peace has made them quarrelsome.'

I nodded. It was true. At the Thing meetings of the previous years, many lords had spoken for campaigns to the east or west, often just for the sake of going on campaign. Harald would not struggle to find willing participants on so grand a scheme.

'You have not answered the most important question,' I said.

'Which is why I am talking to you of this.'

I nodded. I was worried about the likely answer, but excited too, I admit it.

'It is simple, Eric. I want you at my side. One final campaign, one great adventure for Norway. I've never been on such a venture without you, and I need you to come with me. I need your wisdom, and your nose for trouble. It will keep me alive.'

I breathed deeply. 'Harald, I am fifty-five years old...'

'Fifty-six,' said my wife curtly.

'Fifty-six years old,' I said, nodding at my wife before looking back at Harald. 'I haven't been in a real battle for nearly twenty years. Nor do I ever intend to do so again.'

'I do not need you to fight, Eric. I need only for you to follow me on campaign and give me the benefit of your thoughts and words.'

'Ulfr can do all you need, surely,' I said.

Harald's face relaxed a little and his eyes darkened. 'Ulfr is dead.'

That hit me hard. I had seen Ulfr the previous winter. We had remained good friends and he often visited and brought me news of Harald.

'Dead? How?'

Harald shrugged. 'I do not know. I think it was simply a matter of age, and a hard life.'

Ulfr had been a little older than me, about sixty, and true enough, it is old for a man who spent his entire life at campaign and court. But he had always seemed so... invincible. I was greatly saddened. I am still saddened, in fact, thinking about it. Ulfr was perhaps the greatest friend of my life. I had hated losing friends to battle in my youth. In my old age, I hated losing friends to the ravages of time even more. It is more pernicious, an enemy you cannot fight or avoid. And I should know. Every friend of my youth is dead, and I am now all that remains of that time.

'I want you to take his place at my side. I need you, Eric,' Harald said, and his eyes were hopeful. He was, in some ways, still that uncertain boy who first sailed into the Rus. He needed one of us, the great companions of his youth. He was lost without us.

I grumbled, looked down at my hands, flexing my fingers and trying to imagine holding a sword again. Whatever Harald said, any man who goes to battle must be ready to fight in one. Few enemies will grant mercy just because you do not like the inconvenience of defending yourself. Being at Harald's side meant arming yourself for war and facing its trials, ones I had never hoped to face again.

'I do not wish to be your marshal, Harald. I do not know all of your lords and I have not commanded for twenty years. I am not fit for it.'

'Do not worry. Stykarr will be my marshal.'

I nodded. Stykarr was a famous warrior and battle leader, and a good choice, although I did not know him well.

'Then why do you need me?'

'Because Stykarr is not my friend,' Harald said.

'And am I your friend, Harald? Does a King have friends?'

Harald looked at me intently and smiled softly. 'You test me, but I remember Jarl Rognvald's words as well as you do.'

I nodded.

'Yes. Thirty years ago, we stood on the bank of the river in Kyiv, the last time I ever saw him, right after he betrayed me by siding with Magnus. I told him I could not believe a friend would do that to me. And he was disappointed that I was upset. Disappointed!' Harald chuckled to himself, clearly feeling no anger, only fondness. 'He told me that kings have no friends, only allies and enemies, and that both were rapidly interchangeable.' Harald looked down with a smile and kicked at the floorboards. 'I have never forgotten that wisdom. Again and again, it has been proven true.'

He looked up to meet me with his piercing blue gaze. 'But not you, Eric. I never feared that you would be my enemy, and I never considered you my ally. You were loyal, but it was personal, not transactional. You needed nothing from me in return. If that does not make you a friend, what does it make you?'

'A follower,' I said without hesitation, and he nodded softly.

'Perhaps that is merely the very best kind of friend.'

'And perhaps, given that we parted for fifteen years the moment I stopped following you, it was no kind of friend at all,' I said, challenging him, wanting him to rise to it a little bit, to satisfy me by showing a little anger or shame.

'I submit to your argument, Eric,' he said without looking perturbed. 'Maybe what I need you for is because you are a follower, not a friend. Regardless, I need you. What do you say? Can you be my follower again?'

I looked at my wife uncertainly, and I was surprised that I felt uncertain, because if you had asked me the previous day if I would ever go to war again, I would have laughed in your face. But I admit – I was a little excited. I was bored too, because I no longer had to care for my children; my farm was managed by younger and fitter men, and I really had little to do unless I chose to work for the sake of it, which I often did. So I was still fit for a man of my age, and in good health. But I was bored, truly. Happy and content, but bored. The thought of a grand campaign, one founded on sound principles of strategy, was suddenly deeply alluring to part of me.

Finally, and most strongly, I felt a duty to it. I knew that if I let Harald run off to England without me or Ulfr to aid him, he might well not come back, and all my lifelong efforts to help him secure his kingdom might ultimately have been futile. His legacy was *my* legacy, you see. Hardrada's legacy, that is mine own, the work of my entire life, even this very day.

'What do you think, my wife?' I said, looking at Olga, assuming she would rescue me from my temptation and refuse to allow it.

She tapped her finger on the table and looked between me and Harald with a displeased look. 'I think it is your duty to serve your King, and that you should not refuse such a personal request, especially by giving your wife the responsibility to refuse.'

My mouth gaped. 'You think I should go?'

She waved her hand in annoyance. 'I do not want you to go, but equally I see these past years that you are frustrated, itching for some excitement. There is little enough for you to do here and I will not have you hold me for the rest of our lives as the reason you did not go. So... yes, go and serve your King if you wish, and return satisfied. I think you need it, but I do not claim to be happy about it. Either way, be a man and decide for yourself.'

'But I said I would never leave you again.'

'No, you promised never to abandon me, to stay and help me raise our children. That we have done, only our daughter remains at home. You have done your duty to me, so go if you wish. Do your duty to your King and do not hold back with me as an excuse.' She wagged her finger at me with a stern look. 'But I expect you to come back. I will need your help finding our daughter a good husband, when the time is right.'

'Do not worry, Olga. I will not put Eric in danger,' Harald said gravely.

'No, you shall not,' Olga said, staring him down as if he was a servant being instructed not to dirty some linen. 'You will listen to him, and he will keep you both safe, if that is truly your reason for taking him with you.'

Harald smiled. 'It is.' He leaned over to me. 'Stars above, Eric, how did you keep such a wondrous and strong-willed woman as your wife all these years?'

I shrugged helplessly. 'I don't think she gave me a choice.'

Olga snorted. 'No, I just knew what the correct decision was, and guided you to it.'

'That's not how I remember it,' I muttered.

'Well, that is the truth, and don't you dare argue it.' And she gave me a final look and then sat back in her chair looking displeased.

Harald laughed deeply and heartily. 'Then it is decided,' he said, slapping a hand on the table.

'I did not agree yet!' I protested weakly.

'No, but Olga and I did, and thus the matter is complete. Your King alone you might refuse, but the King and your wife?' he said with a mischievous grin. 'That is an alliance you will never be able to defeat.'

I looked at Olga a final time, but there was no retreat in her expression.

My heart thumped in my chest and my stomach churned. But I was filled with an energy that I had not felt for years. I looked at my King. 'I see. Well then, what is it that you need me to do?'

13

SOLUND, WESTERN NORWAY; JULY 1066 AD

In the old days, Harald would have spent months going around Norway, securing support. But by that time there was no need. He sent out word, held court in Anslo, and men simply came to him when they heard the news. So many men wanted to join his great expedition that he was turning away more men than he persuaded. He wanted only the best, the most experienced warriors of Norway. It was not a huge army we were going to sail with; taking 20,000 good men to Denmark was possible, but all the way to England? It would be more a hindrance than a help to do so. So Harald elected only to take less than ten.

I met with his new generation of followers, because a new generation they were. Eystein Orre, a nobleman of the western country and part of the Árnasson clan who were still Harald's allies, was Harald's strongest supporter in that region, and I had not had cause to meet him before he visited.

'Eystein Orre, this is Eric Alvarsson, my new advisor and oldest supporter,' Harald said with a cheeky smile when we met. 'And I do not just mean that he is the oldest man who supports me, although it may be true, but that he has supported me for my entire life when all others have fallen away.'

Eystein looked at me with interest. 'I have heard much about Eric the Follower, but we have never had the chance to meet.'

'I grew out of battle before you grew into it,' I said gruffly, not wanting to explain my fifteen-year absence from Harald's side. That we had fallen out was an unacknowledged matter. We acted as if it had never happened, and men were generally wise enough to play along.

'Well, I am pleased to finally sail at your side. That is what we are doing, is it not?' Eystein said, looking at Harald.

'It is!'

'Where?'

'England.'

Eystein's face lit up with a hunger and delight. 'I had hoped so. Do you intend to face William's challenge, or ally with him?'

Harald slapped Eystein on the back and looked at me. 'See, he is a sharp one! This is why he is to become my son.'

'Your son?'

'He is betrothed to my daughter, Maria,' Harald said with a broad smile. And yes, Harald had named his daughter after the true love of his life and the woman who had betrayed him. Don't ask me why, I found it perplexing. I think he never got over Maria's treachery and never lost his love for her.

I smiled. 'Wonderful news. I am sure that will be a blessed union.'

I took stock of Eystein a little more seriously, because I knew Harald loved Maria the most of all his children. If he had betrothed her to Eystein, he must have believed Eystein to be worthy indeed.

* * *

Well, I was introduced to many new lords in that way, when they arrived at the gathering in Solund in July. Some 300 ships were gathered, for only 8,000 men. Now, that is a large number of ships for that many men, but it is because we were undertaking a long journey and campaign and needed to fill the hulls with supplies and equipment. There were about 200 ships of war, and a hundred fatter vessels usually used for trade.

This seems normal now, but at the time no Norwegian fleet had ever put to sea like that. It was the influence of our time in the empire, you see. Harald had learned that foreign campaigns are won and lost by supply as much as by warriors. It was one of many lessons Harald brought to Norway that we take for granted now.

Harald gathered all the lords and landowners to the meeting place the day before we left.

'As you all know, such a campaign will be dangerous, to me as much as any man – probably more. I suspect some of you wonder why I am going, or what will happen if I fall. Be assured, I do not intend to leave Norway's stability to the whims of fate. I will ensure the continued peace in our realm even if I do not return.' He gestured to his right. 'Stand forwards, Magnus Haraldsson, and be seen.'

Harald's son Magnus stepped forwards. Magnus was eighteen that year and was already going about with his father in the yearly Thing meetings, being introduced to all his future subjects of note, for Harald had made it absolutely clear he intended his sons to rule and that no dissent on the matter was acceptable.

'I ask you all, gathered men of Norway, to support my proclamation that Magnus, son of Harald, King of Norway, be made upon this day as King beside me, so that once again Norway shall have two kings. If I die in foreign battle he will rule. If I return, he will rule beside me and grow into his kingship.'

What reaction could you expect? Only the most loyal lords of Norway were gathered, and they all immediately and enthusiastically stood and acclaimed Magnus as King. The young man, who was good and strong as a boy, stood forwards and smiled, accepting their vocal support. Finally, Harald raised his hand for silence.

'Then it has been said, and no man has opposed it. From this moment Magnus shall be called King in this place, and in every place in Norway where he shall walk. I ask you all to swear it now before him and each other and let it be known to your people.' He held up his hand again to forestall them. 'But first, you all know I have a second son, and no competition or conflict will be allowed between them. Stand forward, Olaf Haraldsson.'

Olaf emerged from the gaggle of family and supporters beside Harald and stood beside his brother with a proud smile.

Olaf was sixteen, and while Magnus was quiet and confident, calm and softly spoken, Olaf was more like his father as a boy: brash and wild, with a fiery spirit and dominating presence. All of you knew him, of course, while he was King. He changed a little over the years, growing into his rule, and as you all know he was a great king to Norway, and father to our King Magnus, but I tell you he was a fine youth too, and well deserved of his father Harald's legacy. And that was the day Harald gave it to him.

'Olaf will accompany me to England, and if we succeed in carving out a kingdom there, it shall be his to rule. If we fail, or when I die, Olaf will take my place as King, alongside his brother, and they will rule Norway together in peace and war, never to be set against each other. I ask you all gathered here, as you have accepted Magnus as King, to support my son's claim when the time finally comes.'

'I will stand behind Olaf's claim,' Eystein said, standing and turning to the crowd with a fervent look and a raised hand. 'And any man who opposes it will call me enemy.'

'And I!' said Thorberg Árnasson, stepping to join Eystein.

Of course, Harald had warned them in advance and told them to voice their support so publicly that the people would be easily persuaded. But he needn't have done so, for the support in the crowd was genuine and rapid. Olaf was already well-liked, as he was throughout his reign, because he was so clearly like his father, and a strong and intelligent young man.

The whole gathering stood forwards for Magnus and Olaf, and they took their oaths for them. Harald celebrated with a great feast the like of which I had not seen in years. It was a feast to celebrate his son's rise and the start of our campaign but also – and I feel it more these days – it was a farewell feast for Hardrada. One way or another, I'm sure he knew it was the last time he would ever sail away on a great campaign of conquest.

* * *

Two days later we set sail for the islands of Orkney, which I had never visited before. The journey was two days at sea, but it was uneventful and the weather was a blessing. I expected them to be rich, for the Jarls of Orkney were always powerful and wealthy, but I was surprised to find windswept, half barren islands of rock and scrubby trees. Their wealth came from war, you see, and their people were hard and tenacious, some of the best warriors you could find.

The earls came to meet us: and Erlend Thorfinnsson. Their father had been the one who had quarrelled with Rognvald and led to his death. But Thorfinn was long dead, and Harald did not hold a grudge against the sons. He made sure to support them, and they were deeply loyal in response.

We took on water there, and what food they could spare to sell us – mostly fish and seal meat. Most importantly, a thousand of their battle-hardened warriors joined our army, and both jarls. That was quite a gesture of faith, let me tell you. It would have been more cautious for one to remain at home, to guarantee the survival of their house if the other died. But as I said, they were true allies of Harald.

I have spoken before of how Harald was not popular in his early years, and that he was given the name Hardrada as an insult because men resented his rule. Well, I can tell you honestly that he was never as popular or loved as Magnus. He never meant to be. But by the year we invaded England the fighting men of Norway loved him almost as fiercely as we in the Varangians had done. Why wouldn't they? He had led them on a dozen years of campaigning where they had seen nothing but victory, and had profited handsomely from plunder. Harald had not won the crown, but the men of Norway had grown rich on the fat carved from Denmark's hide.

Men love generals who win battles and do great deeds, and they did not much care that the campaigns had ultimately failed to gain Denmark. In fact, I suspect many of them were glad because it had allowed them to raid repeatedly. They say the great buildings of Norway are built on Danish silver, and although it is not true, it is also not a lie.

So the army we left Orkney with to sail to England was well-experienced, highly motivated to go to war and fiercely loyal. They were truly the best force of 10,000 warriors I ever saw assembled, with the quality to compare to the Normans, the numbers to compare to the Rus, and a devotion the Greeks could only have dreamed of. Our main problem of discipline was with the various groups within the army competing to prove themselves the bravest and most aggressive.

A lifetime of work had gone into the perfection of that army, which is what makes their fate all the harder to bear.

* * *

We sailed south to the Kingdom of Scotland, where King Malcolm, no particular ally of Harald but more than happy to help weaken England, gave us another 2,000 men. They were of dubious quality and loyalty, but decently equipped and fierce. Ferocity is a quality of its own in battle.

In August we finally sailed to England and landed at the mouth of a great river. I do not know its name; I do not know much of England beyond the area around the city of Yorvik where we spent those fateful final days. Whatever its name, we were met by Tostig's force there.

'King Harald, I am grateful that you have honoured our agreement and brought such a fine army,' Tostig said, and I do not think he knew it was a little insult to Harald, for it implied there was ever a doubt that Harald had intended to keep his word. Harald bristled subtly at the insult, his white-streaked beard ruffling a little as his mouth worked as if he had to chew the words to swallow them.

Tostig was a good specimen of a man. Tall and well-formed, with a real warrior's look to him. But he did not look like us – his face was rounder, his hair short and black, a little curled. He had a sharp nose and a thin mouth, as if he was permanently dissatisfied. Which, as I learned, he was.

'Earl Tostig, I see you have brought rather a small army,' Harald said in reply, and Tostig grimaced. He had not but 300 men.

'It was all I could afford.' He waved at them vaguely. 'Mercenaries from the Flemish shores.'

'Are they worthy of standing alongside my men?'

'They have a good reputation for war. But they don't speak a word of Norse or English.'

Harald frowned. 'I am not sure what use they can be, then.'

'Put them with the Scots,' Tostig said with a glare at the foreign contingent. 'We can find a useful way for them to die.'

Harald smiled at last. Ruthlessness was a trait he prized in his allies.

'Come. Now we are assembled, take us to your enemies, and let's rip this country from their grasp.'

* * *

In late August we sailed down the coast and we went to raiding. It was like Denmark again. We sailed from town to town – and there were a great many towns, far more and in far more verdant land than in Norway or even Denmark – and we burned, killed and plundered. It was not for the sake of riches, for that was not our purpose there; it was all designed to force the English to raise an army to face us, and, within a week, they did.

We were approaching the great city of Yorvik, which our kin settled nearly 300 years ago if the skalds are to be believed. 'It is the key to the northern earldoms,' Tostig told Harald. 'Whoever holds Yorvik owns the north, but if we do not defeat the northern earls first, we will merely be besieged there.'

So we gave them time to gather and we let them know we were coming. We stung their coastal towns hard enough that they might be forced to face us, although Harald was wary, because that strategy had never worked on the Danes.

We left our ships at a place called Riccall, with a quarter of our men to guard them, for we could not risk their destruction or capture. Harald left his son Olaf with the men at the ships, which infuriated him, as you could imagine. But Harald's cautiousness was correct. If he fell, Olaf had ships to sail home and enough men to protect him. It was wise, even if it earned the anger of his son and heir.

Our journey north was at first uneventful but as we approached Yorvik from the south, following the river that passed the city, our scouts reported that an enemy army, a little smaller than our own, had deployed to block our path along the riverbank at a place called Fulford.

Our army had landed in 300 ships a few miles to the south, and let me tell you, 300 ships occupy a lot of riverbank. So our army was a little spread out, and the land we were marching through was boggy in places, with only a handful of tracks piercing it. We were not all together but spread out over a few miles of land when the scouts reported to us that the enemy had been sighted.

'Tell me of their army and their position,' Harald asked the scouts.

'They are maybe four or five thousand.'

'You are sure?'

The scout nodded. 'I was able to observe them from a low rise to their south and could see them all clearly.'

'The land to their south is higher?'

'Yes.'

'Then what ground do they occupy, that they refused the high ground?'

'They are gathered next to the river on their right flank.'

'And on their left?' Harald asked.

'Lower ground – boggy, I think, perhaps impassable. The ground I observed them from is away from the river and can be approached from any angle.'

'Ah, that is why they refuse the higher ground. They intend to defend the narrow gap, where our numbers matter less, thinking we are here to take the city, when really we are here for them.'

Harald smiled at us, the wolf's smile. 'Everything goes well. If they mean to defend their ground we will gather a mile to their south and prepare to make camp. They are fewer than us, and must know our number, so they will not attack.'

'And if they do?' I asked.

'We will have a line drawn up in case. Do not worry.'

Harald looked around the group. 'Árnasson, you will gather the men of Trondelag and take the left flank, on the river. Eystein, you will take the Westerland men and hold the centre. The men of Scotland are near the front and will take the right. The men of Upplond, Viken, Orkney and Tostig's mercenaries are all further back, and we will deploy them as they arrive.'

Everyone who was present voiced their assent. Harald had grown them all used to simply accepting his orders, rather than debating the best course of action. He had fought a dozen smaller or greater battles against the Danes with them and never lost a single one. They trusted his judgement, and I saw nothing wrong.

* * *

We continued the march along the lush riverbank in the early autumn sun. It was unseasonably warm, although for men like me and Harald, who had marched in Sicily and the Holy Land, it was merely a pleasant day. The landscape was beautiful. That river is quite magnificent, with green banks and lush forest stands on either side growing in between areas of marsh and grassland where the locals grazed their cattle. I would have loved to make a home there, if such a place existed in Norway. It was something like paradise.

We soon came to the hill that the scouts had described, although it is nothing like a hill that you men of northern Norway would imagine here. Those lands of England are very flat, and this hill would be accounted a smooth field to our people. But beside that river, it was the higher point for a few miles and afforded a good view of the enemy army.

They were arranging themselves in formation, a single thick line, between the river and the waterlogged marshy lowland on their left flank.

'No easy way around them to attack their flank or rear,' said Stykarr.

'No. They have chosen their defensive position well. We have no choice but to break through their line the hard way, from the front,' said Harald.

'So we will. We have the numbers, and better warriors,' Eystein boasted. He was a young man, strong and brave, and a little desperate to prove himself. I recognised it well, because I had been that man once.

'It seems odd,' I noted. 'They must know our numbers and that they cannot win. They are throwing their lives away for what?'

Harald pointed at the city visible on the hill in the distance behind them. 'They are defending their homes.'

I pointed at Tostig. 'But we have not threatened their homes – we have offered them peace if they submit.'

'Would you submit, Eric, if an enemy arrived outside Anslo and demanded it?'

I shook my head. 'No.'

Harald nodded in satisfaction. 'Then I assume they are merely brave men, or that they hope we will not be willing to spend the lives required to break their good position and that we will negotiate.'

'Then they are brave, but do not know you,' I said with a sigh, because a great many lives it would require indeed to break that line.

'Start moving the Scots out onto the right and then follow up to fill in the centre of our position and finally the left. We should be ready for battle by the afternoon.'

'Do we just leave them there watching us form up? What if they attack?'

Harald looked at the enemy army for a moment, standing there immobile in their ranks. 'Would they abandon a good defensive position to march out here and attack a superior foe? I do not think so. No, they are waiting for us.'

'You would come and attack while your enemy was not formed. Half of our army has not even arrived yet.'

Harald flashed his confident smile. 'They are not me.'

I shrugged. That much was true.

We stayed in position on the crest of the rise as the Scottish warriors moved out towards the boggy fen on the right, followed by the men of the Westerlands and Trondelag filling into their positions. The men of Upplond, Viken and the Orkneys were not even in sight behind us yet, still making their way along the narrow paths. Harald and I went back to the rear of the hill to see where they were, and we could see them snaking along the riverbank and filtering through the trees several miles away.

'King Harald!' a voice shouted, and a man came scurrying down the slope towards us.

'What?'

'The enemy are advancing,' said the warrior breathlessly.

Harald's brows fell. 'How many?'

'All of them, the entire line. They are moving towards our right. The Scottish are about to be attacked.'

'They will not withstand the whole enemy army,' Stykarr said quickly. 'We must send them help.'

Harald's eyes widened, and he looked back up the hill, and then over his shoulder towards the rear half of the army, which was too far away to help.

'We could retreat towards them,' I said. 'Gather all our forces and then attack.'

'No,' Harald said firmly. 'It will take too long and they will fall upon the rear of the army as we retreat. This is good – they have been drawn out of their defence and we have a chance to crush them. But only if we can hold long enough.' He pointed at Stykarr and then to the south. 'Go down there, gather whoever you can and take them to help the Scots, as fast as they can move.'

Stykarr nodded. 'Yes, my King.'

Then Harald gestured to the rest of us. 'Come, back up the hill. I need to see.' We started up the hill at a fast walk.

'And bring me Land Waster!' Harald shouted to no one in particular. 'Let this new enemy begin to learn its meaning.'

* * *

We reached the top of the hill to a view of full battle just beginning. Harald had been right – there was no opportunity to withdraw. It would have been a disaster. The main body of the enemy was advancing into the nervous Scottish line with a hearty roar that we heard even from the hilltop. The other contingents of our army were not yet linked up in a full line, and smaller groups of the enemy were advancing to engage them, no doubt to keep them busy and prevent them forming a cohesive line or moving to help our weaker right flank. The main mass of their army was advancing in a single block, and their wall hit the Scottish even as we watched.

Harald looked worried, but also alive. 'We are facing a good general,' he said, admiring the movement of the enemy army. 'This is exactly what I might have done.'

'They are trying to turn our flank. If they break the Scottish, they will take this hill and cut our army in two,' I said.

'I know. Quite beautiful, isn't it? God be blessed, finally a true enemy. If only the Danes had been so courageous.'

'You are glad of this danger?'

Harald nodded confidently. 'They do not see the full size of our army and they have made a fatal error. Instead of having to crack their line, we will now be able to completely destroy them. This battle is already won. All we need is for the Scottish to hold a little while or retreat slowly.'

I looked at him dubiously, because I did not see how he could be so confident. 'What if the Scottish break? We have nothing here to send to them yet. Stykarr will take a while.'

Harald looked at me, and then at the 500 men of his personal hird, arrayed behind us under Land Waster, which someone had brought up to the front. And he smiled that wolf's smile of his.

'You are right. We cannot let the Scottish break. We must show them they are not abandoned and let them know help is coming.'

My heart fell. 'Harald, no. I did not mean...'

'Advance the banner!' Harald shouted, turning to the leader of his hird, who stood under Land Waster, the great black bird fluttering softly in the light wind and the hot summer air. 'To the right flank!' Harald roared, pointing his spear at the Scots, who were already giving ground under the ferocious assault of the Saxon army.

'Come, Eric. You are right – there is no one else to help them,' Harald said. 'It is our time once more.'

'Damn you, Harald. We are too old for this. You need to stay here and command the battle, not charge into the first fight.'

Harald smiled as we walked, because of course I went with him. Do you think I would refuse?

'Have you learned nothing from our years together, Eric? The first fight *is* the battle. Nothing matters if we lose it and our army is split in two. No, we hold them there while the rest of the army marches to us and surrounds them. They don't need my orders to do that, they will understand.'

I cursed him so much that he laughed while I drew the sword that King

Magnus had once given me on the downslope of the hill, with the fighting only a few hundred paces ahead. 'You promised me I would not need to fight,' I grumbled quietly, because I did not want the proud, excited young men marching behind us to hear me.

Harald chuckled. 'You didn't believe that.'

'No,' I admitted. 'But lied to myself that it might be true.'

'If you did not expect to fight, then why did I see you sharpen your sword last evening?' Harald said, glancing at my naked steel, shining and clean in the sunlight as I rested it on my shoulder.

I gave Harald a dark look. 'Because I *have* learned from our years together, Harald. And I knew you would not resist the call of steel and blood.'

He hefted his axe as the men of the hird formed around us on the move, and Land Waster fluttered over his head. A lord of war, striding to battle with all the joy he had always held for it. He threw his head back and laughed, the excitement and battle fugue flowing through him.

'God knows it, Eric – I was born to war.'

We were a hundred paces from the left edge of the struggling Scottish line now, and some of them were looking back to see us coming down the hill in our rigid mass of maille and steel, the finest group of warriors in the circle of the earth, the black raven banner flying proud overhead. And the Scots gave a cheer and stamped their feet into the earth, pushing back against the Saxon line.

'Forward, men of Norway!' Harald roared, and he pointed his great axe over the heads of the Scots and at the exposed end of the enemy line. 'Death to the Saxon!'

'Death to the Saxon!' the hird roared back, drowning me in their shout, and we broke into a jog, shields coming up and weapons ready. The enemy stopped advancing and tried to align themselves to meet our charge, which meant curling back the corner of their line, putting up a makeshift wall even as they edged back.

They may not have understood our words, but their meaning was written in the bright steel and the thunder of our feet. Harald's men were flush with the prospect of the fight to come, of a nervous enemy caught out of position. They longed to get their steel into the fight, and I could feel it like a heat at my back. And so could the enemy.

I felt it too. I did. I felt that prickling, hot fear in my throat – the excited churning in my stomach and the fluttering of my heart. Any of you that have been in battle know it. My limbs felt light, and no tiredness could infect them. My head felt clear but my thoughts vague, my awareness narrowed only to the enemy at my front and the brothers at my back.

I felt Harald's loping presence at my side, the battle-heat coming off him in waves of noise and violence.

Ahhh, I admit it. I loved it. For that brief moment I felt that I was young again, even though my legs were burning beyond my awareness and my knees were shouting for forgiveness, unheard over the rage of my battle-fugue.

Oh, to be young again.

We hit their line and my youth bloomed for a moment in the sun as my shield punched and my sword sang of my old skill and battle-rage. Blood flowed from its edge again, blood so long forgotten in the greying years of my fatherhood. I shouted with a voice I no longer had and clawed at men half my age with twice the strength I should have owned.

Ah, my friends, it was glorious, and for twenty heartbeats I was Eric the warrior again.

But only twenty, for an old body can only lie to itself for such a short span, and as I battered myself against a third or fourth enemy my sword would no longer rise, and my breath would no longer draw, and my vision hazed. My left knee gave way, the pain suddenly reaching me through my fogged mind, and it would not support my advance another step.

Someone dragged me back from the battle, and I had not the strength to resist.

Bah. That hurts worse than many wounds, when your body will not do what your mind desires. It happens to me all the time now, for as little as rising from a seat, and I am well used to it so it does little more than irritate me. But there, on the battlefield of Fulford, I had lied to myself that I was a young warrior and for twenty glorious heartbeats, my limbs and lungs had let me believe it.

I think I sat down. Yes, it was that bad. The hird pushed on and I sat there among the dead and the injured, while one of Harald's men checked I was unwounded and then left me to return to the fight.

The last, glorious charge of Eric Sveitungr, defeated not by the enemy but by his own left knee. What a story, eh? May the skalds never sing of it.

14

I watched the fight of the Scots from the slope as it moved away from me. Harald's attack shocked the flank of the enemy army, but they had ten times his number and it was never going to defeat them. They were good warriors, the Saxons, and they recovered from it and started curling around the flank of Harald's men, forcing them to move back.

But that did not matter – he had not intended to defeat them with the charge, only to win time for Stykarr to arrive with more warriors and strengthen the Scottish line.

And as Harald's men started retreating up the slope, carefully and in line, Stykarr arrived over the crest to my right with a thousand warriors, men from all over Norway simply grabbed from the heads of their marching columns and thrown together to run to the King.

They pounded down that sunlit slope and into the rear of the flagging Scots, who had fought bravely but were tired and diminished. No one paid me any attention. I was just another wounded man sitting in the field of carnage. To my left, so close that I was almost sitting on him, a Saxon lay with his head downslope where he had fallen with a spear in his guts. He had one hand clutched to his wound, and he was feebly trying to rise with the other.

Eventually he gave up, and lay there, softly moaning. He finally seemed to notice me, and I gripped my sword a little harder in case he might attack, but his eyes held no hostility, only anguish. And it was not fear, that is a little different. I think he was beyond fear. He knew he was dead, and he simply refused to believe it had happened. I have seen it many times. Fear comes before and during a fight, or when a man is fleeing. Fear is driven by a mind's hope that it will survive, and the concern that it might not.

But once men are dying, especially proud warriors, most of them are merely more surprised that it could have happened to them. They refuse to accept that they were defeated, that their last moments on earth have come, and when the realisation finally overtakes them, they are angry and ashamed. It is painful to watch, for I know that I would be the same. I have believed I was dying several times, and mostly what I remember is being furious. Furious that I would not see the results of my sacrifice, furious that I had allowed myself to die.

And the Saxon dying next to me as I sat there watching the battle was furious with his body for refusing to sit up, and furious with himself that he had allowed himself to be brought down.

I leant over him and killed him with my seax. Not because he was my enemy, you understand, but because it was not fair to leave him there in his anger, for when it left him the pain would take over and he would have wished for death. He would have wept and shuddered and soiled himself, and been humiliated and shamed. I spared him that fate. It was a generosity.

When I finally felt the ability to do so, I rose from where I'd been sitting by the dead man, and the battle in front of me was dying out.

Both sides had committed their entire force, and warriors were exhausted in the heat.

Our centre was still fighting, but I could see that on the far left by the river the enemy had been routed, and the men of the Westerlands, with Eystein commanding, were slowly marching around to cut the enemy off from retreat.

The jarls of Orkney arrived and lent their strength to the centre, and that ended the fight there in our favour.

That is when Harald's prediction about the fight proved accurate. The main body of the enemy was nearly surrounded, pinned against the marshland. Harald's men pulled back exhausted from the fighting as more men arrived to replace them, and the battle ground on in a slow, abrasive brawl on the edge of the marshes, bloody and slow, but inevitable in its outcome.

I hobbled down to join Harald, who was standing under Land Waster, shouting orders to two scouts who took them to Eystein to attack the enemy from their rear. I had my sword and shield in my hands, and my shield was heavy, so heavy on my arm that I considered discarding it. I could not even raise it to guard myself, but I refused to abandon it.

'The battle is won, Harald,' I said as I approached him, and he looked around at me with surprise and then relief.

'Damn you, Eric, you disappeared from my side. I thought you had fallen.'

'Oh, I did, but only on my arse. I am fine, although my knee might be ruined.'

He smiled and embraced me. 'I'm sorry, old friend – I should not have let you join the charge.'

'You could not have stopped me,' I said with a laugh.

He smiled and then his smile faded. 'You are wounded, Eric.'

'What?'

I looked down as he pointed at my arm.

'Oh Christ,' I said numbly.

There was blood seeping through my maille below my shoulder, and a few rings were broken. I put my sword in the earth and probed it with my other hand, and pain finally penetrated, exploding through me. That is why my shield felt so heavy – my arm had taken a severe blow, probably from an axe. I could not tell if it was broken but it was no longer working properly. Nor could I remember receiving the blow. That is battle, my friends. It closes off much of your mind. I've seen confused men trying to advance with an arm cut from their body, or ribs open to the sun with their insides spilling out.

'I will survive,' I said, grimacing and finally dropping my shield.

'But you can't fight,' Harald said.

'I don't intend to.'

'I've heard that before.'

'It doesn't matter. As you said, the battle is over.'

'It's won, but it's not over. This enemy is tenacious. They show no sign of giving up so we will have to grind them into submitting. I am going to take my men into the battle again once they are rested,' he said. 'You will not come with us,' he added sternly.

I shook my head. 'I am happy to obey, but you should remain with me.'

'No, the men need to see me fight with them.'

'The only thing that could lose this battle now is your death,' I said to him firmly. 'So remain here and be a general, not a captain. They have seen you fight, now let the army see you in command.' I glared at him as hard as I could, although I knew he could not be persuaded by such pressure.

He considered it for a while and then nodded. 'You are right. I promised your wife I would heed you. And although you are not intimidating...' He smiled softly. 'She is.'

He turned to the leader of his hird. 'We will remain here as a reserve. Tell the men to rest. Send for Jarl Thorfinnsson.'

'Which one?'

Harald shrugged. 'Whichever one you find first.'

The hird commander sent a man running, and Harald came back to me with a sardonic glare. 'Are you content now, that I stand here commanding, being useless?'

'I am perfectly content,' I said, although I was mostly occupied nursing my injured arm, which hurt badly. I was worried what I would find when I finally took my armour off. *If* I could get my armour off over the wound.

Erlend Thorfinnsson arrived from the fighting shortly after.

'My King?' he said.

'This is going to be a long fight, and I wish to lose as few men as possible. Cease your attack, swap your men out for less tired ones where possible, and simply hold the enemy where they are while Eystein moves around to their rear.'

'Cease the attack?' Erlend said dubiously, looking out over the battle from our vantage point. He could see what we could see – that the entire remaining enemy force was in a crescent with the marsh at their back, locked in a brutal struggle with our men in the low ground, with neither side able to do much more than just shove forwards a half step at a time in the churned mud.

'As you command, my King.' He replied and hurried off back down the hill.

Harald settled in, resting against the bank. 'So we wait for Eystein.'

'Will we offer them surrender?' I asked.

Harald shook his head. 'No. I need the Saxon warriors of the north dead, not embarrassed. This army needs to die or we cannot build a kingdom here in safety. It will be a strong message to any that follow and consider opposing us, that a fight with us means a fight to the end.'

Ah, how accurate that was.

'And someone bring us some water. There is enough of the damn stuff around here, there must be some without blood in it,' he grumbled, and I was terribly thirsty myself.

We sat there and watched the battle slowly grind on, with Eystein's tired men marching around the long flank and getting into position to finally trap the enemy against the marsh.

They realised the danger too late and started to try and retreat through the gap while it still existed.

We watched as the Jarls of Orkney renewed their assault on the retreating enemy, turning the retreat into a rout. We drank fresh water as Eystein smashed into the retreating mass, splitting the enemy army in half, and then relaxed as the trapped half was crushed against the marsh in complete disarray, all formation or cohesion lost.

Some of them died fighting, some died retreating and many drowned in their armour in the marsh, stepping over each other's bodies as they were pressed backwards by the crush of our victorious army.

'I've never simply watched a battle before,' Harald commented as the fighting ended. 'It's not so bad as I thought it might be.'

I laughed, shaking my head at my King. 'It is my favourite part of any battle.'

'How odd, that we can have shared an entire life of war together and think so differently of it,' Harald noted.

'We shared the battlefields, but not the experience.'

'How so?' He looked at me with interest.

'You commanded; I was commanded. It is very different.'

'Is it really? I suppose so.'

'Were you ever so enthusiastic fighting under the command of Maniakes, Michael or, God forbid, Strategos Nikephoros?'

Harald snorted. 'No, I suppose not, but that is because they were fools who were trying to get me killed.'

I smiled at him voraciously. 'So you *do* understand exactly what it feels like for me.'

He turned and his mouth opened in protest, but then he grinned. 'A point well made. At least I listen to you. None of those idiots ever listened to me.'

'And they are all dead,' I said with a mock salute of gratitude.

'And they are all dead, indeed,' replied Harald with a nod, before turning and watching the last of the Saxon army die.

* * *

Some of the enemy army escaped. It was inevitable. Our men had marched all day in the heat. Many had run to the battlefield when the enemy attacked, and none had the energy to pursue the broken remnants of the Saxon army. Their leaders escaped, which Harald regretted, but there was nothing we could do to stop them. A man fleeing for his life will always run further through exhaustion than a victorious warrior chasing him with sword still in hand.

The enemy bodies at the edge of the marshland were laid so thick you could walk on them like a dock, and those who went out to strip them of their wealth did exactly that. Thousands of the enemy had died, and nearly a thousand of ours, half of them Scots. Those men had proved themselves well, and with half their men dead or wounded, Harald sent them back to their ships with his thanks and the promise of good reward.

The rest of the army could not wait. We had to follow up the great victory by capturing the city of Yorvik and holding it, proclaiming our domination of the lands around.

'We should not storm the city,' Tostig cautioned. 'Arrive as ruler, not tyrant. The men of the north are proud people, and even though many of them are descendants of the Norse, they will not support you if you cruelly plunder them. You will be their enemy for life. Let me talk to the elders of the city. I know them and they know me. We can negotiate a peaceful takeover.'

Harald nodded. 'I agree. I am not here to strip the land, but to rule it. We will wait outside the city while you negotiate our entry.'

'Then what? How will we secure their loyalty?'

'Hostages. We will demand hostages from all the main families,' Harald said.

'That will take a number of days. Most of their families do not live in or near the city,' Tostig said, looking concerned.

Harald smiled and patted Tostig on the shoulder. 'I am in no hurry. The hostages will come to the city faster than a new army of their people. What escaped from here will not recover quickly. I am sure we will have to fight them again, but not for a while.' He looked out over the churned battlefield by the fen. 'Too many of their best are dead.'

* * *

We marched north along the river towards Yorvik the next morning. Tostig and a few of his men had gone the previous evening, to gather the city's elders and present Harald's offer. Not that it was truly an offer – it was a demand placed against the threat of invasion and death, but the presentation was important. People give in more easily when it does not make them feel like defeated cowards.

We arrived at the city and found the gates were open, and a party of men was waiting outside with Tostig at their head.

'Welcome to Yorvik, King Harald,' Tostig said with a proud grin. 'The city is yours.'

'Congratulations, Tostig,' said Harald, embracing him. 'You took the greatest city of the north with nothing but words. A feat of great distinction. I do hate sieges.'

'I hear you are quite good at them.'

Harald smiled. 'I am good at ending them because I hate conducting them so dearly. I am grateful to be spared this one. Come, take me to their elders so that I might negotiate with my new subjects.'

We marched through the town, which felt almost deserted. Some of the people had fled, others were too afraid to come out and see the Northmen who had taken their city. They were right to be afraid, for ten generations we had scoured those lands, and they feared us the way the deer fears the wolf: instinctually, irrevocably. Their warriors fought so hard because they knew what we might do to their homes and their families, and because they are brave men. Remember, even after 300 years we never really defeated them. Not fully. Do not listen to those who would mock the Saxons. They did not have our sophistication or adventuring spirit in war, but they were as solid in the shield wall as men can be, and they were far more resolute in fighting us than the Danes ever were.

There were armed men in the city, quite a number of them. Some of them were clearly survivors of the battle, but peace had been declared, and they stood in disconsolate groups and stared at us, spears point-down in the earth and no shields on their arms. Defeated but defiant. I liked them for that, for daring to stay and face us, even if their leaders had fled. No doubt, with time, they would have made fine additions to our forces.

We reached the central square of the city, and a nervous-looking party of elders was waiting for us, arrayed in hastily laid-out chairs. A good hundred or so armed men guarded them, standing in blocks on both sides. It was enough to raise the hair on my neck – a deliberate show of defiance, and a threat.

My instinct would have been to demand they disarm or leave, but I am not Harald, and he was a man entirely impossible to cow with threats.

As we filed into the square Harald never stopped smiling, and, motioning at Stykarr to stay with his guards, he walked forwards casually, not towards the waiting elders, but to the armed men on either side. Tostig and I followed him nervously, and my hand never strayed far from my sword, a pointless gesture though drawing it would have been in the face of such numbers.

Harald simply went up to the line with a friendly expression, ignoring their glares and hatred, and inspected them as if they were Varangians on parade. Ha! The spine in Harald was unlike any other man. He went up to the first warrior, who could have struck him down before Harald could act, and looked him up and down before clasping him on the shoulder. 'Thank you for being witness here,' Harald said, and the Saxon looked confused.

'Not many of them speak your language,' Tostig called to Harald.

'Enough of them do,' Harald said, nodding at more of the soldiers. 'Who here knows my words?'

Several men looked at him perplexedly and clearly understood him. 'I do,' said one of the boldest.

Harald looked around and saw a burly man in the second rank. 'Ah, a man of Norse family then?'

The man looked reluctant but nodded. 'My father is the son of a Dane.'

Harald smiled and spread his arms. 'Then we are near to kin.'

'I am no kin of yours, Norwegian,' the man said with a shake of his head.

Harald was again not dissuaded, and he motioned to several warriors to step aside. Reluctantly they did, so that Harald could stand face-to-face with the man who spoke. The warrior bristled but made no threatening move.

'Why do you say that?' Harald said curiously.

'You invaded my home, killed my real kin. I may have Danish blood, but you do not belong here.'

'I have the rightful claim to the throne,' Harald said loudly, and then he inspected the warrior's arm, and saw that it was bandaged beneath his tunic. 'You fought yesterday?'

The man nodded after a pause, and he looked nervous.

Harald turned and snapped his fingers at Stykarr. 'Bring a purse of silver.'

Stykarr looked utterly bemused, but he was not going to disobey his King. He took a purse from the carts behind us, which were loaded with silver so that Harald could bribe and reward as required to secure his power.

It was all a show, you see. It drew every eye in the square to the cart, and suddenly they all understood what was in there, that Harald had arrived with wealth. They could not know that all the silver in those carts had been taken from the towns we had raided down the coast, but it did not matter.

It changed things, you see. They feared that Harald was there to plunder, but he showed in an unsubtle gesture that he was bringing wealth to distribute. It took half the resistance out of those fighting men, and all the resistance out of those elders, in a few heartbeats. A wise man, Harald, as I have often told you.

Stykarr jogged forwards and handed the purse to Harald, who took it and turned around, holding the purse out so that all could see, before offering it to the warrior.

For a moment the warrior was wracked with indecision. He was clearly tempted to refuse, but to refuse would lead to unknown consequences, and none of them good. If he insulted Harald he was unlikely to leave alive, nor were his fellows. So finally, and reluctantly, he took the little leather bag, and his eyes opened slightly when he felt the weight of it. It was a rich purse.

'I give you this to reward you, for few men have the courage to face an enemy again the day after a battle lost. You and your countrymen fought well and bravely, and there is no shame that you were on the side that was forced to leave the field, for you fought until fighting was no longer possible and I commend you for it. Let no man speak against me.'

Men in the ranks chattered to one another, clearly those who understood translating for those who did not.

'I did not fight alone of those here,' the man said, his hostility gone and now embarrassed to be picked out.

'No, I know you did not. Have all those who took the field yesterday come forwards and take reward from me too. For they are men who I wish to be my subjects, and I wish them to understand that I am both generous and fair and hold no grudges against worthy opponents.'

The man looked at him, and then at the cart, which was surrounded by several hundred of our men.

'This seems to be a trick to draw out those who fought you, so that you can take them or kill them in punishment.'

Harald stiffened slightly and froze, and I cursed the fool under my breath. Harald stared at him almost with a hurt expression, and then slowly shook his head.

'You do not know me, so I will forgive you this accusation once and once only.' He gestured back towards our army. 'Did you see my banner flying yesterday, where the fighting was thickest?'

The man's eyes narrowed, and he looked up slightly as he thought about it. 'A black raven on a red banner?'

Harald smiled in pleasure. 'Yes.'

'What of it?'

'Do you see it today?'

The man's eyes flicked across our ranks, but the banner was not there. 'No.'

'That is how you know I mean no violence. When Land Waster flies, there is no mercy for any who oppose me. But today I come not to punish, but to rule. You did your duty to your lords well, but now I am offering a new lord, a stronger one, who will bring prosperity and justice. There will be no harm done to those who opposed me yesterday, as long as they do not oppose me or insult me today.' He stressed the last words carefully, and the threat was clear. It was also, let me be plain, not aimed at the warrior. That whole message was aimed at the elders who stood and sat helpless and ignored off to one side. Harald was already negotiating with them, making his position clear, but without giving them the chance yet to reply. It was masterful, truly.

The warrior looked dubious, but then down at the silver still clutched in his hand. He turned to his ranks and called out to them in his own language. I do not know what he said, and he spoke for some time, but when he was done some of them looked angry, and others looked interested. Eventually, as Harald stood there patiently, another man stepped forwards and looked down the line of his comrades.

He was met with a mix of furious glares and sympathy. You see, Harald had split them in two with just silver and clever words. He did not need all of them to accept him, just enough to prevent them uniting against him.

Someone hissed at the man in Saxon, presumably telling him to get back in line, but he waved the complaint away and shook his head, stepping forwards and heading warily to the cart. He made it all the way there, where Stykarr offered him a fine silver cup. He looked at it as if it would bite him but took it and stared at it intently. It had probably come from some rich Saxon's hall further north. Maybe he knew that. Either way, he clearly didn't care.

Then another man came forward, and a few more, and Harald stood there smiling as his defeated enemy accepted silver from his hand, and all the menace and defiance of the enemy ranks melted away. Some of them even turned to leave in disgust.

As the defeated enemy continued to collect their silver, some of them even thanked Harald or saluted him, and Harald smiled and gestured to them generously in return, far beyond the acknowledgement a king would normally give a lowly warrior. It meant something to them, you see. They wanted to feel their King respected them.

Harald then strolled over to the elders, leaving the warriors he had just purchased milling behind him, and stood facing them, a neutral expression on his face.

'So, who speaks for Yorvik?'

Hah. He had won the negotiations already, and they all knew it.

'We all do, King Harald,' said one of the younger men, stepping forwards.

'That is Eldred, who used to be my man before I was exiled. He is powerful and will be loyal,' Tostig said, leaning in to talk in Harald's ear.

'How loyal can he have been, if he did not follow you into exile?' Harald muttered, unimpressed.

'As loyal as could be expected of him, in an argument between his lord and his King.'

Harald nodded. 'Eldred, thank you for your welcome,' he called, although no one had welcomed him.

Eldred looked embarrassed. 'I apologise... I was distracted by your, uh, generous gifts to our men.'

'Tostig's men,' Harald said with a mirthless smile that did not touch his lips. 'I am going to be the king here. Earl Tostig is your lord, and he is loyal to me. So these men are his men. Do you understand?'

Eldred nodded. 'Of course, King Harald.'

Harald nodded happily. 'So, where are the lords Edwin and Morcar, who faced me yesterday? I would like to meet them. Why are they not here to surrender the city?'

Eldred looked nervous. 'They fled, King Harald.'

'I see,' said Harald. 'How shameful for them. They must not care much for this city if they will neither defend it nor have the courage that these men behind me had to be here to surrender it.'

Eldred looked deeply uncomfortable but he inclined his head in agreement. 'As you say, King Harald.'

Harald looked at him carefully, and then at the rest of the elders. 'I intend for us to be friends, my lords. But I see that it cannot be done in a day. So for now we will negotiate as enemies, although I will not treat you as such unless you give me cause.'

There was concerned chattering in the group, and Harald waited patiently.

'What do you mean, treat us as enemies?' one of them asked.

'It is simple. I cannot trust your loyalty – not yet. So I have two options. I can have my army occupy this city, or...' He raised his finger and paused for a moment. 'I can accept guarantees that you will not turn against me and take my army away from your walls. I am sure your people would prefer that.'

The man nodded vehemently after a short discussion. 'We would much prefer that, King Harald. And we will happily guarantee that this city will remain open to you, and we will not take up arms against you until your matter with King Harold is resolved.'

Harald spread his arms. 'What form of guarantee is appropriate?'

'Well, we could give you gold and silver, in accordance to each family's wealth and station—'

Harald interrupted, palm upraised. 'I have gold and silver, and no need for more. Nor do I believe that will be sufficient. No. I will accept from each prominent family one son or two daughters, as hostages, to be returned when my claim is resolved.'

The man's face went white. 'Our children?'

Harald nodded firmly. 'Your children.'

There was an angry commotion in the elders' ranks as they discussed it, and Harald's patient countenance visibly wore off.

'There is nothing to discuss, my lords. If you are truthful that you intend not to betray me, your children are in no danger. They will be kept safe and treated respectfully in my care.'

'How can we trust you?' the man asked with a shrill voice.

'You have no choice, but you can see that I could have taken the city by force and removed your children from you.' Harald idly inspected a cut on his finger. 'That option is still not removed from possibility.'

The man looked at Harald in fear, and then talked to those behind him, most of which looked utterly deflated.

'We accept,' he finally said. 'One son or two daughters per family. But what of those who have no sons, and only one daughter?'

Harald thought about it for a moment. 'How unfortunate for any great family that only has one daughter. Their future looks very poor indeed. I may have to redistribute their lands to those who are loyal to me. For what use have I for lords without children?'

The man looked aghast. 'I only have one daughter,' he mumbled.

Harald nodded carefully. 'Then for you I will make an exception.'

The man swallowed. 'When shall they be delivered?'

'I have not finished my offer,' Harald said impatiently. 'I do not merely require hostages from this city, I require them from all of Earl Tostig's lands, which were so unjustly seized from him. You will send word to every noble family in these lands – Tostig will help you make the list – and demand hostages from them also. They are to send them here to the city before the fifth day from now, when you will come out of the city to the place…' Harald paused and turned to Tostig. 'What did you say the meeting place should be?'

'The bridge at Stamford.' Tostig said.

Harald nodded and returned his gaze to the elders. 'To the bridge at Stamford, where you will present to us the hostages. If you do not, we will come to the city the next day and take who and what we want, and it will be in terms of war. Am I understood?'

The threat was heavy, and the elder looked utterly miserable. 'I understand, King Harald.'

'Good. In return for this help, Yorvik will be spared any form of violence or depredation, and my men will not enter its walls again in arms. In addition, it will be given special status in my new kingdom, to be the capital city of the north of England, with all the taxes and benefits that will be due to that.'

That, at least, seemed to cheer the elders up again. Rich people are never too miserable to like the sound of wealth, and Harald wielded wealth like a sword and had done all his life, with just as much skill as he wielded steel.

'T-Thank you, King Harald.'

'Then we understand each other. Now, my army and I will leave today, once we have been presented with the first twenty hostages,' Harald said, nodding to himself.

'The... The first twenty? You need them now?'

Harald nodded impatiently. 'Yes. You do not think I would leave the city today with nothing? No. I want the first twenty, against your good conduct in delivering the rest.' He gestured to Tostig. 'Earl Tostig will work with you to identify who in the city is suitable. Be quick about it. You do not want my men sleeping within the walls tonight. They are hungry and thirsty, and we brought no food with us today.'

The elder paled again but Harald was already walking away, needing no reply. Tostig walked over and gave the elders a stern look, then spoke to them in Saxon. I do not know what his words were, but I can tell you that the elders did not like them.

15

RICCALL, 22 SEPTEMBER 1066 AD

The elders of Yorvik gave up their sons and daughters and agreed to a further gift of hostages for five days later, all as Harald demanded. They had no choice and they knew it, but Harald wanted to give them the appearance of having negotiations, to make the bitter draught easier to swallow. Remember, he wanted to rule those people, and he had learned from his campaigns in Denmark, where he had hurt the people so badly that they would never accept him as king, preferring that he destroy their country utterly than submit to him.

He made many mistakes in his life, King Harald, but like all great men, he learned from them.

We set up a good camp on the riverbank at Riccall next to our moored fleet. The weather was God-sent, sunny and fine. We had water, food, silver and victory. It was the happiest of times for an army. A golden time, truly.

My arm wound was annoying – the blow had bruised my entire arm, and despite my armour it had cut into the muscle a little and possibly damaged the bone. My left arm was useless, wrapped in a cloth that held it to my chest. It would heal, but not for weeks. Still, it did not dampen my spirits.

I think the only man there who was not satisfied and happy was Olaf, Harald's son. He had been bitter to have been left behind and denied a part in the victory, and he confronted his father about it while we were sitting on the riverbank after washing ourselves, relaxing in the sun, letting its heat dry our bodies.

Olaf strode out of the water, rubbing it from his face in angry, choppy motions, staring at his father in undisguised anger.

'What troubles you on this perfect day, my son?' Harald said without even looking up.

'You know what troubles me,' Olaf said angrily, anger made more bright by how his father was ignoring his petulance.

Look, do not be angry with me for how I speak of our beloved and recently passed King. We were all young boys once, and there is no insult to saying that our King was a boy like all of us, even if being a son of Hardrada and destined for kingship.

When he was sixteen, he was an arrogant and petulant youth, despite his obvious intelligence and talent. Harald was the same at that age! I simply speak the truths, and we all know it.

'You are upset that I did not take you to battle, which means you are upset that I am wise, which makes you a fool,' said Harald with a lazy gesture of his hand as he lay reclined on the bank.

'If you think I am a fool, why would you be here trying to win me a kingdom? And if you are here to win me a kingdom, why would you not let men see me taking part? What will they say of me, that I guarded ships while my birthright was earned? You have shamed me,' Olaf spat, throwing his wet tunic to the muddy ground.

'It is because you are so desperate to prove yourself that I did not take you to the battle. You are too young, and you would have got yourself killed. What use is there in me earning you a kingdom if you die in a prideful attempt to take part?'

'Too young? I am sixteen! I am a man.' He gestured at his father angrily. '*You* were in battle at my age. You commanded men in the Rus! What a hypocrite you are.'

Harald levered himself up on his elbows with a chuckle. 'And I was woefully unprepared, and lucky to survive it. I nearly died at Stiklestad because I was so desperate to prove myself a great warrior. The most serious wounds I ever took were on that field. And ask Eric how my first time commanding men in the Rus went.'

Olaf looked at me with narrowed eyes.

I was annoyed to have my peace disturbed by being dragged into the argument, but I had a son only a little older than Olaf and I knew well how boys of his age thought. They were desperate to be seen as good as or better than their fathers. When your father is Harald Hardrada, that is a terrible shadow indeed.

'You immediately got yourself captured by a Rus pirate, ignoring all our advice that your plan was stupid, and we had to rescue you, a rescue that succeeded only by luck and the subterfuge of Thorir the Cuckoo. By all rights you should have died that day, entirely because of your own idiocy, because you were trying to prove yourself to us all.'

I looked at Harald, who raised an eyebrow in surprise. 'I wasn't expecting quite such an honest assessment, Eric,' he said with a touch of annoyance. 'I wasn't *that* bad.'

'Yes, you were,' I said with a firm nod. 'It is a miracle you did not get us all killed.'

Harald gave me a filthy look. 'You exaggerate.'

I shrugged and lay down again, flicking my eyes at Olaf just long enough to see that his anger had faded a little and there was a hint of a smile of triumph on his face. I smiled as I closed my eyes in the sun.

You see, I understood teenage boys.

'Well, regardless of Eric's burnishing, it is true that I only survived those battles and my first year in command by luck and by the wisdom and protection of those around me. Until you accept my advice and direction, I cannot risk you in battle.'

'Then why am I here? Why take me on campaign if I am not allowed to fight?'

'To see how a campaign works!' Harald said irritably, waving the boy away. 'You will meet my leaders, see an army on campaign, witness how to organise a fleet and supplies, observe negotiations and kingship. You think being a commander is about battles, but that is only one fraction of it, and the least important.'

'Battles are the least important?' Olaf said derisively.

'Yes,' Harald replied.

'How?'

'Because without doing all the other things correctly, battles cannot be won. I can teach any fool to fight with a sword or conduct an attack on a flank. Real generalship is in the management of an army and everything it needs. Success in battle is built before the battle starts, so you will learn those parts first. You are lucky; it took me a few years to fully understand that lesson.'

They went silent, and I could feel Olaf glaring at his father and Harald staring tiredly back.

'You are making a fool of me. Men will say I am a coward.'

'Men will say a great many things about you – that is the nature of being a king.'

'So when will I be allowed to march to battle?'

'When you are ready!'

'I *am* ready!' Olaf shouted.

Harald sighed hard. 'You think you know better than me.'

'I know myself better than you.'

'And that, my boy, is why I know you are not ready. No one your age knows themselves.'

'Oh, this is all nonsense. You just don't wish to share the glory. My brother is King of Norway, my father is the great general, and I am a camp servant.' Olaf scoffed and I heard his wet footsteps slapping off along the bank into the distance.

Harald muttered angrily to himself for a bit and then turned to me. 'Are your sons so hard to manage?'

'Of course,' I said. 'Although, because I am not a king, the concerns are pettier.'

'Sometimes I wish I was a commoner. What concerns do you argue about with your sons?'

I sat up and smiled at him. 'I had that same conversation with my eldest boy about training a horse.'

'Really?'

'Yes. I told him the horse was not ready to be ridden, and that he was not ready to ride it.'

'How did you dissuade him?'

'I didn't. He bored me to death with his arguing, so I let him ride it.'

'And what happened?'

I laughed. 'It tried to buck him, broke through a fence, and threw him off onto his head. He spent a week in bed recovering.'

'Then why did you let him? He could have been killed!'

I nodded calmly. 'Yes.'

'Yes? How can you be so nonchalant about it? Why would you let him do something that could kill him?'

I shrugged. 'Because I cannot stop him. I cannot protect him from everything in the world that might harm him, or from his own mistakes. Sometimes you just have to let them do the stupid things and make mistakes. Some lessons they will refuse to learn merely by being told.'

Harald looked at me with deep concern and shook his head. 'I think it is different as a king. My sons are my legacy; I cannot risk them. I need them to grow into kingship, and be great kings, so that men will say the sons of Hardrada were worthy.'

'So maybe you need to allow them to find that path themselves. Can great men be made by leading them by the nose through life and protecting them from everything?'

'I can't risk it!'

'Harald, how was your greatness made if not through risk? How can you expect your sons to become great kings if they merely watch?' I shook my head. 'Sometimes you have to let them ride the horse. After all, you rode it, and it threw you on your head many times. God knows I tried a dozen times to stop you riding a horse that you were not ready to ride. Think on it. Where would you be if you had listened to me every time?'

Harald looked at me and his expression had shifted. 'I would not be King of Norway. Perhaps I would still be a guard commander in the Rus or the empire, or dead.'

I nodded. 'Exactly. But where would you be if you had ignored me every time and always ridden the horse?'

'Dead,' he said without hesitation. 'If I had never heeded your warnings, I would be dead.'

I nodded. 'Sometimes you just have to let young men who wish for greatness take risks.'

'Then how can I know what risks to let them take?'

'You can't. You just use your best judgement and let God decide the rest.'

Harald recoiled. 'Since when were you so casual about risk, Eric?'

'Since raising three boys to adulthood,' I said with a grin. 'It is a miracle they all survived for they did so many stupid things.'

Harald's eyes narrowed. 'Three? You have two sons.'

'Yes, I am counting you,' I said with a laugh, and Harald scowled and threw a clod of dirt at me, before laughing and looking out over the river.

'Damn you. It is true. Although not you alone – Rognvald raised me to adulthood with his advice. I am still bitter that I never met him again, could not help him or keep him alive.'

'He was a good man,' I said.

'He taught me things about leadership that you could not, and it was essential to my life.'

I nodded gravely, for it was no insult.

'But I don't know how to deal with Olaf. I don't know why he resents me so much or how to stop him being so infuriating. How can I be sure he will turn out well? I am filled with doubt.'

'You know why he is like that and you know exactly why he will succeed.'

He looked at me oddly. 'How so?'

I smiled at him. 'Because he is exactly like you.'

Harald's eyes narrowed and he stared at me intently. 'Truly? This is how I was?'

'Yes! I see you in Olaf so strongly. The pride, the ambition, the desire for greatness. I do not see those things in Magnus; he is much calmer, more measured. He is more like your brother Olaf, but your son Olaf? He is cut from your cloth. It is why you do not get on well.'

'So what do I do?' Harald asked softly.

'Stop trying to contain him. Could you be so contained? I tell you, you could not. I remember trying all too well.'

Harald looked pained. 'So to avoid losing him, I must cede control?'

'Yes.'

He looked away with a grim expression. 'This is what real fear is like, then.'

'Yes.'

'I have never felt it before. It eats at me.'

'That is because you have never had anything so precious to lose before. You were always willing to risk yourself, because you wanted for greatness more than you wanted for your own safety. But now, you want nothing more than for your son to live and take your place but allowing him to do that risks everything. It is hard, Harald, but you must let him take at least some of the risks you did and guide him. If you restrict him too much, he will reject that guidance.'

Harald sat there for a while in the sun and pondered, his eyes sightlessly scanning the river and the lush foliage on the far bank.

'You are right, and it seems so childishly obvious. How did you become so wise, Eric?'

'I was taught patience by the best teacher – living alongside the most impatient man in the world,' I said with a grin.

'You know I wouldn't let any other man insult me the way you do,' he said with a raised eyebrow.

'I know. It is a privilege I have earned.'

'True enough.' He nodded and groaned, levering himself to his feet. 'God, I am tired after battle. Everything hurts.'

I gestured ironically at my injured and wrapped arm, and Harald smiled. 'Ah, yes – I am complaining to the wrong man. But my knees remind me that I should not be doing this any more, and I do not like it.'

'Eventually, like your son, you will have to learn to listen.'

Harald laughed heartily. 'You know me better, Eric. I will die before that happens. I will always want to ride the horse.'

Ah, how fate mocks our words.

'Then don't complain when it throws you off!' I said, and more prophetic words I have never spoken.

'I will go and find my son and make peace. He will give me a tougher negotiation than the Saxons.'

'Good luck. I will not be joining you this time. Too fearsome an opponent, indeed.'

Harald snorted and winced, hobbling away as he stretched his protesting legs, and I lay down again with a sigh, finally hoping for peace.

I had closed my eyes for only a short time, or so it seemed, when I felt footsteps approaching and I opened my eyes reluctantly, shading them from the sun as I squinted at the visitor.

It was Stykarr.

'I need to talk to you,' he said flatly.

I closed my eyes for a moment and cursed under my breath before I looked at him with my best attempt at a smile. 'What is the problem?'

'The Orkneymen set up camp upriver of the Westlanders, and the Westermen claim the islanders have been shitting in the water rather than walking to the proper place.'

I put my hand to my brow, massaging my temple softly. I could not imagine anything I wished to get involved in on that beautiful day less than an argument over who was shitting where. But that is leadership on campaign.

'Right. Just give me a moment to get dressed.'

* * *

That evening we dined with Tostig. I will not say we feasted, although men who tell of it often like to call it a feast, because we were on campaign in a hostile land and food was always hard to come by, so there was no feast as you would recognise it. But we ate well, better than on most evenings.

The remarkable thing was that we had ale. Ale is rare on campaign, because it is too heavy to bring with you in any quantity. The only times men at war drink ale are when they steal it after the sack of a town or city, and it had been many days since we last did that so there was none to be had.

But Tostig had arranged with one of his friends – a local lord who supported his claim – to buy and ship to us all the ale that could be found, which amounted to perhaps two cups per man in the army.

He did the whole thing secretly, in only two days, without even Harald knowing, and it was a remarkable feat. With those two cups he bought the love of the entire army, for it was a magnificent gift. A wise politician, Tostig.

I sat with Harald and Tostig on the ground around a fire, for we had no benches for the men and Harald chose not to sit on chairs while the men sat on the ground.

Tjodolv was also there, and he entertained us with stanzas about Harald's life, and of the campaign we were on. I know, I have barely mentioned him, which might seem unjust because he was there all the time. He had fought at Fulford in the King's hird and... Look, I just didn't like the man, and I have good reason. I will not tell you why for there is nothing to be gained from discussing petty grievances so many years later, but consider this: did you ever hear me mentioned in a single thing he wrote or said. No? Well, exactly – so why should I gild his memory by speaking much of him now?

Eugh, I apologise. I should not let such bitterness affect my telling. Let me gather myself and continue.

So, we were sitting around on the grassy bank in the evening light and the light of the fires, sipping our ales so that they might last the full meal, while laughing and talking. What was being talked about? Well, what any warriors talk about: the battle they had all just fought! Many tales of bravery and honour were being spoken around those flames, and at least half of them were true.

Harald himself was in fine spirits, perhaps the finest I had ever seen him in. This was his most fervent desire, what he lived for and had spent his entire life striving to attain: to be a king on campaign, defeating his enemy in battle and winning land, wealth and glory for himself and his people. Everything so far in his life had been in service of other empires or nations, or securing his crown, or his frustrating decade-long war against Denmark that led to only one major battle and no gain to speak of.

Now, at fifty years old, he was finally doing the thing that he had always wanted, the thing that he brought that army from Norway for, and he was in the finest mood of his life. Even his argument with his son could not bring him down, and it was clear from their chilly but polite behaviour towards each other that they had made some kind of peace during the afternoon.

And I was happy too. I was happy to see Harald happy, because truly he rarely was. All through our lives together, even when he was smiling and laughing and merry, Harald had always been burning within from some injustice, some desperate ambition, some unquenched thirst or concern that he was missing an opportunity to seek the greatness he so deeply desired.

But there, on that beautiful riverbank in England, with his victorious army about him and in lands he had newly conquered, I believe that for the first time in his life he found true happiness. That is why he had been able for the first time to feel true fear, you see. Because only when he had nothing but things to lose, and nothing left that he needed to gain, could Harald feel the true fear of losing what he had. For the first time in his life, he was focused on preserving what he had, not adding to it.

It sounds strange that I say this about that evening, of course, because you all know that we still had a battle yet to fight. But we did not know it then. We thought the fight for the North was over, and it is what Harald and Tostig talked about that evening: plans for negotiating an end to the war.

After we had eaten, Harald leaned in towards Tostig. The sun was not yet low. 'So, your brother will hear of our victory and our taking over of your northern provinces tomorrow, or perhaps the next day. Are you certain he will send men to discuss peace? If not, we must prepare for the possibility of another battle in the weeks ahead. If I were him, I would raise a new army and march north before the month was out.'

Tostig nodded. 'He would certainly do that, if it were not for the threat of invasion by Duke William of Normandy. He has already gathered an army and waits near the southern coast. He knows William is also ready and awaiting his opportunity, and surely your victory up here will seem to be that opportunity. William will sail when he hears of it, come to finish off the weakened kingdom, if he has not sailed already after hearing of your landing here a few weeks ago.' Tostig smiled thinly. 'So my brother is in an impossible position. If he marches here to try and save the north, he risks losing the south, which is the real core of his kingdom. If he stays in the south, he will likely defeat William but be greatly weakened and forced to make terms with you. This was our assessment before we came here, and I see nothing to change it now.'

Harald looked into his ale and nodded. 'That is what my mind says a good general and king would do, try to preserve his richest and most important lands.' He shook his head. 'But my heart tells me I would march north with everything I had, regardless of the risks. I would fight the enemy I had today, not the enemy I might have tomorrow.'

'My brother is not you, King Harald, even if he shares your name.'

Harald laughed. 'Do you think it is a good thing he is not like me, or a bad one?'

'For us? A good thing indeed,' Tostig said with a grin. 'I would hate to have an enemy like you.'

Harald raised his cup to the compliment. 'Well spoken. I will accept your flattery gladly.' He looked around the fire, and there were a great number of men gathered around its periphery. Many wanted to be near the King and hear him speak. The men of the army practically worshipped him, and that is no exaggeration. 'Who else wishes to flatter their King?' he said with a smile.

There was a good-natured laugh and some men called out jokes and compliments, and Harald waved and nodded at them in good humour, but then he turned to me. 'Eric, why don't you tell a tale of our time in the empire? I think no other man here witnessed me there in my youth. Tell all these proud, young warriors of what I was like when I was not an old man.'

I looked at him in something like annoyance, because – and this will amuse you – I did not think of myself as a teller of stories at the time, and did not do so by habit, although I told my family and friends of my time in the empire, of course.

But it gave me a moment of sadness because he was right. Not even one of his Varangians, let alone any of the blood-marked, was still with us in that army. Many of them were still alive, of course – they were just old enough that they no longer went on campaign.

Now I am thankful for it, because it means none of his Varangians died with him in England, which would have been a sour fate for such loyal men.

I was the last man at Harald's side, as I had been the first man at his side at Stiklestad.

But I could not refuse. My King was in a wonderful mood and I was not going to ruin it, nor embarrass him and the men watching with such a refusal.

'Ah, Harald, there are so many tales. What should I speak of? Perhaps our trip to the river Jordan?'

That always impressed men, you see, because river and the very spot where our saviour was baptised is so very far away and so holy that men almost do not believe it is a real place, or that Harald and I had visited and bathed in its cleansing waters.

'No, that is too serious. Tell of something more glorious.'

'Ah, glory. The siege of Syracuse then?'

Harald smiled. 'That was glorious, was it not? But it is a tale of trickery. No. How about a truly great battle?'

I nodded. 'Something rousing. Well, the battle against the Pechenegs?'

'The Pechenegs!' He exclaimed. 'You wish to tell of a battle that I nearly lost! Heaven, no – let's hear of something that was a crushing victory. Yes, what about the battle against the rebel Petar Delyan? That was a magnificent victory, and I fought like a lion, did I not?' Harald was beaming, utterly satisfied with himself.

The thought of relating that battle sickened me, as it still hurt me when I told you of it yesterday. It would have been unspeakably cruel of Harald to make me joyfully tell it in public, if he knew or could understand what that battle had done to me. But he was not able to, as his experience of it had been so different to mine. He remembered the glory, the magnificence of his charge up to the enemy command position, with Land Waster in one hand and his sword in the other, of how he cut through ten ranks of the enemy and slew the rebel emperor himself, all at the head of his peerless and ferocious Varangian guard.

I remembered a different battle. I remembered 2,000 of my brothers, encircled and trapped in the valley of the Varangians, bleeding and dying in their hundreds while Harald summoned enough of their once near limitless but then failing strength to make one last attack on the summit. I remembered the feeling of despair, and of men I had known for years whimpering and bleeding on the dry ground, cut off, helpless, victims of Harald's ambition and overconfidence.

I remember Styrbjorn, my great friend, falling from the rock that he had won for Harald, from the breach he had cut in the enemy lines that Harald charged through to gain victory. I remember him landing in the dust near my feet, a spear through his chest, gasping and confused. Afraid and muttering as his life drained from him too quickly for him to even know it was over, let alone make his peace.

I remember holding his hand as he died, injured myself, and my mind breaking into pieces.

Harald remembered the glory of carrying Land Waster to the summit, but forgets that he was carrying it because his standard-bearer Sveneld, a fine and fiercely intelligent warrior who would have made a great leader if he had lived long enough, died clasping it, his final act of service and loyalty after receiving his death-wound being jamming it into the hard earth so that it would not fall when he did.

So, you understand that as men called out their agreement and excitement to hear the story of that famous battle, of the greatest of Harald's victories, that I felt numb and sick.

But I told it anyway, for it was Harald's greatest achievement of war, in all his many great achievements. I regaled them with the tale of Harald's cunning in determining the enemy's weakness. Of his boldness in persuading the emperor to listen to his idea, and of his courage in leading the attack into the entire enemy army himself. Two thousand Varangians against an army, deliberately cutting our way through their line and becoming surrounded – the actions of a madman or a hero.

And I told them of Harald's last charge, the pinnacle of his glory, where he reached the top of that unreachable summit carrying his banner, and all the enemy could not stand before him or the axes of his Varangians. They listened spellbound as I told them of my beautiful brothers climbing that rocky slope in the face of overwhelming enemies, and how they carved a path through them with steel and sacrifice.

They cheered as I told them of the moment the clouds broke and a shaft of sunlight flooded that rocky platform, illuminating the black raven on its red background, and the mighty warrior who held it, and how the entire enemy army saw that their leader was dead, and broke. Forty thousand men fled from my King's spectacle, and it was the crowning summit of his legend.

I wish I was a skald so I could have sung of the beauty of it, of the way Harald's form towered over the enemy in that pillar of light, his foes cringing from his feet and the fear of his bright steel, of how he tore the rebel emperor from his horse and killed him, winning an entire war with a single stroke.

But I am not a song weaver like Tjodolv was, so I just told them like a soldier, and the audience understood it all the better.

It was dark by the time I finished my tale, so they did not see the water in my eyes or the way my hand shook. I was telling them of Harald's glory, but all I could see was Styrbjorn's face, and the fear and coldness of his dying eyes, and how that day was the last day I was ever a warrior.

I did not let them see how hard it was for me. I did not ruin my great King's evening for my own weakness. So he laughed and slapped his hands on his thigh and acknowledged the adulation of the audience while I praised him, because that was my duty.

Look, I have told you many times. They call me Eric the Follower, and damn you, I earned that name.

16

TINGHAUGEN, NORWAY; SPRING 1098 AD

Eric's eyes watered a little as he looked around the audience. 'I beg a pause. I am tired and my voice is hoarse – a problem of age – and I need to rest and compose myself. As you all can tell, I am very nearly at the end of the tale, but it is the most difficult part to relate.'

The day was ending, the afternoon fading into early evening with the sun vying with the mountains in the south-west for supremacy, and soon about to lose, as it did every evening.

Magnus stood. 'It is time we all took a pause, for there is much to be prepared for this evening and the great feast. Men must bathe and dress themselves. I suggest all that is left in your tale is the telling of my grandfather's last battle, and that can be done to entertain us after the ale flows and before the food arrives. It is too heavy and important a subject to be related out here in the field, sober and chilling in the evening air. And Eric, if you would be so good, I would take this opportunity to meet with you to seek your counsel about my intentions. My grandfather trusted you, and if I have learned anything from him and your tale, I should do so also.'

Eric smiled and dipped his head in acquiescence. 'I would be honoured, my King.'

'Good! Then I say to you all, come and be welcome in Jarl Halfdan's hall as the sun sets, and be ready for a fine tale, and a feast of celebration before the

Thing!' King Magnus said, smiling and spreading his arms in invitation to the field, who all stood and cheered, voicing their support.

The crowd rose from their benches and Magnus held his arm out, gesturing for Eric to join him on the path back to the hall. Eric shuffled to the King's side and allowed himself to be led away down the path, Magnus keeping his stride slightly faster than Eric would have liked.

'If I may be so bold, I am pleased your mood has improved, my King,' Eric said. 'It was not my intention to upset you with my tale. In fact, I did not know you would be here to hear it.'

Magnus smiled. 'Do not worry. This is a difficult subject for me to hear. I'm sure you understand. I must take my family's reputation extremely seriously.'

Eric nodded. 'Of course, of course, and I apologise for seeming to threaten that. Honesty can sometimes be very challenging, but your grandfather appreciated it, even when he hated it.'

Magnus laughed. 'Yes, I think I perfectly understand his feelings about your honesty now.'

Eric smiled nervously back. 'Good... good, I am glad.'

They reached the jarl's chambers and Magnus let Eric lead the way in. Servants had lit lamps and a jug and two fine silver cups were laid out on the table between two cushioned chairs. Eric noted that with a raised eyebrow. This meeting had clearly not been impromptu.

The King sat and gestured Eric to the other chair, before taking the jug and offering it towards the old man, a fairly outrageous compliment, for a king to offer to pour a drink for another man.

Eric held up a hand awkwardly. 'I thank you, my lord, but I do not have the stomach for more ale.'

The King smiled. 'This is Greek wine. I am partial to it, even if the price is outrageous.'

Eric's eyes lit up. 'Ah, well, that would be a rare treat then.'

Magnus smiled and poured some of the ruby-red liquid into Eric's cup and then his own and set the jug down near himself.

Eric took the cup gingerly and sniffed it, his eyes closing in happy appreciation. 'Ah, now this takes me back to my younger years. A smell of home, almost. I have not had a good Greek wine for years. Normally what we get here, when any wine is to be had, is French, or even that Bulgarian swill.' Eric took a sip and shook his head ruefully. 'And it is not the same. Thank you, Lord King, for this great gift.'

Magnus smiled. 'The benefits of being King. I can have the best of everything and be generous to those I choose to be.'

Eric raised his eyes to the King. 'And why do you choose to be generous to me, Lord King? I did not think you appreciated my tale.'

Magnus sipped his own wine thoughtfully before answering. 'It is not the case that I do not appreciate your telling of my grandfather's glory. I merely question your timing and intent. Let us be honest with each other as you were with my grandfather and be done with the pretence that you started it by chance, and with nothing in mind. You have intentions, and I would know them.'

Eric set his cup down, pursing his lips and looking at it wistfully before turning his eyes to the King with studied care.

'That is quite true, but if we are to be honest, we must also dispense with the pretence that this wine is merely a courtesy, and not an attempt to warm me to your cause before this meeting – and that this meeting is not to hear my counsel, but to make sure my counsel is to your liking.'

Magnus cocked his head a little and smiled. 'Not quite accurate. There is always space in diplomacy for a little gift and a little flattery. But I do not seek to influence your counsel – I wish to hear it first, as I think is my right as King.'

'Hear it first? My King, whatever words I speak to you are private, inviolable. I will not speak to another of what we say here.'

'Really? But you speak freely of the counsel you gave to my grandfather.'

'Not while he lived.' Eric shook his head. 'No, at the time, whatever passed between us was private, unless he needed the involvement of another of his companions. Anything I say to you, or you say to me within these four walls will remain a secret until you choose to speak it.'

Magnus nodded and smiled. 'That is good to know. So we can be entirely honest with each other.'

'We can.'

'Then what will you say at the Thing tomorrow?' Magnus asked with a pointed stare.

Eric looked down at the table, considering his words, before meeting the King's eye. 'I do not know, exactly.'

'Then generally.'

Eric looked uncomfortable. 'It depends on what plans you announce.'

Magnus nodded. 'That is fair. Well, I will announce plans to raise a great fleet and army, and sail to the islands north and west of Scotland, to gain control of them, to invade Scotland and force their King into alliance, and by doing those things create a foothold from which I can later invade England. I may also capture the great island to the west of England and compel its people into alliance. There are already a number of petty kingdoms of our kin in those islands, and if I bring them all to my side, I will unify a powerful force the like of which has not been seen since Harald's time. King William of England is weak and old, and I believe with that power I am describing he can be defeated and my grandfather's dream finally completed.'

Magnus spoke with complete confidence, and Eric clasped his hands on his lap nervously as he listened.

'So what will you say to that, Eric?' Magnus asked.

Eric looked at him with a pained expression. 'I would not advise it, Lord King.'

'I know that. It is plain from your tale of my grandfather that you believe such an expedition would be foolish, but I believe my grandfather's mistake was to be too bold, to try a single strike. I will build my position slowly, over years. I am young and have many years ahead of me. I will do this carefully and with good allies and preparation.'

'That is well thought-out, my King, but I think you under-estimate the danger, and I do not believe the English will ever be conquered by us. They were not after 200 years of trying before they were unified, and they will not be now.'

'I think you have lost your spirit and your nerve, old man,' Magnus said with a shake of his head. 'Just because my grandfather failed does not mean it is not possible. He was not perfect.'

'I know that. I know that more than any man.'

'Then why would you deny me and this generation of Norwegian warriors their chance at gold and glory? Are we merely to sit here, our ships laid up on the stones? You know Norway – if they are left so unused, eventually they will be turned on each other.'

Eric breathed out hard. 'There is some truth to that, my King. The sword left in the scabbard too long calls to its owner's hand. I have seen it many times. But I would give you the same advice I gave to your grandfather: you have secured the nation, so rule it. Be a good King, defend its borders, defy its enemies, enrich its people and its lands, and protect them. That is a king's duty, not conquest. I am sure the opportunity for battle will come and slake your warrior's thirst, but war for war's sake is the fool's path to wealth and glory, and rarely leads there.'

Magnus bristled. 'Strong words, Eric. A man should be careful speaking to his King like that.'

'You asked for complete honesty, my King, and I spoke to Harald like that my whole life. It's why he liked me, even if he hated my words. I am too old to fear for myself, but I will never be too old to fear for Norway and its people. And committing to an invasion of England again? I fear they will not survive it. I fear Harald's legacy will not survive it. You, my King, and all that he and your father have built, could be destroyed by such an endeavour. It is my life's work to protect against that.'

Magnus stared him down. 'So you will oppose me?'

Eric nodded regretfully. 'I will.'

Magnus sat up, raising his head a little. 'And what if I do not let you speak?'

Eric gave a sympathetic shrug. 'I think we both know, Lord King, that it is too late for that. I have already spoken, and in my tale, the men of Norway have heard enough to know the danger better than I could ever describe it in a speech at the Thing.'

Magnus nodded slowly. 'So it is true – your entire performance here has been intended to dissuade them from supporting an invasion of England.'

'Yes.'

'Are you not loyal to your King, Eric?'

'Always, my lord. It is the defining cause of my life. But a loyal man can speak the unwanted truths, and my loyalty to my King has always included that. If I speak against your plans at the Thing, just know it is not a betrayal, but done precisely out of loyalty to my King.'

Magnus stood. 'Thank you for your honesty, Eric. I do not doubt it, or your intentions, even if I believe you are wrong and hope to defeat your attempts.'

Eric stood and bowed. 'That is the most honourable course a king can take, King Magnus, and your grandfather would be proud.'

'Then we have nothing else to discuss. Go now. I must prepare for the evening, and so must you.'

Eric bowed again and turned towards the door.

'One last question,' Magnus said, and Eric turned, already halfway through the doorway.

'Yes?'

'When you say that you do everything out of loyalty to your king... which king do you mean? Throughout your tales, you have referred to Harald as "your king", and to me as "the king" or "our king". So where does your loyalty lie – with him or with me?'

Eric smiled softly and looked at Magnus. 'You are so much his grandson.'

'Answer the question.'

'In my view, King Magnus, there is no difference. I will always have one king, and he is the man I will be loyal to until death.'

Eric bowed again and then left, and Magnus breathed hard as the shuffling footsteps succeeded.

Soon the silence was broken by the sound of another approaching, and Jarl Halfdan appeared in the door and looked at Magnus questioningly. 'What did he say?'

Magnus met his jarl's stare. 'He means to oppose me.'

'I see. As expected. Why is he doing this? It seems insanity for an old man to try and sabotage your plans. Did he give a reason?'

'He claims it is all to protect me, and Hardrada's legacy.'

'But what you are doing is merely what Hardrada would have done. Does he not see that?'

'He does, and I believe that is what he is afraid of. He thinks I will fail as my grandfather did, but that is a belief born of weakness.'

Magnus stroked his beard. 'I also considered that it might be a test, a test to see what I would do, because my grandfather wouldn't tolerate such opposition and neither will I. Perhaps he is just making sure I am ready, in his perverse way.'

'That would be... outrageous. Who is he to test you so?'

'Indeed. It is unacceptable either way, so I will not allow it, although I fear he is right when he says much of the damage is done, I think it is not as complete as he judges it to be. We can still win over the assembly, but only if he does not speak against us.'

'So there is only one thing remaining,' Jarl Halfdan said.

Magnus's jaw set into a hard line. 'Yes. We will use the solution you prepared.'

* * *

The crowd packed into the great hall, filling every bench and standing space, with men gathered around the open doorways to listen. Not even everyone who wanted to listen could, but that did not stop the excitement inside as they prepared for Eric to speak.

Magnus arrived, smiling and looking around the hall, walking through the entire room clasping arms and thumping shoulders, stirring the crowd as he went.

They raised their drinks to him as he took to the dais, where lords were crowded on chairs and benches behind Magnus's seat, and such was the overcrowding that the whole room was thick with smoke and the smell of breath and sweat, even with all the doors and smoke-holes open.

'Welcome, men of Trondelag, to the feast of the Frostating!' Magnus roared, and the men stamped their feet and cheered back at him, for the feasts before the great meeting were legendary for their raucousness and joy.

Magnus waved for silence, and it slowly fell. 'But before we feast, first we will hear the tale of my grandfather, King Harald, and his epic battle with the English.' Magnus looked around and his face was serious. 'Fear not, for we all know how the tale ends and we should not be saddened. Take strength from the tale of our forefathers' bravery and glory, for they dared to dream and had the courage to test their ambitions. No warrior who died by my grandfather's side bears less than glory worthy of remembrance!'

The crowd cheered that too, although more quietly, shouting and thumping their hands and feet.

Magnus waited for silence again. 'So remember, that although we should mourn their loss, we should be proud of their courage and their honour. As men, all we can do is strive to match their worth. Remember that. How privileged we are to have here with us a famous man, a friend and advisor to King Harald, who was there with him to tell us of that day and what happened. Be quiet now, and do not interrupt, as Eric Sveitungr tells us of that final day. Remember, men will seethe with jealousy not to have been here this day to hear his words, so make sure we hear them well!'

The crowd rumbled once more with acknowledgement and Magnus took his seat with a flourish, gesturing to Eric to stand and take the open space in front of him.

Eric stood from the table where he had been sitting with Jarl Hakon, Ingvarr and some other friends and bowed to the King. He looked terribly old and tired, but his eyes were still bright. 'Thank you, my King, for such profound and kind words. And let me say that I appreciate them, and I know that your grandfather would have done so also.'

Magnus nodded his thanks, and Eric turned to the room, staring out over the crowd, which was more numerous than it had ever been so far.

Then he cleared his throat for the last time and began to speak.

PART III

THE DEATH

17

RICCALL, 24 SEPTEMBER 1066 AD

Here we are, my friends. At last, my tale comes to its close. The final full day of King Harald Hardrada's great life. How can I do him justice, as I relate, for what might be the last time, this tale of his achievements? When I am gone there will be no man left to speak of him the way I can speak of him, and although all of you who have heard my words can share them, to the best of your recall, none of you will be speaking from your own experience. The weight of it bears down on me heavily, I can tell you.

The King was awake with the dawn, striding around the camp greeting every man he could while they had their morning meal. He was in a heavenly good spirit. I was sore, my arm was causing me some misery, and a little fever was upon me. Not terrible – not the kind that takes a man's life in two nights of sweating and shivering – but nevertheless it was angry and a little swollen. So I did not immediately share Harald's good mood at the rising of the sun, which I think I can be forgiven for.

The day, by the time I was finally up and about, was hot, hotter than any of the previous ones. It was not quite hot enough to rival Sicily, but certainly it was hotter than any day in Norway that I have ever experienced, and hotter than many days in Constantinople in the summer. The kind of heat that many of you will never have experienced, and many of the men there with us had never experienced.

But it was tolerable if you drank water and spent time in the shade. Anyway,

I make this point because it is important. It changed everything that followed, as I am sure most of you know.

Harald held a meeting in the shade of a big yew tree, sitting on the highest of its roots, and we all stood before him to hear his plan.

'The day is hot, and tomorrow surely will be too, so we will march to the meeting place this evening. I hear the river there is far too narrow to take all of our ships, so we will go overland.'

'Today? Did we not intend to travel tomorrow?'

'Yes, we did, but it is fifteen miles, and we would have to walk there and back, much of that in the heat of the day. I see no need to put the army through such punishment, so we will march there in the cool of this afternoon, camp, and can relax in the morning while we wait for our new subjects to arrive with the hostages.'

'We will be vulnerable, away from our ships. Our ships will be vulnerable without us here,' said Erlend Thorfinnsson.

Harald shook his head casually. 'It is too soon for them to have raised another army in the north. There is no danger to a force our size, and I will leave one in three men here with the ships. That will be enough to defend them from any raiding force, and enough to row them away to safety if a larger one arrives.'

'Who will command here while we are gone?' Thorberg Árnasson asked, seemingly irritated at Erlend's concerns.

'Eystein has earned the rest, I think,' said Harald with a smile. 'He will remain here.'

Erlend looked dubious. 'My King, some men might be insulted if you leave only the Westerland men here, as if you value their contribution to the battle above others.'

'You are quite right, Erlend, which is why that is not my intent. Eystein will remain here in command, but not with his men. One in three men of every contingent will stay with him. Each of you choose those who wish to rest, or deserve the rest. I do not care how. That way you can all guard your own ships and your own loot.' He looked around questioningly, but everyone seemed agreeable to that plan.

'Good, then prepare your men, assign those who are staying and those who are coming with us. We will march in mid-afternoon.'

'What equipment shall we bring? Are we marching armed for war? If you do not expect battle, perhaps just swords and spears? It will ease the men's burden in the heat.'

Harald looked at him thoughtfully and then flicked his eyes towards me. 'What do you think, Eric?'

I gave him a knowing look. 'You know well that no good general takes his army unprepared for battle, even when he does not expect it, for that is the time an enemy would most wish to attack.'

Harald pointed a wagging finger at me, happy to use me to blame for insisting on taking our war-gear. 'Eric is quite right – it would be foolish to march away from our ships unready for battle, even in lands we now control. So we will march ready for war.'

There was a grumbling and Harald looked surprised. 'What is the matter?'

Thorberg Árnasson shrugged. 'We must march half the day, in this heat, carrying everything we need for camping while also all our equipment of war? We have no mules, almost no carts beyond what we took from the locals and only a handful of horses likewise taken. It will be a hard march, and the men will hate it.'

'Soldiers always hate marching, Thorberg, but I acknowledge that this will be more unpleasant than most marches.' He stroked his grey-streaked beard. 'A compromise, then. We will march equipped for war, but without our maille. Any foe we meet is likely not to be formidable, so spears, shields, helmets and bows should suffice with so many men as we have. Not marching in twenty pounds of iron rings will ease the path considerably, do you not agree?'

Thorberg nodded gruffly. 'It will, my King. Your wisdom prevails, as always.'

'My wisdom may not prevail,' Harald said, 'but my will does. I order every man to be properly equipped and ready for battle if the enemy should surprise us, except only for his maille. Good. Any other concerns?'

No one spoke up.

Harald stood with a small grunt and a wince, quickly banished. I think one of his knees was troubling him since the battle, but being the man he was, he did not admit it.

He smiled broadly. 'Then go to your men, prepare them for the march.'

I went over to him. 'Are you sure that is wise?'

'What?'

'Leaving our maille behind?'

Harald shrugged. ‘It is not important. There is no enemy nearby who can challenge us.’

‘Yes, but if we are ambushed with bows, we will take terrible casualties without it.’

‘Not enough to defeat us. Our shields are broad and there are not enough arrows in England to manage it.’ His brow darkened. ‘And our revenge will be so terrible, who would dare? Bah, I spent ten years marching in Denmark, and never needed my maille once, despite wearing it for every step. I am glad to be rid of it for one journey.’

I pursed my lips but looked away. It was not worth arguing over.

‘Not that it matters to you, you will be staying here.’

I looked back at him. ‘I will not.’

‘I am not going to argue with you. You are wounded, you will not march.’ He pointed at my arm in its sling.

‘I am not arguing, I am coming with you. Damn it, Harald, I marched from one end of the world to the other with you. You brought me here to be with you for the final campaign, and if this meeting decides its end I am going to be there and you will not stop me,’ I said, bristling with anger. I think I was angry because of the suggestion that I was not capable of it, not because I truly cared to witness the exchange of hostages. It was just my pride. ‘Anyway, it is my arm that is wounded, not my legs.’

He narrowed his eyes. ‘I do not tolerate dissent in my army from anyone.’

I squared up to him a little. ‘You have always tolerated it from me – you claim it is what you like about me. I am coming with you. It is my place, and it was fucking pointless dragging me from my home to bring me here if I do not.’

He huffed at me, anger swelling at being talked to that way, for no one else did. Then he took control of himself, and a small smile appeared, all his anger washing away in that magical way he had. I never met a man who would switch from hot to cold like he could. ‘It is true that is what I like about you. No one else has the balls to talk over me, except my son, and he does it from resentment, not conviction.’ Harald slapped me on my unwounded shoulder. ‘I will be happy to walk with you again. Just stay out of the fighting if anything happens, eh?’

I nodded and gently shrugged my injured arm. ‘I can’t hold a shield anyway.’

'A shield! Hah! I've seen you kill fully armed men with nothing but an eating knife.'

'I was a lot younger,' I grumbled.

'No, my friend. I have always thought of you as particularly old. It is one of the strange things about you, you see. I have noticed, throughout our time together, whatever age I am, that you always seemed to be an old man next to me.' He grinned and led me away from the tree towards our camp, gently mocking me.

It was punishment, you see, for standing up to him. Nothing like that could ever go unpunished. From other men, he might have banished them, humiliated them, taxed them... even had them killed.

But for me? My sentence was 500 yards of being derided for how he had always been younger and faster than me. I tell you, it was a soft punishment indeed. Ah, how I miss his humour. So few men saw it. He was always Hardrada to them, but in so many precious moments he was sometimes just Harald to me.

* * *

We reached the camp before Harald reached the end of his jokes, and Harald's son Olaf was there, talking to Stykarr. He saw Harald and strode over, all pent-up tension and angst.

'I presume I will be here with Eystein, Father?'

Harald gave me a knowing wink. 'Time to let him ride the horse, eh?'

I nodded subtly.

He turned to his son. 'No. I wish you to accompany me to the negotiations and the exchange of hostages. I think I might even pick you a bride sometime soon from one of the greatest families of this land. That would help secure your future kingship here, and it is time they met you. Let us see if there is anyone worthy among them, eh?'

Olaf was taken aback. He looked surprised and then thrilled. 'You are speaking the truth?'

'Of course.'

Olaf grinned from ear to ear and then controlled himself in an amusingly excitable way. 'Thank you, Father.'

Harald slapped him on the shoulder. 'Now, come and speak with me – I wish to discuss the matter of taxation of this new land and how we will ensure it.'

He stopped and looked over his shoulder at me kindly. 'Go and rest, Eric. You will need all your strength for the march with all the young warriors.'

I rolled my eyes, but he was gone with Olaf, one arm across his son's shoulders, chatting to him happily, and I did not have a quip to reply with.

I looked around to see Tjodolv the skald looking at me in amusement, and I wagged a finger at him. 'If you write a stanza about that to recite this evening, I will gut you.'

He laughed mockingly and turned away.

Well, I needn't have worried. He never wrote a word about me. God, I hated that man.

* * *

The march to the meeting place felt more like a journey to a festival than an army going on campaign. The men laughed and joked as they carried their food, sleeping rolls and equipment slowly in a meandering column through the English countryside.

Harald had scouts out, of course. We had about two dozen horses that we had taken from the English at Fulford and before, and nothing threatening was seen by anyone all afternoon. When we arrived at the meeting place, we got our first look at the site the English had chosen. It was quite far from the city, and even further from our ships, things that bothered Harald now that we saw it.

'I did not realise the meeting place was on the other side of the river. If we go across, we will be cut off from our ships,' he griped.

'I think they just wanted to keep us away from their city.'

'We should have met them at Fulford.'

'Amongst the bodies of their dead, lying there in the heat for five days? I think not.'

No one had cleared the battlefield. We certainly had not had the time nor interest, and several thousand English bodies – and I am sure some of ours that we missed while collecting our dead – were rotting in the marsh and the land beside it. The southern road to the city was completely unusable because of it.

'They should have buried their dead. It is not my fault they did not,' Harald said with a shrug.

'Most of the men who might have done so were lying there in the water. And in this summer heat?' I shivered. 'I would not go near them, not even after two days. Even the next morning our own dead were ripe enough.'

Harald looked at me distastefully at the way I had spoken of them, and I looked away, suitably chastened.

'Whatever the reason, I do not like how far away we are.'

'We could march towards the city, meet them closer.'

Harald scratched his chin. 'No, the land is all open. Although we will be the wrong side of it, the river at least forms a wall we can use if needed.'

I looked at him, suddenly a little concerned. 'I thought you were certain we were not going to need to fight.'

'I know, but I am just being cautious. We have been soldiers for too long to think a battle is impossible simply because we do not expect one.' He looked around, clearly troubled. 'And there is something... a feeling about this place, this situation. It is not advantageous. I should have insisted on picking the place and the terms.'

'It is not too late for us to march back to the ships and send word that the meeting place has changed.'

Harald considered it seriously for a while, gazing at the landscape and at the bridge over the river. Heavens, how the fate of the nation hung on those moments of thought.

'No, I am just worrying too much. A habit you have taught me. We are not wearing maille, and if needed we can retreat down the far bank and cross this little river ourselves to get back to the ships. I will not appear afraid or indecisive in front of our new subjects. Let us boldly accept this meeting and they will see what kind of men we are in peace as well as war.'

I nodded. Honestly, I would like to tell you that I advised against the location, or that I felt nervous or predicted what would happen. But I did not. It seemed perfectly acceptable to me, if inconveniently far from our ships. I feel the irony deeply; I, who was always worried about everything, completely missed the looming danger.

'We will camp on the other side of the river. Get the army across the bridge and leave a good screen of scouts on this bank,' Harald said to Stykarr.

'There are some cattle on the other bank. I heard some of the men talking of taking and eating them.'

'Why not?' said Harald with a smile. 'Allow it.'

Tostig looked at him nervously. 'But my King, those belong to local landowners, men we are trying to make peace with. It will insult them if they arrive and we have butchered their herd.'

'You are quite wrong, Earl. Everything we see here is mine, and no time is too soon for them to learn that. Let the men who own those cattle say they have paid their first taxes to me, and let my men eat good, fresh meat instead of yesterday's bread.'

Tostig wavered but did not relent. 'It is wasteful. We do not have time to butcher and hang them, nor cooking implements. It will be terrible fare.'

Harald laughed uproariously. 'Do not think to lecture me on how butchery is done, Tostig.' He gave the Saxon lord a leery grin. 'I am known as quite the prolific butcher.' He looked away at the cattle grazing on the hillside across the river. 'Besides, my men have eaten far worse than poorly butchered meat cooked over an open fire. They will rejoice at the chance. Let's pray this is the only bloodshed this day. They will cut those cattle with their axes and have their hunger for both food and death satiated.'

Tostig relented; it was clear Harald was not going to discuss it further.

'I will give the word, my King.' Stykarr said, and then went off with some of Harald's hirdsmen.

'Shall we send scouts to Yorvik, to watch and ensure they are coming out in the morning?' I asked. 'I am worried it is the only direction we are not covering. We have our fleet in the south, and our scouts are covering the north and more are going east now. But we cannot see the city or beyond it.'

Tostig shook his head. 'Do not worry. My people are in the city and will watch over the preparations for the exchange. If anything looks wrong, they will come in the morning and tell us.'

Harald waved vaguely at Tostig. 'See, already provided for. The benefit of having allies in the land you are invading, eh?' Then he rubbed his hands together. 'Now, what I really want to address is my need for some freshly cooked meat.' His eyes wandered hungrily over the cattle again. 'Someone bring me my bow.'

Ah, poor Tostig could not have known it, but probably at that very moment the army of King Harold was arriving in Yorvik from the west, beyond the sight of our scouts. The very first thing they did was secure all the gates and the walls, not just to keep us out but to keep news of their arrival in. The enemy was no more than seven miles away, with twice our number, but we were oblivious, consumed as we were with the heat, our tiredness, and soon the beautiful smell of fresh roasting meat.

Harald set a strong guard that night and commanded that those not involved go to their sleeping rolls as the sun set. We had no ale or mead with us, beyond what little here and there that soldiers always manage to scrouge, steal or save, so there was no merriment and drunkenness. We had no tents; we did not need them, for the night was warm, so warm I just lay on my blanket in the pasture where cows had grazed until the day before, and stared at the stars until a troubled sleep took me.

* * *

I woke as badly as I had slept, confused and tired, sitting up like I had been kicked, only to find that I had, in fact, been kicked.

'Time to be up, Eric, you are making us old men look bad,' Stykarr said with an annoying grin as I peered at him in the harsh morning sunlight.

I lay there, sweating and damp in its heat, and my arm throbbed and ached from the moment my eyes opened, welcoming me back into the world with an infuriating level of bearable but sapping pain.

I slowly got to my feet, which in that condition meant rolling with all the grace of a beached sea creature and dragging myself first to my knees and then to my feet. I did all this as I became aware that I was possibly the last man in the army still asleep, and that I was right in the middle of the enormous field. The bustling army around me had probably been amused at my expense for well over an hour, judging by how high the sun was above the horizon.

That embarrassment spurred me to quickly gather my things and head down to the river. I needed to clear my head with some cooling water before I could face Harald.

I washed and then I scrounged some of the previous night's beef, which was quite unpleasant – cold, undercooked and greasy. But it was food, it was hearty, and as you all know, better than dried fish or barley soup.

I finally dragged myself to Harald, looking as ready to face the world as I could manage, and found him across the river on the western bank with Tostig, Olaf and the jarls of Orkney. A few hundred men guarded them in a loose arc, just in case. The leaders were deep in conversation.

I joined their huddle with barely an acknowledgement. Tostig was speaking.

'I don't know. It's still early to have heard anything. I expect they will be here soon,' he said to the King, who was clearly annoyed.

'Who will be here soon?' I whispered to Erlend.

'Tostig's people, the ones he left watching Yorvik. They have not arrived to tell us what the Saxons are doing.'

'That's not good,' I said helpfully.

Erlend shrugged. 'Maybe the city was late opening its gates for the morning.' He looked at me flatly. 'Or maybe it is just that some people are late to rise today.'

I gave him a raised eyebrow at the jibe and looked away.

'We should send men to look for them,' Jarl Paul said.

'No. If your men are seen intercepting them, the identity of my spies will be given away. They might be useful in the coming days. Do not expose them,' Tostig pleaded.

Harald nodded. 'Fine. We will wait awhile and give them a chance. But not too long – spies who cannot arrive on time with the information I need are of no use to me anyway. We will prepare the meeting area. I am certain the Saxon lords will arrive on horseback, and it will not do for us to be on foot like common men. Get some of the horses. We will wait mounted.'

'Yes, my King,' said one of Harald's courtiers, who jogged off towards the river.

'Good of you to join us,' Harald said without even looking at me. But I saw the corner of his mouth curl up in a smile.

'Did I miss anything important?' I asked sarcastically.

'No.'

'Then my timing, as always, is perfect,' I said with a sneer. 'In fact, so little is happening I might return to my bed. I certainly won't be riding a horse.'

'You will sit on a horse like a lord or wait with the army like a commoner. Your choice,' said Harald with a wicked grin, finally turning to look at me.

The bastard; he knew how much I hated horses.

Harald laughed at my annoyance. 'What did you tell me, Eric, the other day? Sometimes you just have to ride the horse.'

'That's not what I said or what I meant!' I protested.

Harald shrugged. 'I don't care. It's the meaning I choose to take.' He let out a contented sigh and stretched his long arms over his head and then behind his back. 'I am the King, and I say it is so.'

'You're a bastard,' I muttered under my breath, not brave enough to let anyone hear it.

* * *

Horses were brought. Harald chose the largest, a black and white stallion, which still looked rather small under his enormous height. I was given a surly chestnut mare, who fortunately for me did not look like she had the spirit left in her to be trouble.

I got atop her with help, grimacing at the pain in my injured arm, and she just stood there. I gently urged her forwards to join the others, and she moved only with great reluctance. I patted her on the neck and leant forwards. 'I know. I feel the same way, but we must make a good show together.'

She did not respond in any way, nor did her mood improve. I am convinced that even if she understood my words, she would not have listened. I knew immediately that she was just that sort of horse.

'You are surly in the morning and don't like to be told what to do or be ridden. I shall call you Olga,' I whispered to her, which amused me far more than it should have. 'Just like Olga, I expect you to tolerate me without too much fuss, understand?'

Olga just stood there chewing air, not even a whinny.

So, she did not have Olga's intelligence.

'I think I see movement,' Erlend said, shading his eyes from the sun and peering at the horizon towards Yorvik.

I looked up in interest and, sure enough, I saw the errant flashing of metal and vague movement that betrayed a large group of people moving just on the edge of our vision across the fields, before the slight rise that obscured all but the top of Yorvik's buildings from view on the extreme horizon.

'That is a lot of them just to escort hostages,' Erlend said.

'They will want to make a show of force but... yes, it is too many,' Harald said. He turned to Tostig. 'What do you think? Who could this be? I see steel flashing. This is an army.'

Tostig peered at them, chewing his lip. 'It is probably allies, coming to join you. Perhaps the people have decided to fully accept our rule without it being forced on us? It would be the wisest course.'

'I think we must assume they are hostile, just in case,' I said.

Harald watched them a moment longer and then nodded. 'Yes, we must. Call the army to battle formation. We have scouts near that treeline. I am sure they will report soon, but let us prepare.'

'Battle formation?' Erlend said, his face aghast. 'We are not ready for battle.'

'Then I suggest you become so very quickly,' Harald said tersely.

He looked at me with a dark expression. 'There is a lot of steel on those people.'

I nodded, and my stomach was churning. 'They would dare march against us again, even when we have their hostages?'

Harald looked at me and cursed. 'The hostages are at the ships – we cannot even display them.'

'But they know if they do anything those hostages will die, here or not.'

'Yes.' Harald turned to look at the appearing army again, for there was no doubt now that an army it was. I could see flags fluttering in the air above them as they marched towards us across the fields.

'It must be someone who doesn't care for the hostages of Yorvik. Maybe another lord of England.' He turned to Tostig. 'There are still other lords in Northern England, within a few days' march?'

Tostig sputtered and shook his head. 'No one who would face us alone.'

'Then they have gathered all of those who would not face us alone into one army.'

'No... They...' Tostig was utterly confounded now, unsure and nervous. 'I still think it is more likely they would come to join us. They know me, they would want to be my allies and show their support.' He sounded deeply uncertain. 'I am sure of it,' he added.

One of the mounted scouts was racing across the field towards us and he slewed his recently stolen horse to a stop with commendable skill.

'King Harald, an army approaches,' he said.

'We see it. Who are they? Do they have the elders and hostages with them?'

'I did not speak to them, but they march ready for war. If there are unarmed people in their column, I did not see them.'

Harald nodded darkly. 'As we feared.'

'What banners did you see?' Tostig asked urgently.

'At their head was a gold eagle on red,' the scout said.

Tostig's brows furrowed. 'A gold eagle? I know of no one with such a banner.' Then he paused and the colour faded from his face. 'Describe the eagle.'

'It was rearing, one claw in the air, wings back. It had an odd, slender face.' The scout looked apologetic.

Tostig fell completely still, and then, with a funerary expression, he turned to Harald.

'What?' Harald said. 'What does this strange eagle mean?'

'It's not an eagle; it's the griffon banner of Wessex,' Tostig said with a hollow voice.

Harald's eyes narrowed. 'So what does that mean?'

Tostig shook his head in disbelief and then stared at Harald for a moment before finally replying. 'It means my brother is here.'

18

STAMFORD BRIDGE, 25 SEPTEMBER 1066 AD

The army of the King of England, which was supposed to be 200 miles away, filed into the fields in front of us as if appearing from a fever dream. It was impossible that they should be there, insane, suicidal. Harold Godwinson had abandoned the south of his kingdom to come and face us, and by some magic or madness, arrived only five days after we defeated his northern forces.

Our army was in a state of barely controlled panic. Men were arming themselves and being organised into formations. Some tried to cross the bridge to join us, but the bridge was narrow, allowing two men at a time, and Harald angrily sent them back. 'It will take too long to bring the army over and it would be impossible to retreat. Stykarr, form them up on the other bank on the slope!' Harald roared across the narrow river.

Stykarr waved his arm in acknowledgement, and Harald turned his horse and trotted back over to where we watched the oncoming army, spellbound and horrified.

'So?' Harald said, moving to our sides. 'How many?'

'Twice our number,' Jarl Erlend said quietly.

'We should retreat at once to the ships,' Jarl Paul said, pleading with Harald.

'No. You see that?' Harald pointed at the mass of horsemen filing out into the fields, thousands of them. 'If we try and retreat, they will run us down, pin us in the open, and we will be destroyed. No, it is too late to retreat, nor do I intend to retreat from an opportunity to win the whole kingdom in one stroke.'

'Win the kingdom?' Paul said, aghast.

Harald glared at him. 'Yes. If we defeat King Harold here, there will be no one left in England to face us.'

'But William will invade from the south!'

'I do not care about Duke William today. I will deal with him when I need to. Now I need only to win this battle, and I need men around who will help me. Gird yourself, Jarl Paul, or flee in disgrace. I will not have the men see weakness in our ranks!'

Paul looked down, chastened. 'I apologise, my King. I support you, as always,' he said.

Harald grunted and looked at me and Erlend, who was much stouter in body and mind than his brother. 'Are you with me?'

'Of course,' Erlend said.

'Harald, how do you intend to win this battle?' I leant in. 'We don't have our armour.'

Harald nodded. 'I know, and they have numbers, but we will fight in such a way that neither matters enough to defeat us.'

'How?'

He smiled at me from his horse. 'Eric, now is not the time to forget your faith in me, or the battles we have shared together. I have won much harder victories than this.'

'And lost one to the Normans in a very similar situation, with our backs to a river and them with cavalry.'

Harald's smile faded to annoyance. 'That was with a useless army of Greeks on our side, and the enemy were Normans. These Saxon horsemen cannot be so good. Besides, we defended that river successfully and can do so again here. Believe in me, Eric! This can be the moment of our glory.'

He turned to shout at the men gathered behind us. 'Bring up Land Waster.' He stretched and settled in his saddle, staring once more at the enemy army. 'The time for peace talks is over. The time for the black raven has come again.'

* * *

As the army organised into line on the hill behind us, and the 500 or so men on our side arrayed themselves for battle guarding our end of the bridge, Stykarr came over to Harald.

'What are your orders, King Harald?'

Harald turned to look at him. 'We will hold the bridge as long as possible and then face them as they try to cross it. Maybe we will stop them there.'

'That does not sound like the decisive battle you seek,' I said.

He grinned, full of heat and excitement. Of course he was – battle was what Harald lived for, and the impossible battles that men thought he could not win but somehow always did, were what he loved most of all.

'No, it is only to delay them.' He pointed at Stykarr. 'Get the three fastest horses and the three best riders we have and send them to Eystein. Tell him to bring every man, fully armoured for battle, as fast as he can. He should cross the river downstream. We passed several fords so it will not be hard and then march up the eastern bank. We will hold the Saxons here, drain them and tire them, let them cross the river eventually and then, when Eystein arrives with 3,000 armoured men, we will smash them between us and him. Their army will then be trapped against that bridge, two men wide, and we will annihilate them.'

Stykarr's eyes widened at the ambition of it. I must admit, I felt a stirring within me. It was a good plan. The enemy could not know Eystein was coming, and that surprise, and the arrival of 3,000 good warriors, armed and armoured for battle, could indeed turn the battle in our favour. We would just have to hold long enough, and the river crossing was a perfect place to do so.

But one thing still tore at me. 'Harald, without armour...' I shook my head bitterly.

He waved his hand irritably. 'We will fight in such a way that it doesn't matter. Not attacking, but defensive, keeping to our shield wall. Not all the army has maille anyway, and many of us are used to fighting without it. Truly, do you believe all the enemy have it? Of course not. I wager most of Harold's army does not have maille. Do you think England is so rich that even their farmers wear iron shirts? No.'

'It is not England's farmers that worry me. It is their huskarls. They will be armoured and we will not. We will pay a heavy price when we face them, and when we face their archers.'

'Men will die, it is true. More men than normal, but men must die to achieve great glories, and an entire kingdom is at stake!' He held up his hand. 'I will hear no more of it. We have our shields and our helmets, and good men of Norway behind them. We will remain disciplined, hold our line and wear the enemy down. It is they who must fight in iron on such a hot day, and we who will remain cool.' He smiled. 'Have faith in me, and also in our people, and victory can still be ours.'

'They are coming,' Erlend said, pointing over the field.

We all turned to look and saw that twenty or so horsemen were riding across the field towards us under the griffon banner, which did indeed look like a gold eagle of sorts, although a poorly drawn one. Apparently, it is supposed to be a sort of dragon, but... Well, the English have a strange idea of dragons, that is all I can say.

The twenty horsemen, all armoured in maille, carrying bright shields, and wearing shining helms, stopped, and they were a magnificent sight. Real warriors. It is not just from a man's equipment that you can tell, but the way he wears it and holds himself. They stood there for a moment judging us likewise, and then three came forwards to talk to us. They stopped a short distance away and one of them, a mid-sized man on a fine grey stallion, with no distinguishing marks about him, confidently rode forwards, almost strutting, if a horse can strut. The stallion was excitable and impatient, tossing his head and kicking with a back leg, turning and side-stepping, but the man upon it seemed not to notice, riding the highly strung beast like an experienced sailor steering a good ship in storm waves, never taking his eyes off us.

He gazed at us, taking us in. 'Is Tostig among you?' he called out, and Tostig nudged his horse forwards.

'I cannot deny that he is here,' Tostig called back.

Harald looked amused not to be addressed, but I must explain that all of this took place in the Saxon language, and one of our men who spoke both had to relay it to us, which was too slow a process to interject as it happened, so Harald was a few moments behind in his understanding throughout.

'The King of England says to Tostig, that if he rejoins his brother, all of Northumbria will be his again, for he would rather give it to you than be enemies.'

Tostig huffed and shook his head. 'That is quite different than the scorn and enmity I was offered last winter. If this had been offered then, many men who have died would have instead returned to their homes, and many more yet to die as well. But if I accept, what do you offer King Harald for his trouble?'

The Saxon knight turned his horse and it tossed its mane, shorting and pawing at the ground, making quite the display. I saw Harald smile at it. He loved a brave man, and he loved good horsemanship.

'For King Harald of Norway, he offers nothing but six feet of English ground to lie beneath, or seven, for he is taller than other men.'

Harald listened as this was relayed to him, and he grinned, throwing his head back and snorting with laughter.

Tostig looked at Harald and then back at the horseman. 'Then go and tell your King to prepare for battle, for I will not allow it to be said that I betrayed King Harald to join his enemy. I would rather fight and die with honour, or gain England through victory, than gain Northumbria through shame.'

The horseman half-turned his horse and saluted Tostig with his arm, before spurring the magnificent beast and riding off, with the other twenty filing in behind him, cantering across the field back towards the King's army.

Harald was staring in undisguised admiration smiling ear to ear. 'Ha! What a man is that who speaks so well. Who is he?' he asked, turning to Tostig, who was sitting motionless, watching the horsemen go.

'That was King Harold.'

Harald's eyes widened. 'That was Harold!' He looked away again at the distant figure as the King of England went to stand his horse under his banner at the head of his army. 'You should have told me. I would have killed him!'

'I know,' said Tostig. 'But I would not be known as the man who rewarded his brother's offer of peace by having him murdered.'

Harald smiled and inclined his head. 'Right you are. That is the honourable thing.' He clapped his hands together excitedly and his eyes were filled with glee. 'Finally,' he said, raising a finger to the sky and half shouting it. '*Finally*, I have a worthy foe. Ha! No more years of chasing Danes too cowardly to face me. These Saxons may not be the men we are, but by God they do not lack for courage or will to fight.'

He turned his horse, starting to head back towards our men, and we all followed him. 'What a man your brother is, Tostig. I should like to know him better.'

'One of you will die on this field, my King. I think England can only contain one Harald. It is fated.'

Harald nodded. 'I think you are probably right.' He smiled and looked at Tostig. 'Let us go and prepare for the fight.' He nudged his mount to turn back towards our men but then his borrowed horse stumbled while Harald was off balance, and the horse pitched the King headlong to the ground, right in front of the entire army, and still within sight of the enemy.

'Harald!' I shouted, slipping off my horse to run over to where he lay sprawled in the grass. It had been a heavy fall, and I feared the worst.

But as I arrived the King rolled onto his knees and then stood, embarrassed and bruised, but otherwise intact.

He looked around at our horrified faces, and the men in the formation in front of us guarding the bridge.

We were not just horrified because the King had fallen and might have been hurt, but because it seemed like the most terrible of omens to be thrown from your horse in front of your army. What can I say? It is a pagan superstition, I suppose, but many of us still believe in such things, even to this day.

Harald knew it too, and he forced a smile. 'What? It is good luck for a traveller to fall from his horse unharmed,' he exclaimed, walking over to the black and white beast, who had clearly hurt its leg and was holding one hoof barely on the ground. Harald saw it and frowned. There was no pretending that was a good omen.

'Well, we should walk now, anyway. Horses will not be needed for this battle,' he said, and we all dismounted, the silence of our worry awkward and prolonged.

Harald let some men take the horses away, and he brushed the earth from his fine gilded helmet. The sound of a horn floated across the field from the Saxon lines, and a great cheer went up.

Harald gestured urgently. 'Come, let us get across the river. It begins.'

* * *

We went across the footbridge. I had worried Harald would want to stay on the western bank with the men chosen to defend the bridge, but he was not so foolish, or perhaps not so young any more. We went up towards the warriors arrayed on the bank overlooking the bridge and stood under Land Waster to watch the battle begin.

Our 500 men guarding the bridge formed a semi-circular shield wall as they had been ordered, a cramped one too, seven or eight men deep, and they all had spears, shields and helmets. It presented a formidable obstacle, even if it had no chance of defeating the Saxon army. It was not meant to; it was meant to be a rock the Saxon army would batter itself on.

Time. It was all about time. Harald was going to spend blood for time.

The Saxons may have known about Eystein and that critical factor of passing hours, they may not have. I will never know. But regardless, they wasted little sunlight and their army deployed several thousand men to attack that precarious defensive line, and did so with precision and discipline.

'So their King is a general, as well as a brave man,' Harald said with a small smile, as a thousand Saxon footmen, clearly levies by the look of them, formed into a solid block and advanced on our outnumbered men with a cheer and a spring in their step that betrayed no terror of what they were about to face.

'They move well, and under control. He is using his least important men to wear ours down, not impatiently throwing his best forces in to be killed.'

'So you think his strategy will work?' I asked.

'Yes.'

'Then why do you look happy about it?'

'Because it will take longer, and because I am glad that he is doing as I expected him to do.'

'Is he a good general if he is doing as you expect?'

'Yes, because it is the least bad of many bad options, and he has no choice. That is how I will beat this Harold, Eric. I will give him nothing but bad choices until he runs out of time or men, and I care not which happens first.'

I nodded and watched as the Saxon attack fell upon the defending shield wall with a clatter and a roar that was so familiar to me. The two lines locked together, the Saxon one curling around like the fingers of a hand, seeking to find the edges and gain leverage. But our men had their flanks to the river, and there was no purchase to be had. A few men wrestled and splashed in the water's edge, but the current was strong and the centre deep, and the Saxons could not turn our flank.

Nor, it became apparent, after a while of hacking and shoving, could they push our men back, compress them into a ball of men at the bridge's end that would inevitably lead to panic and defeat. Our line, being curved outwards, was naturally stronger and needed fewer men to hold it in place than the enemy, who were wrapped around it.

I wish I could tell you of moments of glory or the stories of valour from that encounter, but really it was just a mass of men pushing and hacking, stabbing unseen under shields, and I could see nothing of interest whatsoever in the contest of shoving, other than that our men were holding, and that few men on either side were dying.

Harald's plan was working, you see, for time was wasting. But so was Harold of England's plan, for our men were tiring.

The dance of battle between good generals and good armies – I had known it since my time in the empire. You remember me describing it, yes? The first time I had seen it was in the battle against the Moslems near Edessa, where the empire won a fine victory against a fine enemy. I relayed to you that every part of that battle had been a deadly dance between two generals who knew each other's moves so well. It is a beautiful and terrible thing, a contest so poised, and I had not seen it for decades.

Finally, the Saxon line flagged, started getting a little ragged in its movements. They were only levies, what the Saxons call fyrdmen, and they could not sustain an attack for long. They paid dearly for it too, for when their line finally retreated, the ground was smeared with the bodies of their countrymen, while from the back of our own formation a worrying number of wounded warriors limped or staggered back across the bridge.

'Send some men down to help them,' Harald shouted to Stykarr. Then, under his breath to me, added, 'The rest will fight better knowing we will help them retreat.'

He had the skill of making men be willing to die for him, you see. Well, if you do not yet, I think you will by this story's end.

* * *

The Saxon fyrdmen retreated, and hundreds of archers loosed over their heads, hitting our shield wall while our men were barely reorganised. The arrows did little other than force our men to cower behind their shields. But that was no surprise; arrows alone rarely work against such a formation.

But, of course, the arrows were not alone.

While our men hid blind behind their shields, weathering the storm of iron-tipped wood, we were watching a block of a thousand Saxon horsemen move forwards, spreading out into a broad line and angling to the right of our men.

Then a horn blared and the horsemen charged in from an angle along the riverbank, the archers stopping only at the last moment, so our men were still cowering as the horsemen rode in.

The ranks of the enemy horsemen did not clatter into the shield wall – you know that almost no horse will do that – but ran across the front, and in each rider's hand was a long spear, which they lanced out into the shield wall, looking for the gaps between them or trying to reach over and down.

'Get your spears up!' Harald shouted angrily, although none in the fight could hear him.

Our men were taken by surprise by the new attack and its method, and as the long stream of enemy horsemen rode past them, so close that many horses bounced shields off their flanks. Few of our men managed to get their spears up and many that did had the weapons merely knocked aside by the fast-moving current of horseflesh, leaving gaps that others lunged or threw their spears into as they passed.

I watched nervously as the formation of our men buckled and shivered, shrinking away from the terrible stream of horsemen and the ragged fissure that it had ripped into the shield wall. I fidgeted nervously with my sword-hilt, and thought that Harald had miscalculated, and that our men might break there and then.

They might have, too, if it was not for a warrior on the left of the line, the first act of heroic sacrifice for Harald that I saw that day and, of course, far from the last.

As the line to his right buckled and fractured, threatening to collapse the entire formation, one warrior jumped forwards from it, holding his shield and spear out in front as far as he could reach, putting them right in the face of a rush of horses that had no chance to avoid him.

At least two of those rushing horses hit him, and his spear lodged in the chest of one, the butt digging into the ground and impaling the running beast even as the brave warrior was crushed beneath the other, disappearing to the ground, never to rise.

But the impaled horse turned in pain and panic, toppling to the side and thrashing, and two more horses ran into it and fell headlong in a tangle of breaking legs and thrown riders.

The whole stream of Saxon horsemen pulled out and to the left to avoid the carnage as more than half a dozen horses went down, and in that moment, the pressure on our wall was gone. Our men in the line cheered and stepped forwards, bringing their shields and spears up, presenting them to the rest of the Saxon force, which reined in and stopped their assault.

'That was too close,' I said, letting out a ragged breath.

'Have faith in the men, Eric,' Harald said calmly. 'Or how can you expect them to have faith in us?'

I nodded brusquely, bewildered at his calm. He had a confidence that simply could not be matched by any other man I have ever known.

The Saxons withdrew, and the rain of arrows continued again. But this time our men had learned, and as they hid once more behind their shields the row of spears never wilted, ready for the next attack.

A new block of the fyrdmen came forwards, more of them this time, and they fell upon our line again.

'This is the attack meant to succeed,' Harald said, watching carefully. 'And it likely will.'

I could see he was right. Our formation held, but there was no cheering, and they visibly shrank under the attack. The trickle of wounded trying to escape across the bridge only thickened.

'What happened to faith?'

'I have faith in our men's courage and skill but understanding of the limits of their bodies. You need both.' He turned to Stykarr. 'Get ready to pull them back. I want as many to escape as possible.'

Whatever the enemy was expecting, they had clearly prepared, and as our men across the bridge started to give ground in their exhaustion, crowding in towards the bridge and starting to retreat over it, the Saxon archers came forwards and aimed their bows in the air, showering the area around the bridge with arrows that stooped in like diving falcons.

That was when I first really saw men fall in numbers on our side. They were retreating with their backs to the enemy or their shields down, and the deadly hail skewered into dozens of unarmoured bodies before they realised what was happening and started to protect themselves.

The scene around the end of the bridge was now carnage. Half our men were still on their feet and fighting, the other half were dead, wounded, or trying to escape across the bridge, and I could feel, even from 200 paces away, the tendrils of panic spreading their way through that formation.

You can feel it, you can hear it and you can almost smell it when panic hits a group of brave fighting men. Levies and bandits panic easily, and it happens like a rush of sheep at the sight of a wolf – instantly and irresistibly. But in a formation of good soldiers it takes longer, they resist it. At first, they edge away, then they go quiet and start looking behind, wondering if they will be able to escape when the end arrives.

It is a sort of nervous, shuffling silence that creeps into the formation, not the cries of panic of untrained, unseasoned men. And that is what I saw. I suddenly saw a lot of faces flashing looks our way, instead of focusing on the enemy that was pressing harder than ever.

Everyone has their limits, you see. And the Saxons had found the limits of our warriors.

When the formation broke, it was over in moments. The left flank by the river gave way first. They had borne the brunt of the attack by the horsemen, and a band of brave Saxons managed to drive them away from the river's edge and get around them. The men who were about to be entrapped broke and rushed back, pushing into the centre of the formation, who then lost the thing that had been protecting their backs.

The ripple rolled all the way around the wall and the shock shattered it. They did not turn and flee in panic. No, they were too experienced for that. They simply lost their formation and backed up as fast as they could, shoving and competing to be the first to the bridge, even as they kept their weapons and shields up, defending themselves in their flight.

The end of the bridge became a crush as they arrived and, instead of trying to turn them around, Stykarr and his men helped them across. It was too late to save the fight on the far bank, but not too late to save some of the fighters.

They streamed across the bridge as arrows plunged in around them, flecking the water like hailstones, pattering onto shields held over heads, and striking into any exposed flesh they could find.

The wounded were no longer helped across. Those who became an obstruction were simply shoved over the low rail that bordered the walkway on each side.

The Saxons let out a great cheer and rushed in on the last of our men, and the fighting broke into a desperate melee where dozens of men fell on both sides, but the Saxons had numbers and the smell of victory, and our men knew they were beaten.

'Get our archers ready!' Harald shouted.

The few we had were already behind us, behind the shield wall, prepared to try and stop the enemy when they tried to cross. Harald had not sent them down to the riverbank to help in the fight on the other side because the Saxon archers would have slaughtered them, and we had not more than two dozen arrows for every bow.

We had not come ready for battle, remember.

The last of our men fled onto the bridge or were cut down steps from safety on the far bank.

I expected the Saxons to stop and regroup. Harald had expected them to stop and regroup. Their King maybe thought so too. It was insanity to try and cross into the teeth of our defenders before their army's archers came down and cleared the way, but the enemy had the scent of blood and victory in their nostrils, and they simply followed our men across the bridge, caught up in the excitement of victory.

Our own surviving men, several hundred strong, blocked our archers from a clear target, and we had not the arrows to waste with the trick of firing high and landing among them like rain.

The Saxons were halfway across the bridge before anyone in either army reacted, and Harald was cursing and shouting orders. I could see the survivors down on our side of the bridge were in no condition to fight again, nor were any of our other men close enough to reach them.

Harald had not wanted to sit our line in an arrow-storm down on the riverbank, but we were not ready to let the enemy cross yet. We needed time. It was all about time.

Someone needed to earn us some time.

* * *

I am sure you have all heard the story of the hero who gave his life for Harald's time, and it is exaggerated with every telling.

Someone down there, a warrior with a great axe, stepped back onto the bridge. He should have been cut down in a heartbeat by a hail of arrows, but the enemy archers on the far bank were moving down, preparing to attack our main line. He should have been overwhelmed by the rushing enemy on the bridge, but they were clogged with our own dead and dying. He should have been speared on the spot before he got into range of his own great axe, but the enemy were unprepared, and he was inside a spear's length before they knew he was there.

I don't know his name. No one who could have known who he was survived the battle, but that unknown warrior charged onto the bridge alone between two armies, and he carved the first shocked Saxon from shoulder to groin and burst over his rended corpse like an avenging angel. The enemy were farmers, fishermen, woodsmen and craftsmen. They were brave, they were flush with victory, but they were tired and few of them even had helmets. Two-wide they faced him, and in two heartbeats, two-wide they died, and the axeman built a wall of their bodies.

Now men who tell the tale claim he was alone, or that he slew forty enemies before the Saxons gave up attacking. None of that is true, of course. He killed the first four or five who faced him, and the ones behind could not clamber over the bodies on that narrow walkway without exposing themselves to his axe, so they did not. The entire advance of the Saxon army was halted as the men at the blockage of corpses and axeman baulked, and the ones behind could not move.

Nor was he the only brave man – of course he was not. Others followed his example, rushing back onto the bridge to help him. It was their shields that saved the axeman from the arrows and spears that flew at him, trying to dislodge him from the six blooded feet of wood that he was guarding, and across which the army of England had to cross.

I wish I knew who he was, that man who died so bravely for Harald's dream. I would have shared a cup with him and praised his strength and his courage, but the enemy attacked again, and after he slew the first of them, some Saxon farmer managed to get under the shields with a spear and ended his story by embedding it in his groin.

The axeman howled in pain and anger, a howl we could see and hear all the way where we were standing, and then he collapsed onto the boards and was overrun.

What a terrible tragedy that was, and what a glorious death.

The arrows came thick and fast then, and the enemy pushed our men back and cleared the bridge of bodies as they advanced, until everyone on our side was driven away by the hail of arrows from a thousand bows on the opposite bank of the river.

Our own archers responded, finally given a target too good to miss as several thousand Saxons crowded across the bridge.

Perhaps a hundred or two hundred of them were cut down, but thousands more came behind, and our arrows ran out before their men.

It did not matter. I was no longer standing on the bank with Harald; we had retreated with the army up the slope. The axeman and the arrows had given Harald what he needed: time. And their loss no longer mattered to the mind that marshalled the great and deadly dance. Perhaps 200 Norwegians had died, but the sun had moved across the sky regardless, clawing its way across the face of heaven, and, somewhere to the south, so we hoped, three horsemen had arrived at Eystein's camp, horses blown and flecked white with sweat, and delivered him the message:

Battle is joined and Harald is holding across the river. Don your armour and come up the eastern bank. Come to your King, come to Land Waster. Reach him before the army's strength fails.

Reach him or die in the attempt.

19

Harald drew us back into a great circle on the top of the slope overlooking the river. A solid wall with no end, 7,000 men arrayed six men deep, curled completely around on itself. He knew that enemy would overlap his wall if we faced them in line, causing it to fail. King Harold of the Saxons would know it too.

So he denied them the chance of breaking us so easily, and denied us the chance of victory, and curled us up in a ball of wood, steel and flesh.

There was another aspect to that formation too, that Harald never explained but I knew well: the enemy would surround us, and all our men would see that there was no escape but through victory. No one would be shuffling back or looking for escape, for there *was* no back, no escape.

The only way out of that circle was through valour and victory, through holding on long enough for Eystein to reach us with the armoured hammer of his men. We simply had to live long enough to still be fighting when he arrived.

Time, by God. We just needed time.

When the formation was settled, we watched the Saxon army cross the bridge unopposed, two by two. It was taking them a great deal of the time we needed.

Tostig came over to stand with Harald, looking deeply troubled.

'I don't understand this, Harald. Why don't we charge down and attack them while they are crossing?'

Harald nodded. 'It might work, but he is expecting it. See there, his archers are on each flank on the far side, ready to tear apart the flanks of any attack with their arrows. And that formation screening the crossing? There would be no quick victory, and we would be drawn into a fight on the riverbank with their archers shooting down into us that would be over quickly, one way or another.'

He gestured to the ground at our feet. 'Here, on the crest, their archers will fire up into our shields, unable to see us at all once battle is joined. It is the best protection I can give men without armour. We have built a fortress of our shields atop this slope, and all we need to do is defend it until the late afternoon.'

'That is a long time. Are you sure Eystein will come?'

'I have bet my life on it,' Harald said with a soft smile. 'He cannot marry my daughter if he abandons me, after all.'

Tostig gulped and looked at the slowly developing formations of his kin as they crossed the river.

'Will you stand with me, Tostig?' Harald said. 'You look unsteady.'

Tostig gave the King a hurt look. 'There should be no question of where I stand.'

Harald put a hand on his shoulder and shook his head. 'No, you mistake me. I know you will fight. I mean, will you stand with me here, under my banner, at my side.'

Tostig relaxed, looking sheepish, and then he shook his head. 'I thank you for the offer, but no. I will fight with my men.'

'That is a fine answer.' He clapped the Saxon earl on the back and offered him his hand. 'I hope this battle brings you what you wish for, Earl Tostig. I wish you fortune and honour.'

Tostig took his hand. 'What if I no longer know what I wish for? If I am earl at the end of this battle, it is because my brother is dead. And if my brother lives, it is because I have fallen. What should I want?'

Harald nodded, thinking it over for a moment. 'I know what I would seek, but for you, I merely say I hope you find the answer before the end.'

Tostig gave Harald an odd look that I recognised well, because I had given it to Harald so many times before. Harald did not think like us, normal men like Tostig and me.

'What would you seek?' Tostig finally asked.

Harald smiled more broadly and let go of Tostig's hand. 'What I always seek:

to gain advantage for the next fight to come. In experience, in reputation, in wealth and position. I fight each battle so that I might win the next one more easily.'

Tostig's brows furrowed. 'And then what, to what end?'

'There is no end, Earl Tostig. There is always land beyond the horizon, and time beyond your days.'

'I don't understand. What is your goal?'

Harald nodded. 'That is why you need to find your own answer.' He looked down the hill, his blue eyes narrowing as horns blared from the Saxon lines. 'If you intend to stand with your men, now is the time. Your brother is ready.'

Tostig followed Harald's gaze, and I did too. The Saxons were spreading two formations of levies out left and right, preparing to envelop our citadel of shields. Half of their army was not yet across, but King Harold was wasting no time.

'He is bold, moving to surround us so quickly,' I said.

'He is inviting an attack on his centre,' Harald said, shaking his head slightly with admiration. 'So bold that I am tempted to indulge him.'

'Should we not?' Tostig asked.

'We should not,' Harald said. 'It is what he wants, therefore we will not do it.'

'What if he is relying on you thinking that, so that he can take outrageous risks knowing you will do nothing?' I asked.

'Then he is smart as well as bold. But it does not matter. I am doing what I wish and intended and will not allow myself to be led by the nose. We hold here, that is all there is. I want all his men across the river, and he is happy to bring them to me.'

I looked dubiously at the Saxons again, but I knew better than to argue further. Harald looked utterly serene and confident.

'I go, then. I will return if anything changes,' Tostig said. Harald barely nodded; he was busy watching the Saxons. It did not matter. The circle meant that Tostig's men were only a hundred yards away.

Harald looked back to where the clutch of his closest followers and officers stood under Land Waster. Stykarr was there, and Olaf his son. Even Tjodolv was there, armed and ready for battle.

'Son, come and stand at my side,' Harald said, beckoning Olaf over.

Olaf strode down proudly and stood on Harald's other side, almost in the shadow of the black raven banner.

'We have a little time, and I want to explain to you what our enemy is thinking, and what he will do next.'

'How do you know what our enemy is thinking?' Olaf asked, eagerly looking at his father.

Harald smiled his soft smile. 'That is what I want to teach you.'

* * *

It took a good while, but as the sun rose to its zenith, the Saxons finally had most of their army across the river and advanced to meet us. The formations on their flanks marched around out of bowshot, circling our fortress of shields so that they were on my left and right. The horsemen rode around to our rear, arraying on the flat land behind us facing Tostig and the men of Orkney and the Westlands.

And then the moment had arrived, and both armies were prepared. I wondered whether they would attack all at once or try and whittle us down. The answer came in the form of a storm of arrows from three sides and thrown spears and javelins from the horsemen behind.

'Get low! Shields and spears up!' roared Stykarr as the first missiles were launched. The whole army crouched down, hunkering behind their shields and pressing together to overlap as best as possible. The front rank's shields were practically on the ground, and the ranks behind held theirs overhead. It formed a formidable barrier to the missiles that were seeking to bury themselves in our flesh, but not proof enough.

In the shower of iron rain, and the clatter of iron and wood on shield and helm, there was almost at once a chorus of curses and shouts of agony, as some of the missiles slipped through gaps, or under rims, and found their mark.

The whole army shrank like wet wool in the sun, every man seeking to get deeper behind his shield and that of the man next to him.

The worst were the arrows, fired blindly, that skipped over the shield wall, crossed the space in the centre of our circle where Harald and his entourage stood inside a circle of his hird's shields, and landed in the rear of the wall the other side.

I think more men fell to those stray shots than the ones aimed true in the first moments, and the rear rank quickly learned to face the wrong way, putting their shields inwards, sheltering as best they could the soft unarmoured bodies of the ranks behind them.

It was a miserable thing, to be so helpless, and to hear the cries of the wounded and the dying, and the pant of the man next to you as you huddled together. My injured arm could not even hold a shield, so I knelt near Harald as our men protected us both. Olaf cried out in alarm as an arrowhead punched through his own shield and scored his forearm, but Harald just chuckled. 'That is a sign of good fortune in battle, if ever there was one.'

It was not true; no one said such a thing. He was just trying to steady his boy's nerves, for the prince was wide-eyed and breathing hard, as all men are in their first real battle.

It must have only continued for 200 heartbeats, but it felt ten times that before the deadly hail finally slackened and petered out, and we peered over our shields again to see if it was some trick or if the enemy had really run out of arrows.

'Stand!' called Stykarr, for the enemy was not wasting their time, and their lead formations were moving forwards towards us. Not at a charge, but in a careful, deliberate march, maintaining their wall. They were not coming to break us; they were coming to wear us down.

'They can only do that once. Break up and form in the centre. Be ready to respond to any break in the wall!' Harald shouted to his hird, and the men surrounding us in a crude blob stood and started moving.

'We can stand now, dammit,' I said to the warrior who had been covering my back. He was still leaning against me, pressing my knee into the mud. But the man didn't budge, so I swore and pushed him up and away from me, getting my second foot under myself and forcing myself upright.

I turned to give him a scowl as his weight left my back, but the warrior slumped to the ground as the press around us moved. He was dead, an arrow through his neck. We had all been packed so close together he had had no chance to fall where he died.

I stared at him in shock, and then the man next to him knelt and picked up the dead warrior's shield. He looked at me with cold, sad eyes, offering it to me. 'You need it more now, I think.'

I gestured to my injured arm. 'I can barely hold a shield.'

'Barely will be enough,' the warrior said emotionlessly as he pressed it into my hand. I winced at the weight of it but managed to close my fingers around the grip and not drop it.

I looked up to thank the warrior, but he was already walking away, moving with the rest of the hird to form up, leaving three dead men on the ground around me. Men who had not been so lucky as Olaf.

Harald was watching the oncoming enemy, and the first ones reached our wall nearest the river. They came with horns blaring and flags flying, roars in their throats and steel in their hands, and our men received them almost silently. They needed their strength for fighting, not shouting. It was a grim silence in our ranks that was broken only by the thunder of iron on wood and the ringing clatter of iron on iron as the true battle finally began.

I looked up, seeing that the sun was past its height. There was a bird there circling already, watching. Waiting. I stared at it, almost in jealousy. For that bird, the outcome was certain – a feast. The only question was how long it would be, and it was willing to wait.

That was the question for both of us, that bird and me. How long would it be before the battle was done? I said a small prayer that the black-winged beast would be disappointed for as long as possible and returned my gaze to the ground and looked around, sweeping my eyes across the entire circle.

Everywhere I could see, the wall was fighting. The Saxons had engaged the entire length of it with their first attack, and my whole world was reduced to a sea of struggling, swearing, fighting men.

I felt completely helpless.

* * *

That first attack lasted a long time. The Saxon first line wore themselves out on our wall, scraping at it, hacking at it, tearing souls from it one cut at a time. And each warrior that fell weakened it forever, and those that were still standing were made tired and weakened, from exertion or from injury.

Finally, the attack relented, and the surviving enemy retreated, leaving our men gasping and sweating under the relentless sun.

I looked out over the enemy centre, still near the river, where King Harold's griffon standard flew. He had thousands of armoured warriors with him, the cream of his army. None of them had even swung a blow, not even one had died. They would be hot and sweating in the sun, but they had the river at their backs and we were on a parched hill. We had taken all the water we could carry, but it would not suffice. I looked down at those ranks of killers calmly waiting for the time to finish us and I hated them. I hated them because I was sure that one among them would stand over my corpse in triumph.

I shook that dark thought away and watched Harald, who was circling the army, relentless in his energy, shouting encouragement and praise. I saw spirits raised as he passed, and he made sure everyone in the army had seen him close by, seen the sweat on his brow and the bloodied sword in his hand. I don't even know when he had been down to the fight; it would not surprise me if he had bloodied his blade on a corpse just to show the right effect.

It didn't matter. He rallied their spirits, and they cheered him hoarsely. Finally, he returned to where I stood under the banner with his son and his skald.

'The heat has done worse to them than the Saxons,' Harald said with a grim look. 'This English King has used his worst warriors and is exhausting my entire army.'

'But caused few enough casualties,' I said, with hope I was not sure I felt.

The enemy were withdrawing to rest, for no man could fight for long in that heat, but they were not retreating in panic, merely walking backwards in good order. Far from defeated.

'Tired men die more easily. This attack was just the start. Look, another comes.' Harald pointed, and I saw that, sure enough, the Saxons were sending another wave of men against us, almost everyone who had not fought in the first attack. I saw a big block of the armoured men around the King's standard marching forwards under another banner – a red banner with an image of a warrior in white, helm on his head, shield in his hand and axe held overhead.

'The enemy finally send their true warriors,' I said, pointing them out to Harald.

'We can meet them with our own and beat them,' Harald said. He turned to Stykarr. 'Strengthen that part of the wall. Bring Tostig's men if you have to.'

The back of the circle, where Tostig's men stood, had seen the lightest fighting. The Saxon horsemen there were unable to press an attack against a wall that refused to be lured out of position, eventually dismounting and fighting on foot in what amounted to little more than a skirmish.

Stykarr shouted at a runner to summon Tostig's men, and we watched the enemy come in again as our men reformed the wall and readied themselves for battle.

I glanced up at the sun. It was falling now – still high in the sky but undeniably heading towards the western horizon where it would eventually fade from view. I tried, for the tenth time, to calculate in my head where Eystein would be, if he was close. But the answer was always the same: there was no chance of him arriving yet. It was too far; he had not had long enough.

We needed more time. We had to repel this attack, and surely the next one afterwards.

The second attack landed harder than the first. The Saxons were using better-armed men – real warriors, not fyrdsmen – and they were mostly fresh.

Our wall started bleeding in earnest. Blood traded for time, flowing red and precious into the ground as our men gave their lives for Harald.

They started giving ground too, the circle shrinking as the attack hammered into our ranks. We took a heavy toll on the Saxons, of course. Don't believe for a moment that the enemy's blood flowed any less freely than ours did down that shallow slope into the river, turning its waters rusty-brown at the edge. But the Saxons had more blood to give, and every drop of it spilled was in their favour.

Harald stood watching carefully, judging where, if anywhere, the circle might weaken, ready to commit his hird. Then Tostig arrived with a clatter, hundreds of his mercenaries at his back.

'What do you need, King Harald?'

Harald pointed at the front of the wall, where the men of Trondelag under the banner of the Árnasson clan fought against the armoured enemy attack under the red banner of the white warrior. 'Put your men in the wall there! That is where the battle is being decided. I need my men fresh. Their time will come soon enough.'

Tostig grimaced. 'My mercenaries will not last long in that fight.'

'I don't need them to. Those armoured men cannot fight hard for long in this heat, and I need nothing more than targets for them to waste their strength on. Go, send them!'

Tostig frowned at the callousness of it, but shouted orders at the mercenary officers, who took their men forwards gamely enough. They were surrounded like all of us. They knew they had to fight to survive.

Tostig watched as the Flemish mercenaries and his few Saxon allies pushed forwards and got into the fighting, replacing our exhausted and denuded men, giving them a moment's respite.

The fighting surged anew with the fresh warriors pouring in, and the red banner of the enemy came forwards, a crowd of well-equipped enemy beneath it hacking their way into the Flemish wall, which resisted stubbornly but could not completely stem the assault.

'Whose banner is that? What is its meaning?' Harald asked Tostig, looking concerned.

'That is my brother's personal standard.' Tostig raised his sword and pointed. 'That is Harold fighting beneath it.'

Harald's eyes widened. 'That is King Harold, fighting at the front in the second attack?' He smiled appreciatively. 'A true king then, but perhaps foolish.' Harald turned to Tostig. 'I thought your brother's banner was the golden dragon?'

'No. That is the banner of Wessex, the banner of the King. The red banner is his personal standard, the one he always stands under in battle.'

'That is what it is called, the Fighting Man?'

Tostig nodded.

Harald beamed and shook his head in genuine appreciation. 'What a name for a banner. By the furies, what a man is your brother! The Fighting Man of Wessex? Ha! To finally have a great man such as this as my enemy... I tell you, Tostig, it is the joy of my life. Look at him!' Harald exclaimed, pointing as the red banner surged forwards, the knot of superb warriors at its base forcing themselves into our line, threatening to break it.

Tostig looked saddened. 'If you love him so much, perhaps it would have been better to be allies.'

Harald shook his head, never taking his eyes off the young English King as he and his guard cut into our ranks. 'No. Let me tell you what a wise man once told me: great men have no friends, only allies and enemies, who are frequently interchangeable.'

Tostig looked at Harald in consternation. 'Am I then not your friend?'

'No and take it as no insult. You are my ally, and a very good one.'

'So do you think I might so easily become your enemy?'

Harald finally tore his excited eyes from the fighting. 'I would have said so, until this morning, when you were given the chance to become my enemy and refused it. Now I know that you are one of the few men who cannot be so easily swayed.' He gave Tostig a respectful nod. 'Do not be offended, Tostig, when I say that you are not a great man like your brother or I, for you are a more valuable thing: a good man. Men like you, and Eric here, and all these great lords of Norway around me, you are what makes kingdoms and armies. Your brother and I – there is no limit to what we would do to win, no sacrifice we would not make. In this whole island of England there is only space for one great man, as the mere existence of another is intolerable to us.'

Tostig looked at Harald in something approaching fear and revulsion as Harald talked with animated gestures while men died by the dozen just fifty paces away. I smiled a little, because I recognised Tostig's horror. I had experienced it myself.

'So as you said, one of us must die, and I can know that and love him despite it, for he is clearly a man worthy of admiration.'

'Admiration? He exiled his own brother, drove me from my lands and my country and forced me to return with a foreign army just to claim what is mine by right!'

Harald nodded, his smile never fading. 'As I said, we have no friends, and no limit to what we will sacrifice. Tell me, why did he exile you? It was not for hatred of you, was it?'

Tostig shook his head sullenly. 'It was to maintain his position, ready to take the throne when it became available.'

Harald inclined his head. 'You see? If it helps you, he probably cares for you, Tostig. He simply loves power more.'

I could see from Tostig's grim expression that did not help at all, but Harald would not have understood and did not see it as he had turned back to the battle.

The enemy assault was slackening, the armoured men moving sluggishly and lethargically as the ranks of the Flemish struggled against them.

Finally, the banner of the Fighting Man withdrew, and the second attack ended.

Harald finally tore himself away from watching the enemy retreat, and looked around our battered army, which stood still resolute upon the crest, but painfully degraded. The ground inside the wall was littered with the dying and the dead, and the ground outside was thick with bodies, ours and theirs in equal measure. Thousands had died. The lifeblood of Norway's finest men was soaking into the Saxon soil, while their army was still massive, still organised, and clearly ready to continue the fight.

Harald did not appear concerned.

'Distribute what water we have. Bring the wounded into the centre. They will attack again shortly.'

'Where is Eystein?' Olaf asked nervously, looking south at the empty fields beyond the battle.

Harald did not follow his gaze. 'Do not be concerned, my son, he is coming. All we need to do is hold.'

I looked up at the sun; it was halfway down now, still bright and hot, but the shadows were lengthening. Where was Eystein? *He might be close now*. That is what I told myself. If he had marched immediately, and marched hard, he might be close. All he needed was a little more time. We just had to bleed a little more time into that rich soil.

Just a little more precious, blood-reddened time.

20

'They are coming!' someone called from in front.

I looked up, even my eyes feeling sluggish, tired as I was in that heat. And I had not even fought; God knows how the warriors in the wall got to their feet, even though most of them were so much younger than me.

The enemy had reformed their formations, and I could see that this time every man they had was prepared, their entire army.

We had fought off their third attack, which had been from the same tired formations of levies that had conducted the first. But now their best troops were rested, formed up and ready to come at us again.

'This is the final attack,' I said to no one, for no one was close enough to hear.

The day was fading. My shadow was longer than I was tall, and Harold of Wessex was coming to finish the battle. The golden dragon of Wessex and the Fighting Man of Harold fluttered above the centre of the biggest formation, the one that King Harold had reserved for this death blow.

He had worn us down, weakened us, bled us and tired us. But now the dance of battle was coming to a close, and Eystein was nowhere to be seen. I had hoped he would have arrived by then. He *should* have arrived. I began to think that he was not coming at all. It was possible the messengers were intercepted and never reached him, or that Harold had sent another force to destroy our fleet and that even now the bodies of Eystein's men lay around their burning ships.

It was possible that we were alone.

Harald had only one weapon left to him unused: his hird. Nearly 400 of the greatest warriors in the circle of the world, standing patiently under Land Waster, waiting for their chance to seize victory for their King once more. If they felt my despair, they did not show it. None of them had ever known defeat under Harald's banner. It had been twenty-five years since any foe won the field against Harald, and he had never truly been beaten even then.

That was the hope I clung to – that Harald always found a way. In the black marsh of the Rus, we had come from the darkness and snatched victory from an enemy who believed us dead. In the plains south of Kyiv we had survived a week of being hunted by the mighty Pecheneg, dealing them a sharp blow in return and sending them fleeing from the steppe. In the Holy Land we had defended Theodora against hopeless odds, Varangians dying in turn to protect her until we were delivered. In Sicily we had taken fortresses that could not be taken and defeated armies twice our size.

In the valley of the Varangians Harald had seized an impossible victory, cutting through an army of 60,000 and slaying their rebel emperor by his own hand.

Harald had defeated them all, and a dozen more enemies besides. He *could* lose, I knew that, but he *would* not. He simply would not allow it. Harald always found a way.

The shield wall reformed as the enemy came at us, a smaller and thinner circle than it had once been, with broken shields and gore-smeared weapons, dirty helmets no longer shining in the sun. It looked like an army of the dead, but they were very much alive and defiant, and they put their chests towards the enemy and stood shoulder to shoulder.

I went to stand with Harald. I had nothing else to do. There was no advice I could give, no plan I could concoct. All that was left to me was to stand at his side, as I had done for all of those years, and hope he could find a way to victory.

He was no longer smiling, no longer wallowing in his own confidence. He looked grim and drained. His eyes were still bright as they turned to me. 'I am sorry, Eric, I think you might have to fight this time. I think every one of us will have to fight.'

I nodded emotionlessly. My borrowed shield was lying on the ground somewhere, its weight too much for my injured arm to hold all day. But it didn't matter. I would find another – the ground was littered with equipment abandoned by the dead and wounded. We had more spare shields than we had uninjured men.

'I thought Eystein would be here,' Harald lamented. 'We held, we held, but he is not here.'

His voice sounded hollow, and I was shocked.

'He is coming,' I said, forcing myself to show the confidence Harald's great heart had somehow lost.

Harald just stared at me. 'Perhaps. I am not sure it matters now.' He looked out bitterly at the advancing enemy, who were nearly at our wall. 'This attack may be the last.'

I grabbed Harald's elbow, jerking him towards me, forcing him to face me eye to eye, or as close as possible with a man so much taller. 'These men are expecting you to deliver victory. How can you expect them to have faith in you when you do not show faith in them?'

Harald's eyes widened at the rebuke, and he pulled my fingers from his arm with childish ease, but he straightened and nodded. 'You are right. And thank you, I needed that.'

'Good. They are your words,' I growled.

He nodded and smiled softly. 'I know. I am right sometimes.' And then his smile faded. 'I hope you are right about Eystein. But I fear I gave him too long to march, and not enough time to do so. I was a fool to accept a meeting here, so far from our ships. I have killed us all.'

'It doesn't matter now. Save your self-loathing for later. You are about to send these men behind us to fight and die for you. At least look like you don't think it is for nothing,' I hissed, keeping my voice low even over the din of the armies around us.

Harald gave me a scorching look but dipped his chin just once. 'As you say.'

Well, that was as close to taking orders from me as Harald ever got. It gave me a shiver of energy just to hear it.

Then the enemy attack arrived, their whole army against ours. The cacophony of battle overtook us, and the army of Norway started killing and dying again.

* * *

It was not long before we could see that the main enemy attack, under King Harold's personal banners, was going to be the decisive blow. We had strengthened the wall facing them as much as possible, putting the men of the Westlands in alongside the men of Orkney and Trondelag, but it was not enough. Several thousand armoured huskarls, the cream of the Saxon army, were attacking all at once under their twin banners, and our circle started bowing inwards towards the centre under their irresistible pressure.

Harald watched it carefully and looked around the rest of the army. Everywhere else was holding. There were no men left out of the fight except his hird. The moment had arrived.

He did not give a speech or speak to the ranks of his personal warriors. We were too close to the fighting for him to be heard more than a few paces away, and there was nothing to be said. They all knew what was needed of them. They all knew what it would cost.

They didn't care. Let me tell you, it did not deter them. I think they relished it – the chance to die for their King and, perhaps, to be the ones who gained another of his famous victories, the ones the skalds would sing about for generations to come.

Harald looked at them, and then at the battle, and finally he took his son by the arm and came to me. Olaf looked terrified, and Harald looked suddenly calm and serene.

He put Olaf right next to me so that we could both hear him speaking without having to raise his voice.

He clasped his hand on my shoulder and smiled at me softly, lovingly, his eyes two pools of calm amidst the screaming and the death. 'Eric, you stay with my son. Look after him, in whatever follows.'

Then he took his other hand and clasped his son's shoulder as my legs shook, for I knew the words he would speak next.

'Listen to Eric. He will keep you safe. Mind his words, for even now, he is wise beyond his years.'

Olaf nodded, not fully understanding. How could he? Those words only held true meaning to me and to Harald: they had been the last words his brother and king had said to us, all those years ago at Stiklestad. And now Harald said them to me.

Harald looked between us, utterly calm and smiling, all the weight lifted from him as the battle raged around us and blood flowed from his loyal men, so much blood, so much time, and yet not enough.

That was when I knew he had accepted that he would probably die, that he was happy with it, even revelling in it. All his life Harald had been searching for something to quench the anguish of his brother Olaf's death.

He had retaken his brother's throne, wrought vengeance on his killers, united Norway and fought a dozen campaigns against his enemies. But it had never been enough, it had never satisfied him, even though he had exceeded his brother in power, glory, victory and wealth. He had never been satisfied.

But there, in that moment, he had found the chance to match his brother in the final way: to die as Olaf had, and to leave his son with the same words his brother had left him. And in that final decision, he had finally found his peace.

'Harald,' I croaked, shaking my head firmly. 'Don't.'

He may have accepted it, but I had not. I could not. I was not done. I was not ready to let him fail! I had given my whole life to him, to his ambitions. I was not ready to simply let him give up.

He smiled at me and pointed down at the fighting. 'There stands the King of England, and all I must do is slay him and this battle is won.'

'He has 4,000 against your 400. You cannot!'

'Fear not. I can,' he said, soothing me, lying to me. 'One way or another, my men have given enough while I watch. It is my time to fight. I will go down there to that brave English king, and we will end this.'

'You cannot do this, Harald.'

'I will and I must,' he said with finality.

I wanted to argue, but what power had I to stop him?

None. I was helpless, furious and helpless, because Harald had bound me to his son with words that he knew I could not refuse.

He nodded at me a final time and kissed his son on the forehead, then he turned and walked away towards his hird, stopping in front of them. All their eyes were on him. They stood proud in their ranks as Harald raised his sword to signal them, and they cheered thunderously as he pointed it at the banner of the Fighting Man.

Down the slope they went, those magnificent men, those glorious heroes, with Harald at their head. Stykarr went with him, and Tjodolv and all his other entourage. Every single one of them. Everyone except Olaf and me, for Harald had given me a sacred and final command: to keep his son safe. Harald's legacy survived as long as his son did.

'Why aren't we going with them?' Olaf said, looking at me in confusion.

I looked at him and wrestled with it. There was no safety in the circle; if the army broke, we would die there as easily as we would die down with the hird. My mind hardened around the decision.

'Because you are your father's legacy, and he needs you to survive.' I looked at him. 'But your path is your own to decide, and I will not stand here while he fights. Come with me. Stay behind me and do nothing reckless. We go to stand with your father.'

Olaf nodded and I drew my sword, heading down the slope on the heels of Harald's men, snatching a shield from the ground as I went. I had walked the whole earth with Hardrada, and I was not going to stand back and watch him take those last steps alone.

Harald's men went forwards with Land Waster flying proudly in the gentle breeze, and even as the enemy assault broke through the exhausted men of the front line, his hird let out a thunderous shout and hammered into the enemy attack, axes flashing and shields battering, with reckless rage.

They did not spread out to reform the wall. They did not stop and hold. They had one goal only – to help Harald reach the King of England and cut him down, and they pushed into the stunned Saxon ranks like a spear into a gut. The banners of the black raven and the Fighting Man came almost close enough to touch in the ferocity of that first impact, before the armoured ranks of the massive Saxon force recovered and steadied themselves.

I got into the mass behind Harald, seven or eight men behind him, Olaf tucked into my right side behind me. I could see Harald over the heads of the rest, roaring and carving his way into the armoured Saxon ranks with a ferocity they were not willing, or able, to match.

He lay into them without pause, and his men guarded his flanks with their lives, even as the Saxon huskarls ripped into them, for they were every bit the match for us. We were fresh, they were armoured, and it was a devastatingly even fight.

But an even fight amongst warriors of that ferocity and skill is a terrible, terrible slaughter. This was not a wall fight, a pushing of lines of shields. Neither side had formed a wall, neither side was interested in the slow grind of one. Both forces were trying to end the battle with a single attack, and so the fight was a terrifying brawl, where great warriors with experience in a dozen battles were slain by the bushel and blood misted into the air like deathly rain.

Yet our men kept pushing forwards, even as the flanks of our attack stalled and frayed. They kept pushing forwards, cutting and stabbing, kicking and stamping. Bleeding for every pace of blood-soaked earth they gained. All to get Harald to the Saxon King, so that he could end it.

The best of Harald's men died in their dozens to get him to that red banner with the Fighting Man of Wessex, and yet he strode among them untouched, slaying enemies to his front without pause. At some point he lost his sword and ripped a great axe from a Saxon's hands and cut him down with it, kicking another enemy back and bringing the axe down so hard on the man's head that he killed him through his helmet.

I was only three men behind Harald now, partly because I was forcing my way through the ranks, and partly because so many men in front of me had died to the axes and swords of those fearsome huskarls.

Enough men in both ranks died that suddenly I saw King Harold of the Saxons standing beneath his banner. He was motionless, watching Hardrada carving a path towards him while Saxon knights vied to get between their King and the attack that was coming, as bravely throwing themselves into the slaughter as Harald's own men were.

There were only twenty paces between them now, and Harald showed no sign of flagging. Although I could see he had wounds on his arms and chest, they were not slowing him.

Harald was now bleeding into the sodden ground himself, and it was not time he was trying to win with his blood sacrifice, but an end to all of it.

A spear lanced out at him, perfectly timed between blows, straight and true for his stomach, but somehow he knocked it off course with the shaft of his axe and it only scored his thigh. Harald roared and took a half step forward, using the angle of the axe to cut diagonally down from the high side towards the spearman, who looked shocked as the axe tore out his throat, unable to comprehend how quickly his winning blow had been defeated and reversed.

The Saxon fell to the ground in a heap and Harald grunted, testing his wounded leg while I batted away another spear to try and get my shield to his side.

But Harald did not wait for me, nor did his leg seem to slow him – he simply advanced again, with a half dozen of his hird hacking their way forwards to stay with him, shoving and clawing past me to do so even as I screamed curses at them.

I wanted to be with him, I wanted to fight with him, but my body was too slow and too old, and those young men were equally desperate to stand with their King.

Harald knew of none of this – he was focused on his goal, his axe rising and falling, swinging in arcs, punching out with the tip of the blade at eyes and throats, blocking blows with the splintered haft.

Still he cut men down with impunity, every bit the lord of war that I had known from our time in the empire, and brave men cringed from his size, power and the ferocity of his attack. His stolen axe-head ran red with blood in the afternoon sun and its movement never ceased. He was carving his way to Harold, and Saxons and Norwegians alike died in his wake, paving his way with the bodies of the fallen.

All to reach the enemy King, to bring the battle to an end. I started to believe in him. I roared and I shoved and I fought my way to be at his side. To be there at the end, to be there when he faced the Fighting Man of Wessex.

I could see the Saxon King waiting to receive him, that brave man. Resting and preserving his strength, watching the storm of Harald's attack inch ever closer. I saw his guards urge him to retreat, and I saw the English King shake his helmeted head firmly. He was going to face the storm; he believed he could weather it.

I reached Harald's back again when we were only ten paces from the Saxon King, because so few of his men nearby were still alive or able to advance with him. I cursed and swore as a wounded Saxon tried to cut at me, trying to get my shield up to guard Harald's flank, even though my arm screamed with pain. I could not get my sword around properly so I kicked at the desperate Saxon, who was so close in the press of combat that I could smell his breath, and I could see his wild, pain-filled eyes and the blood dribbling across his bared teeth.

He grunted and fell back half a step, so I brought my pommel down on the bridge of his nose and he disappeared from view.

I looked back to the enemy King. We were so close. Olaf was fighting now, on Harald's right, and I do not think the King noticed, for surely he would have sent his son back. I considered going to drag the foolish boy back out of danger, but I was the only man guarding Harald's left flank and Olaf had a half dozen of

Harald's men around him. I hoped they would have the sense to keep the boy alive.

I fended off a spear that was seeking Harald's side and someone to my left cut the spearman down with a victorious howl. Harald took another step forwards, and suddenly there was no enemy on the other side of my shield, and only five paces of open ground in front of us.

We were close, the enemy King was *there*. Harald had his chance to end it, to win his greatest victory and become King of all of England. He paused, just for a moment, perhaps to catch his breath, as he stared at Harold of Wessex.

There was a dark blur of motion and a soft thump. I felt Harald's back twitch against my shoulder as an arrowhead sprouted from the back of his neck, near his spine. I was so close that his blood speckled my face. I could taste it in my mouth.

He just stopped, his axe slowly falling from his hands. He swayed on his feet even as I failed to understand what had happened. Then my King toppled backwards, falling into me, tangling with my shield and knocking my sword from my hand as he fell to the ground. I collapsed at his side, scrambling to get up and kneel over him.

His confused face looked up at me and his hands scrabbled at the arrow that was protruding from his neck. Blood was frothing at his lips, but he was still breathing.

The enemy saw and pressed in, shouting in excitement, and Harald's men roared in outrage and surged forwards to protect his prostrate form.

I had lost my sword, but it did not matter. I did not need it. I grabbed Harald's tunic with my empty hand and put my shield over him. My stomach churned and panic threatened to overwhelm me.

'Pull him back!' I shouted desperately, not knowing who would hear me, but someone did, and we started dragging the big man back.

Blows were hammering on my shield, which I could barely hold up on my injured arm, but the pain did not matter. I had to get Harald back, I didn't know if the wound was fatal, but regardless, I had to get him back. Blows were also landing on Harald's legs, but there was nothing I could do to stop that, so I just kept pulling him with all my strength.

The remaining warriors of the hird threw themselves into the rush of armoured enemy to stop them hacking at Harald and there was a terrible slaughter all around me. But more came, more and more brave and loyal men, heedless of anything except saving their King, giving their lives for him without question, throwing themselves onto the steel of the enemy to give their King a chance at survival.

We dragged him back, further and further. An axe-blow shattered my shield and broke my injured shield arm, but it did not matter. I did not need it any more. Tjodolv appeared, grim-faced, and got his shield over Harald's legs.

'Pull!' he shouted, and I leant into it with all the strength I had left. Olaf leaned in and grabbed Harald's belt, and the King gurgled and pawed at us, trying to stop us. I didn't know why and I didn't care. I wasn't leaving him for the Saxons.

I just kept pulling, dragging him along the ground to escape the fighting as his men died in a rearguard defence, but the enemy were rampant and they were desperate to finish Harald off and claim his body. Above me, almost shading me from the sun, the banner of the Fighting Man of Wessex loomed, mocking me. The King of England had come to finish his foe.

I despaired, but all I could do was pull.

A spear lanced into my leg and I felt it go numb below the knee, but I could still put weight on it, and I was leaning on my other leg. It didn't matter; I just needed to keep hold of his tunic and keep pulling. I just had to keep moving.

My injured leg buckled. Harald's frenzied hand grabbed at me, pawing at my tunic as the enemy crowded us. Tjodolv was fighting back now. They were so close and Harald was staring at me, trying to say something, but the arrow had taken his voice if not his life, and his face was full of anger and frustration.

It didn't matter. I couldn't have heard him even if he had spoken, and his banner had fallen, lost behind the Saxon ranks somewhere. I looked up at them as they came for us, those armoured men with their joyful eyes, joyful at the prospect of finishing the great Hardrada. There was a moment of calm as I realised what it must have been like for all those enemies we had faced in the empire, for those huskarls looked very much like Varangians. Lying on the ground, half-draped over Harald, I had a moment of clarity as I faced the fate that we had delivered to so many enemies over the years.

I watched helpless, defeated and broken, as the banner of the Fighting Man of Wessex towered over us, and the King of England and his armoured men came to finish their task. Behind me, I heard shouting, and I heard Olaf's protesting voice fading as someone dragged him away.

I smiled. That was good. I was glad that Olaf would survive my death, even if it was only by a little.

Someone grabbed me, trying to drag me back in the chaos, and I lost my grip on Harald. For a moment no one had him, and I thrashed and raged at the unknown man to let me go, to let me get back to Harald.

But he did not hear me or did not heed me, and then a rush of huskarls arrived and he was cut down above me, falling on top of me and rolling onto my legs as he died.

I watched in distraught helplessness, wriggling with one working arm and leg against the body pinning my legs until a Saxon thumped me on the back of the head with his axe-haft to persuade me to remain still.

A dozen of the huskarls gathered around my wounded King, fighting off any attempt by our men to get to us, and the hatred of him was clear. Many of them were Danish mercenaries, you remember, and Harald was ten times the enemy to the Danes as he was to the English, who barely knew him. They all relished his death.

They cleared the last of our men away and made half a ring around Harald as the Saxon King stepped forwards and stood over him, regarding him with curiosity with a tilted head, sword in hand.

Hardrada levered himself half up on one elbow, his legs shattered and useless, snarling and staring, the two foes facing each other down as battle raged around that small clearing in the chaos. Harald glared defiantly at the English King, coughing and bubbling, never taking his eyes off him, perhaps never believing that it was possible that he could truly lose.

I forced myself to watch as Harold of Wessex set his feet and raised the bloodied sword into the air and held it there for a moment, the red banner and white warrior hanging in the sky behind as if bearing witness.

I cried out Harald's name, the strength to do anything but watch gone from my body, weeping at my own weakness for not being able to put myself between my King and his enemies. Between that bloodied sword and Harald's prostrate form.

And then the sword fell.

And my King died.

And an age ended.

21

I collapsed onto my back and waited for death, insensate to what was happening around me.

So I did not see Tostig and some men of Upplond arrive and drive the over-stretched huskarls back, did not see Harold of Wessex being pulled back to safety by his guards and abandoning the body of his dead rival.

I did not hear Tostig shouting orders to the survivors of Harald's hird to pick his body up and carry him back, but I felt their hands under my armpits when they came for me, and I shouted and raged feebly at them as they dragged me away.

They carried us both back from the fighting and Tostig led another charge of the men of Upplond to earn us more room. He died in front of me as I watched, helpless, when the massed huskarls countercharged his brave but doomed act of resistance. Don't let anyone ever say that Tostig was a weak or treacherous man. You tell them that when all other men would have laid down their banner, Earl Tostig Godwinson did what I had failed to do, and he died for Hardrada.

The Saxons advanced again once Tostig and his brave charge were expended, and there was nothing left to stop them. All around us the tattered remains of the army were dying, falling back into the centre of the charnel house that was the crest of that ridge. There was nowhere to run when they reached the middle, so men died where they stood, or simply lay down and waited for the end.

Everyone knew that Land Waster had fallen and not been recovered, and they all knew what it meant.

The enemy paused, taking their breath. They were probably, I realised later, about to offer us terms to end the bloodshed with surrender. But we did not know that, so we sat there atop that hill in our misery as the little that remained of our forces huddled together and tried to make some sort of wall of those who could still stand and fight.

Tjodolv, who was badly wounded, sat morosely by the King, staring at his body. 'He deceived us. Look at the price we have paid! He has died for nothing. His life of great deeds is ended and we with him.'

Well, you wondered why I hated him, and the truth is I always disliked him, but while other men died for Harald even after his death, Tjodolv – who I think only ever followed Harald to bathe in his glory and for his own fame – insulted him and pronounced him to be a deceiver and a fool.

I do not even care if he was right, but saying it then, to those suffering men around him, was unforgivable. He died sometime later in the battle from his wounds. I do not know when and I do not care. For me he died when he spoke out against his dead King as we mourned over his body. Curse his soul.

The jarls of Orkney appeared, bloodied but alive, and they had Olaf with them. I felt a moment of guilt, for I had not known where Olaf was for a while, and I had promised to stay at his side and protect him. But what could I do? Leave my dying King to stand by his son?

Well, yes. That is exactly what Harald wanted me to do, asked me to do… Regardless, I did not and you may judge me for it as you like. Others have before you.

Then we heard the Saxon horns blaring, and for a while nothing happened. They did not attack us, nor approach us to talk of peace. I sat there, confused and disappointed, for I was ready and hopeful for death to spare me the shame and the pain. Then I saw the mass of Harold's armoured huskarls turning and reforming, facing across the slope towards the south. Much of the Saxon army was hurriedly realigning in that direction and panicked-looking horsemen were riding to and fro, shouting orders and gesturing to the south.

'Eystein is here!' someone shouted.

I tried to stand but could not, so I could not see far enough to see over the crest to the south. But then I heard it – beyond the chatter of the warriors around me, and beyond the din of battle. I heard another peal of horns beyond the Saxon lines. They were our horns, I could tell.

'Get me up!' I shouted, and someone came over and helped me to stand on my uninjured leg.

There, in the south, I saw the glittering of armoured ranks and the 3,000 men of Eystein Orre were arraying into a single battle formation, facing the still much larger Saxon army, preparing to attack.

God, how I wish I could have called out to them, told them Harald was dead and to make terms, not waste their lives against the Saxon lines. But I do not think they would have listened even if they could have heard me. The men around me cheered weakly and waved their weapons in the air, the few banners we had left standing proud. To Eystein it must have appeared that Harald was still holding on. Even if he could not see Land Waster flying, he must have believed Harald still lived.

I found it hard to accept Harald was dead, and I was standing over his body.

'We must go to them,' Erlend Thorfinnsson said, looking around. His brother shook his head.

'We cannot move from here – we are more wounded than living. Perhaps less than a thousand men who can fight, and all the Saxon army between us!'

They argued for a short time, and other men joined in, but the Saxons decided the matter for us when they sent several thousand of their battered levies to guard us.

I say guard us because they did not really attack. They were almost as badly mauled as us, and beyond a few desultory attempts to finish us off, they mostly just surrounded us and prevented us from moving. Prisoners in all but name.

So we could do nothing but watch as Eystein attacked.

And what an attack it was. They were outnumbered, and they were as exhausted as the Saxons, if not carrying wounds. They had marched fifteen miles in the heat and in armour without stopping. I hear tales that they left a trail of men who collapsed from exhaustion and died where they fell in the latter stage, where Eystein had them almost at a run.

What fabulous men they were, and how glorious was their assault on the killers of Hardrada. It was a tragedy, a pointless gesture, but men will speak of their valour for a thousand years, and that is worthy.

I cannot tell you anything about the fighting; for me, it was almost a smear on the short horizon, but some of the few who lived to tell of it have done so, and it is called Orre's Storm with good reason.

They charged straight at the English King's centre and almost broke it. Three thousand of Eystein's men attacked perhaps eight thousand Saxons, and they nearly won. They and the Saxon huskarls fought to a standstill and the carnage on both sides was terrible, for they were so evenly matched.

But eventually the Saxons manoeuvred their larger force around Eystein's flanks, and his men were slowly slaughtered. It pains me to think of it, watching from that hill, as helpless as I had been when the Saxons killed Harald, when we saw the last of Eystein's banners fall, and the banners of the golden dragon and the Fighting Man fluttering over the survivors unchallenged.

Eystein died there, as did almost everyone else. I think fewer than 300 of his 3,000 survived.

Those men died for Harald not knowing it was already too late. The glory and the greatness of that is only matched by its terrible sadness. What men were those, and what they could have achieved if they survived to return home. You all know this, for some of them were your fathers and grandfathers, men who never came home to teach you the ways of war.

And then it was over. We had been defeated, in the most terrible defeat Norway ever suffered, even if it was the boldest and most courageous. Whatever you say of those men, and whatever we think of their actions, remember them with honour, for they were brave and loyal and none of us are worthy to say a bad word of their memories. Men such as them built Norway into the nation we live in today. So honour them with your words, and make sure others do the same. They died for what they believed in: courage and loyalty. What more needs to be said?

* * *

After the fighting ended, the jarls of Orkney agreed terms with Harold's emissaries – that we would leave and never return. So we took everyone who still drew breath and we went home. We did not even bury our dead – it was impossible, for they outnumbered us nearly ten to one. We filled twenty-seven ships, and left nearly three hundred behind, such was the scale of the loss.

Prince Olaf was allowed to leave with us, probably because the Saxons did not know who he was. We took him home and we crowned him alongside his brother, and the two of them ruled peacefully and without conflict until Magnus's untimely death just three years later.

The tragedy only deepened when we learned that Maria, Harald's beloved daughter, had died on the same day as her father and husband-to-be. Somehow, her heart had known of their deaths, and it had failed from the grief of it. Perhaps it was a blessing that she did not live in that misery.

Norway's strength was gone for a generation, and I watched it die. Don't think that I resent the shame you feel on my behalf, for I have felt a lifetime of it. I should have died there on that field with my King, but fate was not kind enough, or I was not strong enough. Either way, I shall not relate the tale of our surrender, or the sad journey home. I came here to tell you the story of Hardrada's life, and care not to tell you of the events that came after his death.

You all know it, and it is not my story to tell.

All that is left to me is to tell you how great those men were, my glorious and fallen brothers, and how much I loved my King, and how I regret not dying with him. I would like to claim that I stayed alive in order to watch over his son and protect his legacy, but I think that is a lie. I think I simply ran out of strength. Strength of the mind, strength of the body. I was not killed because those Saxons around me did not even consider me a threat, pathetic and prostrate as I was. That is the final insult, in many ways, and I live with it still.

But although that was the end of Harald's life, it was not the end of his story. He knew, as I do now, that a man's true worth is measured by his legacy – what he leaves behind. Harald and his bloodline have built the country of Norway we proudly live in today. Norway is united like never before, because his brother, his nephew and he himself united it, and his son and grandson have maintained it. We are wealthier, holier, more respected than ever before. Those things and more are Harald's true worth, not the years of his life or the manner of his death.

Harald's legacy lives and breathes today, both in his son – wise King Olaf, who was at his side when he died – and in his grandson King Magnus, and in the men who fill these benches, proud and full of the stories of his life. Harald will not truly die until his legacy dies, and so I have spent the rest of my life defending it, telling his story, protecting his achievements and his family. I tell you this story so that you can repeat it, and those you tell it to can repeat it. In such a way may he never truly die.

I have learned to live with the shame of surviving his death, and I have become content with relating his story and defending his legacy. I do this not for myself – my name will be forgotten to history – but for Harald, because he was worthy of it, because I was sworn to it, and because I refuse to allow his achievements to fail, for in their failure, my own life and efforts would have been wasted. I dedicated my life to his, and that duty never ends.

His was not an easy life, nor everything he wanted it to be. He was not without failings, and his failings threatened to ruin everything he ever achieved. But in his wisdom, his ambition and his ability, a greater man I never met, and in my travels, I met them all. It was my place merely to stand by his side when it mattered, and to be his protector when he needed it.

They call me Eric the Follower, and I swear to you, despite all my own failings, I *earned* that name. For I walked the earth with King Harald Hardrada, and now, finally, you all know what that means.

22

TINGHAUGEN, NORWAY; SPRING 1098 AD

Eric sat heavily as the hall erupted into the thumping of hands, feet and drinking vessels on wood and earth. He looked exhausted, drained and grief-stricken, but he smiled and acknowledged the grateful crowd with a wave.

Magnus stood and clapped his hands together until the room stilled. 'Wonderful. Thank you, Eric, for your telling of Harald's campaign to England and his final battle. I have heard it many times before, but it is heart-warming to hear of his courage and skill in battle from one who stood beside him, and of his achievements and wisdom as king. We will drink to their memory, and as Eric bids us we will tell the stories of their courage for as long as we live. I swear it.' Magnus beamed at Eric as if there had never been any tension or disagreement between them.

Magnus looked out at the crowd and beamed at them. 'And now, men of Trondelag, we feast!'

There was a thundering cheer around the room, and the door at the back of the room opened, revealing a line of servants and cooks bringing in a seemingly endless procession of platters, bowls and then a half dozen roast boars, still steaming on their spits.

The servants fought their way through the packed hall, batting away hands as if they were children so they could set the food on the tables, where the men eagerly dived in to claim their share.

Magnus ate with his lords and chatted with them cheerfully as the feast began, and Eric sat with Ingvarr and Hakon and looked drained.

He turned away most of the offered food, merely nibbling on some bread and a little roast boar.

'Are you well, Eric?' Hakon asked with concern.

Eric smiled weakly. 'I think the labour of these days speaking has exhausted me beyond my expectation.' He nodded to himself. 'I think I must rest.'

Hakon looked downcast. 'Now? Before the feast is done? But men will want to speak to you, ask questions.'

Eric looked pained. 'That is exactly what I intend to avoid. I can return and speak to them later; this feast will last well into the night.' He gripped the table and levered himself unsteadily to his feet. 'But for now, my lord, the ravages of age...'

'I will escort you from the hall. It is difficult enough to move in here,' Hakon said.

'I would appreciate it,' Eric replied, and Hakon gave Eric a shoulder to steady himself. They carefully made their way through the crowded hall to the side door. Ingvarr watched them a little and then saw Magnus watching Eric leave before the King leaned over to Jarl Halfdan and spoke to him. The jarl nodded and left the room.

As Ingvarr was watching, the King's gaze suddenly turned back to the room, scanning the area where Eric had been sitting quickly, before resting on him.

Ingvarr was rooted to the spot as the King pointed to him and beckoned him over.

Ingvarr's heart pounded and he looked around and behind him to check the King really meant him, but no one else was paying attention. The King nodded and waved his hand impatiently again, so Ingvarr broke from his stupor and trotted over.

'My lord Magnus,' he sputtered, bowing deeply.

'Eric has already gone?'

'Yes, my lord. He is tired.'

'Hmm, I was hoping to speak to him and share a drink. He is very fond of Greek wine, you see.'

'Uh, yes, my King.'

Magnus smiled. 'Maybe you could do me a favour, young man.'

Ingvarr nodded. 'Of course.'

Jarl Halfdan arrived at that moment bearing a jug and a fine silver cup. The King took the cup and Halfdan poured some wine into it.

The King offered the cup to Ingvarr. 'Take this to Eric as a gift from me. He will appreciate it. A little wine can rejuvenate a man's spirits, especially good wine such as this. It is my personal supply.'

Ingvarr's eyes widened and he carefully took the cup, which was worth more than everything he owned. 'Yes, Lord King, I will take it to him. I am sure he will appreciate it.'

Magnus smiled and sat up again. 'Good lad.'

Ingvarr took the hint as the King broke eye contact and turned, carefully hurrying from the hall.

* * *

Eric was sitting on the stool in his room, exhausted, throat hoarse and legs shaking from the exertion of his day of speaking. He rubbed his knotted old thighs with hands that would not fully unclench, and he moaned a little at the dull ache it elicited. He had never felt so old, but underneath it all he was happy.

There was a knock at the door and he looked up in surprise, and with a little unexpected spark of fear.

'Yes?'

The door opened and a boy appeared in the doorframe.

'Ah, Ingvarr. What is it?'

Ingvarr stepped into the light from the oil lamp on the shelf near the bed and proffered the cup. 'It is a gift from the King. Greek wine from his own supply.'

He placed the silver goblet carefully down next to the oil lamp, and Eric smiled. 'Ah, very good of our King.' He sighed and looked at the cup with a wistful smile. 'I do like a little good Greek wine, especially before bed.' He laughed to himself. 'The King knows my weakness.'

But then he looked up. 'I am very tired, however, so perhaps I should not.'

Ingvarr frowned. 'Oh. Uh, what should I tell the King?'

Eric looked a little perplexed. 'Why would you tell him anything?'

'Well... he asked me to give this to you.'

'What, he asked you personally?'

Ingvarr nodded. 'That is what I said.'

Eric looked at him oddly. 'I thought you meant he sent it to you with a servant or something, but he gave this to you, from his own hand?'

Ingvarr nodded, and Eric looked at the wine again. 'That is... generous. It would be rude to refuse him, and of course I would not expect you to have to admit the gift was rejected.' He took the cup and looked at it before taking a good draught. His wizened face creased with pleasure, and he smacked his cracked lips together. 'Ahh, I do like a good Greek wine.'

He looked at Ingvarr and gave him a wink.

The boy turned to leave, but stopped and then looked back at Eric, looking troubled.

'What is it, my boy?'

'Why did you come here to tell your tale?'

Eric smiled softly. 'I have always served Hardrada. Even after his death, I wished to preserve his reputation and his legacy. A life seeking to repent for the sin of failing to die at his side.'

'Dying with him would not have saved him.'

'No, but dying to fulfil your duty, even if you know it will likely fail, is still a good death.'

'And now it is too late, and you regret it?'

Eric laughed. 'Yes and no. It is complicated. It may also not be too late. I feel old and tired in a way I have never felt before. Perhaps my time has come and this journey has hastened it. Who can know? The way home may be too hard on my old bones. Either way I feel my time is coming to an end. But I am not saddened, I do not fear it. I came here to tell of Harald's life, and I have done so. If it is the end of me, I do not regret it in the slightest.'

'Are you feeling unwell? Shall I call for someone?'

Eric laughed weakly and then coughed and waved Ingvarr's concern away. 'No, it is not like that. Ah, a young man like you cannot possibly understand what it feels to be old. Your body talks to you, you know, and sometimes it tells you very bad things, and you believe it and you think "finally, this is my time!" I have had it a dozen times, yet I am still here. Maybe I will still be alive to return next year.'

Ingvarr looked unconvinced. 'So why risk so much to tell King Harald's tale? Men say it will speak against the King's ambition. How does this protect Harald's legacy?'

Eric waved a finger. 'Harald's legacy and what Harald wanted are not the same thing. He was a great man, perhaps the greatest, but he failed to control his ambition, and I failed to help him do so. Perhaps, if I can save his grandson from the same fate, I will have finally finished my duty to him and secured his legacy as the greatest of Norway's kings, as he wanted. You are wrong to think I speak against Magnus. No, it is my duty to try and advise him and speak the truth.'

'I see. Well, what did you advise the King?'

'That is for the King alone to know.'

Ingvarr was uncomfortable but he nodded. 'So, do you think I should go on campaign?'

Eric's brows creased as he considered it. 'I think every man should decide for himself. I am not going either way, so you must choose your own path.'

'But your whole life has been advising people. Can't you advise me?'

Eric smiled and took Ingvarr's hand, and he felt the old man's hand was shaking slightly.

'My boy, my advice to you is to forge your own path. Remember what I have told you and make up your own mind. Be honourable, be honest and have courage. Be good to your friends and your family and loyal to your lord and your King, even if you disagree with him. After all my life, that is really all I can say that matters. A man who follows that path can only say he lived well, no matter the result.'

Ingvarr nodded slowly. 'I think, then, that I should not go on campaign. I see the folly in it.'

Eric smiled. 'Then you have made the right decision, because it is what you believe is correct.'

'But I will have to go if my father goes.'

'That is also correct, because it is honourable and loyal.'

Ingvarr looked perplexed. 'But how? If both are correct and honourable, and both have different outcomes, how can I know what is right?'

Eric smiled and clasped Ingvarr's hand between both of his own. 'Young man, if you ever find the answer to that, be sure to let me know.'

'That's not very helpful,' Ingvarr said with a pout.

Eric nodded and laughed a little. 'I've heard that many times.'

Eric sipped the wine and looked into the cup thoughtfully. 'I think I will not return to the hall. Could you give my thanks to the King for his gift?'

'Of course, but they will be disappointed not to have you return to them. What shall I tell them?' Ingvarr asked.

'They have heard enough from me. Let the next generation be heard.' He smiled and patted the boy weakly on the shoulder. 'Tell them that I am tired, but happy to have done my duty to my King. Now go, tomorrow will be a great day. Leave me to my peace.'

'Yes, of course. And I am sure King Magnus will appreciate your service,' Ingvarr said, and left with a respectful nod.

Eric chuckled softly as Ingvarr closed the door, leaning against the wall and smiling softly. 'That is not the King I meant.'

Eric reached out a tired hand, lifted the cup to his mouth and drank deeply from it, quickly and with relish, and smacked his lips together weakly. Then an odd look came over his face. He peered into the cup and he was still for a moment.

Then he snorted in something like amusement. 'Maybe there is more of Hardrada in his grandson than I thought.' He put the cup down and leant against the shelf with his wrinkled hands, staring at it.

He was unsure what to do, and his hand shook. Then a flash of an old memory came unbidden to him, and he remembered Afra the Constant, standing at the rail of his burning ship in the Golden Horn of Constantinople as the fire raced towards him. He remembered the way his friend had been still in the chaos, smiling at him across the water that separated them – separating death from life so cruelly. He had always marvelled at how Afra had found his peace in that moment, how he had accepted the fate that his duty had led him to, and smiled in the face of it.

He picked up the cup again, with a steady hand, and drank the rest of it, setting it back down with a thud and staring at it.

And he smiled.

* * *

The meeting field was abuzz with chatter and excitement the next morning as Ingvarr and Hakon waited for the King to arrive and begin the Frostating. The day was cloudy and damp, with the threat of rain and a chill in the air, but it did not bother the men of Trondelag – they were well used to such weather.

Hakon saw someone making their way through the crowd towards them and he smiled.

'Morning, Torvald. You look like you have a sore head. I wondered after last night whether we would see you at all!'

Torvald gave Hakon a filthy look. 'I am surprised to find I am even alive. The King's ale is strong, and the night went on forever. How are you so happy?'

Hakon grinned. 'Because I am an experienced man and a good drinker... and because I voided my stomach before I went to bed. Did you not?'

Torvald looked queasy even at the mention of it. 'There is still time,' he gasped.

Hakon laughed and embraced his fragile friend. 'You are a fool, but I am glad you are here. Soon we will find out the King's intent!' Hakon noticed his son, who was standing silent and brooding. The boy had not got drunk the night before, through simply not being in the hall for very long, nor drinking his share of the ale.

'What is wrong, boy?'

'Nothing.'

'Don't *nothing* me, son, you look like a horse pissed in your breakfast. What has you so moody?'

Ingvarr's shoulders hunched for a moment in annoyance and then relaxed. 'I just... It is something Eric said last night.'

'What?'

'I can't... It doesn't matter.'

'I'll know it doesn't matter when you stop looking so miserable about it.' Hakon sighed and looked around. 'Where is the old goat, anyway?'

'I don't know.'

'Well, he will come when he pleases. He earned his rest. Come now, there are men I wish to introduce you to.'

* * *

Finally, the King arrived, his entourage surrounding him. He conducted the traditional ceremony and welcomed the men to the assembly, then they all took their seats.

'Men of Trondelag, I know what you are all waiting to hear from me, what you wish to debate at this assembly, and I shall not waste another moment leaving you waiting. The lawgiving and the petty matters can wait until tomorrow. Today, we must speak of my plans for the campaign season, and whether I intend to raise the leidang.'

The crowd fell to a hush, hanging on his words and staring at him as he swept his gaze around the space.

'It is my intention to raise a great expedition and sail to the islands of Orkney, and then to the southern isles, where we shall impose our rule on our kin in the petty kingdoms there, and expand it to all those who live in those islands. From there, in the next years, we can force the submission of the Scottish or conquer them if they refuse, and even, if all goes well, expand our conquests to include England itself!'

There was a ripple of shock through the crowd, excitement and apprehension, as the King finished.

'Now, we must discuss this venture, and I hope to receive the support of this assembly, for without the men of Trondelag, how could any such campaign succeed? Come with me, brave men of the north, and we will gain new lands and wealth, blood our young warriors, and become the most powerful nation of those that surround the northern sea!'

The King stood back as men raised their hands to be seen, and the old man who kept order pointed to some and directed them to the speaker's bench.

The first man thus picked stood there and nodded to the King, and then the crowd. 'I am Styrken of Nidaros, and I am honoured to speak to you today.'

He nodded with the formality done and looked at the King with an emphatic nod. 'I support your intentions, Lord King, and I will bring my men to your army for this campaign.'

There was a cheer of support from some of the crowd at Styrken's words, and the King nodded his thanks.

Several others in turn said similar things, to the point where Hakon knew with a soft smile that they had been prepared to say them in order to try and sway the meeting, and that the old man had instructions from Halfdan who to choose first.

Finally, a man was given the speaker's bench who did not look so pleased.

'My King, I wonder at the wisdom of invading England. Do we not know the likely outcome of such an adventure?'

'The likely outcome is success, otherwise we will not do it.'

'I am sure your grandfather thought the same, my King, as Eric Sveitungr related to us yesterday.'

'I heard the story as well as you, and from my father too, and we will learn from the mistakes of the past.'

'I believe you would, King Magnus, but it still might not be enough. There are ten men in England for every one of us.' Then he looked around. 'And where is Eric? What advice did he give you, and what would he say here to us today?'

'I will not speak for him,' Magnus said, waving to the crowd. 'Let Eric speak for himself, and I am sure you will be satisfied.' And he gestured to the audience.

The crowd shuffled as men looked around, but Eric did not step forwards.

Magnus waited impatiently, and then Jarl Hakon spoke up. 'I noted that he was not here earlier, my King. Perhaps he is still in his room? He was exhausted yesterday, and it is early.'

The King nodded. 'Then send someone to get him, for his words will end these concerns.'

Jarl Hakon nodded to Ingvarr. 'Go, boy, and fetch him.'

Ingvarr nodded and headed off, weaving through the assembly and disappearing into the town.

'Let the next man speak,' Magnus said, and another man stood under the tree at the head of the assembly.

'My King, I will wait until Eric has spoken, for I too wish to hear his words.'

Magnus looked a little irritated but nodded, and they stood there waiting. Men spoke to each other in animated debates all across the field as Magnus watched them in silence.

Ingvarr soon reappeared, and he cut across the assembly towards Hakon, and Hakon noted his son's wide eyes and pale expression.

'What is it?'

'Eric is... dead,' the boy gasped. 'Father, he is cold and still in his bed.' There was a ripple of shock from the men around them.

'Well, where is he?' the King called out, looking at them in irritation, too far away to hear.

Hakon looked at his son intently. 'You are sure? You checked him?'

Ingvarr nodded miserably. Hakon gave him a sympathetic nod and turned towards the king.

'King Magnus, Eric has died in the night. My boy found him in his bed, cold and still.'

There was a murmur of shock around the crowd and some calls of grief. Magnus looked disturbed, then he held up his hand for silence.

'Men of Trondelag, that grieves me, for Eric was a good and wise man. We will honour him tonight, but we cannot be distracted from the purpose of this gathering, nor would he want us to be. He was an old man, and we cannot be overly surprised that his efforts on our behalf, to entertain us and educate us, have used the last of his strength.'

He turned to the man who was under the tree. 'You have your chance to speak your mind, so do so.'

The man looked at the King uncomfortably. 'I would ask you, Lord King, what Eric advised. We should all like to know.'

Magnus tapped his fingers on his sword hilt and considered it. 'It is unusual at this assembly to speak another man's words, especially when they affect him and were given in private. But... in this case, I see that none of you will be satisfied if I do not.'

He turned to the audience. 'Let us be honest. You all know that Eric and I had our differences of opinion, and none of you would be surprised to hear that he counselled caution. I heard his stories of his campaigns with King Harald, and the mistakes that were made. Because yes, it is no insult to my grandfather to admit his mistakes, as Eric was brave enough to do.

'So Eric and I spoke of those mistakes, and how we could correct them. And this was his counsel: not to be greedy, nor overly bold, but to secure good harbours, supplies and allies before marching for any great battle. Not to rely on local men who might fail us, but our own kin and people we trust. To ensure we keep watch and scouts around us, as not to be surprised.'

Then the King smiled and looked around the crowd, nodding to himself. 'And of course, to wear our maille.'

There was a nervous laugh from the audience.

'Eric supported your campaign?' the man asked, looking surprised. 'It seemed from his tale that he would not, that he spoke against such conquests?'

'He did support it, as long as it was conducted carefully, and learning from the lessons he related.'

There was a rumble from the crowd as the King stared out over them, his face rigid and confident. Some men looked dubious, a few even angry, but none raised their hand to speak against him. Who would claim the King lied?

The man under the tree nodded. 'Then I will support you, King Magnus.'

Magnus turned to the man under the tree and smiled softly. 'I am glad to hear it.'

The assembly ended and the agreement of the great majority to support Magnus's expedition was secured. As the men in the field rose from their benches and gathered in groups to discuss it, Magnus stood under the tree and watched them carefully. Jarl Halfdan came over to stand with him.

'I think that went well, my King.'

'It did, and my thanks to you. I will not forget your support.'

The jarl dipped his head, and then nodded at Jarl Hakon's boy, who was in a sombre little group near the edge of the field, deep in conversation.

'What of the boy? Do you think he will work out that he delivered Eric's death?'

'How could he? He could not know the wine was poisoned.'

'No, but maybe he could know Eric's true opinion. It appears they were close, after all, and they spent a lot of time together.'

Magnus pursed his lips. 'Even if he knows, he would not dare speak against me.'

'We could use the same solution for him,' Halfdan said.

The King gave the jarl a reproachful glare. 'It would look bad if he were to suddenly die too. An old man? No one will suspect anything. But a healthy young boy who was close to him? Such a thing will cause whispers, and whispers have a power all of their own.'

'As you say, my King.'

At that moment, Magnus saw Hakon catch his eye, and the jarl nodded in salute. Magnus smiled and raised his hand a little in acknowledgement, then turned back to Halfdan.

'Good. Let us leave the problem of Eric the Follower behind us forever. He can follow us around causing trouble no more, as it should have been long ago. A king should have his own council, his own ambitions. That coward should have died with my grandfather. I want men of conviction and courage to follow me, men who share my ambition and vision. We will make Norway into a nation to be respected and feared once more, and rule over all the peoples around the northern sea. I need loyal men with me, my own followers, ones who will not restrain me but support me.' He turned to Halfdan. 'Can you be that man? Can you be a better follower to me than Eric was to my grandfather?'

Halfdan smiled. 'My King, I can.'

Magnus nodded and then looked at Jarl Hakon again, cocking his head. 'But maybe the boy is a worry I don't want. His father declared support for me this time, but he opposed me once and may do so again. He is not important. I will put his men under your command in the campaign ahead. Perhaps the opportunity will come to put that father and his boy in the front line of a difficult battle, and the problem will take care of itself.'

Halfdan nodded and smiled, casting his gaze to the father and son in the crowd. 'Do not worry, King Magnus. I will take care of it.'

* * *

MORE FROM JC DUNCAN

AFTERWORD AND HISTORICAL NOTE

And so, we have reached the end of this series and of Harald's epic life. As always, I took pains to ground this book in reality while adding the parts that were needed to make a good narrative fiction and interesting characters and conflicts within it. The latter parts of this book hew closer to the known history than others, but even with the Battle of Stamford Bridge little is known for certain other than its vague location. Just because I wrote about it in great detail, do not think that it is supposed to be the objective truth. Almost everything I wrote about Harald's campaign in England is taken in whole or in part from at least one source, but I patched it together how I felt best for the story, and in some aspects it diverges from the mainstream opinion or common narrative.

There is, for example, some testimony/rumour that Harold of Wessex shot the arrow that killed Hardrada. I doubt it's true – it's a little too perfect to be true, and I don't think the King would have spent the battle trying to 'snipe' his opponent with a bow, but either way I decided it was more appropriate that Harold killed him face-to-face, not from a distance, although there is nothing in the sources suggesting that happened. I made that up entirely. That is the fun of writing historical fiction, after all.

I have mixed emotions coming to the end of the tale of Harald's life. I am thrilled to have had the chance to relay it, almost in its entirety. I have spent the last two years living and breathing Harald Hardrada's adventures, researching and writing them and then seeing the reader's reaction to it, and it has been a joy.

But there is also sadness, because he is a unique figure and I can only write about him once. There will be, as you might have guessed, no sequels!

I am also sad to see the end of Eric, who unlike most characters in this story, was entirely fictional. I needed someone who saw Hardrada from the outside, not a perspective from his own mind. I don't think it's straightforward to convincingly or perhaps interestingly portray such a person from their own point of view, because they are so arrogant, so sure of themselves and so self-obsessed. I needed an outside viewpoint who, although biased, could see Harald's flaws and his failings as well as his achievements, and who could try and help us understand why men would love and follow such a man. A major theme of this book and interest for me in living 'with' Harald for so long, was why so many men loved or followed him. Eric is in part my way of trying to explore and explain that. Harald's own POV would be largely unable to show that. Because although Harald was a 'great' man – of that there is no doubt – he was not a 'good' man. This is not some historical revisionist view; he was a tyrant and was thought of as such in his own time. The sagas, written about 800 years ago, are painfully clear in that, showing with surprising candour how many of Harald's own people hated him and opposed him for it, and the lengths he went to to murder them or suppress them, and how the brutality of his methods shocked his people. They had a strict culture of law and punishment in that time in Norway, even for kings, and Harald's disregard for the law and persecution of those who opposed him, even when opposing him legally not through any form of rebellion, was shocking to his own people in his own time.

And that is the impression taken from a set of written sources that, on the whole, are trying to burnish and uplift his reputation and present him in a positive and heroic light. Amusingly, quite often in the sagas, after describing how Harald murdered an entire family/region, they would throw in a note about how 'Harald was generally regarded as very wise and a good ruler' at the end, as if to try and give a counterpoint.

But the truth is that Harald was worse than I depicted. I left out entire parts of his rule in Norway, the middle part of which was characterised by massacres and privations against his own people whenever they dared to speak out against him or defy his demands. I did this not to attempt to whitewash his actions, but because it is simply more interesting to write about a flawed man, not spend a book trudging through the actions of a brutal tyrant who burned his entire home region of Upplond to the ground for refusing to pay him taxes during a dispute (and yes, he did that). He was called Hardrada: The Hard Ruler, and trust me, dear reader, he earned that name.

So why did he inspire such loyalty and devotion? It is true that Eystein Orre and his men died for Harald after he had fallen. They probably knew he was dead, and they probably could have made terms with King Harold of England, who had no need or interest in wasting his best men fighting them once Hardrada had fallen.

But almost all of Harald's army fought to the death for him, an extremely rare event in history. Nine in ten of Harald's men died or were so terribly wounded they could not leave after the battle. There are only a handful of battles in history where that rate of casualties happened – the battle of Cannae, for example – and mostly it is where the army in question could not escape, not where they *decided not to*.

The Battle of Stamford Bridge is overlooked in that historical context as a complete outlier in the history of medieval conflict. It is simply almost unheard of for an army of that size to fight to the death in that manner. In almost all medieval battles, once it was clear one side had lost, they would retreat, rout or make terms. Last stands and armies fighting to the death are exceptionally uncommon in the period, especially in battles of that size. But that is the loyalty and devotion that Harald inspired.

And Harald was loved and revered after his death too, despite the enormity of his disaster at Stamford Bridge. It is also not the only time where his men's utter dedication to him is apparent. It is clear throughout his time in the Rus and the empire that his men were devoted to him despite the very high casualties they sustained in his service, and his brutal methods. It is quite remarkable, and he must have been an extraordinary personality and force of nature to acquire such devotion.

So in Eric's narration I tried to show in a way we can understand why he inspired such love and devotion, despite such tyranny and sacrifice, and I tried to show how it could have happened. That is why I had to make Eric up from whole cloth, because there is no one in the historical record who is attested as having spent their entire life with Harald, except maybe Ulfr, but Ulfr died before Stamford Bridge.

I was also quite unfair to Tjodolv Arnórsson, Harald's favourite skald (he loved skalds and was a patron to a whole gaggle of them). I almost wrote him out of the story, and I did that because he is too important to pretend he did not exist, but I needed to replace him with Eric. I can only apologise to his memory. He, like so many others, died for Harald at Stamford Bridge, a warrior-poet in the truest sense.

So what do we take from the life of Harald Hardrada? Well, he was one of the most remarkable and fearsome leaders in European history. Fantastically talented, utterly ruthless, enormously ambitious and able to inspire fanatical devotion. His impact, especially on this country (England), was massive. There is a very solid argument, and not original to me in any way, that the battle of Hastings was lost at Stamford Bridge. Harold Godwinson's army was shattered there, even in victory, by the last stand of Harald Hardrada's fearsome veteran warriors. By the time the King confronted William of Normandy, most of his best troops were dead, and his army lacked that solid core that had defeated Hardrada, so he was overwhelmed and killed.

As for the Norwegian legacy? Harald laid (or arguably finished his brother Saint Olaf's work in laying) the foundations for the modern nation of Norway. It was a unified nation from then until now, despite periods being in unions with Denmark and/or Sweden, and various border changes. The brothers Olaf and Harald are commemorated heavily to this day, and Saint Olaf has a national holiday in his name.

Militarily the disaster of the Battle of Stamford Bridge ended the Norwegian age of conquest forever. No Norwegian army ever invaded England again, although minor raids in Scotland, Ireland and the various islands continued for a while. And that brings us to Magnus Barefoot, grandson of Hardrada, and King during Eric's retelling in Tinghaugen. He did indeed take a modest army to the northern end of the British Isles in 1098. He campaigned there on and off for a few years, gaining a little territory, and he died there in 1103 in a pointless death in an otherwise minor ambush. The last King of Norway to die in battle, in a waste of what was otherwise a promising reign. But he did not lead thousands of warriors to their deaths in another attempt at large-scale conquest of England, a fact I decided to leave as Eric's legacy, although it was more to do with funding, logistics, strategy and political factors... not the machinations of an old man trying to make up for old failings.

Maybe he did not have, as I depicted with Eric, wiser heads to advise him on a better course. We will never know. But he did not fully learn the lessons of his forefathers and it cost him his life.

But the legacy of Harald Hardrada survived his foolish grandson, and his direct descendants ruled in Norway on and off until at least 1184, or much longer, depending on how you treat some varyingly dubious paternity claims.

It is interesting to note in that context that the much-maligned King Sweyn of Denmark, who was Harald's enemy for so many years and had a terrible reputation in battle, survived Harald. Sweyn's descendants, in unbroken paternal line, still sit on the throne of Denmark today.

He made no conquests, won no glory, but his family have worn the crown for nearly a thousand years. Make of that what you will.

And so it is time to leave Eric behind, a character I completely invented and whom is much more sympathetic and likable, much more human, in fact, than the main subject of this series. He kept insisting that 'this story is not about me,' but more and more it was. I must admit that at first I intended to end with him leaving to return home, his duty of spreading Harald's story and protection of his legacy complete.

But when I got to the final chapters it just didn't feel right. I didn't want him fading away into the shadows.

So I gave Eric the one thing he wanted, perhaps the thing that he deserved and something that gave the series and myself a more definitive closure: I let him die for Hardrada.

I hope you all enjoyed this series half as much as I enjoyed writing it, although I suspect that is too much to ask. It has occupied two years of my life, tumultuous years at that, and has taken me from the remains of Constantinople, where I traced Harald's history through the chaotic ruins that lie under the modern city of Istanbul, to the battlefield of Stamford Bridge. I had the chance to walk in the footsteps of Hardrada, both on the page and in the world, and it has been a huge pleasure.

So, to the future! My next series is coming swiftly on the heels of this one, and it is about the Jomsvikings – the semi-legendary Viking mercenaries who sold themselves to the highest bidder in the wars of the Norse kings just prior to Harald Hardrada's time. In fact, Harald's brother, King Olaf fought alongside the Jomsvikings in their twilight years, so perhaps expect to see him pop up again in the story, making the next series almost something of a prequel. It will be a classical Viking revenge and adventure saga, darker and wilder than the political machinations of kings and empresses that I have portrayed in this series. I am going to enter into the mythical world of an army for hire, pagans in a Christian world, who developed a reputation for bloodthirstiness, ferocity in battle and for ending the reign of kings. The series is called the 'Kingbreakers Saga', and the first novel will be published in September 2026. It is available on pre-order already, and I hope you will enjoy reading it!

For now, though, that is all. I want to thank Boldwood Books, and all the wonderful editors, illustrators, proofreaders, and marketing team for helping me make it a successful series, and the CEO Amanda and my editor Caroline for believing in this story enough to publish it with me. It has been a pleasure, and I look forward to working through my next series with them.

And I thank you, those of you who walked all the way in Harald's footsteps with me, for reading to the very last words of this series.

J. C. Duncan

September 2025

ABOUT THE AUTHOR

JC Duncan is a well-reviewed historical fiction author and amateur bladesmith, with a passion for Vikings.

Download your exclusive bonus content from JC Duncan here:

Visit JC's website: www.jcduncan.co.uk

Follow JC on social media:

x.com/jcduncanauthor
instagram.com/j.c.duncan
facebook.com/JCDuncanAuthor

ALSO BY JC DUNCAN

The Last Viking Series

Warrior Prince

Raven Lord

Emperor's Axe

Wolves of the Empire

Viking Conqueror

www.ingramcontent.com/pod-product-compliance
Ingram Content Group UK Ltd.
Pitfield, Milton Keynes, MK11 3LW, UK
UKHW040418030326
11028UKWH00009B/63

9 781806 563555